mR. bERZERKELEY II

Big Games, Big Lies, Big Decisions

Jack McLaughlin

iUniverse, Inc.
Bloomington

mR. bERZERKELEY II
Big Games, Big Lies, Big Decisions

iUniverse books may be ordered through booksellers or by contacting:

iUniverse
1663 Liberty Drive
Bloomington, IN 47403
www.iuniverse.com
1-800-Authors (1-800-288-4677)

ISBN: 978-1-4759-4574-4 (sc)
ISBN: 978-1-4759-4575-1 (hc)
ISBN: 978-1-4759-4576-8 (e)

Library of Congress Control Number: 2012915114

Printed in the United States of America

iUniverse rev. date: 8/31/2012

PART ONE
Go Bares

Chapter One
Best of Times

A FULL MOON IN dark skies begins to sink into the silent ocean beyond the Golden Gate Bridge, chased by morning light in the east rising over Berkeley's tree-covered hills. City streets are empty, and traffic lights on Shattuck flash yellow on and off. Bakery smells dance in a soft, cool breeze that hardly moves the evergreens around Hamilton House, a block away from the university. The sounds of a BART train taking the first load of Cal rooters into San Francisco can be heard in the distance. Homeless men, women, and children curl up in their sleeping bags and blankets under cardboard shelters or in doorways, trying to stay warm. This day's early hours hide the fact that the entire community will be energized later as Cal takes on Stanford in Bay Area football's Big Game.

The boarding house kitchen door opens and Winston Churchill—Winnie—dressed in black trousers, tennis shoes, and a dark-blue Cal sweatshirt walks to the center of a driveway adjoining Mayor Sain's home and stops. He looks across Durant at a van used by the pickets Bertha Potts has hired as a timeout station and then continues on. He almost steps on Trojan, the Hamilton House mutt, as he makes his way toward the doggy door. "Sorry!"

Mayor Sain—or mR. bERZERKELEY, as Josh, one of the boarders, labeled him in cartoons during his recent reelection—sits at a small table in his kitchen smoking a joint and drinking beer. His six-foot frame is covered by khakis and a dark-blue Cal sweatshirt. His Birkenstocks move back and forth as his feet try to find a comfortable place to rest. His black hair is bedraggled. The two-story, hundred-year-old craftsman has been around almost as long as Hamilton House. Inside, the clutter of papers, books, and clothes suggests he doesn't have many visitors. The fact that dust and cobwebs can be found in the kitchen indicates he hasn't spent much or any time preparing food, either. And why should he, with his mother and her great cooking a few steps away?

It is clear to Winnie that the mayor would rather be naked at the moment. "Isn't it a little early to get started?" Winnie says as he sits at the table.

"Started? I'm still up after partying all night getting ready for the Big Game. Want a juicy one or a beer?"

"Nah. I got to pace myself. I wanna be sober when we kick Stanford's ass!"

"You sorry you came back to Berkeley and restored the old house?" Mayor Sain says, taking a hit.

"Not at all. A little time away from Kansas politics and a return to my roots has been the best thing I've ever done. Even a little shit from our old classmate Bertha hasn't dampened this adventure."

"Fat Bertha! When's she gonna get her pickets off our backs?"

"After the primaries when Gerry gets the nomination. I'll be out of the picture. She'll leave you alone, too, even though she's still pissed at you for mooning her in the third grade."

"If those pickets keep slandering me with those libelous signs, I'm going to have an ordinance passed to require a truth squad before exercising 'free speech'! Ha!"

"Come on, you know how Bertha operates: guilt by character assassination. She gets you; she gets me! It all makes good reading back in Kansas."

"You don't want to go back and run for governor, do you? Stay here with me and be free!"

"In my household, I do have a vote. But sometimes it gets vetoed."

"Your better half, Babe, is a good one, that's for sure. You did all right, old chum. Sure you don't want a juicy one?"

"Better not. They are all going to be getting up soon and ready to take the train to Palo Alto. Better be on my best behavior. Who knows where Bertha has her spies ready to take a picture of any mistake I might make?"

They hear the Hamilton House kitchen door open and shut and see Asia moving quickly toward her scooter, her black hair tied back and her large breasts bouncing inside a dark-blue Cal sweatshirt.

"I can't wait to get close to China Girl," Mayor Sain says. "She has a way about her that turns me upside down every time I see her."

"She'd rip you apart, you horny bastard," Winnie says as he laughs. "Maybe you should follow Trojan's example and concentrate on legs."

"What a way to die!" Mayor Sain says. "Me and the Asian beauty!"

"At least you stopped stalking Sarah," Winnie says.

"Oh yes, Miss Gorgeous from Kansas—our naïve freshman that you are supposed to protect from us evil old men and every other swinging dick. Didn't work with Surfer Boy Josh, Mr. Muscles, the great cartoonist, did it? Or all those fraternity guys?"

"Now that she's gone lesbian, she's at least safe from sex, at least with men."

"The lesbians, Stephanie and Judy—maybe I can change their minds about men?"

"You are really horny, aren't you?" Winnie says.

"Like a twelve-point buck."

"Maybe you should take up with the vice-chancellor again," Winnie says. "She's enough woman for all of us."

"The evil bitch! We had a son together—my son. She's the last person on earth I would ever touch. Look at what we produced! Michael, even with the hole in the side of his face, the hood and the mask, is the best thing that ever happened to me. I have a son!"

"Down, boy, down," Winnie says. "You have a wonderful son. Bessie will be proud—when she finds out!"

"Mom," Mayor Sain says. "What am I gonna do? She's going to die if we don't get her a new liver. Her quart of Jack a day finally caught up with her. Asia, with all her scientific mumbo jumbo, will figure out a way. She has to!"

"Old chum," Winnie says, pushing back and standing up, "we've been through a lot since I came back. These past three months have been some of the most stressful in my life. But you know what? They have also been some of the best. Your reelection was classic, our little foray to Kansas a hoot, and just being around you again has given me new energy. Now, all we have to do is go and kick a little Stanford butt to make my return perfect."

"You sure you didn't smoke a little before you came over here?

"No, old buddy. With mR. bERZERKELEY around, who needs anything else? Think I'll go back over and see if I can wake Babe up."

Mayor Sain stands and gives Winnie a big hug. "Get out of here before I turn bi, would you, you son of a bitch?"

Chapter Two
I Have a Son!

"Stop that, you naked-ass commie!" seventy-year-old Bessie yells, fidgeting with her long black work dress at the stove in the Hamilton House kitchen. Mayor Sain rings a dinner bell several times. "You'll wake up those damn pickets in the vans across the street and whoever is left upstairs."

"It's Big Game day, Mom!" Mayor Sain yells. "They all got to get up and hit the rooters' train in San Francisco. Winnie came back over to wake 'em up. I'm going to bring the Victory Axe back from Stanford!"

"If you don't stop yelling I'm going to use my axe and cut off the part of your body where your brain is housed!" Bessie grabs her cleaver and waves it in the mayor's direction. "Stop it!"

"This is important. The Bears need all the help they can get this year."

"Some of the inmates have already left."

"They go to Palo Alto?"

"The lesbians took off to go geocaching—whatever that is—and Asia went to see needle dick about her experiment."

"Geocaching is where you use a GPS to locate a treasure someone has buried. It's this new thing people do for fun."

"Maybe they can find your father's grave so I can piss on him for what he left me with these past fifty years."

"Come on, Mom. Look at all the fun we've had."

"Fun? Like a barrel of monkeys—you running around naked, smoking dope, and chasing women. It's a comedy gone bad."

"Is the experiment the one Asia is doing in the basement?" the mayor asks softly, not wanting Bessie to know he knows Asia is trying to grow liver cells to save her life. "I wonder what she's doing."

"It's none of your damn business what China Girl is up to! Leave her alone."

"What about the others ... Winnie and Babe, Josh, Sarah and Michael? Are they still upstairs?"

"As far as I know. Trojan left, so Michael is probably stirring around. I don't think Josh came home last night."

"Michael seems like a nice young man, doesn't he?" Mayor Sain says, not wanting Bessie to know Asia told him Michael is his son. "It's a real tragedy the way the vice-chancellor raised him. He is squared away in spite of her."

"He is a nice boy. He has more sense in his little finger than a naked-ass commie I know."

"Would make some father pretty proud, don't you think? If I ever had a son I would want one just like him."

"Shit! If you had a son he'd probably be in San Quentin by now."

"What would we do without you around to keep us in line? You always tell it like it is!"

Mayor Sain reaches out to touch her tenderly on the shoulder. She turns and hands him a plate of eggs and a small steak on top of pancakes. "Why don't you give us all a break and take this next door for breakfast? Get some food in your stomach to cut the booze and weed."

"You really know the way to my heart. Can I send Jefferson, Sylvia, Jack R. Abbott, and Doreen over for some? They should be at my house by now. We gotta make final plans for the game."

""Shit! Are you gonna embarrass me again on national television?"

"Not me. Some of my friends might! We've got to keep sending a message to the president that his underlings are messing with us and the stimulus money he gave out. The cities are waking up and fighting to keep the money. This will be a big day at the Big Game."

"Shit—double shit! Send them over, and the Jack Rabbit had better not bring that smelly bulldog. If he does, I'll go for a long walk off the pier!"

Mayor Sain looks at his mother for a second. "Bye, Mom. I love you and will always love you."

"Get the fuck out of here! Weed has finally swallowed your mind!"

The mayor almost trips on Trojan popping through the doggy door. "What happened?" Bessie yells at the mutt. "The little white puff next door turn you down again?"

Trojan makes a small sound, walking with his head down toward Bessie. "Here," she says, reaching toward an open cabinet beneath the sink and taking out a bottle of Jack Daniels. "Start the morning off right. I've got a little left from last night." She pours a small amount in Trojan's dish. "As a matter of fact, with the way this day has started, I might join you." Trojan makes another soft sound as he laps up the booze.

* * *

Mayor Sain sits at the small table in his kitchen again. He gets up and opens the refrigerator, the one appliance that is well used, takes out a cold beer, and returns to his breakfast as the kitchen door opens. Jefferson, wearing his dark-blue Cal sweatshirt and jeans, and Sylvia, wearing a yellow Cal sweatshirt and a wraparound blue skirt, walk in. The past fifty years have been good to the bearded, spry Jefferson, but not so good to his drugged-out partner Sylvia, who barely knows her own name.

"Mister Mayor?" Jefferson says, looking at the plate of food. "Your mom trying to keep you from getting drunk and disorderly at the Big Game again?"

"She's got a lot more," Mayor Sain says, with food in his mouth. "She's ready for you."

"I am always ready for you," Sylvia slurs.

"Go get your food and come back," an excited mayor says. "I've got something to tell you."

Jefferson and Sylvia leave and walk across the driveway to Hamilton House while the mayor clears the small table and a couple of hanging cobwebs. "I have a son!" he says happily to himself. "Michael is my son! The evil bitch and I have a son! Oh! The evil bitch! I'm going to tell her I know at today's game. Yes. That's it! I'll make her squirm and scratch her butt because I know what she's been hiding all these years. Michael is our son!"

A familiar smell fills the air, making the mayor's nose twitch. Jack R. Abbott, slight and short, opens the kitchen door and peeks in. "Where's Doreen?" the mayor asks.

"She had to do an emergency gonad extraction on a Schnauzer," Jack R. Abbott says, rubbing his scraggily beard.

"You didn't bring Winston, I hope?" the mayor says, rubbing his nose.

"No. He's real pissed! Cable went out and he's gonna miss Raider reruns. His butthole opened up, and he let me have it just before I left."

"Want to take a quick shower?" Mayor Sain asks, hardly able to stand the stench.

"Nah. It'll drift away soon. Your mom is cooking, I see."

"Wait a minute," the mayor says as he stands and walks into a small bathroom, grabbing air freshener. "Spray on some of this evergreen. It'll cut the smell—or she'll throw you out of Hamilton House."

Jack R. Abbott groans as he catches the spray can the mayor underhands. He covers his body, including under both arms and his holey green tennis shoes, before tossing the can back.

Mayor Sain takes a whiff. "That'll do for now," he says. "Go on over. Jefferson and Sylvia are already there. Bring your food back. We've got plans to go over, and I've got something very important to tell you."

"Sounds like material for another mystery novel," Jack R. Abbott says.

"It'll be a good one," the mayor laughs. "More like a horror novel!"

"Was that *horror* or *whore*?" Jack R. Abbott chuckles.

"Both," the mayor says. "Go get your food and hurry back."

Jack R. Abbott leaves. "I've got a son! I really have a son!" Mayor Sain repeats to himself, holding both hands over his head signaling a touchdown. "I'm going to have him be just like me. Well, maybe not JUST like me—he does have that hole in the side of his head. I'm going to teach him how to make a lot of money in real estate ...a lawyer ... no, a professor, and invent something to cure cancer ... no, like Asia, and grow body parts. I will teach him how to play an instrument and sing so we can be a father-and-son act and make CDs and hits and be famous. Maybe he will call me Dad and Mom Grandmother. I've always wanted that! Yes! I've got a son!"

* * *

Mayor Sain and Winnie's school classmate Willie, a muscular African American, walks into the station on Martin Luther King Jr. Way in his police uniform, rubbing his eyes. "Sergeant Williams," a uniformed African American female says loudly. "Your son Jamal is in the conference room waiting for you."

"What now?" Willie groans. "What trouble is my prodigal son, Mr. Big Man on Campus at Berkeley High, going to cause me today?"

Willie walks into the room where the handsome and muscular Jamal sits at long table. Willie sits in a chair beside him. "What now?"

"Mom kicked me out of the house for the day," Jamal says. "She wants to watch the Big Game with her new boyfriend and doesn't want me yelling and screaming and making a scene."

"Esmeralda has a new boyfriend? How many does that make since we got divorced?"

"I can't count that high. It's been a swinging door since you left."

"Why don't you hang out with your friends, like you usually do?" Willie asks.

"I'm kinda hidin' after last night. Me and a couple of brothers rode our bikes to Union Square and had a misunderstanding with some Asian gang members during the Big Game rally. I had to work one over to get away."

"I told you to watch it!" Willie says sternly. "You got too much to lose with the scholarships and pro ball and all. The big schools don't take kindly to trouble makers."

"We got away clean," Jamal says. "But you know how word gets around."

"Why don't you ride with me today? Berkeley will be empty, and we got to keep the peace. We'll listen to the game on the radio. What you say?"

"Are you still trying to get me into the force? You know I'm going after a scholarship and a spot in the pros, like you should have done."

"I'm not trying to do anything except keep you off the streets while your mother ruins another man's life. The last person I want you to be like is me. The only good thing I ever did was have five great children and one who can make it to the Hall of Fame in at least two sports. Come on. Ride with me!"

Chapter Three
Dawn of a New Day

BABE, IN A YELLOW Cal sweatshirt and blue pants, walks slowly down the stairs, followed closely by Winnie. "Well, Governor. You woke me up, made your moves like you were in your twenties again, and dressed me in these horrible colors. What's next?"

"This is a new day," Winnie says as he smiles. "And you make me feel that way every time you give in."

"It was either that or you giving me the evil eye all day," Babe says as she hits the bottom step. "When are we getting the elevator? I'm finding it harder to walk up and down."

"You're not kidding me again, are you?" Winnie asks.

"About what?"

"About being pregnant," Winnie says, pinching her slightly on the butt.

"If I am you'll be the second to know."

"Who'll be the first?"

"My shrink"—Babe laughs—"when I find one that isn't goofy in this crazy place."

"Maybe Josh can work it into one of his cartoons," Winnie laughs. "'mR. bERZERKELEY is pregnant with ideas on how to give back the president's stimulus money.' I can see the headline now."

"You are sick, mister," Babe says, jumping forward slightly as Winnie pinches her again.

They walk to the large cutting block used as a table for twelve in the center of the boarding house kitchen. "What was all that noise?" he asks Bessie. Winnie's nose twitches slightly. "And what's that smell?"

"My naked-ass commie son was over trying to wake up the dead, including those fucking pickets across the street, because you didn't," Bessie growls. "And he sent his friends over for food to take back to his house to plan their stunt for the game."

"It smells like that one guy's bulldog," Babe says.

"He got butt-bombed before he came over and tried to hide it with deodorant or something. I had to take a swig of Jack to get rid of the odor. It even sent Trojan out the doggy door."

"That's right!" Winnie says, pulling out a chair at the block for Babe. "He and his cronies are planning some spectacular prank for the Big Game."

"You told me he was going to sit in the president's box and behave," Babe says.

"His friends will do his dirty deeds for him."

"The only dirty deed was done by his father fifty years ago," Bessie growls. "I think I'm going to take a long nap today, after I finish a bottle of Jack."

Sarah walks down the stairs in her short nighty, leaving nothing to the imagination. "What's that smell?" she asks, rubbing her nose.

"Turn around and go back to your room and get dressed, hon," Babe says. "You'll have all the men in heat and force them to take their dirty minds off football."

"Yes, Mrs. Churchill." Sarah yawns as she stretches, moving thin fabric away from her large breasts."

"Go now, quickly," Babe says. "I don't want a certain man to take his eyes off me."

"Never happen," Winnie says as he smiles at Babe. "I got all I can handle."

"Holy shit!" Bessie mutters as Sarah goes back upstairs. "I got crazies, lesbians, naked people, humping mutts, perverts, romantics, and the Lone Ranger living here. I AM going to take that nap today."

"What are they planning?" Winnie asks.

"I heard something about the scoreboard, body paint ... You should go over and ask him." Bessie sighs. "What's a mother to do?"

Josh and Michael come down the stairs at almost the same time. Josh is bare-chested and wearing jeans, and Michael is wearing his dark-blue hoodie and a black mask. "Surfer Boy," Bessie says, "I thought you were still at the sorority house. And Lone Ranger! You want some more Wheaties?"

"That noise!" Josh says. "It sounded like someone was calling in the cows."

"The bullshitter next door ... who else?" Bessie says. "His majesty wants everyone to get ready for the Big Game."

"Are you going?" Winnie asks. "You'll get more material for your mR. bERZERKELEY cartoons."

"Who needs it?" Bessie growls. "Make it up like you did before."

"I've got one for you," Winnie says as he nudges Babe on the shoulder, ready to share his pregnant idea.

"Don't you dare," Babe threatens.

"Sit down, boys," Bessie says. "Get the food while it's hot. I'm so tired I may fall asleep before I finish."

"Can I help?" Babe asks.

"Forget it. I've done this in my sleep so long I can do it again. Besides, you've got to save your strength for the rooters' bus, the train ride, the game, and whatever my naked-ass commie son has planned for your entertainment."

"I'm staying," Josh says. "I'll do a little work at the store and do my duty at the sorority."

"Duty?" Bessie says. "Is that what they call sex these days?"

"Can I go with you to the store and learn how to draw cartoons?" Michael asks.

Sarah, dressed in a yellow Cal sweatshirt and skintight jeans, bounces from the stairway over to the block. "Aren't you going to the game?" she says to Michael as she sits next to him. "It'll be so much fun!"

"Shit!" Bessie growls. "That's all I need now—Miss Bubbly Energy."

"Did I say something wrong?" Sarah asks.

"No, hon," Babe says. "Bessie's just being Bessie, you know what I mean?"

"I guess," Sarah says naively. "I just think going to the game will be one of the highlights of coming to Berkeley. I've never been on a train before."

"Another first for you," Josh says sarcastically. "I'll add it to the list on *Veronica's Lives*."

"I don't care what you do anymore, Mr. Horrible Person," Sarah says crossing her arms. "I am immune to you and your bad sense of humor and those horrible cartoons."

"Can you teach me how to draw *Veronica's Lives* too?" Michael asks.

"That's it!" Sarah yells. "Turn that bad boy cartoon stuff over to someone who has class like Michael here. He's not a loser like you."

"Now, now, let's calm down," Bessie says, walking toward the table, wielding her cleaver. "Let's leave all the hostilities for the football teams and my naked-ass commie son. Eat and go do whatever you're going to do today and leave me alone. You all hear? I'm tired, hungry, and thirsty. Shut the fuck up!"

Bessie turns, puts the cleaver down, and grabs several trays of steaming food, placing them in the middle of the block. "Anyone want anything else?" she yells. She turns to Winnie. "And if you go next door, pass the word that the kitchen is closing in thirty minutes so I can take a shit and rest. Got it?"

Chapter Four
Tweaking

ASIA GINGERLY CARRIES A container from her parked scooter into Professor Spears' laboratory. Her black hair shines in the morning sun, and her large breasts bounce from side to side, loose inside her sweatshirt. She punches in a code and enters. The professor, a stereotypical geek, sits at a computer in a room filled with state-of-the-art scientific instruments, equipment, and technology. She walks to him, carrying the secured container.

"Well, Miss Asia. Did you bring me breakfast instead of going to the Big Game?" he says, adjusting his circular, wire-framed spectacles.

"I'd rather have a Big Game with you, Professor," Asia says in a dripping sexual tone.

"You need me for something, I can tell."

"Actually, I do, Professor. And, I have what you want in exchange."

"You know the way to my heart."

"It's not your heart I'm after. A little lower."

"My God!" the professor says. "This WILL be a good day after all."

"What do you mean, 'after all'?" Asia asks.

"Your favorite person and mine ..." the professor starts.

"The wonderful vice-chancellor?" Asia interrupts.

"She called me at six o'clock and chewed my behind from one side to the other about you. She said in no uncertain terms I was never allowed to let you use DNA equipment ever again. She was still fuming about how you caught the rapist and proved Michael was her son."

"She'll get over it. The chancellor will keep her in line."

"What is it with you and Chancellor Lim? What do you have on him? Did you and he ... you know ... do what we do?"

"Let's just say he and I have an understanding that he doesn't want made public," Asia says, smiling and leaning over so he can take a gander inside her loose sweatshirt.

"I do understand, Miss Asia," the professor says, hardly able to talk, his glasses steamed. "Just like you and I have."

"Just like we have."

“Well, then, what do you want from me before we … you know?” the professor stutters.

“It seems my liver cells need a little help. I keep taking the temperature but it looks like nothing is happening. Could you see if they are still growing? It’s real important, professor. It’s a matter of life and death.”

“Might I ask whose life you are trying to save?”

“You can ask, but I won’t tell you. Shall we?”

“Let’s take them over to the table and see. They may need a little boost just like I do.”

“That’s a good one, Professor. I haven’t heard that one before.”

Chapter Five
Game Plan

WINNIE OPENS MAYOR SAIN'S kitchen door. Inside, sitting at the table under a green cloud, Mayor Sain, Jefferson, Sylvia, and Jack R. Abbott pore over a piece of paper while they smoke joints. "Winnie, my man, come in," Mayor Sain says, looking up. "You want a hit? Jefferson scored some good skunk."

"At least it cuts that bulldog smell," Winnie says as he smiles.

"Goddamn cable. I think I'm going to get a satellite dish after I publish my first novel so he can have more football games to watch," Jack R. Abbott says before taking a drag.

"Your first novel?" Mayor Sain laughs. "How many years have I been hearing that?"

"It'll happen. I'm on a roll right now with my latest, *Murder by Panther Piss.*"

"I hear you have some excitement planned for the Big Game?" Winnie says.

"Excitement?" the mayor laughs. "We're gonna put the president's stimulus funds up Stanford's butt. Ha! We got streakers with messages on their bodies, a scoreboard with a message straight from mR. bERZERKELEY, and the Stanford band's tubas have been filled with soap. What a brilliant plan!"

"Bail for the naked people?" Winnie asks.

"Covered with Josh's leftover mR. bERZERKELEY cartoon money," the mayor says as he takes a hit.

"And your contingency plan?" Winnie asks the mayor.

"We got Martin and an airplane just in case. His Japanese mother's father was a kamikaze, and his Italian father was a skydiver. He lives to jump out of airplanes to honor both. And that will be your responsibility."

"Me?"

"If we are all in trouble—and who knows what the vice-chancellor will do to me—it's up to you to contact Martin and tell him he's on."

"Great plan, Mr. Mayor," Jefferson says.

"I am on too, Mr. Mayor," a stoned Sylvia says.

"Couldn't written it better myself," Jack R. Abbott says.

"Maybe I will have some skunk after all," Winnie says. "Too bad Bertha isn't here to see me smoke it in person."

"Fat Bertha?" the mayor laughs. "We'll make sure it hits all the social networks and give her pickets more ammunition. The more publicity the better."

* * *

Bertha Potts, wearing a red power suit, her graying hair piled on top of her head to expose her long, size-twelve neck, exercises her fifty-year-old body, pacing back and forth at the Kansas Central Committee Headquarters. The dark-paneled office with antique furniture and expensive carpets covering a hardwood floor, sits atop the tallest office building in downtown Topeka. The door opens and two elderly men wearing expensive suits walk in and look around for a bottle of scotch. "Sit," Bertha orders as she points. "No time to drink."

"What did you call this emergency meeting for?" one of the men asks as he sits in a soft chair.

"On a Saturday?" the other man says. "I gave up my warm water exercise class for this meeting."

"Warm water, cold water!" Bertha says as she groans. "We've got to get our act together or we'll all be in hot water if Winston Churchill and his buddy the mayor get the national attention I think they're going for this afternoon. Fucking Big Game! There's no way two bum teams need to be on national television."

"You mean the Stanford and Cal game? Is that what you are talking about?" one man asks.

"Yes!"

Sarah's father, Gerry Armstrong, enters Bertha's office, trying to put his graying hair in place using his fingers. "What's all the fuss on a Saturday?" he asks.

"Bertha thinks your friend Winston and his friend are going to suddenly get national attention at the Big Game out west and take the spotlight away from your becoming our candidate for governor," one of the men says.

"And how is that possible?" Gerry asks.

"Who knows what trick mR. bERZERKELEY has up his butt," Bertha says. "He is so sneaky and crooked."

"The Stanford president is one of us, isn't he?" one of the men asks.

"Yes, he is," Bertha says, stopping in her tracks and rubbing her chin. "Maybe a call and guarantee of funds to beef up security might help. Yes, that's it! Let's use some of our campaign money to have him double—no, triple—his security force, with a special eye on Winston, Jim Sain, and his band of weirdos. No tricks, no national spotlight, no publicity."

"You have my approval, Bertha," one man says.

"Now, can we get on with our weekend?" one man asks.

"Go on, get out of here," Bertha says. "Gerry, hang around."

The two men groan, stand, and leave. Gerry Armstrong sits down. "What else do you have up your sleeve?" he asks.

"I mentioned before that I am going to file a criminal complaint against Winston on behalf of your daughter and you with the Berkeley police," Bertha says.

"I told you I don't want my daughter involved in any way," an angry Gerry says, the veins popping out on his neck as his face turns red.

"I am going to ask our picket captain to watch what happens today very closely. In addition to an underage drinking charge, I am looking for anything else."

"She's eighteen, now," Gerry says.

"I know. But feeding alcohol to a minor is still a crime, along with smoking dope. And if I can throw in a little sex or a come-on, what the hell? If the dumb bastard mayor does anything like that, we'll have pictures and drag Winston under the bus with him. You don't want your daughter drinking and doing drugs, do you?"

"No, I guess I don't," Gerry says. "I'm sure glad I'm on your side. I wouldn't want you against me."

"Like I have said many times, I am yours, and you will win the primary and be the next Kansas governor, or my name isn't Bertha Potts."

"This is the 'Big Game' for you, isn't it?" he says as he smiles slightly.

"When it comes to Winston and Jim Sain, it isn't a big game for me," Bertha says. "It's the only game."

Chapter Six
Lessons

Oxford and Bancroft streets are jammed with students wearing blue and gold heading for BART and a ride into the San Francisco to catch the train to Palo Alto. "Go ahead, sit in my seat at the table," Josh says to Michael as they enter Babe's Art Store. The Campanile rings nine times in the background.

"That's your chair," Michael says softly from behind his black mask. "You go ahead, and I'll watch."

"I'll show you a few tricks and turn you loose. I gotta go and take care of my girl's needs. It'll give you a chance to play around a little, be creative, hang a mR. bERZERKELEY on the world. I'll be back in a couple of hours."

"What if I make a mistake?"

"One good thing about working on a laptop is that mistakes can be erased, changed, altered, deleted," Josh says, putting his laptop on the desk and turning it on. "Go ahead. Make yourself comfortable."

"I would rather try a *Veronica's Lives*, if that's all right with you?"

"Whatever turns you on, Michael. The lesbian wannabe provides a lot of material to work with, that's for sure. I'll show you both files. You pick."

Josh steps aside, and Michael settles in the chair, waiting for the laptop screen to clear. Josh looks over his shoulder. "There," Josh says. "See those two folders? One is marked 'Naked,' and that holds all the mR. bERZERKELEY drawings and frames, and 'Stupid' for the *Veronica's Lives* stuff."

"'Stupid'?"

"Yeah." Josh laughs. "I had a few other titles, but that one seems to fit at the moment."

"I don't think she's stupid. She's wonderful."

"Michael is in love," Josh teases. "That's okay. At least you have good taste. But you'll have to wait until she gets through this lesbian phase, if she ever does. Say, that's a great idea for a Tuesday cartoon—when she's a wild teenager turning down the most handsome guy in school for a girl."

"Won't she get mad?" Michael asks.

"Who cares? The madder she gets, the more material she provides."

"I don't want to make her mad at me."

"Don't worry about that," Josh says as he laughs. "I don't. Just draw it the best you can, follow the prompts that pop up when you click on 'draw,' paste the pictures you think fit from 'bank,' and I'll look at it when I get back. No one will know."

"What if I don't do it right or delete something important?" Michael asks.

"Just play around and see what happens," Josh says, reaching into his jeans. "I got a backup for everything." He holds up a flash drive.

"After this, will you teach me how to paint like you?" Michael asks.

"Sure. I will teach you everything."

"Thanks, Mr. Josh."

"Mr. Josh? That's a good one."

*　　　*　　　*

Naked Josh and the gorgeous, brunette, nineteen-year-old Jasmine lie on their backs in her plush bed at the sorority house on Piedmont, just off campus. "Wasn't that worth skipping that horrible football game for?" she asks softly.

"So was the first couple of times," Josh says as he smiles.

"Everyone is gone to the game. We can go again and make all the noise we want, just like if we had our own apartment."

"That's right. You want an apartment."

"Or a house in the hills so we can raise our baby."

"That's right," Josh kids. "You're pregnant!"

"With your baby, you oaf. And today, at ten, we're going to learn how to take care of our baby."

"We are going to do what?" Josh asks, turning serious.

"There is a free clinic at the high school health center to learn how to take care of newborns. I signed us up."

Josh rolls to look at the digital clock. "It's almost a quarter to ten right now. We better get going."

"We have time for one more. You know my needs."

*　　　*　　　*

Pickets walk back and forth in front of Hamilton House and the mayor's home. Asia's scooter stops at the top of the driveway between the two after she carefully dodges the sign carriers. Asia gets off, holding the secure package containing the liver cells. About that same time, the mayor,

Jefferson, Sylvia, Jack R. Abbott, and Winnie are leaving the mayor's house. "Our Asian beauty!" Mayor Sain yells. "Are you going to the Big Game with us and watch real men and a woman in action?"

"No. I've got important work to do, if you know what I mean?"

"I think I do," Mayor Sain says, winking at Asia. The others walk down the driveway toward the pickets, and Winnie walks into Hamilton House. Alone, Mayor Sain and Asia talk softly. "Is Mom going to be okay? Are you still growing the new liver?"

"Everything is going as planned. The professor tweaked the cells a little and gave them an energy boost."

"Thank God. I can't have anything to happen to Mom."

"The professor assured me that the cells will be just fine, and, hopefully, enough. The energy boost really helped."

"Speaking of an energy boost," Mayor Sain says, "when are you and me, you know, boosting together?"

"You can fuck me anytime you want, Mr. Mayor. Right now I've got a job to do. Maybe when you get back."

"I'll think of nothing else at the Big Game. I gotta go now and give the Bears their energy boost. You'll be thinking of me and later?"

"How could I forget?"

Mayor Sain kisses Asia on the head and walks off.

* * *

Thirty-year-old Ron Smith, Bertha's picket captain, watches the common driveway with a cell phone to his ear. "They are all in the driveway except Sarah Armstrong and Mr. and Mrs. Churchill, Miss Potts."

"Get pictures of everyone?"

"I will."

"Good! Forward them to me and I will send to the Stanford president. He and his hired security force will take it from there."

"We were all wondering if we can take the rest of the day off since they are going to the game," Smith says.

"Don't even think about it. You follow them to the bus, the train, and the game. Don't give up. We'll teach them a lesson in how politics works—Bertha's politics."

* * *

Mayor Sain, Winnie, Babe, Sarah, Jefferson, Sylvia and Jack R. Abbott walk west on Bancroft, headed toward Shattuck and the rooter bus to San Francisco. A line of pickets carrying signs bashing the mayor and Winnie follows them. The sidewalk is filled with Blue and Gold fans. "There's a lot of people headed for the buses," Winnie says. "Maybe we should jump on BART."

"It'll be full, and those BART cops are vicious, especially to those of us who might have a little refreshment on the way," Mayor Sain says. "The bus drivers all know me. I've been down this path a few times before."

"That's what I'm afraid of," Babe says.

"You all mind if I stop at the art store on the way?" Mayor Sain yells.

"Maybe I'll stay there with Josh and Michael," Babe says.

"I don't want to stay with Josh!" an angry Sarah says. "He's an asshole."

"My!" Babe says sarcastically. "Our vocabulary has certainly changed since Kansas."

"I can see Michael in the window, but no Josh," Mayor Sain says.

Hooded, mask-wearing Michael is concentrating on the laptop and doesn't see the group walk up. The mayor taps on the window, and Michael almost jumps off the seat. He opens the door. "Where's Josh?" Babe asks.

"He had to do something with his girlfriend," Michael says sheepishly. "He taught me how to make cartoons. I was just practicing."

"Let me see!" an excited Sarah yells, moving to the tilted table.

Michael slides back into the chair and pulls up a *Veronica's Lives* cartoon, and Roni, the rascally teen, helping an old lady cross a busy street with the caption "Everyone needs a little help once in a while." "That's a great one!" a pleased Sarah says. "You're better than he is—a lot better. He'll never use it, though. It's not horrible enough."

"You are good," the mayor says, looking over Michael's shoulder. "You learn real fast."

"Josh is a good teacher," a shy Michael says.

"Good teacher?" Sarah yells. "He's a real bastard, that's what he is. But you, Michael, you're the best."

"Good work, young man," Babe smiles. "Maybe we need to put a second artist's table in here."

"Michael," the mayor says. "I've got something for you." Mayor Sain pulls a cell phone from his khakis and hands it to him. "I got it last night. I taped the number to it and put my number, Winnie's, Bessie's, and Willie's in by their names."

"I wasn't allowed to have one. My mother didn't want me talking to anyone but her."

"That's what my daddy said to me!" Sarah yells. "He's a real bastard, too. I'll put my number in so you can call me any time you want."

"It's my present to you," the mayor says. "I don't want my ... a friend of mine to be at the mercy of the world without the ability to call for help."

"Thank you, sir. This is the best present I've ever received."

Mayor Sain and Winnie go outside the store while Babe checks the letters on her desk. "You almost told him you are his father, didn't you?" Winnie says, standing on the sidewalk next to the mayor. "Almost slipped out."

"Yes," Mayor Sain says nervously. "When do you think I should let him know he's my son? I am so happy I could run up to those fucking pickets and shit all over them."

"I'm sure the right time will come," Winnie philosophizes. "He'll probably know pretty soon, because you never could keep a secret. Remember when I stole Gertrude's panties from the locker room as a prank and you couldn't wait to tell the principal, even though you swore on your honor you wouldn't?"

"Yeah. I was getting even with you for stealing Priscilla Partridge away from me."

"You would never have gotten anything from Priscilla," Winnie laughs. "She wasn't your type—buck teeth, frizzy hair, and in-grown toe nails."

"She had small, pointed boobs and I wanted to see if I cut my hand or not when I grabbed 'em."

"You really are one sick bastard, like those picket signs say." Winnie laughs.

"We'd better get going, Mayor!" Jefferson yells. "It's after ten and the game starts at one."

"Shoulda brought the real Winston and blasted a few pickets," Jack R. Abbott says. "They are getting on my nerves."

"They've been around so long, I don't even see them anymore," Mayor Sain says.

Babe and Sarah rejoin the group. "Is Michael ready to use his cell?" Mayor Sain asks.

"Call him and see," Sarah says.

Mayor Sain punches in a number. "Michael?"

"Yes, sir, Mr. Mayor, it's me," Michael answers. "Thank you for the great present."

"You're welcome, Michael," the mayor says. "After you finish drawing a cartoon about Sarah, give mR. bERZERKELEY a whirl."

"I will, Mr. Mayor," Michael says. "Have fun at the game."

"The Big Game," the Mayor says. "The biggest game of them all!"

* * *

As the group walk toward the bus, Mayor Sain notices a bearded young man holding an expensive video camera on his shoulder pointed at him and another bearded young man carrying a large boom mike walking his way. "What do we have here?" the mayor says.

"Probably another one of Bertha's gimmicks," Winnie says.

"Wait a minute," an agitated Mayor Sain says. "I'm going to find out if they have a permit to film in my town!" He walks toward them. "Who are you and what are you doing?"

"We're university students, and we are shooting a sizzle reel for a possible reality show about you, mR. bERZERKELEY," the young man holding the boom mike says. "I'm Jed and this is Ken."

"A sizzle reel?" the mayor asks.

"Yeah, you know, a three-to-five-minute short to see if anyone wants to buy our idea and turn it into a television series," Jed says.

"You have a permit to be doing this?" the mayor asks.

"We do," Jed answers. "You want to see it?"

"Who put you up to this?" Mayor Sain asks, obviously irritated. "Who is financing this craziness?"

"We got the idea from the cartoons about you," Jed says, sensitive to the mayor's concern. "We're using our own money. You're okay with it, aren't you?"

"Well, I suppose so," Mayor Sain says. "I guess the notoriety will serve my purposes. If you sell it will I get a cut?"

"That'll be up to the studio that buys it," Jed answers. "That'll be up to you and them. Without you there's no sizzle or series. You have them over a barrel, if you know what I mean."

"You're right!" the mayor says. "What do you want me to do?"

"Just be yourself," a confident Jed replies. "Forget we're around."

"Just like with those fucking pickets?" the mayor yells.

"Just like that," Jed says, looking at the sign carriers.

Mayor Sain walks back to the group watching him deal with the film crew. "What's that all about?" Winnie asks.

"They are filming me for a possible television series. They are going to follow me around."

"Do they need someone to write a script?" a suddenly excited Jack R. Abbott asks. "I've got boxes of them back at my apartment. I've got experience."

"They want me to be my normal self with no script," Mayor Sain says.

"R or X rated," Babe laughs. "Did they tell you to keep your clothes on?"

"I could be a star?" Sarah asks.

"You are a star, hon," Babe says.

"Come on, gang," Mayor Sain says. "Let's give that camera crew a lesson in how real people celebrate freedom and beat the shit out of those Stanford whatever they call themselves. It's Big Game time."

"I don't know about this," a suspicious Winnie says. "Once we all get on film anything could happen to it."

* * *

Josh sits on a carpeted floor inside a portable classroom on the Berkeley High campus with Jasmine and twenty pregnant women. He is the only male. In front of them are a naked rubber baby, a stack of disposable diapers, baby powder, and wipes. "I'm the only father that's here," he whispers to Jasmine. "The rest of them are probably going to the game."

"I am so proud of you," Jasmine says, rubbing Josh's leg. "I'll give you your reward on the way back to the sorority."

"I can hardly wait. This is highly embarrassing. But it would make a good cartoon."

"Keep those going! Father told me to marry someone filthy rich and I got lucky. You make it and I'll spend it!"

"That's what I'm afraid of. I should be at the store cranking them out."

"Speaking of cranking them out, how about having several more of these little items?" Jasmine says, lifting the rubber baby to look at its blue eyes. "I want a house full."

"I guess I'll have to create a few more strips or paint more nudes."

"I'll pose again for you anytime you want, before, after, or during. You take care of me and I'll take care of you."

"Okay, okay," the teacher, a tall, heavy-set African American woman says, standing over the class looking at Jasmine and Josh. "Enough of the lovey-dovey stuff! That's what got you pregnant in the first place. Time to pay the piper, so to speak. Grab the little love child in front of you and let's get on with the real work!"

"You aren't going to make me change diapers, are you?" Josh asks, taking the rubber baby from Jasmine. "I mean, I changed my sister's little girl once, and they had to clean her up after I barfed."

"You'll get used to it. You change the baby while I get ready to make love. You know my needs."

"You mean ..." Josh starts.

"You know what I mean," Jasmine says touching his leg.

"Hey, you two!" the teacher yells. "Stop cooing and start changing."

*   *   *

With the mayor holding the bus door open, Winnie, Babe, Sarah, Jefferson, Sylvia, and Jack R. Abbott step aboard. The film crew is next. The mayor holds up his hands as the sign-carrying pickets try to board. "Sorry!" the mayor says. "This rooter bus is full, and it's the last one." He steps back and yells as the door is closed, "Go Bears! Driver!"

The pickets watch as the long, extended bus loaded with Blue and Gold fans pulls onto Shattuck. Ron Smith takes out his cell. "Ms. Potts, we've got trouble."

"What are you talking about?"

"The mayor and his buddies got on a bus and wouldn't let us on. It was the last bus."

"Well, get cabs, cars, or something, you idiot!" Bertha yells. "I need you at the Big Game."

"Why go? We'll hardly be noticed with the thousands that will be there."

"I'll make sure you're noticed," Bertha says. "I've hired a photographer and a reporter to make sure your picket signs are in all the papers with the stadium and the crowd behind you."

"Take cabs to Palo Alto? That'll break out budget."

"Money?" Bertha yells. "We've got a lot of money! Spend it! Teach those pricks a lesson! Trying to get away from Bertha! Those bastards!"

*   *   *

Asia finds Bessie sitting in a chair at the block, having trouble breathing. She puts the secure container down and moves in next to her. "Bessie? What's the matter?"

"China Girl," Bessie whispers. "I can't stand up anymore. Did they all leave? I don't want them to see me like this."

"They are all gone. They left, and so did the pickets."

"You and needle dick look at my liver cells?"

"They are coming along real well. He gave them an energy boost and taught me how to do it myself."

"How long until they're ready? I don't know how much longer I have."

"Hold on. They are growing and multiplying fast. It'll take a lot of them. Maybe a couple of weeks before testing."

"I don't know if I can wait two weeks. I can't walk and can't breathe. I feel my heart going this way and that. I don't even feel like drinking any Jack. I must be almost dead."

"Come on, Bessie. You're just tired. I used to get so tired from all the fucking that I wanted to die myself. Life in a whorehouse isn't much fun."

"I love when you talk about whoring. Keeps me alive thinking about the next time you'll tell stories about Lily Liu Lu."

"How about I take you into your room, put you in bed, and tell you a couple of stories that'll make you heal up fast?"

"Come on, China Girl. Let's go. I want a little excitement around here, other than my naked-ass commie son and his naked people."

"That's my Bessie. Let me help you up."

Asia, with one arm around Bessie's waist, helps her sit on the bed. "You get changed, and I'll put the liver cells back in the basement and get them going. I'll be right back and tell you a couple of tales you won't believe."

"Oh, I'll believe them, all right. Nothing shocks me anymore after fifty years of you-know-who."

Asia watches Bessie try to untie her work dress and goes to the block. After taking the cells to the basement and turning on the equipment and the grow lights, she returns to Bessie's room. Bessie is under the covers, eyes closed, arms at her side, looking to be deader than a doornail. "Bessie? Bessie?"

Bessie's eyes open. "I was just practicing dying. Go get me a little glass of Jack and start telling me those whoring stories and about all the men you fucked."

"You have that much time?" Asia laughs.

"I want to hear about everything, how you learned to fuck, how you turned men on, how much you made—everything. I want to die hearing about sex, men, all kinds of men … things I've dreamed of for the fifty years I've been stuck behind a stove."

"Where are the medications the doctors gave you?"

"I stopped taking them a week ago. Those quacks don't know shit."

"Why did you stop?" Asia asks.

"I read the bottles. No alcohol allowed. Can you imagine me making a decision between a little Jack and a goddamn pill?"

"Those pills will keep you alive until the cells are ready," Asia says with a stern voice. "The alcohol warning is just that. It usually accelerates the effects of the pills."

"You mean it wouldn't kill me if I took both?" a surprised Bessie asks.

"Too much and they could. Trust me about pills. At the whorehouse everyone used pills, for everything you can imagine. Uppers, downers, oxis, abortions—you name it. When it came time for drug testing I supplied them all with my urine because I didn't take any. Where are your meds?"

"In my bathroom," Bessie says, pointing feebly to a closed door across her room.

Asia walks inside the bathroom and opens the medicine cabinet, seeing a dozen bottles of different sizes. She carefully looks at each one.

"Hurry up. I want to hear stories."

Asia, carrying three pill bottles, turns to leave and sees a man's picture on the wall. She pulls close, and her face turns pale. She pulls back. "It couldn't be," she says to herself as she walks back to the bed and sits down next to Bessie. She hands Bessie two pills from each bottle. "Take these. They will keep you going. Two of them will help you sleep."

"Can I wash them down with Jack?" Bessie asks.

"Of course," Asia says, handing her the glass by her bed. "Why not?"

Bessie takes the pills from Asia, pops them in her mouth, and follows them with a sip of booze.

"That picture on the wall in your bathroom? Who is that?"

"That's the bastard who took advantage of me and knocked me up fifty years ago. That's the father of the naked-ass commie next door. I keep that picture there so every time I take a dump I can think of him and pretend I am shitting on his head."

"Sure looks a lot like the mayor—and someone else I knew. Is he the Sain in your life?"

"Sain? He and I never got married," Bessie says. "He got what he wanted and took off."

"What is his name, then?" a nervous Asia asks.

"Johnny Blood," Bessie says. "Can you imagine me, Bessie Blood? Or Mayor Blood? Thank God for little favors."

Asia's face turns ashen as she dwells on Bessie's words. Bessie notices her demeanor. "What's the matter, China Girl? You look like you've seen a ghost. Do I look that bad?"

"It's nothing," Asia says, trembling. "How about you get some sleep? I'll come back and tell you all the whoring stories you can take."

"Sounds good. Either those pills or the Jack is working. I feel a whole lot better."

"Great. Sleep!" Asia says as she stands and walks toward the door.

Once outside Bessie's room, Asia wants to scream but holds back as she covers her mouth and heads for the stairs and her room. Once inside, she locks the door and goes into her closet for a locked case. She sits on her bed, puts in the combination, and opens it. She takes out a red outfit with gold tassels, puts the case on the floor, and lies down, the outfit on top of her body. She tries to close her eyes but can't as the recurring, haunting vision of her past fills her head. She sees a room full of Johns and the whores lined up like a meat market—an expensive, exotic meat market—looking for their next fuck, their next roll of greenbacks, their next trick. She stands next to an older, tall, voluptuous blonde squeezed into a tiny see-through outfit they all called Lady Gretchen who whispers out of the side of her mouth, looking at an older man with salty black hair coming their way. "That's him. That's Johnny Blood. I'm sure of it. He's much older, but I'm sure he's the one who killed your mother."

The late-sixties, tall, staggering drunk, unshaven man dressed in baggy dark slacks that haven't been off his body for days and wearing a droopy gray sport coat covered with fragments of grime and sludge, takes a sip of beer from the bottle he holds. He spills liquid on the carpet while he looks straight at Lily Liu Lu.

"Are you sure? I guess the grapevine was right about him getting out of prison."

"I will never forget that face," Gretchen says. "He beat your mother with his bare hands and hit her so hard so many times in the stomach she gave birth to you early before she died. He beat others, too."

The older man walks toward Lily Liu Lu and stops. "So, you are the Chinese whore's daughter? Let's see if you got the same talent."

"Take me," Gretchen interrupts. "I've got everything you want and more, and I'm not nearly as expensive as she is."

"Shut up, old bitch. I want her. If she's half as good as her mother, I'll pay double anything she asks. And I might give her a lesson or two about fucking."

"Half as good?" Lily Liu Lu says. "I'm twice as good, and I want to see what you got, old man. I'll be the teacher, not you."

"Excellent," Johnny Blood slurs. "Go get ready for the ride of your life."

He walks off with the madam while Lily Liu Lu watches him. "Why?" Gretchen says.

"I've been waiting a long time for him to come and see me," Lily Liu Lu says. "I'm more than ready."

"Oh, he is the one," Gretchen says. "There's no mistake about that."

Lily Liu Lu goes to her private room wearing her red and gold outfit, tassels moving side to side as she walks. She sits on her bed, legs apart, ready for Johnny Blood. Suddenly, without warning, a revolver is thrown through an open window and lands beside her. She fingers it and slips it under a pillow. She waits. Johnny Blood opens her door and stands naked with his hands on his hips. "There you are, you baby Chinese whore," he says, wiping beer off his chin. "Your mother said I am your father. She deserved to die. She was a liar. I hate liars, especially whores that lie. I am not your father.

A thousand others could have been. Not me. It's time to show you what a real man can do."

The older man steps forward. Lily Liu Lu takes the revolver from under the pillow and points it at the man. "You going to stop me with that, you little whore?" he says. "You don't have the guts."

"For my mother and all the others you have beaten," Lily Liu Lu says as she pulls the trigger and shoots him in the dick. He grabs himself in severe pain. Lily Liu Lu shoots him again, aiming for his balls. He falls to his knees, looking at her. She pulls the trigger again and shoots him between the eyes. He falls dead at her feet.

Gretchen runs into her room. "What the?" she yells, looking at the dead man on the floor and Lily Liu Lu holding a smoking revolver. "You gotta get out of here. Where did you get that gun?"

"Someone threw it through the window," an unemotional Lily Liu Lu says, dropping the gun on the bed. "I was going to use this." She pulls back the pillow to show a stiletto. "It belonged to my mother."

"I'll hold them outside," Gretchen says. "Get out of here."

Lily Liu Lu climbs out the window and walks low to avoid being seen. In the parking lot, she jumps in a sedan and drives away.

Asia sits up in bed, grabs the small suitcase, and carefully puts her red and gold outfit away, turning the lock before she sets it down on the floor. She lies down, staring at the ceiling. "Oh. My. God," she says to herself as a sudden new thought comes into her mind. "If JohnnyBlood is my father and he is the mayor's father and Michael is the mayor's son—oh my God! I gotta find out if we are related!"

Asia gets up quickly, grabs her keys, and heads down the stairs. After taking a peek at the sleeping Bessie, she hurries outside, almost tripping over Trojan coming in through the doggy door. She fires up her scooter and speeds down the driveway.

Trojan goes inside and looks around at the empty house, walks to his empty dish, turns, and goes back outside. He looks in both directions and then lies down to rest on the kitchen steps. Mimi has been locked in her house, and all the available legs have disappeared. *What's a horny dog to do?* he thinks to himself. He hears a noise coming from Mimi's house. He perks up. It's the doggy door. He can hear plastic move against metal. Mimi IS coming out! *Yes! Game on!*

Chapter Seven
Mr. Mayor's Wild Ride

The train to Palo Alto waits in San Francisco. Hot steam comes from under the train in the cool air. Two African American men wearing blue conductor uniforms and hats watch the train fill with Blue and Gold fans. "Have you seen him yet?" one of the conductors asks.

"No," the other conductor says. "And you don't have to see him. Put your nose in the air and you can smell the marijuana from a hundred yards."

"He's reserved several seats in the bar car again," the conductor says.

"Good," the other conductor says. "Keep him and his animals away from the rest of the train."

"You see those cartoons?" the conductor asks. "Does he really go naked that much?"

"Oh yeah," the other conductor says. "I got a brother who lives in Berkeley. He says he's always naked in his office at city hall."

"What a freak!" the conductor says.

"Go Bares!" the other conductor says.

"That's a good one. Uh-oh, here he comes," the conductor says.

The mayor jumps aboard the train, turns, and helps Babe with an outstretched hand. Winnie climbs aboard followed by Sylvia, Jefferson, Jack R. Abbott, Sarah, and the film crew. "This is so neat!" Sarah says.

"Follow me," the mayor says, walking down the aisle leading toward the bar car.

"Go get 'em!" one of the Blue and Gold passengers yells.

"Go mR. bERZERKELEY!" another passenger yells. "You gonna keep your clothes on this year?"

"Only if they put me in chains!" Mayor Sain yells, holding out his hands as if they were handcuffed.

"He's a rock star," Babe says.

Sitting in adjoining seats, two large men watch the mayor and his entourage walk by. After they pass, one of the men talks low into a microphone near his watch. "They are aboard and headed to the bar car. We can see in there from our seats."

Mayor Sain enters the bar car and spots a guitar in the overhead rack. "Whose?" he asks.

"Go ahead, Mr. Mayor," a bearded young man says. "I brought it just for you, like two years ago."

"My hero," Mayor Sain says, smiling and patting the young man on the shoulder. "I'll put it to good use after we get started."

Mayor Sain stands at the bar with Jack R. Abbott while Winnie, Babe, Jefferson, and Sylvia sit. The two-man film crew sits in front of Winnie and Babe. Sarah sits next to a pale white girl dressed in Goth garb, a piercing through her nose holding tiny blue and white pearls on a chain strung across to a ring in her left ear. Black hair sticks out of both sides of a tall black hat and falls over her black coat. Black fingernails, black eyeliner, and corpse makeup complete her image. The black pants she is wearing are short and expose tall, black, laced-up boots and striped black-and-white socks. "Where did you get all those neat clothes?" Sarah asks the young girl.

"Haven't you ever seen a Goth before?" the cynical girl says. "Everyone knows how to go Goth. What planet are you from?"

"I'm Roni from Berkeley. But before that, I was from Kansas, and I've never seen great clothes, makeup, and chains like you're wearing before. Are you a lesbian, too?"

"You're from Berkeley, don't know what a Goth is, and you're a lesbian? Do I have it right?" the girl responds.

"Yes. Are you?" Sarah asks. "I am looking for a new lesbian friend. My lesbian roommates are in love with each other. You know … three's a crowd."

"I am a Goth and I am not lesbian and my name's Death," the girl says, bordering on impatience. "But even though I am not a lesbian, I respect one who is and is willing to admit it."

One of the conductors walks through the bar car. "Everyone sit!" he says. "The train is departing—and that includes mR. bERZERKELEY." He laughs and walks off.

"Yeah! mR. bERZERKELEY!" one of the passengers yells. Mayor Sain waves in acknowledgement as the train moves. "Guess we should sit down, eh, Jack?"

"Kind of reminds me of one of my mystery novels," Jack R. Abbott says. "*Murder by Lingerie.*"

"Sounds like a sex novel to me. Did you ever finish it?"

"No, but I'm going to."

"How many does that make?"

"Probably in the hundreds by now. One of these days I WILL finish one."

"I'll drink to that," the mayor laughs. "Got my Jägermeister?" he yells at the bartender.

"Yes, sir," the bartender says, bringing down a large, chilled bottle. "Fully loaded at your request and on your tab."

"Did you see those two guys in the long-sleeved winter shirts in the car behind us?" Jack R. Abbott whispers. "They look like private dicks to me. I think they're packing."

"You and your imagination," the mayor says as the train begins to pick up speed, the bar car rocking slightly. "Just more material for your next unfinished mystery novel."

"I tell you, I can pick 'em out," Jack R. Abbott whispers. "No one knows private eyes better than me."

"Well, then, let's give 'em something to look at," the mayor says as he stands and goes for the guitar.

The film crew scrambles to stand.

Mayor Sain returns to the bar, takes a big swig of Jager, and wipes his mouth. "Okay, you Bears!" he yells. "What say we get this road trip off on the right foot—or track, so to speak?"

"Go for it, mR. bERZERKELEY!" a Blue and Gold fan yells.

"All right!" the mayor yells. "Time for a little song about the road trip. You'll all know this one, except for the few words that have been changed for just this occasion." He begins strumming the guitar and singing.

"One, two.
"One, two, three, four.
"On the train to beat Stanford again.
"Just can't wait to get on the train again.
"The life I love is making music with my friends,
"And I can't wait to beat Stanford again."

"He's good, no doubt about that," Babe says as the mayor keeps singing. "Maybe we should name our baby Jim in his honor—if it's a boy, of course."

"Come on! Knock it off with the pregnancy stuff. There's no way. You are kidding, aren't you?"

"Just conversation. Got you good, didn't I?"

The two men sit looking into the bar car, and the mayor continuing to play the guitar, laugh, and drink Jägermeister. "He's playing a guitar and drinking, sitting next to some real weirdo," the man says into the hidden microphone on his shirtsleeve.

"Don't let him or his friends get out of your sight," Kennedy, a tall, gray-haired man says, sitting in a room inside Stanford Stadium with three other men and a gorgeous Hispanic female. "We've got enough security to keep those bastards from doing anything stupid."

"Isn't he the greatest, Death?" Sarah says, jumping out of her seat with excitement.

"Anyone who runs around naked isn't *that* cool," Death says sarcastically.

"How did you get a neat name like that, anyhow?" Sarah asks.

"I chose it," Death says. "Our group all have names symbolizing what we are."

"That's so cool! I should dress like you and choose a neat name, too. Maybe Murder, Horror, Dracula—something like that. Of course it would mess up Josh's cartoon strip. Hey! That's not a bad idea!"

"You have a cartoon named after you?" Death asks.

"Yes, *Veronica's Lives*. This guy who I loved before I became a lesbian draws it. I hate it! He accuses me of everything I don't do."

"*Veronica's Lives*? I've never seen it. My friends and I read horror books and Victorian novels. You ever read about the real Dracula?"

"No," Sarah says sadly. "My father would never let me read anything like that."

"Too scary for his little girl?" Death says cynically as a long, black tail suddenly erupts above the top button of her black coat, stroking her chin.

"What's that?" a surprised Sarah says. "Is that part of your Goth outfit, too?"

Death opens the top two buttons of her coat to expose the black face and green eyes of a purring cat. "This is Voodoo," Death says. "Meet Roni."

"How neat! A little black cat. How fun! I have a dog named Trojan, but all he wants to do is hump everyone's leg. What does Voodoo do? Hey, that's cute. 'Voodoo do'!"

"We're going to meet our friends in Palo Alto and sit outside the stadium while the do-gooders and rich people watch the horrid football game. We can't imagine people and their insanity of cheering and rooting for big guys running around after a little ball. How stupid people are, don't you agree?"

"I guess. I only went to one other game, ran naked on the field, and was thrown in jail, along with the mayor over there."

"And politics. There's another game for dummies. Why waste your time?"

"Can I hold voodoo?" Sarah asks.

"No!" Death responds. "I'm not supposed to have a pet on the train. You do know how to keep a secret, don't you, Roni the lesbian?"

"Of course," Sarah says. "Where do you meet in Berkeley? I want to be a part of your group."

"You'll have to do a lot of changing if you want in," Death says. "We meet in the park next to the high school. You know where that is?"

"Sure do. That's where we finished the parade."

"What parade?"

"I'm one of the naked people, and we got dressed in that park afterwards."

"You're one of the naked people?" Death says with a slight laugh. "You do have a long way to go."

Babe watches Sarah and Death talk and sees Sarah's excitement. "I suppose we have to get out the black clothes now. She's going to do it all, isn't she?"

"I suppose so," Winnie says. "I wonder how Gerry is gonna like a few piercings."

"Bertha will probably blame that on you, too," Babe groans. "How did I let you talk me into going to this game, anyhow?"

"Better do it all now, if you got one in the oven."

"If I do I'm gonna use Bessie's cleaver and cut off what caused it."

"Better knock off the garbage talk," Winnie says. "The film crew is panning our way."

"Why not give them something that'll make their sizzle reel—like flipping Bertha off?" Babe laughs.

"That would be appropriate, I suppose," Winnie laughs. "Want a drink? We are in the bar car."

"Go ahead," Babe says, shifting her weight slightly in the seat. "I've got indigestion bad."

"Sounds like another girl in the family," Winnie jokes. "Remember our daughter Katrina? What a pain! Son Billy never moved a muscle in nine months."

"And look what a pain he turned out to be," Babe says.

"So are you really pregnant, or you just having gas?"

"Go Bears," Babe says as the camera is pointed at her with the boom overhead.

Chapter Eight
I Am Who I Am

Asia is bending over a keyboard when Professor Spears walks up. "What are you doing?" he asks. "You were just here. Did you forget what I told you?"

"Where are the DNA results from the vice-chancellor and the others? I've looked everywhere, and I can't find any of them."

"The vice-chancellor told me to delete them. She was very upset, like I told you earlier this morning. I was ordered to keep you away from anything to do with DNA."

"You didn't tell me she told you to destroy everything," Asia says. "I thought you and I had an agreement."

"She said she would guarantee me the cloning equipment if I did what she wanted. I need that equipment. We need that equipment."

"I need those results," Asia says. "It's very important. You really destroyed them? I thought we agreed to keep them and have something to hold over the vice-chancellor's head, just in case. I need to look at them—not hers, but the others."

"Well," Professor Spears says, coyly pulling out a flash drive, "I guess you and I can make a trade, if you know what I mean?"

"Professor, I love you," Asia says, taking the flash drive from his hand. "You're going to get the treat of your life after I look at these—even better than this morning."

"I was hoping you'd see it my way," the professor smiles. "You won't tell her, will you?"

"Are you kidding?" Asia says. "You can have me anytime, anywhere forever."

"I will be waiting in the sterilization room," the professor says. "You never saw anything."

The professor walks away as Asia inserts the flash drive. She looks at the icons and clicks on "DNA," pulling up the results. After studying them side by side for a few minutes, she loads the icon on the desktop and pulls it out. She takes a second flash drive from her scooter key chain and inserts it into the computer. She loads the "DNA" icon on her flash drive and takes it out before dragging the icon into recycle and emptying the bin. She straightens up and has a pale, ghost-like color on her face. She stares into nothing for a moment and then remembers the deal she has made with the professor. "I am who I am," she says to herself. "And the mayor and Michael are who they are. We are related. Johnny Blood is my father, and I am the one who killed him!"

Chapter Nine
A Driving Lesson

The Campanile rings eleven times as hood and mask-wearing Michael sits at an artist's table working on Josh's laptop. The sun peeks through white clouds moving over Berkeley from west to east as his cell phone rings. After fumbling with it for a few moments, he answers, "Yes?"

"Michael," the mayor says, with train noise in the background. "It's not too late to come to the Big Game. Call Willie and he'll bring you in a squad car."

"I've got a lot of work to do. But thank you, sir."

"This is your chance to see me take down the president's stimulus fund," Mayor Sain says. "It's going to make national news. I'll see you later tonight."

"Yes, sir," Michael says, closing his cell and returning to the laptop. Almost immediately, the cell rings again. "Yes, sir," Michael says, thinking it is the mayor again.

"Michael?" Bessie says, her voice hardly audible. "Can you come home quick? I need you."

"Bessie? What's wrong?"

"I need you, now," Bessie says, her voice trailing.

"Yes, ma'am." Michael folds his cell, closes the laptop and runs out the store door at full speed toward Durant and Hamilton House. He dodges cars crossing at Bancroft and runs like he's never run before. Puffing hard, he runs up the driveway past Winnie's SUV and into the kitchen. "Bessie!" he yells. Hearing nothing, he opens the door to her room. Bessie, wearing her flimsy robe, lies on the floor, the cell phone in her hand. He crouches down next to her. "Bessie?"

"You got to get me to the hospital. I'm dying."

"I'll call a cab."

"No time for that. I gotta go now. Winnie left his car in the driveway, and the keys are on the block. Let's go?"

"I don't know how to drive," Michael says frantically.

"Fuck it. Let's go!"

Michael helps Bessie to her feet and moves slowly out of her room and across the kitchen, where he grabs the SUV keys. They move outside, where a curious Trojan watches at the bottom of the steps. "Come on, boy. I need your help."

Trojan scratches himself with a hind foot and watches Michael open the SUV's door and lean Bessie in, moving her feet inside. "I'm not kidding. Get in and help me!"

Michael opens a door and Trojan jumps in the backseat, putting his front paws on the back of the front seat. Michael moves around to the driver's side and jumps in. "What do I do now?" Michael says, holding the car keys and looking at the dash. "Do I put the key in here?"

Trojan barks. Michael puts the key in the ignition and the SUV starts. Bessie lies against the seat, out cold, her head almost on Michael. "Now what? The car is running. How do I make it go backwards?" He fingers the steering wheel and the gearshift. Trojan barks again. Michael looks at the letters. "I'll bet *R* is for reverse." Trojan barks again.

Michael puts the SUV in gear, presses the accelerator, and begins backing down the driveway. The car starts going sideways, and Trojan barks again. Michael straightens the car. The car backs toward the sidewalk and the street. "What if there are cars coming? What do I do?" Trojan moves to a back window and barks. The car continues to move backward and begins to enter the street. Trojan barks several times loudly. "That must mean stop." Michael slams on the brakes, knocking Trojan off his feet. He rolls over and goes back to the window. "Sorry. Let me know when it is safe."

Trojan barks once, and the car begins to move slowly. Michael turns the wheel, and the SUV backs into the street. Trojan puts his paws on the back of the front seat and barks once. "I guess *D* stands for drive. You ready, boy?" Trojan barks once. The SUV begins moving slowly up Durant. "I remember going to the hospital for a checkup. I think it's this way."

Asia, aboard her scooter, works her way around the university and takes the long way, going to Andronico's for a six-pack of beer she is going to drink by herself to get over what the DNA has uncovered. As she pulls from the store on Telegraph, she is almost hit by Michael driving toward Ashby. "What? Michael? I didn't know you could drive."

Asia quickly turns around and chases the SUV. Michael stops at Ashby, puts on a turn signal, and turns left. Asia is on his rear bumper. Michael moves slowly toward the hospital. "Now what?"

Trojan barks once. "Emergency! Yes, that's it, boy. This is an emergency."

Michael pulls the SUV up to the curb in front of emergency and stops. Asia is at his window. Michael opens the door. "What are you doing?" Asia says, before she sees Bessie passed out in the passenger seat. She runs toward the automatic glass doors and immediately returns with two attendants pushing a gurney.

"She called me!" Michael yells at Asia. "I went to Hamilton House, and she was passed out on the floor."

The attendants gently load Bessie on the gurney and wheel her inside. Michael and Asia follow. Trojan watches from the backseat of the car, barks three times and jumps in the front seat. He presses a button and opens the driver's window. He looks around and jumps out. It's not that far back to Hamilton House. He is a hero! Maybe Mimi is waiting.

* * *

Bessie lays in the emergency room. Michael and Asia are with her. Her eyes open. "Where am I? Heaven?"

"You're in the hospital," Asia says. "Michael drove you here. He did great."

"Thank God! Probably better than my naked-ass commie son would have done."

"What happened?" Asia asks. "When I left, you seemed to be doing real good taking your meds."

"I felt so good, I decided to take a few more and wash them down with a glass of Jack," Bessie says. "My feet never touched the ground on the way back to bed. Before I knew it I was higher than a kite. It felt great, but then *boom*—like a ton of bricks fell on my head. I never felt like this since the mayor's father stuffed a joint in my mouth in the backseat at the drive-in. My clothes came off just like that!"

"Enough detail," Asia says, looking at Michael. "We've all had our moments."

A doctor walks up. "What's going on here?" he says, looking at Asia and the hood and mask-wearing Michael.

"She took too many of the pills she has for her condition," Asia says. "Look at the charts. She took several of each one."

"I have her chart here," the doctor says, looking at a clipboard. "Did she try to commit suicide? Is that what you are saying?"

"Suicide?" Bessie quips. "I feel like that every day when my naked-ass commie son comes into my kitchen looking for food."

"That's right!" the doctor laughs. "You are mR. bERZERKELEY's mother, aren't you?"

"The one and only. Shoulda had that abortion fifty years ago."

"We'll get a stomach pump and refill the meds," the doctor says. "We'll give her condition a fresh start. Just watch it from now on. We'll keep her overnight for good measure. You two can go, if you want."

"China Girl and Michael, go back to Hamilton House."

"We'll hang around awhile," Asia says. "Just get some rest and do what they say."

"What condition?" Michael says softly to Asia as they step away from Bessie's bed.

"She has a very bad liver," Asia whispers. "I'm trying to fix it by growing new liver cells in the basement."

"Why don't you use the university laboratory?"

"I would, but a certain vice-chancellor would fire me and destroy the cells if she knew."

"That bitch," an angry Michael says. "She's the worst person on the planet."

"That's true. Right now, we got to take care of Bessie and get the SUV and my scooter in the parking garage before we have another problem."

"Can you drive it for me? I almost killed several people on the way over. If it weren't for Trojan helping me …"

"Trojan? He knows how to drive?"

"Yes, ma'am," Michael answers, looking out the open window. "It looks like he found a way to get out. Will you help me now?"

"Sure," Asia says, putting one hand on Michael's arm. "I'll do it."

"You sure are nice to me," Michael says.

"Hey," Asia says as she smiles. "If I had a brother or a cousin, I'd want one just like you."

"Thanks," Michael says. "I'd like you as a sister or a cousin, too."

Asia smiles slightly as she gets into the SUV.

Chapter Ten
Tailgating Bears and Vipers

Mayor Sain, Winnie, Babe, Sarah, Jefferson, Sylvia, Jack R. Abbott, and the film crew climb off the train at the Palo Alto Station across the street from Stanford Stadium. Hoover Tower rings eleven thirty from the middle of the campus. "Come on, gang!" the mayor yells as the film crew takes it all in. "We've got several tailgates to visit before we go inside."

"Where does that boy get all his energy?" Babe says. "I want to find a bench and sit for a while."

"Come on," Winnie says. "Last chance to party before you give birth."

"If I am pregnant, I'm going to party you, you bastard," Babe says.

"I met the nicest person on the train," an exuberant Sarah says to Babe as they walk toward the stadium. "Her name is Death. Isn't that neat?"

"We saw," Babe says, puffing as she walks. "I suppose you want to look like her, too."

"Yes. How did you know? I want to be a Goth."

"We'll work on that back at Hamilton House," Babe says.

"Sure, Mrs. Churchill. I am so excited!"

"You're the most excitement I ever had, Mr. Mayor," a stoned Sylvia says. "Are we almost there?"

"Almost," Mayor Sain says. "Jefferson, you bring the good stuff?"

"I got plenty," Jefferson says. "Better smoke 'em at the tailgate because they'll search us going inside."

"Maybe we can stick 'em up our butts like we did last time we were here." The mayor laughs.

"Ruined the taste," Jefferson says.

"I couldn't tell the difference," Jack R. Abbott says.

"There," Mayor Sain yells, pointing at four tie-dye-painted vehicles one row from the stadium in a tree-lined parking lot. "They're waiting for us."

* * *

The two long-sleeved-shirt-wearing men who were watching them on the train follow several yards behind. "They are stopping at a tailgate just outside," one man says into the microphone hidden in his sleeve. "Want us to hang around?"

"We see them," Kennedy says, standing in a room with three men and the gorgeous Hispanic female looking at television monitors. "Go into the stadium and get into position."

A door opens and Vice-Chancellor Kris walks into security with Stanford President Tafoya. Wearing spiked heels, she towers over the diminutive, graying president of American Indian descent. "This is our security center," President Tafoya says. "From here, with a dozen monitors, we can check out every corner of the stadium."

"Impressive!" Vice-Chancellor Kris says. "I'm going to tell Chancellor Lim about this and all the security you have available."

"We had an anonymous donor give us enough to beef up our security for this game," President Tafoya says. "It seems there's quite a bit of interest in keeping your mayor and his friends under control. I don't know what they could possibly do, but we welcome the extra money."

"Are you kidding?" the vice-chancellor says. "He's the most devious, underhanded wacko in the world, and he could do anything, as long as it suits his purpose."

"Purpose?" President Tafoya asks.

"He's in a pissing match with the president of the United States over stimulus funds," Vice-Chancellor Kris says. "Imagine! Against the president. What a jerk! mR. bERZERKELEY!"

"The naked guy in the cartoons! Of course," President Tafoya says. "One of my favorites!"

"Mr. President," Kennedy says. "We've got pickets coming toward the Berkeley guy's tailgate. Should we bust 'em?"

"Can you pick up what the signs say?" President Tafoya asks.

"'The mayor and Winston, child porn mongers' and 'the mayor and Winston encourage underage drinking' and 'ask the mayor about raping young girls.'"

"Good." President Tafoya sighs. "At least there's nothing about Stanford. Nothing like they carry around here: 'Stanford Indians' Indian makes too much wampum'!"

"I saw that one last year when you got a well-deserved raise." Vice-Chancellor Kris laughs.

"Are those things on the signs true, Vice-Chancellor?" President Tafoya asks.

"You wouldn't believe what he and his friends are capable of," Vice-Chancellor Kris says. "Those are the least of his crimes."

"Shouldn't they be in jail?" President Tafoya exclaims.

"That one," Vice-Chancellor Kris says, pointing at Winston on the monitor, "is a real slick lawyer and keeps them free."

"Is he Winston?" President Tafoya asks.

"Yep," the vice-chancellor says. "Mr. Winston Churchill, political bigwig and a possible candidate for governor of Kansas."

"That's why!" President Tafoya says, rubbing his chin. "This Bertha Potts from Kansas, who provided all the money for the security—now I get it. She's probably connected to the signs, too."

"That why you're the president," Vice-Chancellor Kris says. "You see through everything, and the more you know about mR. bERZERKELEY and his friends, the more you'll support Bertha's efforts."

"As long as the pickets don't hurt Stanford's reputation, let them have their fun," President Tafoya says. "Ready to go to my box?"

"Sure," the vice-chancellor says. "Let's have a couple of belts before HE arrives. I don't know if I can take him sober."

* * *

In the parking lot, the mayor sits in a folding chair, smoking a joint and drinking a beer. He grabs a copy of the *Daily Cal*. "Look! I'm featured!" he says, pointing at an article that has a mR. bERZERKELEY cartoon and a full-page essay. "They call me their greatest alum and Berkeley's savior! How about that? When I take down the president's stimulus patrol and their evil doings the students might even support me for chancellor. First thing I'll do is fire that bitch. Imagine—me, Chancellor Sain!"

"How many of those have you smoked?" Winnie laughs, sitting on one side of the mayor. "With those signs and Bertha, you'll be lucky you get supported for dog catcher."

"When you get out of jail," Babe chimes in, sitting next to Winnie.

"You're right!" Mayor Sain says. "I think I'll talk to the pickets about those horrible untruths they're spreading here in enemy territory."

"Where's he going?" Jack R. Abbott says, the zipper of his walking shorts wide open as he stands in front of Babe and Winnie, holding a flask in one hand and a joint in the other.

"He's going to talk to the pickets. Say, aren't you a little drafty?" Winnie says as he motions with his head toward his crotch.

"I'm just giving junior some air after being cooped up on the train," Jack R. Abbott says as he takes a hit. "Gotta keep the snake alive!"

"Maybe you should go and help the mayor," Winnie says.

"Good idea," Jack R. Abbott says. "The boy needs someone with a little sense by his side."

"Can we go home?" Babe says, watching Jack R. Abbott leave. "He makes me nervous."

Sarah walks over, carrying a beer and a hot dog. "Mr. and Mrs. Churchill," a bubbly Sarah says, "thank you for letting me come to the game. This is so much fun! First I met Death on the train, and now I am eating a real hot dog. My father would never let me eat one, because they are made of bad things, he said."

"Your father is just looking out for you and your health," Babe says. "That beer doesn't help any, including the fact you are underage."

"Mr. Jefferson said beer is the fruit of the gods and will make me strong," Sarah says.

"Mr. Jefferson is probably into his second or third joint by now," Babe says. "Maybe you should give the beer to me and go have another hot dog."

"Sure, Mrs. Churchill. I'll be right back."

"Those signs are right," Winnie says. "I'm sure Bertha has already been e-mailed a picture of Sarah drinking beer."

"She's a real snake, too," Babe says. "Can we go back to Berkeley now?"

"The game will start in less than an hour," Winnie says. "We'll be nice and comfy in our seats in the new stadium."

"Can we hide from all these goofballs?" Babe asks.

Mayor Sain walks up to the five male pickets. "Okay, which one of Bertha's babies is in charge?"

"I am," Ron Smith says, holding a sign saying "mR. bERZERKELEY rapes little girls."

"Why don't you guys give it a break? Here we are, on the verge of kicking Stanford's ass, and you guys are still trying to pick on me and Winnie. Tell Bertha to give it up for a while. We'll be back in Berkeley late tonight."

Jack R. Abbott walks up to join the mayor. "Yeah!" he yells, half-stoned. "If you don't quit I'm going to go home and bring back the real Winston to show you how we fumigate the neighborhood and everything else!"

"It's okay, Jack," the mayor says in a calm voice. "I'll handle this. Go on back and entertain the troops."

Jack R. Abbott staggers away.

"Look, Mr. Mayor," Smith starts, "me and the guys don't have anything against you and the other guy. We just need work, and Bertha pays us real good. She can cut us off just like that!" He snaps his fingers. "I got a wife and kids, and I haven't had a job for almost a year. The rest of them are in the same boat. We need the money. Besides, the signs don't bother you none, do they?"

"No, actually, they don't," the mayor says. "Like I always said, any publicity is good publicity. But the signs, being bold-faced lies, bother some of my friends."

"We have no control over what the signs say. I don't like them either. But what Bertha wants, Bertha gets, as long as we get our money."

"I got you," the mayor says, understanding their predicament. "Seems like we are both in a pickle."

"Yeah." Smith groans. "Sorry."

"You guys hungry?" the mayor asks. "We got a hotdogs, beer, and soda—and if you're real brave, some of Jefferson's finest."

Smith looks at the other pickets, who shrug their shoulders. "Why not, as long as you let us hold the signs while we eat and drink, and don't tell Bertha!"

"Come on, gang," the mayor says, walking back toward the tailgate.

"What in the hell is he doing now?" Babe says, watching the pickets follow the mayor toward her.

"He's doing his political thing again," Winnie says. "He knows the real enemy is back in Kansas pulling the strings. These guys might even be potential voters in the next Berkeley election."

"Shit!" Babe sighs. "I want to go back to Hamilton House, where everything is now seeming to be normal."

"Never." Winnie laughs.

Inside security, the vice-chancellor watches a monitor as the pickets join the mayor's tailgate. "Why, that bastard! He's bribing Bertha's pickets with booze and dope. Can't you have him arrested for dealing drugs or something?"

"If we arrested everyone in the crowd from Berkeley and a few from Stanford that were smoking joints, we wouldn't have anyone to watch the game." Kennedy laughs. "It's time for you to go to the president's box anyhow. We'll bring the mayor to you. Kickoff is only a half hour away."

"You son-of-a-bitch," the vice-chancellor growls. "I'll take care of your naked ass once and for all!"

Two large men dressed in black suits approach the tailgate and walk up to the mayor. "Sir," one the men says, "we are here to escort you to your seat."

"You from the police or an escort service?" Mayor Sain laughs, smoking a joint. "I'm hoping it's an escort service."

"We have been asked to take you to the president's box, sir," the other man says sternly.

"I guess it's time for me to leave this esteemed company. Here, don't let this prized one go to waste," he says as he hands a half-smoked joint to Smith, the picket captain. "Winnie, you got the tickets?"

"Got 'em, Mr. Mayor," Winnie says.

"That's mR. bERZERKELEY to you." The mayor laughs as he sticks out both elbows toward the men in jest. "Shall we?"

The picket captain watches the mayor and his escorts leave, looks at the joint, takes one hit and then another, and lays down his sign. "I guess we'll have to wait until he comes out after the game, won't we, boys?"

All the pickets lay down their signs and go for the food and drink.

"Is this for real?" Babe asks Winnie.

"It is," Winnie says, looking around. "Where did Sarah go?"

Chapter Eleven
Stand In

SARAH HAS WANDERED AROUND the stadium to the players' entrance, where the Stanford Band is getting ready to storm the field. Dressed in whatever they feel like at the moment, band members laugh, tune their instruments, and pass alcohol and joints around. Sarah walks up to a tall, slightly bent over, extremely thin young man with acne covering his face, leaning against a tuba. "Hi!" she says excitedly. "Your instrument is very big. How are you going to carry it?"

A short young man standing next to a tuba laughs. "You have no idea how big his instrument is. He's got his pants on!"

"It's no joke," the thin young man says. "I partied all night and barfed all morning. There's no way I can play right now. I tried, and bubbles came out."

"How heavy is it?" Sarah says, grabbing the tuba.

"Not too heavy for someone with muscles like yours," the short young man says.

Sarah lifts the tuba. "It's not *that* heavy. How does it go?"

The short young man gently lifts it in place on Sarah's body, brushing her breasts rapidly with a hand. "How did that feel?" he says. "You feel just fine."

"This is easy," Sarah says. "And you can touch me all you want and it won't do any good. I'm a lesbian and a Goth."

"Some of my best friends are lesbians," the short young man says.

A male band director wearing a red coat yells through a bullhorn. "Shake the soap out of the tubas. It's time! Let's go!"

"I already did it," the young man says. "Keep the tuba around you and get in line with the rest.

"What do I do now?" Sarah yells.

"Just pretend you're one of us." The band moves into the stadium entrance. "Pretend you're blowing into the mouthpiece. No one will know!"

"This is going to be fun!" Sarah yells as the fans erupt seeing the Stanford Band enter the field helter-skelter, uncontrolled, and yelling. They stop at the fifty-yard line. Sarah watches the short young man and does what he does. The band breaks into the Stanford fight song, and fans go crazy. Sarah begins moving her tuba up and down, her lips in the mouthpiece copying the short young man. Suddenly all the tubas run to the sideline. Sarah follows. They form a line and blow a loud chorus and then retreat back into the band. Sarah lags slightly behind but catches up. The fans think she's a plant because of her yellow Cal sweatshirt and start cheering her.

The song ends, and the band lines up, semi-organized in the center of the field. The drums roll, and the fans stand for "The Star-Spangled Banner." As soon as it is over, the band scrambles undisciplined to its section on the home side of the field. Sarah sits with the tubas. "That was so much fun! I want to do that again!"

"I want to feel what you got again," the short young man says. "Lesbians don't mind, do they?"

"I got to go find the Churchills. Wait until I tell them what I just did!"

Sarah moves to an aisle and runs toward the top. Her yellow Cal sweatshirt brings some boos and some cheers as she raises her arms high. She is stopped at the top by a man from security looking at pictures. "That's her. Escort her to her seat."

The two men grab Sarah by her arms and take her to the reserved seat section on the visitor's side, where the Cal fans give her a rousing ovation as she raises her hands, signaling a touchdown. She sees Winnie and Babe sitting next to an empty seat. Sarah sits down hard. "This is her, isn't it?" one of the security men asks.

"The one and only," Babe says.

"You will keep her under control, won't you?" the other security man asks.

"If that's humanly possible," Babe says. "We haven't been able to do that in several months, but we'll do our best."

The two men walk off.

"Did you see the picture they had of Sarah?" Winnie whispers in Babe's ear. "It was of her walking down the driveway at Hamilton House. It looked like they had a stack of them."

"Thank God!" Babe whispers. "It helped them find her."

"Did you see me?" an exuberant Sarah yells over the noise of the Cal football team running on the field. "I was down there—in the band!"

"You were in the band doing what?" Babe asks.

"I was blowing a tuba for some guy who barfed all night. It was so much fun. I want to play a tuba!"

"Well, a tuba-playing Goth!" Babe says. "Sure glad we came to the game."

"Those pictures," Winnie whispers. "I've got to tell Jim something is up."

"Good luck," Babe says. "He's probably locked up with the vice-chancellor by now, ready to stick a tuba up her you-know-what."

"I gotta find the rest and let them know, too," Winnie says, looking around. "I wonder where they are sitting."

"I heard them say something about the student section," Babe says.

"Shit! I'll never find them in that mob!" Winnie says as he stands and starts to walk to the center aisle. He is stopped by a man wearing a blue security blazer and an earpiece. "You'll have to sit down, Mr. Churchill," the man says in threatening tones.

"Do I have to hold up one or two fingers?"

"Don't kid around with me. If you do I'll have to escort you from the game."

"I can't even go to the bathroom?" Winnie says again.

"As I have already stated, Mr. Churchill, sit down! You just went to the bathroom five minutes ago. You're up to something. Go back to your seat."

Winnie, sensing he has pushed security as far as he can, returns to his seat. "What was that all about?" Babe asks as he sits down.

"We are prisoners. He won't let us out of our seats. Something is really wrong. We are in big trouble!"

"Wanna bet Bertha has something to do with this?" Babe says.

"I don't want to lose," Winnie says.

Chapter Twelve
Where's Your Momma?

The stroll home from Alta Bates brings several memories to Trojan, memories of his time as a free man—a stray—after leaving the young girl who brought him to the university as a pup. Willard Middle School, where he used to dig up goodies left by students, is along the way. He loved the delicious organics from their large garden and left his mark on the gymnasium wall mural. *I wonder who's been visiting lately,* he thinks to himself as he sniffs the wall. *A German shepherd who has been eating pizza scraps—gross!* He covers the mark with pure Trojan and leftover Bessie's Jack. *That'll fool 'em and show them who's the real man around here.*

He cuts through a hole in the fence beside the Willard swimming pool and takes a detour through the baseball field and the small park next door. He stops dead in his tracks. There is something across the grass under a bush, and it's not Michael, because he's at the hospital with Asia and Bessie. He sniffs the air. It's not a homeless person sleeping off a night of alcohol and drugs. He takes a few steps then stops again, his nose in the air. Coyote urine! It's a den! Maybe he should turn and run. Maybe he should walk slowly back toward Telegraph and continue on quickly to Hamilton House. He sniffs again and stands motionless. A pair of tiny eyes peer from underneath the bush, looking straight at him. It is a baby coyote!

Trojan takes a step toward the small, gray animal, and then another. If mother or father coyote were around, they would keep this little one hidden, and their eyes would be looking at him—and then he WOULD run like hell. But no other eyes appear. A baby! How much trouble can he get into with a baby? Maybe he should teach the little one not to mess with him and to stay away from Hamilton House and Mimi next door? When was the last time he got to bully a coyote? Why not?

Trojan prances toward the bush and the small pair of eyes that haven't moved. He stops within two feet and wiggles his stub of a tail a couple of times, trying to entice the little creature out. The eyes move slightly, and a head appears, followed almost immediately by a tiny creature barely able to walk, probably recently born. *Come on out and play, you little beast, you,* Trojan thinks to himself. *I'll show you not to mess with a real stud.*

The tiny coyote's nose is within inches of Trojan's face as his beady eyes fixate on the black-and-white mutt. Trojan turns to let the coyote sniff and then lifts his leg and drenches the dirt, some of the urine splashing on the small beast. *That's from a real man,* Trojan indicates by using his back feet to make dirt fly in the coyote's face. Unfazed, the tiny coyote watches Trojan's antics and backs up into the den. *You're crazy if you think I'm going to follow you in there. Mommy or Daddy might just be snoozing. I may be a man about Berkeley, but I'm not stupid.*

Trojan walks up to the set of unblinking eyes, lays down the last of his urine on a bush, and prances off, proud that he has bullied a coyote and backed him down. What a story he will have to tell his offspring—that is, if Mimi would ever give him a chance. He stops at a watering can in the Willard Garden and reloads. *Ah! Nothing like staring down a fierce beast! All in the line of duty! Speaking of Mimi, it's about time for Mrs. McPherson to take off her shield and let her out for an afternoon pee. Maybe this hero will just have to stop by.*

Chapter Thirteen
Doctor's Orders

Bessie lies in a hospital bed while a technician rolls equipment from her room. Asia and hood and mask-wearing Michael sit in chairs reserved for visitors. "What time is it?" Bessie demands. "I can't hear the Campanile in here."

Michael looks at a digital clock outside the room on a wall. "It is almost one o'clock, ma'am," he says softly.

"One o'clock! Shit! I'm going to miss the kickoff. I haven't missed the Big Game since I gave birth to what's-his-name! Get me out of here!"

"The doctor wants to keep you overnight to observe you and the effects your pill rampage had," Asia says. "They want to make sure no further damage was done to any of your organs."

"Organs? I'll show them an organ when I get up and piss all over their floor, after I take a dump on it. These quacks have no idea what's the fuck is going on."

"You want me to leave?" Michael says timidly.

"No," Asia says. "You need to stay here with me and do what we can for Bessie. She doesn't have anyone else right now."

"That's fucking right. My naked-ass commie son is off in Palo Alto, probably to do something real stupid at the game. And I want to see him do it!"

"Why not watch the television in the room?" Asia asks.

"This fucking place doesn't get the channel. I already asked. I want to watch my own television on my own couch in Hamilton House in my own robe, not this open-air, flimsy gown! Get me out of here!"

A doctor walks in, hearing Bessie's yelling. "Is there a problem, Mrs. Sain?"

"I ain't no 'Mrs. Sain'!" Bessie yells. "And the problem is I want out of here now, or there will be a problem, and you'll have to clean it up!"

The doctor takes his stethoscope and leans in on the brooding Bessie, holding it just above her right breast. "If you want to feel me up you're going to have to go a lot lower than that."

"I was just checking your heart. It's been irregular for some time. You know that."

Bessie grabs the stethoscope and pulls it, bringing his face nose-to-nose with hers. "Listen to me, you quack," she says softly so Asia and Michael can't hear. "China Girl knows all about my innards and their problems, but I don't want the boy to know. How about you just say, 'Okay, Bessie. You can go home now. Be careful with those pills, and be a good little girl.' I want out of here. I'll be back soon enough for the last time."

Bessie lets go of the stethoscope, and the doctor stands up. "I guess she can go home. She'll have to sign a waiver and agree to take her medications properly."

"That's a good doctor," Bessie says. "Now let's get the fuck out of here. It's almost kickoff, and I don't want to miss whatever my naked-ass commie son is going to do to embarrass me."

"Michael," Asia says. "Stay with your—stay with Bessie, and I'll bring Mr. Churchill's SUV around. Meet me at the curb."

"Yes, ma'am."

"You are the politest young man I've even known," Bessie says. "Wish I could train my naked-ass commie son to be polite just once."

* * *

Bessie, wearing her tattered maroon robe, sits on a couch in front of a flat-screen in Hamilton House, her feet propped up on a hassock. Several pill containers are beside her next to a half-filled glass of Jack. "Now, this is what I call livin'," she says to Michael, who is next to her and Asia standing in the doorway leading to the basement.

"I've got to go and check my experiment," Asia says. "Michael, you're in charge."

"Yes, ma'am," Michael says, adjusting his black mask.

"It's almost kickoff," Bessie says after sipping Jack. "I wonder what my 'nature boy' is up to."

"Can I get you something?" Michael asks.

"I already got everything I need. Just beat those damn Indians or Trees or Cardinals one more time for old Bessie. That's all I want to make my day, my year, my life."

"There'll be a lot more games," Michael says softly.

"You never know, do you? Maybe for you, but for old Bessie, this could be the last one."

"No, ma'am. You're going to be around for a long time. I'll make sure. You're the nicest older person I've ever known."

"Older person? Yeah, I am an older person!"

Josh walks into the kitchen and sees Bessie and Michael sitting on the couch. "Kickoff yet?"

"No," Bessie says. "I think they're waiting for some game in the east to finish. It's been delayed a few minutes."

"Great!" Josh says. "Has the mayor done anything stupid yet?"

"Nothing—at least not on television," Bessie says.

"Hey, Michael, I went by the store and looked at what you did. Your bERZERKELEY is better than any of mine, and you really put a lot of love into *Veronica's Lives.* I think we've found ourselves an artistic genius."

"My mother wanted me to be a scientist and hide in a lab," Michael says. "She said no one would want to look at my ugly face, so I needed to be a hermit or something."

"Ugly face?" Bessie says reaching for Michael's hood and mask. "Let old Bessie see."

Michael doesn't move as Bessie slowly pulls the hood back and lifts the mask off his face, exposing the hole where his right ear should be and several deep scars. "Looks like any other face to me. Better than most. But you know what's the most important? You are real handsome on the inside. Outside doesn't mean shit! Right, Surfer Boy?"

"I agree. Michael, you want a beer or something before the game starts? You and I got to talk about forming a corporation. We're gonna take cartooning to another level, and the way my girlfriend is spending money, I'm gonna need to do just that."

"Me and you?" Michael asks.

"Who else? You are better than anyone I've ever seen, and I went to USC and Hollywood to learn how to do it. You're phenomenal!"

Asia walks into the room from the basement and sees Josh, Michael, and Bessie waiting for the game to start. She notices Michael's hood and mask off. "Now, that's better," she says. "No more Lone Ranger! We got the most handsome man in the house uncovered."

"Now wait a minute," Josh says, smiling at Asia. "Have you forgotten about me?"

"No, and I haven't forgotten about the little arrangement that has been proposed worth one and a half million dollars, either."

"That's right," Josh says. "Painting you naked in some red thing. I may need that money, too."

"What about a little of it for me? Doesn't the model get a little? No model, no money."

"How does fifty-fifty sound?" Josh says as he smiles back, getting excited.

"Hey!" Asia yells at Michael and Bessie. "You heard him. I've got witnesses. A fifty-fifty split!"

"You want to get started?" Josh says. "To hell with the Big Game!"

"Maybe later. I got an experiment to monitor. When it's time, we'll get it right. Got it?" Asia touches Josh's nose tenderly with her right index finger.

"Hey, you two. Go do it and get it over with. Michael and I have a game to watch."

"What are they talking about?" Michael whispers to Bessie.

"Sex. What else? Some rich Chinese guy offered Josh a whole lot of cash to paint a picture of Asia naked."

"Oh."

"I'll explain later. Right now, I escaped those fucking quacks, and the game is gonna start. Forget sex!"

"You can make a lot of money being an artist," Michael says. "He's gonna teach me how to paint, too."

Chapter Fourteen
Locked and Loaded

FROM A SKYBOX, PRESIDENT Tafoya and Vice-Chancellor Kris watch the team captains for Cal and Stanford shake hands after the coin toss in the center of the field. The bands play loudly from the stands, and the cheerleaders and yell leaders are winding up their fans. The December air in Palo Alto is cool, crisp, and clear. The teams are jumping on each other, getting ready to start the Big Game. The Stanford Tree is moving back and forth in front of the home side, and the new, giant television monitor is flashing "BEAT CAL!" Kennedy from security enters the box. "Mr. President, Vice-Chancellor, all of the Berkeley mayor's folks are in their seats and under our watch."

"Where's his majesty?" the vice-chancellor says sarcastically. "Is he running naked through the corridors?"

"He's on his way, ma'am. He's being mobbed by Cal fans and asked for his autograph in the strangest places. He even took a couple of quick drags on a joint he was handed before my men could take it away. He's more difficult to escort than the President of the United States was when he visited the campus last year."

"Good ol' mR. bERZERKELEY," Vice-Chancellor Kris says. "Can't wait to lock him in chains and foil whatever nonsense he has in mind."

"Do you really think he'll try something?" President Tafoya asks.

"I would bet my life on it," the vice-chancellor answers. "He'll do anything to draw the spotlight his way."

"I can't wait to meet him in person," Tafoya says. "I brought one of my favorite cartoons for him to autograph."

The door to the skybox opens, and Mayor Sain enters, being escorted by three dark-blue-blazer-wearing men and the gorgeous Hispanic female. "Thanks, guys, and miss, what's your name and phone number? Why don't you get rid of these three thugs, and you and I can go sit under a tree, smoke a few joints, and listen to the crowd roar? We can have our own Big Game."

"My God," an exasperated vice-chancellor says, "I heard that line a long time ago."

"It worked then, didn't it?" Mayor Sain says, turning toward the vice-chancellor and smiling.

"Have a good game, Mr. Mayor," the female Hispanic security guard says, shutting the door in the mayor's face.

"It looks like they're finally going to start the game," Kennedy says. "It's time for me to do my duty."

"What duty is that?" the mayor asks. "Guard the prisoners? Why can't my film crew come inside the stadium?"

"Film crew?" President Tafoya asks.

"They're from the university, shooting a reality show about me. What could be more real than me locked up in the Stanford President's skybox at the Big Game?"

"That's highly unusual," Tafoya says. "Maybe next time."

"They don't have tickets, sir," Kennedy says.

"Then they'll have to remain outside," President Tafoya says.

"Mr. Mayor, Mr. President, Vice-Chancellor," Kennedy says, as he heads for the door. "I'll be outside if you need me."

"Don't leave on my account," Mayor Sain says. "I might need someone with snake bite experience in here, sitting next to one of my dearest and oldest former friends."

Kennedy opens the door and shuts it behind him without saying a word. The mayor looks around, and the only seat available is between President Tafoya and the vice-chancellor. He looks at the spread of sandwiches, beer, and wine. "Can I get anyone anything?" he asks. "Where is the Jägermeister and weed?"

"University policy only goes so far, Mr. Mayor," Tafoya says. "We are allowed beer and wine."

"Excuse the animal," Vice-Chancellor Kris says. "He's used to groveling and getting what he wants. Don't give in."

"You mean like someone else did a few years back," Mayor Sain says.

"Would you please sit down," Vice-Chancellor Kris says. "You are embarrassing yourself and the university."

"Yes, your highness," a sarcastic mayor says, sitting down and holding a beer and a sandwich. "Do I have your permission to breathe?"

"If you two can't keep it civil," President Tafoya says, "I'll have you both join the film crew."

"Got it," Mayor Sain says. "I'm glad I have someone to protect me."

As the crowd yells loudly from both sides of the stadium, Cal kicks off and the game starts. Mayor Sain's evil look at the vice-chancellor is returned with an equally vicious and nasty glare as both sit silently. The mayor holds up a sandwich as if to offer it to her. She shrugs her shoulders and turns her attention on the game. "Go Bears!" the mayor says with his mouth full.

Chapter Fifteen
Taking Care of Business

Josh, Michael and Bessie sit on the couch, watching the Big Game with Stanford on offense and Cal trying to stop them from scoring. Asia stands to the side nearest the basement door. "Sit down and take a load off," Josh says to Asia.

"Can't," a nervous Asia says. "I'm waiting for a timer to go off. I am at a critical stage with my experiment."

"What experiment?" Michael asks.

"Hey, everyone!" Bessie yells. "Can you all stop talking? This is the Big Game, and I want to hear every word in case this is my last one. I know my naked-ass commie son is going to do something stupid. I want to hear everything."

"Sorry," Michael whispers, reaching for his mask nervously.

"And keep that damn thing off," Bessie groans. "No hiding out around here!"

"Yes, ma'am," Michael says softly.

Trojan comes in through the doggy door, stops, goes to his bowl, and paws at the empty dish. "Could you drop a little Jack in his dish?" Bessie yells at Asia. "He's the only smart one here. Drinking and screwing—a one-track mind."

Asia walks to the cupboard and takes down a half-full bottle of Jack Daniels and pours a little in Trojan's dish. Hearing a buzzer ring, she hurries down the basement steps. Trojan sips, licks the bowl, and then walks over to Michael and starts humping his leg. He stops, looks up at Michael's uncovered face and his deformity then humps even harder. "See!" Bessie says. "The real you don't scare him!"

Josh's cell rings. "Speaking of drinkin' and humpin'," Bessie says as Josh stands and moves away from the couch.

"What's up?" Josh asks.

"I need you," Jasmine says. "You know my needs, and I suddenly have a big need for you right here in my room."

"We just did it a few minutes ago before I dropped you off."

"I was laying here thinking about what we did this morning—the baby, the diapers, the wipes, the breast feeding, the burping. It just came over me ... *boom!* I need you now!"

"I'll be over in a few minutes."

"Better hurry. You know how desperate I can get."

Josh closes his cell and walks past the couch toward the kitchen door. "Gotta run. I'll catch up to you later."

"Don't let her get the best of you," Bessie says. "There's always another fish in the pond."

"This fish has big hooks and very sharp teeth."

"And I thought it was all about her tail," Bessie laughs.

"Now, that IS a good one," Josh says, pointing at Bessie on his way out the door. "That WILL be in one of the strips."

"What did all that mean?" Michael asks.

"Bessie will explain it to you later," she says, tapping Michael on one leg. "No sense cluttering up your mind with garbage. You keep close to ol' Bessie. I'll teach you all the tricks."

Asia, who has come back up the stairs, stands beside the couch, smiling as she listens to Bessie's unknowing grandmotherly advice.

*   *   *

Josh stretches his arms over his head, lying in Jasmine's bed as she has one arm over his chest. "I can go back to Hamilton House now?" he says softly, moving one hand down around her shoulders.

"Now that my needs have been satisfied, I'm ready to go shopping. We've got a lot of baby clothes and things to buy. And after that, we'll go house hunting."

"Buying baby clothes and house hunting? We are going to spend the rest of the day shopping?"

"Well, we might take a few moments out to take care of my needs."

"Now I know what a prisoner feels like." Josh laughs.

"What?" Jasmine says slapping Josh on the chest. "You think I'm chaining you up?"

"Nah. I was just thinking about tying a ball and chain on one of my cartoons, that's all. It'll be one of my best."

"You better not pull that on me, buster. I'll make life miserable for you."

"Forget it," Josh says. "Ready to go shopping?"

"I think I need you again after you stirred me up!"

*   *   *

Kennedy's cell phone rings as he sits in security, watching several monitors. "Yes, Miss Potts? What can I do for you?"

"Do you have everything under control?" she says, sitting in a soft chair in her office. "I gave you a lot of money to keep the crazies from getting any attention during the game."

"Everything's under control, Miss Potts. I can see them on the monitors. We have them virtually locked up. It's business as usual for me and our team."

"What about my pickets? I have been calling them for an hour. Did they arrive?"

"I can see them on our outside monitor. They are sitting around a fire in the parking lot waiting for the mayor and your friend Winston to leave the game."

"Shit! There's money down a rat hole."

"I'm telling you, Miss Potts, everything here is under control. Watch the game. Nothing will happen."

"I would, but I can't get the channel here in Kansas. If they pull any tricks, the second half of your money will not be sent. Got it?"

"Yes, Miss Potts, got it!"

Chapter Sixteen
Geocaching Babies

Stephanie and Judy walk through a dense Marin Headlands forest dressed in camouflage outfits and lace-up boots following three women, each carrying a tiny baby in a specially designed backpack. "Whose idea was this, anyhow?" Judy grunts. "Following three lesbos and their babies through the forest looking for hidden treasure! I would have rather stayed in bed!"

"Relax," Stephanie says. "I thought you'd like to rough it once in a while. We can only go to our bar in San Francisco so much. Time to think outside the box."

"This is more like out of the universe, if you ask me," a puffing Judy says, trying to keep up. "I can think of a whole lot of other ways to use our time."

"Such as?" Stephanie says.

"Look at our friends," Judy says. "They have their hands full with those babies. That might be fun."

"What?" Stephanie says, surprise in her voice. "Have a baby? You've been working with those young high school mothers too long."

"I'm not kidding," a serious Judy says. "You and me, a little baby. The lesbians ahead of us did it. Why not us?"

"You want us to have a baby? A real baby?"

"Why don't we both have babies? We're getting tired of doing the same old thing, same old bar, same old weed, same old sex."

"Wait a minute," Stephanie says. "Same old sex? You getting tired of me? Is that it?"

"That's not what I meant," Judy says. "I love you and you love me. But I miss having something to devote my life to, like a baby."

"We are lesbians. We don't have sex with men."

"At the high school we talk about sex a lot in the health center, about having babies and the several ways eggs get fertilized," Judy says. "I'll bet the three lesbians ahead of us didn't have sex with a man. Let's ask them when they stop—and I hope that's pretty soon."

Judy and Stephanie walk a few steps and stop as the three baby-carrying women holding small GPS devices look upward at a large tree. "It's up there," one of the women says. "Who's climbing?"

The three girls look at Judy and Stephanie. "What?" Judy says.

"You two don't have a baby," one of the women says. "One of you has to go up or agree to take care of my baby while I do."

"I'll go up," Stephanie says. "But if I do, you will tell us how three lesbos had babies. Agreed?"

The three girls nod yes.

Stephanie climbs up the large tree and finds a small gold box buried in a squirrel hole inches above the first giant limb. She brings it down and hands it to one of the women. "What's inside?" Judy asks.

"Our friends hinted we would like it a lot," one of the women says.

Three silver baby rattles and three miniature bottles of Buena Vista Irish Whiskey are inside. "I love it," one of the women says. "What are we gonna leave for the next geocacher?"

One of the women pulls out a small box of chocolates and a miniature bottle of Cutty Sark. "That'll sweeten them up," she says, handing the gold box back to Stephanie.

Stephanie puts the box back in place. She climbs down the tree and confronts their three friends who are sipping on Irish whiskey. "Okay, how did you get these babies?" Judy asks.

"In vitro," one of the lesbians answers. "We don't do men, at least not anymore. We saved our bucks and had a doc farm our eggs and fertilize them with sperm from his bank, and voilà, we got babies."

"Did you use the same sperm?" Judy asks.

"We did," one of the women says. "Big, strong, handsome, and worth a lot of bucks. We want our babies to take care of us when we get older."

"Why all of you?" Stephanie asks.

"We wanted to go through this together," one of the women says. "My partner didn't want to do it with me, so she took off. No problem. I'll find another one who likes babies."

"What do you think, Stephanie? You and me? Babies together?"

"You know I love you and would do anything for you. I just don't know how we can do it. I don't have the money and neither do you."

"Let's ask Asia," Judy says, putting her arms through one of Stephanie's and holding tight. "She knows all about this kind of stuff."

Chapter Seventeen
The Biggest Game

MAYOR SAIN AND THE vice-chancellor have not said a word to each other. The negative energy generated from their bodies fills the skybox. The game is in the second quarter, and there is no score. Kennedy from security enters and whispers to the president. "One of the alums wants to talk to you. He says it's urgent and that he must see you now or he will hold off on his donation and tell all his friends to do likewise."

"Is it one of the Silicon Valley boys?" the president asks. "Does he want me to order the coach to play his son again?"

"He won't say. You could be right, though. The last time he wanted his friend's daughter to be a cheerleader."

"Okay, okay. Where is he?"

"At the stadium house bar."

The president turns to the vice-chancellor and Mayor Sain. "Can you two keep from killing each other while I attend to a donor matter downstairs?"

"Don't be gone too long. I have no idea what the wild man sitting next to me is gonna do next."

"No problem. As long as you have enough steak sandwiches and more beer, I'll behave."

"Good! I will be right back."

The door shuts behind the president and Kennedy, leaving the vice-chancellor and Mayor Sain alone. "Last time we were alone, we had great sex," Mayor Sain says through a mouthful of food. "Remember that night under the bright moon in the middle of the empty stadium?"

"You evil monster," the vice-chancellor says. "I have repressed any and all memories of you and everything you do and stand for. My only wish is that the earth would open up and drop you into the hell I have lived in since that time."

"Come on. We could have sex right here, right now, and relive those past moments of glory. Imagine … at the Big Game, of all places."

"I hate you more than anyone could hate anything and anyone," the vice-chancellor says, her teeth clenched. "You have made my life more miserable than even you can imagine."

The mayor hesitates. "This is all about Michael, isn't it?"

The vice-chancellor turns her head and looks at him. "Why, you fucking bastard! I have no son!"

Mayor Sain holds up an index finger. "I beg to differ. He's a great young man, ear hole and all, and I know because he has a room at Hamilton House."

The vice-chancellor stands and towers over the mayor, hands on her hips. "You are really a prick, aren't you? You have no right to lay any sort of guilt on me, you condescending, righteous bastard."

"Sit down, sit down, or the television cameras will swing this way and catch you as you really are, not the sweet academic you pretend to be in front of Stanford brass."

The vice-chancellor sits down and folds her arms across her breasts. "You are out of your fucking head, Jim Sain, like you have been since I met you."

"What I can't figure out is why you never told me you were pregnant. All these years, you kept this from me, kept our son locked up in the basement, made him wear a hood and a mask in shame and hide from me and the rest of the world. He's a great young man with oodles of talent and personality. I have no idea where he got the personality from. Certainly not you!"

"Like I said," a calm vice-chancellor says, "I have no son. You have no proof whatsoever of your ridiculous and idiotic claim."

"Oh, but I do. DNA doesn't lie."

"You have no DNA proof of anything."

"I do. Miss Asia ran it several times. There is absolutely no doubt about it. We have a son!"

"Miss Asia! I hate that name almost as much as yours. How can you trust anyone who stripped in front of a class of young college students when she was a teaching assistant?"

"How about testing yourself?" Mayor Sain asks. "You and I and Michael will go to a lab of your choice, be tested, and then let the results stand. What do you say?"

"I'll do no such thing. I have no son, and that is that!"

"Are you going to continue to be the evil bitch? The bitch that picks on young boys and girls, men and women and ruins their college lives? Who keeps a great young man locked up in her basement because he rebels a little against her wishes? The bitch that makes a young lady take an experiment home, fearing destruction or being ruined by one of your fucked-up moods?"

"What are you talking about?" the vice-chancellor says, looking at the mayor. "What experiment did Miss Asia take to Hamilton House?"

"Nothing. Just a figure of speech to make the point that you are nothing but a raving snake of a bitch, the worst kind of person to have in charge of young minds, and a horrible mother."

"In listening to you I am considering the source."

The door opens and the Stanford president returns. "Well, there's no blood on the floor," he says with a smile as he returns to his seat. "The game is still scoreless, too."

"The game has just started," a cool vice-chancellor says while the mayor squirms in his seat, knowing his mouth has just committed an egregious blunder.

Chapter Eighteen
What's Up?

WINNIE AND BABE WATCH the scoreless game in the middle of the second quarter from their reserved seats. "I haven't had to sit this long in one place forever," Babe says. "Can't we get up and walk around a little? This is getting ridiculous!"

"See those guys wearing the dark-blue blazers at both ends of our aisle?" Winnie says. "They are our keepers. Something is up, really up."

"The only thing that is 'up' is my patience," Babe says. "Why don't you try some of that Berkeley bullshit you've used your whole life? Why not try it on one of those guards?"

"Why not let me try?" Sarah says. "They've been smiling at me this whole game."

"They are human," Babe says. "Maybe that's not such a bad idea. Wiggle away and see what happens."

Cal has marched to the Stanford ten-yard line. It's fourth and inches for a first down. Cal fans stand and begin to cheer and yell loudly. "Go Bears!" Winnie yells. "Come on, Babe, stand up and yell."

"If I stand up and yell, I'm liable to pee all over the seat," Babe says. "I suddenly got to go bad."

"Come on," Winnie says, holding out his hand. "Let's try to escape while everyone is standing."

Winnie starts moving in front of the shouting crowd. "Me, too!" Sarah yells as she follows Babe. "I'm going, too."

A quarterback sneak gets the first down ... barely. Cal fans sense a score and yell even louder. Winnie, Babe, and Sarah reach security. "My wife has to go real bad," Winnie says.

"You are not supposed to leave your seats, the president's orders," security says with authority.

"Then I'll pee on your shoes. And maybe I'll do even more than that!"

"I suppose you can go, but you have to stay here," the man says, looking at Winnie.

"How about me?" Sarah asks. "I need to help her."

"You'll both have to wait until I call it in," the man says reaching for a walkie-talkie. "The females in the thirty-fifth row have to use the facilities. Do we have an escort?"

"Yes," Kennedy's voice says over the speaker. "She'll be waiting at the bottom of the steps."

"Stand aside, Mr. Churchill," the man says. "Let your wife and the young lady pass."

The crowd yells as Cal moves closer to the goal line.

"Just what are you all worried about?" Winnie asks.

"Just following orders, Mr. Churchill. Just following orders."

"We're here to watch Cal beat Stanford. That's all."

"I have no idea why we're doing what we're doing. And if you're here to see Cal win, forget it! Stanford is ranked and Cal is in the toilet. No chance."

The Cal tailback dives over the line and rolls into the end zone with the Cal fans going crazy, high-fiving and yelling. The Cal band plays loud and lively. "You sure about that? This is the Big Game!"

"Your team got lucky. We got a whole second half coming up. It'll be a different story."

"You gonna keep us locked up in our seats the rest of the game?"

"I just do what I'm told."

* * *

"What is going on?" Sarah asks Babe, putting cold water on her face in front of a mirror in the ladies' room. "That woman over there won't take her eyes off us." The gorgeous Hispanic female from security stands with her arms crossed, watching them.

"I guess we're lucky she didn't use a mirror while we peed," Babe says.

"Why are they following us and keeping us from having a good time?"

"We don't know, but we think it's about Bertha Potts and not letting the mayor or any of his friends do anything during the game to bring attention to themselves. She doesn't want folks back home to think Winston is willing to do more for their state than your father."

"My father? What a joke. This whole thing is a joke."

"No joke. The mayor is up to something. They know it, and so does Winston."

"What?" an excited Sarah says. "Are we going to run naked on the field again?"

"You can go ahead if you want. I just want to go back to Hamilton

House and get some rest. Why did I ever come to the game? Why did I ever come to Berkeley?"

"Naked? How fun! I wonder what Death will think if I run naked again."

* * *

Kennedy walks into the skybox and asks the president to talk privately with him near the door. "We have the mayor's people under surveillance and basically locked in their seats. Do we try to keep them there during halftime when the crowd is up and moving?"

"We were given a lot of money to make sure they don't create an incident at halftime or during the game," the president whispers back. "They are behaving, aren't they?"

"Mr. and Mrs. Churchill got up with the young girl to visit the facilities," Kennedy whispers. "Mrs. Churchill and the young girl did visit the restroom with no incident, and Mr. Churchill returned to his seat. Maybe our intelligence is wrong about the whole group."

"Intelligence doesn't matter. Maybe the best plan is to eject them from the stadium before halftime—peacefully, of course. That will solve everything."

"Take them out, now?" Kennedy whispers.

"Why not? We have the right to refuse seating to anyone we want."

"What about him?" Kennedy looks at Mayor Sain.

"What can he possibly do inside here under my watchful eyes? If he is outside with the rest of his crew, all hell can break loose. I say split them up."

"Yes, sir. You are the boss."

Kennedy walks from the skybox and the president returns to his seat.

"You seem to be full of emergencies, Mr. President," the vice-chancellor says.

"Goes with the territory, I suppose," the president says. "How's the game going?"

"We're kicking your ass," Mayor Sain says. "The axe will be ours!"

"I apologize for our guest," the vice-chancellor says. "But the Bears are winning."

"It's almost halftime, and we always do better the second half," the president says.

"Do you mind if I go outside to the bathroom?" the mayor asks.

"We have one in my box," the President answers. "It's available."

"Thanks," the mayor says. "I apologize in advance for tinkling too loudly. I wouldn't want to upset you or my darling vice-chancellor."

The crowd cheers as Stanford moves the ball fifty yards to the Cal twenty. "Go ahead, Mr. Mayor," the president laughs. "Stanford fans will drown out any loud noise you can conjure up."

Mayor Sain goes into the bathroom and quickly takes out his cell phone. He punches in numbers and listens. "Jefferson," he says as softly as he can, just loud enough for Jefferson to hear. "Are you ready? It's almost halftime."

"We are surrounded by security and they are taking us out of the stadium," Jefferson yells over the loud crowd noise. "All of us!" Jefferson's cell cuts out.

"What in the hell?" the mayor says as he punches in Winnie's number and listens. "Winnie? Are you and Babe all right?"

"Jim," Winnie says. "They are coming to take us somewhere. Whatever you've planned is in deep trouble." Winnie's voice trails and the mayor can hear him talking to someone. "This is my personal phone," Winnie says. "You can't take it. I may need it in an emergency." Winnie's phone cuts out.

"Shit!" the mayor says as he flushes the toilet. He walks back into the booth and sits down with a distressed look on his face. Cal fans are screaming and yelling, as Stanford has fumbled on the five-yard line. The mayor looks across the field and sees Winnie, Babe, and Sarah being escorted from the stands into a tunnel. He looks at the student section and sees Jefferson, Sylvia, and Jack R. Abbott also being escorted by security. The vice-chancellor sees the look on his face and smiles. "What's the matter, big boy? Baby's little plan go astray?"

A slightly laughing vice-chancellor stands and goes to the restroom. "I'll show her astray," an angry Mayor Sain says to himself. "Go Bears!"

* * *

"Miss Asia?" the quivering voice of Professor Spears says in her cell. "I just got a call from the vice-chancellor asking all kinds of questions about you and your experiment. She heard from someone that you are doing something at the boarding house."

"Who? What?" a suddenly surprised Asia asks. "What did you tell her?"

"I played it cool and told her nothing. She told me to be ready to open up all my records when she gets back from the game. She was very upset."

"Remember our deal, professor? She gets nothing, or you get nothing."

"I remember, Miss Asia. But she can be very convincing."

"Hang in there, professor. I'm sure everything will be all right. Don't tell her anything."

"Yes, Miss Asia," the nervous professor says. "I'll do my best. Can you come over later?"

Asia folds her cell and looks at the game, her face white as if she has just seen a ghost. "What do you want for a halftime snack?" Bessie asks. "Michael wants a big dish of vanilla ice cream drowned in chocolate syrup. How about you?"

"I need to go upstairs and take a short nap. Getting up at the crack of dawn after no sleep is getting me down."

"Speaking of cracks," Bessie says, "was that needle dick?"

"He wanted some information on the experiment. I told him I did what he said."

"Isn't life funny? Here, a few years back, I was trying to rape him and threw him aside when I discovered he had very little to offer, and now he's saving my life. What do you think about that?"

"You can't judge a man by the size of his dick," Asia says as she walks toward the stairs. "Trust me! I'm an expert!"

Asia disappears up the stairs. "She's an expert at what?" Michael asks Bessie.

"About everything important."

Asia locks the door to her room and lies on her bed for a few moments. She stands and takes the small suitcase from her closet. She sits down and dials the combination, opening it and taking out the red outfit with gold tassels. She sets the case on the floor and lies on the bed, the outfit on top of her. A vision of a naked Johnny Blood walking into her room at the whorehouse starts to fill her open eyes.

A knock on her bedroom door brings her back to reality. "Yes?" she says, hardly able to talk.

"It's Michael. Bessie warmed up a cup of soup to help you sleep."

Asia puts the red outfit in the suitcase, closes it on top of her bed and opens the door to see Michael, without his mask and hood, holding a steaming cup with Trojan at his side. "Thanks, Michael," Asia says as she takes the cup. "You're right. Bessie's right. I need this."

"Miss Asia, Bessie says you're an expert at everything."

"Well, I don't know about that," Asia says before she blows steam off the cup. "There are things I DO know a lot about, that's for sure."

“What about this?” Michael says gently fingering the hole on the right side of his face. “Can you fix this?”

“That would be a challenge,” Asia says. “But you know, I just might have some answers.”

“That would be great. That would give me a whole new life.”

“Here at Hamilton House, you’ll always be just who you are. A new ear won’t make any difference. But maybe helping you feel like you have a new life might just make some of the demons that are haunting you go away.”

“Demons?” Michael says.

“Just a figure of speech. We all have them.”

“You have demons, too?”

“Do I? You’ve got to be kidding.” Asia reaches for the closed suitcase. “Do you have a space in your closet for this?”

“Sure,” Michael says. “Can I ask what it is?”

“You can ask,” Asia says, “and one day I will open it for you and tell you a story you won’t believe—a story about Bessie, the mayor, you, and me that is beyond imagination. And maybe when I do, demons will go away forever. Could you store it for me?”

“Sure, Miss Asia,” Michael says, taking the suitcase. “I can’t wait. I love a good story. It might help me make my own cartoon strip.”

“It would be a good one. It would truly be unbelievable.”

Chapter Nineteen
Halftime

As halftime nears, Winnie, Sarah, Jefferson, Sylvia, Jack R. Abbott, the two-man film crew, and the pickets sit on logs around a blazing fire in the parking lot, hearing the roar of the crowd over the top of the stadium. Babe sits in a soft folding chair. "Anyone got the score?" Winnie asks. "Our keepers took my phone."

Smith, the picket captain, takes out his cell. "Still Cal seven and Stanford zero with twenty seconds to go."

"Who would have believed?" Winnie says. "Cal is leading the mighty Trees at halftime. They are doing a whole lot better than we are."

"I want to go home," Babe says. "This has been my worst nightmare. I am tired, sick, and my butt is killing me."

"Anyone want some of my good stuff I saved for after the game and overnight in jail?" Jefferson asks.

"I wanted to stay in jail, too," Sylvia says.

"Let's do our stuff anyhow," Jack R. Abbott says. "The mayor would be proud of us, even out here in the parking lot."

"Do you mind if we film it?" Ken says. "It'll be a part of our sizzle reel, even if the mayor isn't in it."

"I don't mind," Sylvia says stripping off her loose sweatshirt to show "Don't Take Away My Stimulus" written across her sagging breasts. "It's the best one I ever had."

"I'm with her," Jefferson says taking off his sweatshirt and pants quickly to show "The Only Stimulus I'll Give You" with an arrow pointing at his genitals.

"I am all in," Jack R. Abbott says as he peels off his sweats and exposes "I Need All the Stimulus I Can Get" and an arrow pointed at his penis. "If you guys need me to help you with your sizzle reel, just say the word."

"I am going to throw up," Babe says, looking at the naked bodies. "I suppose Sarah is next."

"Me? No way! I'm a Goth now, and I'm not supposed to strip anymore."

"You pickets going to join us?" Jefferson asks the five men sitting around the fire, their signs lying behind them in the dirt.

"No way," Smith says. "You guys are certifiable, just like Bertha says."

"I'll second that," Babe groans. "Can you turn my chair around so I can look at the stadium and not at bare asses?"

A loud cheer comes from the stadium. "It must be halftime," Winnie says. "I wonder what magic Jim is going to pull now that his troops are on the outside."

"Nothing, if Bertha has anything to say about it," Smith says.

"Yeah, nothing," one of the pickets says. "She is in control."

"Hey!" Sarah yells, looking beyond the parking lot toward a large field. "There's Death. I'm going over to see her and her friends." She leaps up from the log and runs toward the young men and women dressed in black.

"I wonder how Goth will play in Kansas." Winnie laughs. "Why don't you go film her?" he says to the film crew. "It'll definitely sizzle someone!"

"Why not?" Ken says. "We've got enough of the naked people anyhow."

The film crew follows Sarah.

"What a nightmare!" Babe exclaims. "I suppose Bertha will blame this one on us, too."

"Whatever she can," Smith says. "It'll probably be on our next set of signs."

* * *

Kennedy enters the skybox. President Tafoya stands and goes to him. "Everything under control?" the president asks.

"Everything but the score," Kennedy whispers. "All his people are sitting around a fire in the parking lot. Some of them are naked."

"What?" President Tafoya laughs. "Naked? I gotta see this."

President Tafoya walks to the vice-chancellor. "You want to visit security with me?" he asks. "I hear it's a sight to behold."

"What about him?" the vice-chancellor says, looking at a silent and bewildered mayor.

"Kennedy will stay with him while we are gone," the president says. "He'll stay right here."

The president and the vice-chancellor leave. Mayor Sain looks around at Kennedy, arms crossed in front of the door. "I don't suppose you have a joint I can smoke while I'm incarcerated, do you?"

Kennedy doesn't answer.

"I don't suppose so." The mayor grabs a bottle of beer and a sandwich and sits back down. "Okay, guys. Let's hope the scoreboard trick hasn't been discovered."

The Cal band performs and the fans show their appreciation with loud applause. As they finish and march off in an orderly fashion, the Stanford Band streams helter-skelter onto the field. "Okay, this should be it!" the mayor says, his eyes on the scoreboard. With a brilliant flash of light a *mR. bERZERKELEY* cartoon, with the mayor pissing on himself and the Stanford Tree pissing on him and a slogan "The Tree Scares the Piss Out of a mR. bERZERKELEY" appears on the screen to the loud cheers and applause of Stanford fans.

"Cute," the mayor says, looking around at an unsmiling Kennedy. "They got the butt mole in the wrong place. But cute."

Mayor Sain watches the Stanford band and its antics. "Winnie," he says to himself, "you are my only hope." He slowly takes out his cell and texts "911" to Winnie without Kennedy seeing him.

*   *   *

President Tafoya's cell rings as he and the vice-chancellor stand in front of security monitors, looking at the parking lot and the naked people. "Yes, Miss Potts. Everything is under control here. The mayor is in my skybox being attended to by the chief of security, and his friends are sitting around a fire in the parking lot, many of them naked. Your pickets are there with them."

"Are they holding my signs up?" an angry Bertha yells.

"No, they are sitting around, drinking and smoking," the president says.

"I guess I'll have to find some new pickets," Bertha groans. "Can you put the vice-chancellor on if she's with you?"

"Sure," Tafoya says, handing his cell to Vice-Chancellor Kris.

"Is there any chance the mayor is going to pull something at the game?"

"Over my dead body! I think we got him, thanks to you and your money. Speaking of money, can I call on you in the future? I might need some help keeping him and his friend Winston from causing any trouble."

"Yes, anything that will stifle their naked butts," Bertha says. "It will be my pleasure."

"Thank you. You're my kind of person. Good luck in Kansas."

The vice-chancellor hands the cell to President Tafoya. "Will you be wiring the remainder of the agreed upon amount?"

"It's on its way, President Tafoya," Bertha says. After folding up her cell she yells, "I got you, you son of a bitch!"

Chapter Twenty
Bait and Switch

WINNIE AND BABE SIT around the fire with the pickets and the naked Jefferson, Sylvia, and Jack R. Abbott. "I wonder if he was able to pull off his scoreboard stunt," Winnie says.

"That's was pretty good," Smith says, looking at his phone. "But I don't think it was what he planned." Smith hands the phone to Winnie. "The tree is pissing on mR. bERZERKELEY. These Stanford students are pretty creative."

"Shit!" Jefferson says. "Our guys must have been found out. The mayor must be beside himself. Got to be time for the contingency plan. That's your job, Mr. Churchill."

"He can't text me. Security has my cell."

Winnie takes out a slip of paper. "Can I make a call from your phone?" he asks Smith.

"Be my guest."

Winnie punches in the number. "Martin. You're on!"

In the skybox, the vice-chancellor takes a seat in between the Stanford President and a brooding Mayor Sain as the teams line up to begin the second half.

"What's the matter, big boy?" Vice-Chancellor Kris says, leaning in to the mayor. "Your little scheme fail?"

"The only schemer around here is you," an angry Mayor Sain says. "No wonder Michael calls you a bitch!"

"Michael? Who's Michael?" Vice-Chancellor Kris says. "I don't know anyone named Michael."

"How did you become such a snake—a real queen cobra?" Mayor Sain asks.

"That's the nicest thing you've ever said to me," a sarcastic vice-chancellor says. "Coming from you that's a real compliment."

"I'm going to help our son become one of the greatest people on the planet in spite of you," Mayor Sain says.

"Is he going to walk around Berkeley naked and smoke pot like you? Or maybe chase every skirt in town, windsurf, and get drunk and high in

People's Park? Or never learn how to cook and eat Bessie's food day and night?"

"He's going to be polite, smart, and learn how to tame snakes like you and keep them from hurting people's lives and help them fulfill their dreams. You don't know anyone named Michael, and that's all right, because he and I don't want to know anyone like you."

"Are you two going to watch the game?" President Tafoya asks. "Stanford is driving, and they are going to whip the Bears."

"You've been whipped," the vice-chancellor says, looking at the mayor. "Admit it. For the first time you've been foiled in your dastardly deeds."

"Don't you think saving Berkeley, Kansas, and a lot of other cities and states from going bankrupt because of an error in judgment by overzealous feds is a worthy cause? You think this is all about me and Winnie? This is about millions of others and their pain and suffering when budgets are cut and millions are out of work because of confusion."

"The only stimulus you've ever had was Jäger and a joint." The vice-chancellor laughs.

"I did have another stimulus a long time ago with a woman who I thought was my one and only. It produced the greatest young man I've ever known."

"You are truly one of a kind," the vice-chancellor says. "Did you smuggle in a juicy one and indulge while we were gone?"

Stanford fans cheer and scream as the team scores a touchdown and the extra point ties the game. "I told you!" President Tafoya yells happily. "We're going to give the Bears a whipping!"

"Just like Bertha Potts and I gave you at halftime," the vice-chancellor whispers.

"A real whipping," the mayor laughs, looking at the late afternoon skies as a small plane approaches. "Go Bears!" He squints and can barely make out a figure jumping from the plane and, after a few moments, a parachute opening.

Winnie, standing by the fire, looks up after hearing the small plane and sees the skydiver. "Plan B completed," he says to Babe, who looks up into the late afternoon sky, shielding her eyes.

"Is that one of the mayor's friends?" Babe says.

"It's Martin, the guy who remodeled Hamilton House."

"Why isn't he at the house hooking up the elevator instead of jumping from an airplane?"

The teams are lined up, and Stanford kicks off. Mayor Sain tries hard not to look up to give away what is about to happen. Martin, parachute open, naked as a jaybird, heads straight for the field. Someone from the crowd sees him coming down high above, using ropes to circle as he approaches the stadium. Blue and gold smoke starts streaming behind him as he descends.

"What the?" the president says, looking up.

"What in the hell?" the vice-chancellor says, looking at the skydiver.

"He's naked!" the president yells, looking through his binoculars. "I can't read what's written on the parachute."

The vice-chancellor looks at the mayor.

"Yup," the mayor mocks. "A real whipping!"

Both teams stop and look skyward as Martin circles the stadium. He reaches into a pouch and begins throwing leaflets that fall on the crowd and the field like rain. "Kennedy! Where's security?" the president yells.

Martin circles, throwing more leaflets.

"'Save our cities! Save Kansas from the stimulus! Go mR. bERZERKELEY! Beat the Tree!'" President Tafoya says, focusing binoculars on Martin. "He's ruining the game!"

"The stimulus is the real game," Mayor Sain says. "The real president's people have to stop trying to bankrupt us!"

"It isn't about the stimulus!" Vice-Chancellor Kris yells. "It's all about you!"

The crowd cheers as Martin circles and lands perfectly in between the teams into the waiting arms of security. He is handcuffed and taken off the field as the players watch. "That boy's pecker must be frozen," a Stanford cornerback says to a Cal wide receiver standing next to him.

"I think *penis* is the proper name," the Cal player says. "Maybe you Stanford boys would have a better time playing with him than us."

"Maybe you Cal boys will shove that penis up your butts after we beat the shit out of you."

The umpire blows his whistle. Kennedy walks into the president's skybox holding several brochures.

"What do they say?" Tafoya asks, grabbing a brochure. "'Stop the president from bankrupting Berkeley,'" he reads. "'Look up at the Stanford President's skybox and see the present the mayor of Berkeley has for the stimulus fund!' What does that mean?"

"I'll show you what it means," Mayor Sain says, standing up and reaching for his zipper. He puts his back to the president's skybox window, drops his pants, and presses his bare ass against the glass. The crowd cheers loudly, stopping the game again. The mayor wiggles his bare ass back and forth.

"Mr. Kennedy!" President Tafoya yells. "Will you please escort the mayor outside?"

Kennedy grabs the mayor, who has now shed his pants completely, and begins to drag him out of the skybox. "Ciao," the mayor says to the vice-chancellor. "Not the first time you've seen my dick!"

The mayor is escorted naked through the stadium and outside to the parking lot. Kennedy throws him his pants. The mayor watches the gates close, looks at his pants, and then decides to join his friends and the pickets naked.

"Oh my God," Babe says as he walks near. "I have to get out of here!"

"He did it!" Winnie says. "He actually did it!"

Sarah comes running, followed by the film crew. "Was that Martin?" an excited Sarah yells to Babe.

"I'm afraid so," Babe groans. "Can you call me a cab?"

Sarah moves to Winnie. "I thought I recognized him!" Sarah yells. "I want to learn how to do that. It looked so neat! Even my new friends liked it!"

"So the Goths liked a naked skydiver?" Winnie says.

"They also liked the video on YouTube, especially when the mayor puts his bare bottom against the glass in the president's box. It was so neat!"

The mayor reaches the campfire. "Anyone find the stash and the Jäger in one of the cars?" the mayor yells.

"I found the stash," Jefferson says, throwing a joint in his direction. "Saved the Jäger for you." He tosses a small, ice-cold bottle to the mayor.

"And my guitar? I feel like singing!"

Jack R. Abbott grabs a guitar lying against a car and hands it to him. "First, let's light up, take a swig, and then have some fun." He takes a deep hit, turns the Jäger upside down, and sits on a log. The fire is going down. "Anyone got any wood?" he asks. "This fire's going out."

"We got a couple of logs left," Jefferson says.

"Throw 'em on," the mayor says. "Let's play while Stanford burns!"

The stadium erupts sporadically with cheers in the background as the mayor strums the guitar and sings "California," finishing with a "Go Bears!" "You all know 'Hey Lotty.' Let's make up a few appropriate verses. I'll start."

"Hey, lotty lotty lotty,
"Hey, lotty lotty lo.
"Hey, lotty lotty lotty,
"Hey, lotty lotty lo.
"I know a school in Palo Alto.
"Hey, lotty lotty lotty,
"Hey, lotty lotty lo.

"The Bears will eat them like a Ho Ho.
"Hey, lotty lotty lo.
"Come on, join in!"

The mayor continues, with the group singing the chorus.

"Hey, lotty lotty lotty,
Hey, lotty lotty lo.
Hey, lotty lotty lotty,
Hey, lotty lotty lo.
I know an Indian that thinks it's a tree.
Hey, lotty lotty lotty,
Hey, lotty lotty lo.
It grows at Stanford and smells like pee-pee.
Hey, lotty lotty lo."

"An Indian that thinks it's a tree?" Sarah says as the mayor strums.

"It's all just his imagination," Babe says. "And he has a real doozie!"

"Hey," the mayor yells at the picket captain, "what's your name?"

"Ron Smith."

"You know Bertha has been watching you sit here by the fire, don't you?" he says while he strums.

"You've got to be kidding," Smith says. "We're toast."

"Why don't you join us?" the mayor says, playing chords on the guitar.

"Might as well," Smith says. "We've been fired, that's for sure."

"Hey, lotty lotty lotty,
"Hey, lotty lotty lo.
"Hey, lotty lotty lotty,
"Hey, lotty lotty lo.
"I know a guy named Mr. Smitty.
"Hey, lotty lotty lotty,
"Hey, lotty lotty lo.
"He carried signs that were real shitty.
"Hey, lotty lotty lo."

"That's a good one," Smith says as he and the other pickets look at each other, grab their signs, and throw them into the fire.

"I got one," Winnie says.

"Hey, lotty lotty lotty,
"Hey, lotty lotty lo.
"Hey, lotty lotty lotty,
"Hey, lotty lotty lo.
I know a naked-ass commie named Jim.
"Hey, lotty lotty lo.
"He gets real pissed when Bertha tries to beat him.
"Hey, lotty lotty lo."

"Good for an amateur," Mayor Sain laughs while strumming.

"Hey, lotty lotty lotty,
"Hey, lotty lotty lo.
"Hey, lotty lotty lotty,
"Hey, lotty lotty lo.
"I have a friend named Winnie the Pooh,
"Hey, lotty lotty lo.
"Cross him once and he will screw you.
"Hey, lotty lotty lo."

"Uh-oh, the party's getting rough," Babe says.
"You got a better one?" Winnie says to Babe as the mayor strums.
"Anyone can do better than that!" Babe laughs.

"Hey, lotty lotty lotty,
"Hey, lotty lotty lo.
"Hey, lotty lotty lotty,
"Hey, lotty lotty lo.
"I know a place where crazies run wild.
"Hey, lotty lotty lo.
"It's hardly a place to raise my child.
"Hey, lotty lotty lo."

"Are you trying to tell us something?" Mayor Sain says.
"Just making up rhymes, that's all," Babe says.
"She was probably talking about me," Sarah says. "But I'm not a child anymore."
"You got one, Kansas?" the mayor says as he plays.

"Hey, lotty lotty lotty,
"Hey, lotty lotty lo.

"Hey, lotty lotty lotty,
"Hey, lotty lotty lo.
"I love a city where great people stay.
"Hey, lotty lotty lo.
"They work and they laugh and they all play.
"Hey, lotty lotty lo."

"That was a great beginning," the mayor says as he strums. "I'll sing another one if you'll take off that sweatshirt and join us."

"Sure, why not?" Sarah says and she pulls her sweatshirt over her head, stripping to the waist. "I can go back to being Goth anytime I want."

"Hey, lotty lotty lotty,
"Hey, lotty lotty lo.
"Hey, lotty lotty lotty,
"Hey, lotty lotty lo.
"Kansas has given us two great girls.
"Hey, lotty lotty lo.
They're rough and they're tough but give us all thrills.
"Hey, lotty lotty lo."

"Are you sure we can't just call a cab and go back to Berkeley?" Babe says. "This Girl Scout stuff is getting me down. Next thing I know, you'll be stripping alongside Sarah. Bertha's cameras are hiding somewhere."

"That has crossed my mind," Winnie says.

Chapter Twenty-One
Momma's Boy

BESSIE SCREAMS WHEN CAL scores a touchdown near the end of the Big Game and scares Trojan off Michael's leg. He heads posthaste out the doggy door. He stands on the porch in the late afternoon and listens intently, trying to pick up any sound coming from Mimi's house next door. Nothing! The sounds of the BART train and a fire engine can be heard, but nothing from the little cutie next door. The smells of garlic and spices dance in the soft breeze, but nothing like the sensual smells of the little white puff. But why not take a chance in going over? It's only next door, and it's a whole lot better than dry humping Michael's leg. Why not have his way with a real female?

Trojan moves around the bushes and heads next door. *What's with the football game, anyhow? Just a bunch of legs running up and down, trying to knock each other over. What's the sense in that? There's a much better use for those legs.* He stops as Mimi's doggy door moves a little. *Ah! Can it be true?*

Rounding the corner of Hamilton House, he stops dead in his tracks. What's that standing between him and the doggy door? It's the baby coyote from the park next to Willard—the baby he bullied. How did he find Mimi? He must have followed Trojan's scent. But what could he do with her? He doesn't even know he has a dick yet.

Mimi peeks through the doggy door and sees the small coyote. She also spots Trojan, her hero, just beyond the baby animal. She darts back inside.

You little bastard, Trojan thinks. *She was ready, and you stopped her from becoming mine! I'll show you!*

Trojan moves toward the baby coyote with a low snarl coming from his mouth, raising his cheek slightly to show his teeth. Sensing danger, the baby coyote begins to walk toward the sidewalk and away from Mimi's house. *I have your little gray ass on the run,* Trojan thinks to himself. *You know who the man in this neighborhood is.*

The baby coyote's pace picks up a little, and Trojan follows behind. The baby moves a little faster with Trojan keeping up. As they move east on

Durant toward Telegraph, they approach a large bush, and the baby coyote turns sharply behind it. *I'll teach you once and for all to stay away from me and Mimi,* he thinks to himself as he snarls and moves in to bite the little guy on the butt.

Trojan rounds the bush, and Momma and Daddy coyote wait with their teeth exposed. Trojan jams on his brakes and stares at the angry adult coyotes with the baby safely behind them. *They already taught him the bait and switch*, Trojan thinks to himself. *Draw me in and eat me for dinner. Well, I've been down this path before!*

Standing his ground, Trojan exposes his teeth. The coyotes snarl. Trojan barks loudly. The coyotes begin moving closer, ready to attack. As the standoff is about to become a life-and-death battle, Josh's car comes into view and stops. "Trojan!" Josh yells through an open window. "Get in here now!"

Trojan looks at the coyotes and barks before sprinting and leaping into Josh's open door. "What are you doing?" Josh yells. "Those coyotes woulda made a meal out of you. You gotta watch out from now on."

Trojan looks out the window at the coyote family. *You were saved by the bell,* he thinks and raises his cheeks to show his teeth once again. *I would have a ripped you all a new one!*

Chapter Twenty-Two
Whiskey Run!

WILLIE AND JAMAL SIT in a squad car at the curb near Cedar and Shattuck listening to the game. "They gonna hold 'em or not, Jamal?" Willie says. "How 'bout if they do, you go to Cal; if they don't, go to USC?"

"I'm not going to let some game determine who I am. I hope they do hold them so we get happy in this town. I'm tired of 'protest this' and 'protest that.' I need a little love and happiness."

"Love and happiness," Willie philosophizes. "Don't we all."

"What's that?" Jamal says, looking at Andronicos. "Those guys are moving pretty fast with that shopping cart."

"What the?" Willie says focusing. "Stay here. They might be carrying."

"Stay here?" Jamal says. "Finally a little action."

Willie jumps from the car at about the same time as Jamal does. Both start running after the men pushing a shopping cart with a box inside. The men see Willie and Jamal, leave the cart, and start running west on Cedar. Willie hustles with a limp. Jamal runs all out. "You get the runt in front and save the last one for me," Willie puffs, seeing Jamal ten yards ahead of him.

Jamal runs past the first man and pushes the second man over a white picket fence. Jamal glowers over him while Willie handcuffs the first man. Willie pulls the first man over to a fence. "Jamal, hold this one while I take care of his friend."

Willie opens a gate and walks to the second man. "I only carry one set of cuffs," he says. "You be a good boy until my backup gets here, or I'll turn my son loose on you."

"Yes, officer," the man says. "We were just thirsty, that's all. We mean no harm. We're homeless and wanted a little drink."

"A drink?" Willie says. "A case of Jack Daniels?"

"We got a few friends over at the park listening to the game. We want to celebrate."

"The game isn't over," Willie says.

"Either way, we'll celebrate," the man says.

"Wait right here," Willie says as he walks from the yard and over to the shopping cart. He opens the box of whiskey, takes out a bottle, and brings it back to the yard and the homeless man. "Don't say Berkeley doesn't have a heart. Go celebrate. Go Bears!"

Willie takes the cuffs off the first man. "We got a lot of friends, Mr. Policeman," the first man says, rubbing his wrists.

Willie goes back to the box and brings a second bottle. "Get out of my sight! I never want to see you in my jail," Willie says, trying to act angry. "Come on, Jamal. Let's take the booze back inside."

"Won't they want us to pay for the bottles you gave away?"

"Guess this box was light two bottles, wasn't it?" he says. "Get back to the squad car and see if Stanford scored or not."

After a while, Willie gets back in the car. "Well?" he asks.

"Cal held them," Jamal says. "Is that how you handle justice in Berkeley?"

"The jails are full, and if the Bears win, they'll be overflowing after all the parties. If they lose, the drunks will be angry and they'll be even more arrests. One way or another we don't need to put more people in jail just because they were thirsty and can't buy their own."

"This town is crazy," Jamal says.

"Yeah." Willie smiles. "Want to get a burger?"

"I promised my buddies I would meet them at the pier for skate fishing. Can you drop me off? We could use one of those bottles, too."

Chapter Twenty-Three
Success

Asia sits with Bessie and an unmasked Michael on the couch watching the final seconds of the Big Game. Stanford is driving for a score to tie. Cal is putting up a valiant effort to stop them. "Don't let them score, you fucking Bears!" Bessie yells. "I want to go out a winner!"

"What is she talking about?" Michael whispers to Asia.

"Just a figure of speech. You know Bessie by now. She's full of them."

"She is all right, isn't she?" Michael asks in a low voice.

"I will make sure of it," Asia says. "Don't worry. Bessie is gonna be around here for a long time. I've got to see if my experiment is progressing like it should."

"Can I watch?" Michael asks.

"No," Asia says, patting him on the leg. "You stay here and keep Bessie from doing anything rash if Stanford does score and the Bears lose."

"Should we hide her cleaver?"

"No. She'll raise the roof with her language, but she won't hurt you."

"Okay," Michael whispers. "You are coming right back, aren't you?"

"Sure."

"Come on, you fucking Bears!" Bessie yells. "Stop goddamn Stanford!"

Josh walks in, followed almost immediately by Trojan. "Who's winning?" he says, moving quickly to the couch.

"We are!" Bessie yells. "But the fucking Tree is about to score and tie us."

"What did the mayor do?" Josh asks.

"Nothing. Not a goddamn thing!" Bessie yells. "I've been sitting on the edge of this fucking couch for hours waiting. Nothing."

Trojan moves to one of Michael's legs and starts humping feverishly.

"We better watch our little friend," Josh says. "I saved him from a pack of coyotes around the corner."

"Coyotes?" Bessie says. "They come and they go, knock over the trash once in a while. They're harmless. Besides, the mutt would probably try to hump them."

"It didn't look like a friendly gathering," Josh says. "I'd say we should watch him a little closer."

"That'll be my job," Michael says, patting Trojan on the head. "Nothing is going to happen to the boy. I'll make sure."

Asia reappears from the basement and moves next to Josh, watching the game. "Everything going okay downstairs?" Bessie asks, her eyes glued to the television.

"It is coming along better than expected," Asia says. "I'd call it a success."

"Yes!" Bessie yells throwing her hands in the air. "We stopped 'em at the goal line. Now just hang onto the fucking ball and we win!"

Josh turns to Asia. "The mayor did nothing at the game? He said he had this great plan to publicize his protest of the president's stimulus fund and that the whole world would know. Something musta happened."

"Nothing was on television," Asia says. "Let's try YouTube!"

Josh brings up YouTube on his phone. "Put in Big Game and see what comes up," Asia says.

"Oh my God," Josh says. "Bessie, this you gotta see!"

"What are you talking about?" Bessie yells.

Josh walks to the couch and hands the cell phone to Bessie as he and Asia look over her shoulder. Martin's skydive comes on with him dropping naked into the stadium, throwing pieces of paper in all directions. Next, a full screen of the mayor's butt pressed up against the Stanford President's skybox glass runs for several seconds. "Now, that's my naked-ass commie son!" Bessie says. "He came through, but not on national television. No one will see it."

"Are you kidding?" Asia says, grabbing the phone. "It already has a million hits!"

"Yes!" Bessie says, throwing her hands in the air again. "We did it! We beat the fucking Tree! Dumplings and Jack all around! This has been a good day for everyone!"

Trojan pauses and switches to Michael's other leg. *I'll say,* he thinks. *I would have torn those coyotes apart!*

Chapter Twenty-Four
Spoils!

"CAL FANS ARE GOING crazy and the stadium is emptying," Winnie says over the crowd noise and the mayor playing the guitar. "We must have won!"

"By a touchdown," Smith says, looking at his cell phone. "Cal stopped them on the one-yard line."

"One-yard line, ten-yard line—it doesn't matter," Mayor Sain says. "We beat those bastards. Time for more Jäger and another joint."

"Can't we go home now?" Babe asks. "Isn't the torture over?"

"I want to go back with the Goths," Sarah says. "They are so neat!"

"I have to wait for the axe," Mayor Sain says. "It's tradition. The train and the axe."

Fans are streaming into the parking lot. "There's no way we can get out of here," Winnie says to Babe. "It'll be a while."

"This is my last game," Babe says. "I can't believe I let you talk me into this. This is worse than sitting through one of your political meetings."

Kennedy from security, followed by three men and the gorgeous Hispanic female, walk up to the group sitting by the almost extinguished fire while the film crew continues to capture the action. A naked mayor stands and is joined immediately by naked Jefferson, Sylvia, and Jack R. Abbott. "Here are your cell phones," Kennedy says, holding out several instruments. "We have laws here about nudity. I suggest you all get dressed or spend the night in the Palo Alto jail with your parachuting friend."

"Can she hang around and watch us?" Mayor Sain says, looking at the gorgeous Hispanic female. "We'll show her how we celebrate a Big Game victory in Berkeley."

"I think we've all seen enough of you and your friends," Kennedy says. "Get dressed and get out. Have I made myself clear?"

"Quite," Winnie chimes in. "Please give Bertha Potts our best."

"And give the vice-chancellor an enema for me," Mayor Sain says. "She's so full of shit you better watch out!"

"Would you all like to go to jail now?" Kennedy asks. "We can add drunken and disorderly to the nudity charge."

"They will get dressed immediately," an angry Babe yells. "or I will help you throw them in jail!"

"Excellent," Kennedy says. "By the way," he says, turning to the pickets, "I have a message to you from Miss Potts. You've all been terminated."

Kennedy and his security staff leave, the gorgeous Hispanic female looking back and smiling at the naked mayor. "See," the mayor says, pointing at the young woman. "She likes me. I told you she wants to see more of me."

"Is that possible?" Babe says sarcastically.

"She was looking at me," Jack R. Abbott says. "She wants a real man who's hung like a horse."

"A miniature pony." Mayor Sain laughs. "Say, that might be a title for one of your books."

"I think she was looking at me," a stoned Sylvia says. "She might be the best I'd ever have."

"A lesbian?" Sarah asks. "Too bad I'm a Goth now."

"I want to go home," Babe says.

Chapter Twenty-Five
Little Bares

The kitchen door opens and Willie, in full police uniform, walks in. Bessie is at the stove preparing dumplings. Unmasked Michael stands beside her peeling potatoes. "Have you heard from the mayor yet?" Willie asks. "That was some game!"

"Sit down!" Bessie yells without turning her back. "The dumplings will be ready in a minute."

"I didn't see him on television," Willie says, sitting hard in a chair.

"You should look at YouTube," Josh says, sitting on the couch watching the post-game commentators. "He's already had three million hits and it hasn't been an hour."

"Let me see," Willie says, putting out his hand. "I'd get up but I've been chasing a couple of homeless men who stole a case of Jack Daniels from Andronicos." Trojan starts humping one of his legs. "Go ahead," he says. "I stepped in a mud puddle, and I got to get this uniform cleaned anyhow."

"Jack?" Bessie yells. "Did you bring one for me?"

Josh stands and brings his cell phone to Willie. "He's given me a whole bunch of ideas for *bERZERKELEY*." Josh laughs.

Willie watches the video. "That tops them all," Willie says. "I'll bet the vice-chancellor shit her britches!"

"She's a real bitch!" Michael says, turning around, holding a knife and a half-peeled potato.

"Well," Willie says, "the Lone Ranger is outed!"

"Looks pretty damn good, don't you think?" Bessie says. "A whole lot better than my naked-ass commie son and his butt mole on YouTube!"

"Not bad!" Willie says. "You do sort of look like him, now that you mention it."

Asia smiles as she sits down next to Willie.

"I'm going to put a hole in the side of my naked-ass commie son's head, too, when he gets home. He promised me he would be on television."

"Looks like he figured out a way," Willie smiles. "Let me see that again."

Willie looks at Josh's cell as the kitchen door opens and Stephanie and

Judy walk in, dressed in their hiking outfits and laced up boots. "It's about time you lesbians showed up!" Bessie yells. "The dumplings are almost ready."

"Who won?" Stephanie asked.

"The Bears!" Bessie answers. "They finally beat the Tree!"

"Did the mayor do his thing?" Judy asks.

"Here, look at this," Willie says, handing Josh's cell to her. "It's a classic."

Judy and Stephanie look at the video. "Is his butt getting bigger, or is it my imagination?" Stephanie asks.

"The only thing bigger than his butt is his fucking mouth," Bessie says.

"What a trip!" Judy says, handing the cell back to Willie. "Think it will force the president to give up taking the money from Berkeley?"

"I guess anything's worth a try," Asia says. "You guys find anything?"

"We did," Judy says. "But it was a setup for our friends and their babies."

"Your lesbian friends have babies?" Bessie asks. "Little bare asses?"

"Yes, they do," Judy says. "It was really fun."

"I wish I could have given away my little bare ass fifty years ago," Bessie says.

"Then what would the world watch on YouTube?" Willie laughs.

"Asia," Judy says, "can we talk to you for a moment?"

"Better hurry," Bessie says. "The dumplings are about out, and the Jack will be poured. Extra portions all around to celebrate."

Asia follows Stephanie and Judy into the living room so no one else can hear them. "Asia," Judy starts, "we have a couple of questions."

"No," Asia says, folding her arms across her breasts. "I've never done a lesbian."

"It's not about sex," an excited Judy says. "Well, sort of. You see, we want to be like our friends and have a baby."

"You want to have a baby?" Asia says. "Which one of you?"

"Both," Judy answers.

"You, Stephanie? You want to have a baby? I didn't think you'd ever want a little one. You don't seem the type."

"If she wants us both to have one to stay together, that's good enough for me," Stephanie says. "After I thought about it, if I am going to take care of one, I'd like it to be a part of me."

"Yeah," Judy says. "We would have brothers, sisters, playmates."

"That means you gotta have sex with—shudder—a man. You both up for that, so to speak?"

"Not necessarily," Judy says. "Our friends had theirs through in vitro and a sperm bank."

"That costs a lot of money, and I thought you two were just barely above water."

"We want you to help us," Judy says. "You know everything about that sort of thing. How can we do it?"

"Well, we need to farm some of your eggs and then get some sperm," Asia says, rubbing her chin. "I suppose it is possible, with a little help from the professor. Whose sperm did you have in mind?"

"We've talked a lot about it on the way back from our hike," Judy says as her head turns to look at Josh.

"You want his?" Asia says.

"He's a hunk and very talented," Judy says. "We want to have his babies."

"That means I have to ask him to make a donation?" Asia asks.

"We thought you would figure out a way," Judy smiles. "That's why we are asking for your help."

"Lesbian babies from Josh," Asia says as she continues to rub her chin. "Why not?"

Chapter Twenty-Six
Axe, Axe, Axie!

Mayor Sain, Winnie, Babe, Jefferson, Sylvia, and Jack R. Abbott sit around a dwindling fire. The parking lot is emptying and the sun has disappeared. "When are we going to leave?" Babe says. "The pickets and the film crew and Sarah got on the train with the Goths. What about us?"

"He's waiting for the axe," Winnie says. "He won't go without it."

"Call me a taxi, then," Babe says. "If you don't, the next lawyer you see will be handling our divorce."

"I guess we should go?" a disappointed Mayor Sain says. "Help me put out the fire, will you, guys? You can help, too, if you want, Babe."

"What's he talking about?" Babe asks Winnie.

"You don't want to know," Winnie says, standing up and moving toward the fire, grabbing at his zipper.

Mayor Sain, Winnie, Jefferson, and Jack R. Abbott piss on the fire and put it out while Sylvia and Babe watch. "I would have helped," a stoned Sylvia says, "but I just went."

"All right," Mayor Sain says, turning around while he zips up. "I guess we gotta go to the next train without the axe. I will still sing, though."

"Great!" Babe says. "I can hardly wait."

"Come on, gang," a dejected Mayor Sain says. They cross El Camino and make their way to the train. "What's that?" Winnie says, looking back. "It's some of the football team and the coach."

The group stops as the team approaches. The coach holds out the glass case containing the victory axe. "Mr. Mayor, we trust you will take this back to Berkeley safely." He hands the axe to Mayor Sain, who is almost in tears. "You bet!" he says. "Go Bears."

Team members step forward and high-five their infamous alum. "Yes!" the mayor says. "Now we can go back in style."

"That's not something you see every day," Winnie says with his arm around Babe. "Almost brings tears to my eyes, too."

"You must be joking," Babe says. "I want to go home."

"How come you've been so angry and sarcastic lately?" Winnie asks Babe. "You're usually up for anything and positive most of the time."

“I don’t know, probably chemistry,” Babe says. “Maybe I am pregnant.”

Mayor Sain sits in the bar car with Winnie, Babe, Jefferson, Sylvia, and Jack R. Abbott. He has a guitar and a half-full glass of Jäger. “Come on, gang,” he says. “It’s time to sing.

“My axe, axe, axie, good-bye.
“My axe, axe, axsie, don’t cry.
“That little choo-choo train
“That takes you away from me—
“No words can tell you how sad it makes me.”

“Go Bears!” the mayor says before he turns his glass of Jäger upside down and continues singing.

Chapter Twenty-Seven
Post-Game Planning

THE VICE-CHANCELLOR IS FUMING as she walks from an upscale Palo Alto restaurant across the street from the stadium. "Please tell Chancellor Lim that we will get the axe back next year," Stanford President Tafoya says. "It was that skydiver that distracted us."

"I will relay your message, President Tafoya," the vice-chancellor says graciously. "And I will take care of whoever sent that naked man into your stadium—as if I don't know."

"And tell mR. bERZERKELEY it was good to see him in person." The president laughs. "All of him!"

"That man," Vice-Chancellor Kris says. "Maybe we can convince him to move to Palo Alto!"

The vice-chancellor walks on the sidewalk toward her Mercedes. "That son of a bitch! I'll cut off his dick and his balls and take that Asia with him."

She talks into her cell. "Professor Spears? I'll be there in an hour. Have everything ready, or you'll be teaching Biology 1A for the rest of your career." She folds her cell and continues to walk in the cool evening air. "Miss Asia! What are you cooking up at your house? And Michael! You sniveling shit! I'll take care of you so you won't forget what I've done for you all these years. I'm going to get all of you! All! You think I'm a queen cobra, do you? Wait until I'm done. There will be nothing left. You bunch of bastards!"

PART TWO
Cobras Strike

Chapter Twenty-Eight
Fangs Out!

JOSH WATCHES THE POST-GAME commentators review Cal's improbable Big Game victory as he waits for Bessie to finish the dumplings. His cell phone rings. "Yes, dear," he says, seeing Jasmine's number come up. "Cal won! Isn't that great?"

"You left me alone!" Jasmine yells. "You better get back over here or else!"

"You said I could leave for a while, freshen up, and come back after dinner."

"I changed my mind. I am entitled. I have your baby inside of me, and I can do anything I want!"

"Can't you wait for thirty minutes? I'll grab a quick bite and be back over."

"You better get over her right now or I'll bite you where you don't want to be bitten."

"I'm leaving right now. Keep it together for a couple of minutes. I'll be there shortly."

Josh walks by Michael on his way out of Hamilton House. "Weren't we going to go to the store after dinner and finish a couple of cartoons?" Michael asks.

"I'll see what's wrong with my girl and give you a call," a harried Josh says.

Josh fires up his old Honda and takes off up Durant toward Piedmont. "Fucking bitch!" he yells as loud as he can. "Who the fuck does she think she is? Who does she think I am? Her slave? I need an abortion now! Goddamn it!"

The Honda pulls to the curb, and Jasmine is waiting outside, tapping her foot on the porch with her arms crossed. Josh approaches and attempts to kiss her on the cheek. She pulls her face away. "Just who do you think you are, mister? When I need you, I expect you here immediately. Now! Not ten minutes from now."

"Pull back your fangs. Daddy has arrived."

"Daddy? You bastard. Is this how it's going to be the rest of our lives? I need you and you are off watching some game or something?"

"We are not married. I am not your husband."

"We have a child! You and I have a baby inside of me. Don't you have any respect for that? What kind of monster are you?"

"Monster?" Josh says, starting to get angry. "Is that the best you can do? Now that I think about it, that's not a bad line for one of my cartoons!"

"You and your fucking cartoons. All you think about is drawing those cartoons—not me."

"Why don't we go to your room and talk about what's best for you and the baby?" Josh says, pulling close and rubbing one of her breasts.

"That's not a bad idea. You always know the way to my heart."

"Pull in those fangs and get ready for one of my best efforts. It has been over two hours, hasn't it?"

"Now that you mention it. Maybe watching that game a little stirred you. Maybe football isn't so bad after all."

Chapter Twenty-Nine
Snake Bit!

Mayor Sain, Winnie, Babe, Jefferson, Sylvia, and Jack R. Abbott walk up the driveway into Hamilton House. The smell of Bessie's dumplings from a block away gives them an energy boost. Willie is already into his second helping, and Michael is busy peeling more potatoes. "Come on, gang," Mayor Sain says, carefully setting down the case holding the victory axe. "Let's turn on some wild music and party!"

"Shit! It WAS peaceful around here all day without your naked commie ass yelling and screaming."

"We won, Mom! And the team gave me the axe to bring back. My best day ever!"

"Your ass had a good day, too!" Bessie yells. "It's already been hit on over five million times."

"Michael," Mayor Sain says, walking up behind him, "your mask is gone! You look great! Are you proud of me?"

"Yes, sir, I am. I wish I could have seen it in person. I'll bet you really made my mother squirm."

"I did," the mayor says. "I'll bet she shit her panties twice!"

"Oh, please," Babe says to Winnie. "Can't we go somewhere quiet and peaceful? I've walked a hundred miles, rode a bumpy train, listened to him play the same songs over and over, sat around a campfire like a Girl Scout, seen grown men put out a fire with urine … can't we get out of here for a while, just you and me?"

"Sure," Winnie says.

"I'm already in the car," Babe says.

"Where are you guys going?" Mayor Sain yells. "The party's just starting! Say, where are the girls and Asia? China Girl promised me something special after the game."

"She and the lesbians are having a confab," Bessie says.

The kitchen door opens and Sarah walks in, her face covered in pale white makeup. "Look, everyone. Death did my face. Isn't it cool?"

"This is great!" Jack R. Abbott says. "I got new titles for books: *Murder by a Hole in the Head* and *Murder by Goth Grease*!"

"Your hole is the best I ever had," a stoned Sylvia says.

Trojan barks at Bessie, demanding Jack in his dish.

Babe looks at Winnie as the craziness continues in the kitchen. "Get me out of here!"

* * *

Winnie and Babe sit at a corner table at Skates looking out at the Berkeley pier, the San Francisco skyline, Alcatraz, and the Golden Gate. The ocean moves beneath them. "Thank God Skates was still open," Babe says. "I couldn't stand it one more minute with the wackos in the kitchen doing their thing. I had to get out!"

"They don't mean any harm," Winnie smiles. "They're just happy about beating Stanford and being themselves."

"Like I said, they are all wacked! I can't wait to get back to Lake Quivira and find out."

"Find out what?" Winnie asks.

"If I am or not," Babe says coyly.

"Pregnant?" Winnie asks.

"Yes," Babe says.

"Why not go get one of those testers?" Winnie says.

"I didn't use them with Billy or Katrina," Babe says. "I'll go and see our doctor."

"They weren't invented then," Winnie says.

"I guess I'm just an old-fashioned girl. I want to see if I have a baby inside, and if I do, I want to raise it in Lake Quivira, not here in the home of mR. bERZERKELEY."

"Come on, Babe. We haven't made that decision yet, have we? This is a great place to raise kids, go to school, and be on the cutting edge of what's going on in the world. We tried two in Kansas. Why not one in Berkeley?"

"Right now, I want to relax, look at the lights, have an over-the-top dinner, and live in the style we should be living in for a moment, at least," Babe says, leaning back. "God knows what's next."

"You've got it," Winnie says. "Let's cool our jets, take a deep breath, and relax before we go back to reality. Let's get back to the positive Babe for a change."

Winnie leans across the table and kisses Babe on the cheek. He sits back, takes a deep breath, and looks out at the Bay at night, the moon making a quivering trail across the water. His expression changes suddenly. "What the hell?" Two police cars with sirens blaring and lights flashing are on the pier, speeding toward the end. Another police car with flashing lights blocks the entrance. "Something's happening on the pier."

Customers in the restaurant crowd the windows, trying to get a peek at the police action. "Great!" Babe says. "We can't even sneak out for some privacy without something happening. I hate this place!"

"Come on," Winnie says. "The police have whatever it is under control. Willie will tell us all about it in the morning. Let's pretend it never happened and have that great meal you were talking about."

"I'd have several drinks if I weren't questioning my insides. On second thought, who gives a shit? Bring on the booze!"

Ignoring the flashing lights on the pier and enjoying their drinks and dinner, Babe and Winnie walk from Skates into the cool night air. The Campanile's eleven rings are faint in the distance but audible over freeway noise. Winnie looks at the pier and the police car with flashing lights still blocking the entrance. "Can we ask the officer?" Winnie asks a staggering Babe.

"Why not?" Babe slurs. "You got me drunk and ready for sex. You want to wait a little? I might pass out."

"What happened, if I might ask?" Winnie says to the officer.

"Looks like another gang fight at the end," the officer says. "A local boy was killed, and another one severely injured by San Francisco gangbangers. One of the gang was killed by a third boy who jumped over. There's a Coast Guard boat looking for him, but nothing yet."

"Sounds horrible," Winnie says. "Is Sergeant Williams here? He's a friend of ours."

"No, but I understand he's on his way. He's finishing up at another crime scene."

"*Scene* is one way of putting it," Babe slurs. "He'll leave no dumpling uneaten."

"She okay?" the officer asks.

"She's overwhelmed by Cal's victory this afternoon," Winnie laughs. "She's never been better. Come on, honey, time to tuck you in!"

Winnie, with some effort, walks Babe to the SUV and opens the passenger side. He places her gently into the seat. He shuts the door and walks around, sliding behind the wheel. Babe throws her arms around him. "How about a kiss, my handsome man?"

Winnie's nose twitches. "Do you smell something?"

"I don't smell anything," Babe slurs. "You want to smell something?"

Winnie puts his hand on her arms to hold her off then takes another whiff. "It smells like someone with wet clothes." He turns his head slightly to look in the backseat.

"Keep looking forward," Jamal's quivering voice says as he lies on the floor. "Take me out of here."

"What?" Winnie says. "Jamal? Is that you?"

"Yes, Mr. Churchill," Jamal says, having a hard time talking. "Get me out of here now!"

Babe looks around and almost screams when she sees Jamal. "Oh my God!"

The SUV leaves the marina and moves toward the freeway, bouncing on the washboard road. "Where to, Jamal?" Winnie asks.

"I gotta go home. I gotta get home to my mother before my father finds me."

"Where's home?" Winnie asks.

"In Oakland, near Kaiser. I gotta get there quick."

"What happened?" Winnie asks.

"The guys we messed with in San Francisco last night," Jamal says with effort. "They found us and came to the pier to settle up. They killed one of my friends before I killed one of them and jumped over."

"You killed someone?" Babe asks.

"Maybe we should go to the police," Winnie says. "You shouldn't have any trouble under the circumstances."

"You don't understand," Jamal says. "When my father finds out I'm a dead man."

"A dead man?" Winnie says as he enters the freeway. "I've known your father since childhood. He's so proud of you. He won't do anything."

"You don't know him. He'll make me wish I'd been killed on the pier."

"You know he'll find you sooner or later," Winnie says.

"Mother will protect me like she has before. She knows how to handle him."

"You're talking about Esmeralda?" Winnie asks.

"Yes, sir," Jamal answers.

"I've known her since childhood, too," Winnie says as he turns on the freeway toward the MacArthur off-ramp. "She was always a tough one."

"She and my father got into it one too many times so she kicked him out. She'll know what to do."

The SUV moves on MacArthur toward Kaiser. "The house over there," Jamal says, peeking up from the backseat.

At the curb, Winnie opens the back door on the passenger's side. Jamal looks both ways, holding one arm. "What happened?" Winnie says.

"The guy I stabbed," Jamal says. "He got lucky before I took his knife and cut his throat."

"Oh," Winnie says. "Lucky!"

Jamal runs and pounds on the front door. "Mother, it's me, Jamal."

In a few seconds, Esmeralda—fifty, curvaceous, and bosomy, of Puerto Rican and African American descent, wearing a silk nighty covering only her top—opens the door halfway and looks out. "Jamal? What the fuck happened?"

"I was attacked on the pier by this guy. I got stabbed, but I slit his throat. I jumped over and escaped."

"You did what?" Esmeralda asks.

"Mom. Let me in! I'm hurt and I've got to hide out."

"There's no fucking way!" Esmeralda yells. "I told you to behave or I'll turn you over to your father. You're just like him, the fucking bastard. Two of a kind."

"He needs some first aid!" Winnie says, standing behind Jamal.

"And just who in the fuck are you?" Esmeralda yells at Winnie.

"Esmeralda," Winnie says. "It's me! Winnie. You remember, Winnie the Pooh from school."

"Shit. Do I?" Esmeralda says. "You're one of my ex's fucking friends. You and that naked Jim Sain! How could anyone forget you sons of bitches? I heard you came back."

"You gonna let him in?" Winnie asks.

"Fuck no," Esmeralda says. "You brought him here. Get his nigger ass back in your fancy car and drop him in the ocean for all I care. He's not my son anymore."

The door is slammed just as the sirens and flashing lights of a Berkeley police car slamming on its brakes appears in front of the house. Willie jumps out and runs full speed toward Winnie and Jamal. "Shit!" Jamal says. "I'm a dead man."

Willie grabs Jamal by his wounded arm. "You mother fucker!" Willie screams. "You really did it this time!"

"Hold on," Winnie says, grabbing Willie's arm. "You can't do this!"

"I can do anything I want!" Willie yells with blood in his eyes and extreme anger in his voice. "He's my son and he just murdered someone in my town."
"He was involved in an altercation in Berkeley," Winnie says. "But this is Oakland and you have no jurisdiction here."

"Winnie!" Willie yells. "Let me have him. When I'm through with his dumb ass, there won't be anything left in any town."

"Willie," Winnie says sternly. "Do I have to call the Oakland PD to get over here and keep you from hurting one of their residents?"

"Winnie!" Willie yells. "Don't do this to me. He's going back to Berkeley to take his punishment for what he did."

"I will bring him to you at the station," Winnie says calmly. "Now, take your hands off his hurt arm, leave him with me, and go back to Berkeley. We'll meet you at the station after we tend to his wounds."

"This arm," Willie says, almost crying. "It was going to Cal or USC to play ball and maybe even the pros. What the fuck is he gonna do now? He'll be in jail and ruin his life. He'll have no future."

"We'll see how it all works out," Winnie says calmly. "Leave him with me. Go back to Berkeley."

Willie lets go and backs off. "This is no way for a friend to act," an angry Willie says to Winnie. "If this were reversed you'd understand."

"We'll see you in a while," Winnie says.

"You're dead, mister," Willie says, pointing at Jamal before he turning and walking to his squad car.

"I told you," Jamal says to Winnie.

"Let's go to Alta Bates and stitch that up."

"I told you my mother was a piece of work, too," Jamal says. "She's a snake in women's clothing … when she wears any."

"Some things never change," Winnie says.

"She was like that in school?" Jamal asks.

"How do you think she landed your father?"

Winnie and Jamal climb into the SUV. Babe's head is back against the headrest. "Are we going home now?" she asks.

"After we take Jamal to the emergency room we'll go to Hamilton House. You haven't eaten in a while, have you, Jamal?"

"No, sir," Jamal says. "Not in quite a while."

"That's it," Winnie says. "After he eats we'll take him to the police station so he can turn himself in."

"My head is starting to throb," Babe says.

"Come on," Winnie says. "The night's young, and we beat Stanford!"

"You and your football," Babe says. "I'm voting to ban the sport from here on out."

"I'm hoping Jamal will be able to get back into the game," Winnie says. "I've pulled off miracles before."

"How will I be able to do that after my father kills me?"

"I'll take care of Willie," Winnie says. "Above everything else, he is a father."

Chapter Thirty
Bitten!

It is almost midnight as Asia carries silverware and three empty plates into the kitchen, where Bessie bends over the sink, her head almost touching the faucet. "Bessie! Are you all right?"

"China Girl. I can't move."

Asia puts an arm around Bessie's midsection and helps her to a chair at the block, where she rests her head on her outstretched hands. "How long have you been standing at the sink?"

"I don't know. After Michael left to meet Josh at the store and the rest went next door to smoke dope I couldn't move. Sarah ran out before I could stop her, headed somewhere carrying black clothes. I'm too old for all this shit!"

"Rest a little and I'll walk you to your room. What about your meds? Did you take them like you're supposed to?"

"I did, but they didn't help. I think I need to go back to the hospital."

The kitchen door opens and Mayor Sain walks in. "Mom! What's wrong?"

Bessie straightens up quickly. "Nothing, you naked-ass commie bastard! Too much Jack, I guess. I'll be all right in a moment or two."

"Phew!" the mayor says letting out air. "You had me worried."

"What do you want now?" Bessie says.

"The gang has all left, and I was sneaking back over for one more dumpling. After listening to Jack R. Abbott's description of the gonad operation Doreen did this morning and her removal of hemorrhoids from a Dalmatian, I got a sudden empty feeling in my stomach. Or maybe it was the three joints I smoked with Jefferson and Sylvia before they left. I don't know. I am hungry!"

"There's some left. Get it and get out."

"I will," the mayor says, heading for the refrigerator. He stops and turns to Asia. "Didn't you promise me a little fun this morning before we left for the Big Game? I've been thinking about it all day and night."

"I did," Asia says. "But I just started my period, and it'll have to wait a few days. When it starts I'm like Old Faithful, if you know what I mean."

"Wait? I can hardly wait much longer. Just thinking about you turns my Old Faithful on."

"Get your fucking dumpling and go away. China Girl and I are having a talk."

"Okay, okay," Mayor Sain says, opening the refrigerator. "You take all the fun out of everything."

The mayor grabs a dumpling and heads out the door. "Bye! I'll take a rain check!" he says as the door slams behind him.

"I'm going to chop off his Old Faithful with my cleaver and save you the torture," Bessie groans. "You aren't really having your period, are you?"

"No. I think helping you is far more important than fucking him right now."

"That's my China Girl. He's wacked out anyhow."

"Come on. Let's get you into bed."

"I don't think that will help. I think I need to go back to Alta Bates."

"We don't have a car."

"You got that scooter, don't you? Get me on the back and I'll hold on. I can do it!"

With Bessie clinging tight and her housedress blowing behind, Asia steers her scooter toward Ashby. Asia cannot feel her breathing. The scooter moves toward the emergency entrance. "Shit!" Asia says. "There's Mr. Churchill getting into his SUV right in front. He'll help us."

"No, no," Bessie says, gulping slightly. "Hide until he's gone. I don't want him to know what's going on."

"He's gonna know sooner or later."

"Those cells you and needle dick are growing are gonna work so he'll never have to know," Bessie says. "Hide, I tell you!"

Asia pulls into the parking garage with Bessie clinging tight, stops, and watches as Winnie loads Jamal with a sling on his arm into the SUV and pulls away. "We can go inside now," Asia says. "You okay?"

There is no sound from Bessie. Her grip remains strong but there is no movement. Asia pulls up on the sidewalk and the front wheel touches the glass door. It opens automatically, and she drives the scooter inside as an astonished female attendant jumps. "She might not be breathing!" Asia yells.

A male attendant grabs a wheelchair and moves quickly to Asia's scooter. Bessie is lifted off and placed in the chair. The attendant takes her pulse. "She is still with us," he says. "Get her into a bed immediately."

"Her name is Bessie Sain," Asia says. "She was discharged around noon today. You have all her records."

"Don't leave me, China Girl," a weak Bessie says, her eyes opening slightly. "Tell me more whoring stories."

"Whoring stories?" the male attendant says. "Is she drunk or high?"

"That is a long story all in itself."

Chapter Thirty-One
Seeking Out Prey!

As THE CAMPANILE RINGS eleven forty-five the vice-chancellor's Mercedes convertible speeds on the winding road behind the university leading to Professor Spears' laboratory. *You better be there, you freak! I WILL find out what Miss Asia is up to or you WILL be teaching Biology 1A for the rest of your miserable life.*

"Let me in, you bastard!" the vice-chancellor yells into the intercom. The gate is opened. She parks beside the building and walks to a nervous, twitching Professor Spears.

"Yes, vice-chancellor?" the professor says, hardly able to speak. "What is it you want?"

"You know what I want, you ungrateful piece of shit! I want to know what Miss Asia and you have been up to behind my back and what experiment she's doing at her boarding house. What the fuck is going on at my university in the laboratory I have supplied with exotic and state-of-the-art equipment these past several years?"

"Nothing unusual, I assure you," a quivering Professor Spears says. "Miss Asia has been a model student and laboratory assistant. There's nothing going on that should upset you."

"You're not going to make this easy, are you?" Vice-Chancellor Kris says, towering over him in her spiked heels. "What did she do to you? A little action? She take off her clothes?"

"She has been a tireless worker," the professor says. "Nothing unusual has been happening."

"I guess we're going to have to do this the hard way. Bring me your inventories and we'll see what's missing. Maybe then you'll tell me what she is doing at home."

"The inventories? We are going over inventories? That'll take all night and tomorrow."

"Then why not tell me what's going on at her boarding house? I got all night, Sunday and next week. I WILL find out what she has been doing behind my back. I will get that little demon if it's the last thing I do—and a couple of others, too."

Professor Spears walks away and then walks back. "You won't get mad if I tell you, will you?"

"Not nearly as mad as I will if you don't tell me and I find out. What the fuck is she doing at Hamilton House?"

"She is doing an experiment, that's all. Just a little experiment."

"What kind of experiment?"

"She's growing special cells—very special cells."

"What special cells?"

"She is trying to grow a new liver."

"For who?"

"I have no idea about that. It's the first time I've ever seen such a great start to growing a liver. Not in all the time I've been at this laboratory …"

"You've been helping the bitch behind my back? I told you not to let her do anything but sterilize equipment, and you're letting her conduct experiments?"

"She's a brilliant scientist," the professor says. "I've never seen anyone like her before."

"I'll bet she showed you more than test tubes," the vice-chancellor says, standing up. "Whose equipment is she using to grow these liver cells?"

"The laboratory's, of course," the professor says.

"She's using our property for her own purpose?"

"Yes. And she's doing unbelievably well with it!"

"You're mine!" she says as she walks toward the door, raising a fist in the air. She stops and walks back to the professor. "I'm going to let you off the hook this time, professor. If you warn her, call her, or let her know I know what she's up to, I will assign you to Biology 1A. You understand me?"

"Yes, Vice-Chancellor," the professor stammers. "I understand perfectly."

The vice-chancellor leaves a shaking professor standing in the middle of the laboratory and jumps in her Mercedes. She opens her cell, punches in a number, and waits for an answer as the Campanile rings midnight. "Dr. Ford?" she says into the cell. "Yes, I know it's midnight and we won the Big Game, but I have an emergency. I need you to help me get a search warrant immediately."

"A what?" a sleeping, bald Dr. Ford says from underneath the covers as his wife rolls over and puts an arm across his naked chest.

"A search warrant!" the vice-chancellor yells. "You are the Boalt Hall dean. You have all the legal connections. This is a matter of university security. I need a search warrant now."

"Can't it wait until Monday?" Dr. Ford says. "No judge is available at this hour on Saturday night—or I guess it's Sunday morning now."

"You find one now, or you'll be looking for your next case out on the street by Monday," the vice-chancellor says, yelling into the cell as loud as she can.

"Yes, Vice-Chancellor," Dr. Ford says, throwing back the covers and sitting on the edge of his bed. "Whatever you want!"

The vice-chancellor closes her cell and throws it on the seat next to her. "Bitch! I got you now! I am going to win my Big Game. With one fell swoop I'm going to get that naked son of a bitch, my bastardly son, and Mr. Churchill! What a night! I wonder if I have any wine left."

Chapter Thirty-Two
The Snake Strikes!

WINNIE'S SUV PULLS UP the Hamilton House driveway and stops. "Let's get you some food. I'll tuck Babe in, and then it's off to the station to surrender like we said we would."

"He will kill me," Jamal says. "Will you stand by me?"

"Count on it. He's had enough time to cool off by now."

"He will never cool off when it comes to me," Jamal says. "Trust me. I know what I am saying."

"Are we home yet?" Babe yawns. "I had a dream we were back in Kansas looking out at Lake Quivira, rolling around in our bed."

"Come on," Winnie says. "We're at Hamilton House."

"Oh, no!" Babe yells. "The zoo!"

Winnie helps Babe from the front seat while Jamal watches. Trojan strolls up, sees Jamal's legs, and starts to hump. "Hey, little guy," Jamal says, reaching down. "I remember you from Thanksgiving. Come on inside and take either one or both. I need a friend."

"I wonder where Bessie is," Winnie says, moving Babe toward the stairs with his arm around her waist. "Sit down at the block," he says to Jamal. "I'll be right back."

"Told you an elevator IS a top priority," Babe groans, half asleep. "Go Bears!"

Winnie reappears downstairs and walks to Bessie's door. Listening, he opens it slightly and then all the way. He turns on her light and looks at an empty bed. "This is highly unusual."

He walks to the refrigerator and takes out a plate of dumplings covered with plastic. "Let's throw a few of these in the microwave before we take you to the station," he says. "You probably won't eat for several hours."

"Can I take a quick nap?" Jamal asks. "Those shots and pills put me out. Just a few quick winks?"

"Why not? That'll give more time for your father to cool down."

"Never! He'll leave more bruises before he kills me with his bare hands."

"I never saw that in him," Winnie says. "It doesn't sound like the Willie Williams I knew."

"He tried to make me be like Junior," Jamal says. "You know—a smart, handsome do-gooder lawyer. Didn't work! I'm too much like him, I guess."

"That's right," Winnie says. "Your older brother is an assistant district attorney. It must be hard to live up to him."

"Hard?" Jamal laughs. "How about impossible?"

Trojan switches legs as the kitchen door flies open and Sarah bursts in, her face painted white and her blonde hair dyed black, dressed from head to toe in black with lace-up black boots. "Sarah? Roni?" Winnie says. "That is you, isn't it?"

"My new name is Dream," Sarah says. "Death gave it to me. We're sisters now."

"Dream?" Winnie asks.

"Isn't it perfect? It's a real Goth name."

"I don't get it," Winnie says.

"You take this little pill they gave me, and that's what you do all night for your initiation," Sarah says. "I took it, and I can't wait to go to sleep and see how it works."

"What was the pill?" Winnie says.

"They called it ecstasy, I think. Isn't it exciting? Good night. I'm going to bed now."

"This is Jamal," Winnie says. "You remember him from Thanksgiving?"

"Yes, I think," Sarah says, starting to hallucinate and stagger. "Wow! Good night. The pill is starting to work." She holds onto the rail and disappears upstairs. Winnie and Jamal hear a door slam.

"X is bad," Mr. Churchill. "You can die from that shit. First we'll take you to jail, and then I'll work on our new druggie."

Josh and unmasked Michael walk in. "Hey, guys," Winnie says. "You want some of Bessie's leftover dumplings?"

Jamal looks at Josh and Michael. "I'm Jamal," he says.

"Sorry," Winnie says. "Josh and Michael, this is Jamal, Willie's son. He was in an accident and he's as hungry as a horse. How about you two?"

"We grabbed a burger after we finished the cartoons," Josh says. "I'm going to bed. Michael, you can stay up if you want."

"No, I'm tired, too," Michael says as he yawns.

"He's a star," Josh says, looking at Michael. "I don't know which is better, his *mR. bERZERKELEY*s or his *Veronica's Lives*. He outdoes me ten times."

"You might have to change your strip again," Winnie says. "Sarah now wants to be called Dream because she's Goth now."

"Dream?" Josh says. "That's kinda stupid, isn't it?"

"The other Goths gave her ecstasy so she could dream all night as her initiation," Winnie says.

"X?" Josh says. "That's dangerous stuff!"

"Maybe you should see if she's okay," Winnie says. "And don't be shocked. She's in black from head to toe, including her hair. A whole lot more cartoons for you guys."

"Cartoons?" Josh says. "This is no laughing matter. That stuff can start her on a real slide to nowhere. Come on, Michael, we'd better check her out."

Josh and Michael head up the stairs, followed closely by Trojan. "Is it always like this around here?" Jamal asks.

"Never a dull moment," Winnie says, carrying a steaming plate of dumplings to the block. "Eat, sleep if you can, and we'll take a trip downtown."

"I might need some X myself." Jamal laughs.

Josh bangs on Sarah's door. No answer. Josh tries the handle and the door opens. Sarah lies face down on her bed, moaning. "What should we do?" Michael whispers.

"Why don't you go to bed," Josh says. "I'll lie beside her and see if she can make it through without hurting herself."

"Well, okay," Michael says. "Call me if you need me."

Michael and Trojan leave Sarah's room. Josh lies beside Sarah, his head propped up on a pillow. He puts one hand on the back of her head. "Little girl from Kansas what in the world are you doing to yourself? First you're the best thing I ever knew, and then you're running around naked and calling me names, then a lesbian, and now a drugged-out Goth. What will you be next?"

Winnie takes Jamal's plate and the glass he used to kill off a quart of milk and puts them in the dishwasher. "Go and lie down on the couch for a while. I'll wake you up and take you to the station."

"Yes, Mr. Churchill. Thanks."

While Jamal moves to the couch, Winnie goes inside Bessie's room. "And where are you?" he says to himself. He walks into the kitchen and notices the lights on in the mayor's kitchen next door. He goes outside, walks across the common driveway, and opens the door. The mayor sits drinking Jäger at the table, watching the late late news. "Come on in," Mayor Sain says. "You got all the animals tucked in after a glorious day?"

"You got any more Jäger?"

"Grab a glass. And when this bottle runs out, I got several more in the refrigerator."

"What are you watching?" he says. "Pictures of the asshole of some nut at the Big Game?"

"You got it," Mayor Sain says. "They got to show something and make some comment. My butt is already up to eight million hits on YouTube, and Martin's fantastic entrance from the sky over five!"

"I guess people like your butt better than his dick," Winnie laughs.

"I'll drink to that," Mayor Sain says as they touch glasses.

"I got Jamal next door," Winnie says, after a pause.

"Willie's Jamal?" Mayor Sain asks.

"He got into a fight at the end of the pier, got stabbed pretty good, cut one of his attacker's throat and killed him, jumped over, swam ashore, and hid in my SUV."

"Whoa! He did what?"

"You heard me," Winnie says. "We took him to his mother's house—"

"Esmeralda?" Mayor Sain interrupts.

"Yes," Winnie says. "She locked him out and said she didn't have a son named Jamal anymore. Willie showed up in Oakland at her house and was ready to finish the job the gang started. I've never seen him so angry. I got him to let me take Jamal to Berkeley and turn him in. Jamal's worried Willie will kill him."

"He probably will. He's been pretty angry since Esmeralda kicked him out for beating on Jamal and the other kids a few years back."

"I never saw that in him," Winnie says. "He was always Willie, the nicest kid on the block."

"Marriage and a bunch of kids can do that, I guess," Mayor Sain says. "Another good reason to stay single. You've had quite a day!"

"That's not all," Winnie says. "Sarah just came home dressed like a Goth with black hair and all and a new name: Dream."

"Dream?"

"The Goths and her new friend Death gave her an initiation pill that will let her 'dream all night,' hence the name."

"What kind of pill? In the old days it would have been LSD, remember?"

"Ecstasy. Josh is upstairs making sure something bad doesn't happen."

"X?" Mayor Sain says. "Took it once and tried to screw a waitress at Skates in broad daylight with a hundred people watching."

"That IS bad," Winnie says.

"That shit can hook you good if you're not careful," Mayor Sain says.

"Remember LSD and—what was the name of that chick we undressed and chased around the park?"

"That was Esmeralda," Winnie says. "Don't you remember? That was when Willie took one look at her naked and decided she was the one for all time."

"You're right!" Mayor Sain says. "I'll bet she remembers, and when she saw you with Jamal—*bam*! He had no chance."

"I never thought about that until you brought it up," Winnie says. "You're probably right."

"So where is Sarah or Roni or Dream right now?" Mayor Sain says. "I might have to give her a little of my drug counseling expertise."

"You horny old bastard," Winnie says. "You never stop trying, do you?"

"Learned from my mom."

"Where is Bessie?"

"Probably snoring away in her room. It is after midnight, isn't it?"

"No sign of her next door. I thought maybe you knew."

"She does disappear now and then. I think she has a boyfriend somewhere in the neighborhood she doesn't want me to know about. This isn't the first time she has vanished."

"Then you're not worried?" Winnie asks.

"I never worry about Mom. She's as tough as a nail, indestructible, ornery, and never misses a chance to set me straight. That's why I love her. What I AM worried about is why the news isn't saying anything about what we did at the Big Game. I need the publicity so the president will take notice and call off his dogs and let us keep the stimulus money."

"I'd be more worried about your mother, if I were you," Winnie says. "Your naked ass will be on television another day, if I know you."

"You're right. Hey, I almost got laid by the Chinese tonight! Now that would have really made my day. You want to go down to the basement, smoke a joint, and listen to me rehearse for the presentation of the victory axe Monday?"

"No. I'm going to rest my eyes for a few minutes and then take Jamal to jail."

"My rehearsal sounds a whole lot better than that. Want some Jäger for the road?"

Winnie declines and walks back across the common driveway and inside Hamilton House, where Trojan is whining at his empty dish. "Hey," Winnie says to Trojan, trying to whisper loudly. "You'll wake him up."

"It's okay," Jamal says. "I can't sleep anyhow. There was a scream upstairs that woke me."

Winnie goes up the stairs and sees Babe outside Sarah's room. Judy and Stephanie are peeking from their room. Babe opens the door and sees Michael and Josh trying to undress Sarah with throw-up everywhere. "What is going on?" Babe asks.

"I was lying next to her making sure she could sleep off the X," Josh says. "She suddenly woke up, saw me, and started screaming. She hit me several times and then started throwing up. Michael and I are trying to put her to bed."

"What in the hell is X?" Babe asks.

"A drug the Goths gave her for initiation," Winnie says.

"And what's with the black hair?" Babe asks.

"Her name is now Dream, and she is a Goth," Winnie says.

"Dream?" Babe laughs. "That's what this whole thing is, isn't it? A bad dream? You boys get out of here, and I will take care of whoever she is tonight."

"You okay?" Winnie says.

"I got at least ten minutes of sleep," Babe yawns. "Did you take Willie's son to jail yet?"

"Momentarily," Winnie says. "Guess I'll see you later."

Winnie walks down the stairs and sees Jamal sitting on the couch with Trojan humping his right leg. "Isn't that the leg that kicked a winning field goal last season?"

"Yeah," Jamal says. "A lot of good it'll do me after my father beats me to a pulp."

"Come on," Winnie says. "Let's go make history."

* * *

Winnie and Jamal head toward the Berkeley Police Station. "Just be as humble and apologetic as you can. I'll talk to your father."

"I appreciate anything you can do, Mr. Churchill. If I make it through this night, I'll be lucky."

"It's going to be daylight in a couple of hours. By the time we get you fingerprinted, your father will be exhausted and give you a break."

"Nice thinking. Just seeing my black face will give him the adrenalin he needs to rain havoc on my head."

"I'll think of something, Jamal," Winnie says. "Trust me."

The SUV parks in front of the police station. Winnie leads Jamal inside, where they are greeted by a uniformed female African American officer. "Jamal Williams?" she asks. "Your father is expecting you. Please step inside and go into the conference room."

"I am his counsel. He has engaged me to represent him."

"Sergeant Williams is his father. Jamal is underage, and his father has not given his consent to have Jamal engage an attorney. Therefore, you are not allowed inside with Jamal."

"Mr. Churchill is my lawyer. I know my rights. Even a young child can engage an attorney, if he feels his parents or parent have or will abuse him."

"Are you accusing Sergeant Williams of abusing you? Is that what you are saying?"

"I am stating my case for having my attorney in the conference room with me. He is coming in with me."

"Okay, okay," the female officer says. "You can deal with Sergeant Williams about this. I'm out of it."

Winnie follows Jamal into the conference room, where Willie and a female officer sit behind a table. Willie's eyes are red with fury, and his fists are clenched. "Sit down!" Willie orders. "Winnie, what are you doing here?"

"Jamal has asked me to represent him," Winnie says calmly. "He is concerned that he won't get fair treatment from you."

"He gets into a fight on the pier and cuts someone's throat before jumping over and running away, and he wants fair treatment?"

"He has voluntarily turned himself in to be judged for what he did in defending himself," Winnie says. "You, as his father, should be proud of him for doing that."

"I am not his father," Willie says. "I am a Berkeley police officer in charge of investigating two murders that occurred late last night. Being his father has nothing to do with these crimes. It is my intent to bring the full power of the police into this situation, and I will."

"I told you, Mr. Churchill. He will throw the book at me, and when you're not looking, he will beat me to a pulp."

The conference room door opens, and the female officer walks in. "Sergeant Williams," she says. "There is someone from the university at the front desk holding a search warrant that needs your attention."

"Can't anyone else handle it?" Willie asks.

"There's no one else on duty," the female officer says.

"Who is at the desk?" Willie asks.

"She says she is the vice-chancellor," the female officer answers.

"What?" Winnie says. "Vice-Chancellor Kris?" Winnie gets up from his chair and looks out at the front desk and the vice-chancellor, still wearing the power outfit she wore to the Big Game. Willie leaves the conference room and looks at the paper she is holding. He walks back into the conference room.

"Jamal Williams," Willie says with authority. "You are hereby arrested for murder. The officer here will go through the proper procedures and admit you to one of our jail cells without bail. There will be a hearing on Monday."

"Can we talk privately?" Winnie says.

"No," Willie answers. "I have to serve and implement a search warrant on Hamilton House immediately. I suggest you might want to be there."

"What?" Winnie says. "A search warrant for what?"

Chapter Thirty-Three
Twin Vipers

Bertha Potts sits at her desk watching the sun rise in the east. She hasn't slept all night and has viewed Mayor Sain's YouTube video dozens of times, trying to figure out what to do next to keep Gerry Armstrong's campaign moving forward.

"You bastards," she says, her voice cracking. "Maybe hiring cousin Guido isn't such a bad idea."

Bertha's cell rings. She looks at the number. "Five one zero? Must be one of the new pickets I hired late last night."

"Miss Potts," Vice-Chancellor Kris says. "Sorry to bother you so early in the morning."

"Early for me?" Bertha says. "It's a lot earlier out there, and you're up, too. I haven't been to bed yet."

"I never went to bed, either," the vice-chancellor says. "I've been chasing down a devious young lady who lives in the boarding house owned by your favorite, Mr. Winston Churchill."

"You're not talking about Sarah Armstrong, are you?"

"No. A Miss Asia, who has been wreaking havoc on my life for months ever since I tried to fire her for teaching naked."

"Sounds like one of my old friend Jim Sain's prodigies. So what are you going to do to my favorite bunch? Why did you call me?"

"I've got a search warrant to recover stolen lab equipment and arrest the little vixen who stole it. And I thought I might be able to stir up enough trouble to energize your campaign to destroy Jim Sain and Winston Churchill by default. What do you think?"

"My old pickets caved in and are in Jim Sain's camp. My new ones are supposed to start in a couple of hours."

"I can give you some new slogans for your signs," the vice-chancellor says.

"Such as?"

"'Winston Churchill harbors criminals' and 'Winston Churchill bares all in public,' for starters."

"I like those," Bertha asks. "How did Winston 'bare all'?"

"I got an infrared picture of him and others with their privates out pissing on a fire in the Stanford Stadium parking lot," the vice-chancellor says. "Of course Mayor Naked was sitting there in the buff for all to see. You can say anything you want about him, and it'll probably be true."

"I like the way you think, Vice-Chancellor. When you gonna break into Hamilton House?"

"I'm on my way now. I've got three big policemen and a piece of paper that is going to open up the lion's den. This is going to be a great morning!"

"I really DO like the way you think, Vice-Chancellor. We DO have a lot in common!

Chapter Thirty-Four
Seek and You Shall Find

WINNIE PULLS INTO THE Hamilton House driveway at top speed and slams on the brakes. He notices the lights on in the mayor's house. He opens the mayor's kitchen door and hears music coming from the basement. He moves quickly down the steps and sees the mayor playing his flute. "Jim! The police are on the way."

"What are you talking about? What did I do this time?"

"Your old friend the vice-chancellor is coming with a search warrant."

"For me?"

"No. For me!"

"What does the queen cobra want from you?" Mayor Sain asks. "If she wants a snake to keep her company, I've got one available."

"This is no laughing matter. You're the mayor. Can you stop them?"

"What have you got to hide?" Mayor Sain says.

"I have no idea what's going on in all the rooms. For all I know one of them could be doing something that'll get us all in trouble."

"Mom will take care of them. She'll chase them out with her cleaver."

"When I left she wasn't in her room."

Mayor Sain drops his flute on a music stand. "Let's go check."

The mayor follows Winnie inside Hamilton House. They open Bessie's door and see her bed made and unused. "I have no idea where she is," Winnie says.

A tired and woozy Babe walks down the stairs. "What's going on? I haven't been able to sleep after dealing with Dream.

"The vice-chancellor and the police are headed this way with a search warrant," Winnie says. "You better go back upstairs and lock the door."

"A search warrant?" Babe says, rubbing her eyes. "What for?"

The kitchen door swings open and the vice-chancellor walks in, followed by Willie and two male officers. "For the basement and all rooms," The vice-chancellor says. "I heard Miss Asia is conducting an experiment using stolen university equipment. Isn't that right Mr. Mayor?"

"Well, I ..." Mayor Sain stutters. "I was just making small talk at the game, that's all. You all should turn around and leave. There's nothing to what I said."

"I believed what you said, so I followed up," the vice-chancellor says. "I believe what Professor Spears said—that Miss Asia has stolen university equipment for her own use."

"Willie," Mayor Sain says, "can you please straighten this whole thing out?"

"It's Sergeant Williams," an uptight Willie says. "We have a legal document that gives us the right to search the entire house, and that's what we are going to do."

"We have sleeping boarders," Winnie says.

"Not anymore," Willie says. "Officers, please assist the vice-chancellor in searching Hamilton House for stolen university equipment and anything else you can find."

"We are going to have a talk about you continuing on the police force," an angry Mayor Sain says.

"Whatever you want. You are the mayor. Search 'em, officers."

The officers, with the vice-chancellor watching, open every cabinet and drawer in the kitchen. Winnie goes upstairs and knocks on Michael's door. "Get up, Michael," he says. "The police are here to look in your room." He goes to Stephanie and Judy's door and does the same.

Michael, his mask and hood off, Stephanie and Judy in robes, and a bare-chested Josh sit on the couch. Babe and Winnie sit at the block with Mayor Sain.

"Check out Bessie's room!" Willie yells.

The officers and the vice-chancellor go into Bessie's room next to the kitchen and emerge moments later.

"Let's go upstairs," Willie says. "All the way upstairs."

"That's our room!" Babe yells.

"The search warrant is for the whole house," an angry Willie yells, "and that means every room!"

"You're a real bitch!" Michael says as the vice-chancellor walks by him.

"Officer," the vice-chancellor says. "This pervert just swore at me. Is defiance a crime?"

"Isn't that your son?" Willie asks.

"I don't have a son," the vice-chancellor says.

"We'll deal with that later," Willie says.

Trojan jumps on Michael's lap, out of the way of the officers and the vice-chancellor.

"I really blew it," Mayor Sain whispers to Winnie. "Me and my big mouth! If they take Asia's experiment, Bessie has no chance."

"No chance at what?" Babe asks.

"Asia's little secret?" Mayor Sain says. "It's about Mom."

"Maybe they'll forget about the basement," Winnie says.

"Anyone want coffee?" Babe asks as she gets up from the block. "I am desperate."

Willie and the officers, the vice-chancellor in tow, walk down the stairs and over to the block. "Where are you hiding the university equipment?" the vice-chancellor asks Winnie.

"I have no idea what you are talking about," Winnie says.

"I have some equipment you can look at," Mayor Sain says.

"Since we found nothing, the officers and I are leaving," Willie says.

"When I was here a long time ago, I remember going into the basement," the vice-chancellor says. "Seems some asshole wanted to show me his etchings."

"Worked, didn't it?" Mayor Sain says.

"I think we've searched enough," Willie says. "We are all tired from yesterday and last night."

"The basement, Sergeant," the vice-chancellor says. "I want to see the basement."

A disheveled Sarah, dressed in black with splotchy white face paint, comes down the stairs, yelling. "Who in the fuck are you guys? Why did you wake me up?"

She staggers as she walks up to the vice-chancellor. "Get out of my house! I'm going to call the police!"

The vice-chancellor smells vomit on her clothes and backs off. "Young lady, and I use the term loosely, if you don't stop harassing me I'll have the officers here throw you in jail."

Josh walks to Sarah. "Come on, back to bed. These are the police, and they WILL throw you in jail."

"You!" Sarah yells at Josh. "They should throw you in jail for slandering me."

Michael walks up. "I'll take you to your bed."

"You're the nice one. I'll go to bed with you."

Michael puts an arm around Sarah's waist and moves her to and up the stairs.

"Looks like your son has a little kindness in him, unlike you," Mayor Sain says. "I wonder where he got that from."

"I don't have a son," the vice-chancellor says.

"We're finished here," Willie says. "Let's go and leave these folks alone."

"Not before we look in the basement," the vice-chancellor says. "Do your job!"

Willie opens the basement door and the officers descend, followed by the vice-chancellor. Willie looks at the mayor, knowing what's down there, before following the vice-chancellor.

"He tried to keep them from going down," Winnie says. "What's Asia doing?"

"She's trying to save Mom's life by growing liver cells," Mayor Sain says. "Mom doesn't want anyone to know, but Asia told me."

"Liver cells?" Babe says, standing beside Winnie. "What's that all about?"

"She only has a few days left, according to Asia. The new cells could jump-start her liver and save her life."

"Oh my God!" Babe says. "That explains a lot."

The vice-chancellor reappears, holding a secure package containing the liver cells. "Looks like university equipment to me," she says, holding the package out from her body. "I'd say Miss Asia is going to spend time in jail and be looking for another school to attend."

Trojan, sitting on the couch, jumps down and goes straight for the vice-chancellor's legs. He bares his teeth and bites her above the knee. "Ouch! You fucking mutt!" the vice-chancellor yells, swatting Trojan aside with her free hand. She looks down at the blood oozing from her leg. "And that will cost you plenty."

"You want first aid, Vice-Chancellor?" Willie says.

"I want to get out of here and have you put out an all-points for Miss Asia, Sergeant. I have what I came for."

The vice-chancellor walks toward the kitchen door. "You must not take those," the mayor says. "They are being grown to save a person's life, or do you care?"

"She stole university property, you asshole," she says. "They are mine."

"I'll get a restraining order this morning," Winnie says. "Do not destroy the evidence."

"Threats, Mr. Churchill? Bertha said you would try and stop me with all your legal mumbo jumbo. Go ahead. Try and stop me."

The vice-chancellor walks through the kitchen door, following the officers. Willie lags behind. "I tried to keep her from going down there," Willie says. "Sorry."

"Thanks for putting on a show and trying, old friend," Mayor Sain says.

Willie leaves.

"What are we sitting here for?" Winnie says.

Mayor Sain and Winnie follow Willie and the vice-chancellor across the lawn to the squad cars. Bertha's pickets are gathering with new signs. "I demand that you keep that evidence intact!" Winnie yells.

"See you in court!" the vice-chancellor yells, climbing into a squad car.

Asia, with Bessie on the back of the scooter, slows to turn into the driveway. "Hold on, Bessie," she says. "It looks like we have company."

"Shit!" Bessie says. "You can't let them see me this way."

"We have no choice. Those drugs they gave you will take care of you for a while. I'll drop you near the kitchen."

Asia speeds past the officers up the driveway.

"There she is!" the vice-chancellor yells. "Arrest the bitch!"

Chapter Thirty-Five
Get the Snake!

WINNIE, BABE, SARAH, JOSH, and Michael sit at the block. Mayor Sain stands next to Bessie while she cooks breakfast. "Mom. You've gotta sit down or go to bed. Let me do the cooking."

"Not while I have a breath left," Bessie says. "This is my job, and I will do it until I die."

"That's what we're all worried about," Mayor Sain says. "Everybody knows now. We can't live without you. Go rest, and we'll think of something."

"With China Girl in jail and my cells gone, what chance do I have? There's no transplant list for seventy-year-olds. Go sit down and let me finish cooking. I'm not ready for a rest yet. Get the fuck away from me!"

Mayor Sain sits down hard next to Michael. "What's going to happen, sir?" Michael asks.

"She'll die on us if we don't get those cells back."

"She can't die," Michael says. "She the nicest older person I've ever met."

"She ought to be," Mayor Sain says. "She's your grandmother."

"What?" Babe says. "She's …?"

"Yes," Winnie says.

"That means the mayor is Michael's father," Sarah says. "How neat!"

"You are my father?"

"Yes. I am the one who, in a weak moment, made love to the evil monster. You are everything she isn't."

"She told me my father took off after seeing this hole in my head. She's a lying bitch."

"The important thing right now is taking care of Bessie," Mayor Sain says.

"You knew all along, didn't you?" Babe says to Winnie.

"Does it matter now?"

"It's a piece of information I would have liked to have known."

Bessie walks to the block with a tray of eggs and bacon.

"Mom," Mayor Sain says, "there's something you should know, and I guess now is as good a time as ever."

"What the fuck are you gonna try and pull on this dying woman now?" she says.

The mayor stands up, takes the tray and sets it on the table. He puts one hand on Michael's shoulder. "Mom, meet your grandson."

"What? You've been saving that joke for a while, haven't you?"

"Mom, you know when I'm serious. Michael is your grandson."

Bessie looks at the mayor and at Michael. "Last time you had that look on your face was when you were told you had to have a hernia operation. You mean ...?"

"Yes. You have a grandson. You remember how his mother and I had a fling a long time ago before she turned bad? Well ..."

Michael stands and hugs Bessie, who wraps her arms around him. "I knew there was something about you."

"Grandma!" Michael says. "I always wanted one, and I'm glad it's you."

"Shit!" Bessie says, pushing back. "Now I really need those fucking cells. I want to be around for a long time to see how everything works out!"

"Why don't we do what we're best at," Sarah says. "Let's protest the bitch!"

"Michael and I can draw cartoons," Josh says. 'We got YouTube, Twitter—you name it."

"I'll get a restraining order immediately," Winnie says.

"I'll get Asia out on bail ASAP," the mayor says.

"Jefferson and I can organize a march by noon," Sarah says.

"I will walk naked through the campus wearing a sign," Michael says.

"That's my son!"

"Two bumps on a log," Bessie says. "Maybe I won't stay around much longer if I have to put up with two of you."

"What about the president's stimulus and Berkeley going bankrupt?" Winnie says.

"To hell with that! Mom comes first!"

"What are you going to do, Mrs. Churchill?" Sarah asks.

"I am going back to bed and put in my earplugs so I don't have to listen to those pickets."

"Yes!" Mayor Sain yells. "Let's get those cells back! Let's save Mom's life!"

"I'd say let's all drink to that. But one day without booze might give me one more day with my new grandson. Hell, who gives a shit? Jack in their coffee, anyone?"

Chapter Thirty-Six
Dead Or Alive

ASIA AND JAMAL SIT side by side in a holding cell inside the Berkeley police station. "Guess you'll have to keep that trash-talking mouth of yours shut for a while."

"I'll be lucky if I'm still alive once my father gets ahold of me."

"Can't be that bad. He's just a big teddy bear."

"A grizzly when he gets mad. Between him and my snake of a mother it's been rough this past year. Now, with my arm all cut up, sports might be over, too."

"Let me look at it," Asia says, reaching for his arm. She turns it over and over. "Doesn't act like the tendons or ligaments were cut. You might heal just fine. A lot of power lifting and you should be as good as new."

"How do you know all this stuff?" Jamal asks.

"No one knows the human body—especially the male body—better than me."

"Where did you learn about it?"

"That's my secret. Trust me, you'll be all right."

"Unless I'm dead! Why are you in here?"

"The vice-chancellor has it in for me. I was doing an experiment in the basement using university equipment. She has been trying to find something on me for a while."

"She used that for an excuse?"

"She did, and here I am. The worst part is I was growing a liver for Bessie. Without it she will die."

"That's the mayor's mother, the great cook."

"Yes."

"What did the vice-chancellor do with the experiment?"

"They may be dead now. I had them growing at the right temperature in a controlled environment."

"Shit! We both may be dead."

"I got to get out of here and see if I can save the cells. It's her only hope."

"Miss Asia? You've been bailed out," a female officer says, standing outside the cell.

"What about me?" Jamal asks.

"You?" the officer laughs. "Your father told us to throw away the key."

"I'm sure Mr. Churchill will take care of you," Asia says. "I'll talk to him."

Asia leaves the holding area and is greeted by Mayor Sain. "Come on," he says. "We got to find those cells."

"She probably destroyed them by now," Asia says.

"They can't be. That's Mom's only hope."

They leave the police station. "I brought your scooter. I know where the bitch lives. Jump on." Mayor Sain fires up the motorbike and Asia jumps on the back. "Go ahead and put your arms around me. You can grab my joy stick, if you want."

"You are incorrigible, Mr. Mayor."

"What are friends for?"

*   *   *

The scooter moves quickly around the campus to the vice-chancellor's home. Her Mercedes is nowhere in sight. "Try the laboratory," Asia says. "She may have gone to see the professor."

Inside the laboratory, the vice-chancellor stands in front of Professor Spears holding the secure bag. "This is what we found in the basement," she says. "I want you to destroy whatever it is immediately." She hands the bag to the professor.

"If these are the cells she was working on, they are cutting-edge science and need to be preserved. It would be a crime against science and whoever she was growing the cells for if we destroy them."

"You want to teach Biology 1A the rest of your life, professor?"

"No. But I don't want to be party to destroying what might be the finest scientific work I've seen in years. Can you imagine what we might be able to do if the experiment is successful? We could start a whole industry and bring millions to the university and fame to all of us. She has used every technique I taught her and kept the cells multiplying rapidly. It might work!"

"If you won't destroy them, I will," the vice-chancellor says, grabbing the bag from the professor. She walks to a sink and tears open the bag. "No, don't!" the professor yells. "You can't destroy what might save someone's life."

"I can and I will," the vice-chancellor says, ripping the bag apart and opening the sealed dishes. She empties the contents in the sink, turns on the water and washes the cells down the drain. "There. That ought to do it," she says, washing her hands.

The professor's face is white and tears are in his eyes as the door is thrown open and the mayor and Asia run in.

"Professor?" Asia yells.

"You evil bitch!" Mayor Sain yells. "Do you know what have you done?"

"I have confiscated university equipment and put it back into the inventory," the vice-chancellor says.

"And killed my mother," Mayor Sain says. "Those cells were growing a new liver for her. You just murdered her."

"That is not my concern. The equipment is returned, and you, Miss Asia, are on administrative leave while the chancellor and I terminate you from the university."

"You won't get away with this, bitch!" Asia yells.

"I already have," the vice-chancellor says as she walks to the door.

"You haven't heard the last of this," Mayor Sain says.

"What are you gonna do, Mr. Naked? Wiggle your dick in public at me again?" She slams the door shut behind her.

"I am so sorry, Miss Asia!" the professor cries. "She is an evil woman."

"Is there anything we can do now?" Mayor Sain asks.

"I'm afraid not," the professor says. "Those cells are gone, and so is Miss Asia."

"So is my mother. There's no hope."

"It's not over until it's over," Asia says. "Take the scooter. I'll stay and comfort the professor."

"Thank you, Miss Asia. You don't know what you staying means to me."

"Don't worry," Asia says. "Miracles are my specialty."

Chapter Thirty-Seven
It's Never Over!

ASIA WALKS UP THE sidewalk into Hamilton House, where Winnie, Babe, and Mayor Sain sit at the block while Bessie labors at the stove. She slumps in a chair.

"You tell her?" Asia asks the mayor.

"Yes, the naked-ass commie told me my life was flushed down the drain," Bessie says, overhearing the conversation. "Nothing new. It's the kind of luck I've had for the last fifty years after the mayor's father took off."

"What are we going to do?" Babe asks.

"Hell. Drink Jack, eat my dumplings like they were the last ones you'll ever get, be happy, and kiss my ass good-bye. What do you think you can do? You guys better get the bitch, though. I don't want to be in an urn knowing you didn't hang her from the highest tree. My ashes will get inside your bodies and never let go."

"Okay, Grandma," the mayor says. "How about that? Grandma Bessie. Quite a surprise, wasn't it?"

"A little late to enjoy it, don't you think? You knew a few days ago and didn't tell me. Michael is my grandson and I didn't know until it was too late."

"That was my fault," Asia says. "I tried to keep it a secret so you wouldn't have any more stress than you already have."

"Stress? What do you think I've had for fifty years with what's-his-name over there?"

Asia's cell rings. She listens and folds her cell. "The chancellor wants to see me in fifteen minutes."

"Want me to go with you?" Winnie asks.

"I got myself into this mess, and I can get out of it. I'll see you all later."

"Kick her once for me, won't you?" the mayor says. "Mom's going to haunt her forever."

"Bessie isn't dead yet," Asia says. "I'll think of something."

*   *   *

"Here we are again," Chancellor Lim says, sitting behind his desk with the vice-chancellor off to one side and Asia in front. "The vice-chancellor says you stole university equipment, and that is a crime. The university has strict rules about taking equipment off campus without proper written permission. Is this true?"

"Yes, Chancellor. I did take three dishes, a grow light, and a secure container to Hamilton House to conduct an experiment."

"That is a crime no matter how large or small the equipment is, Miss Asia. What were you doing?"

"I was doing preliminary work for my dissertation."

"I gave you cloning a dog for your doctoral study," the vice-chancellor says with authority. "You said you were growing liver cells to save some one's life."

"You were trying to save someone's life?" the chancellor asks. "Whose?"

"Bessie, our cook and the mayor's mother."

"That's very admirable, but it doesn't sound like it relates to your doctoral study."

"Actually, it does," Asia says rubbing her chin. "If I could grow enough liver cells to create a functioning liver, then I could surely grow enough regenerative cells to create a dog, something that has never been done before around here."

"That's a stretch," the vice-chancellor says.

"Might be possible," the chancellor says. "Why did you do it at home and not in the laboratory?"

"The vice-chancellor has ordered Professor Spears to keep me from conducting any experiments. In order to do my work, any work, I have to be secretive about it."

"You told him that?" the chancellor says, looking at Vice-Chancellor Kris. "She's studying for her PhD, and you won't let her do experiments in the laboratory?"

"After her stunt in the classroom, I wanted to keep her on probation of sorts. With her record, who knows what she might do? And she proved me right."

"Dr. Lim, I'm sure there has been a misunderstanding about all this. I see the vice-chancellor's point, and I didn't know about the need to fill out paperwork to take home a few cell dishes and other small pieces of equipment. I meant no harm and no disrespect to you or the university. I only hope I can conduct myself properly and get my experiment back on track immediately."

"Where is your experiment now?"

"The vice-chancellor flushed the growing cells down the drain."

"You did what?"

"I returned the equipment to its inventoried condition," the vice-chancellor says.

"Those cells were being grown to save someone's life?"

"Yes, Chancellor Lim," Asia says. "According to Professor Spears, they were further along than any he's worked with before. They might have actually produced enough stem cells to repair a dying liver and save someone's life."

"The mayor's mother?"

"Yes. And she is the grandmother of the vice-chancellor's son, Michael."

"I've heard enough," a disturbed chancellor says. "Miss Asia, I will have my office call you later with my decision after the vice-chancellor and I have a little chat. You are excused."

"Thank you, Chancellor Lim." Asia stands, bows slightly, and leaves the office, shutting the door behind her.

"Vice-Chancellor Kris," the Chancellor starts, choosing his words carefully. "In all my time as a scientist and a university professor I have never heard of such vindictive, vengeful actions by a supposed intelligent individual in a position of high responsibility—or any responsibility, for that matter. Miss Asia will be reinstated, will be allowed to conduct experiments in the laboratory as part of her doctoral study, and has my full support to continue with the vital work she has been doing. I hope she is able to restart it immediately. If she is unable to develop cells successfully, that will be one additional fact I will add as a reason for terminating you from the university. Am I understood?"

"But Chancellor Lim—"

"Am I understood?"

"Yes, sir."

* * *

"I should be happy, but I'm very sad," unmasked Michael says, sitting next to Josh at the store and working on a laptop in the late afternoon.

"The new laptop confuses you?" Josh asks.

"No. Bessie is my grandmother, and the mayor is my father. But she is going to die because my mother took the liver cells away. It's impossible for me to think about making funny cartoons when I'm so sad."

"It all seems like a bad movie, doesn't it?" Josh says.

"Can you imagine taking the liver cells Asia was growing for my grandmother and flushing them down the drain because she hates me and the mayor? She's insane!"

"There you go," Josh says. "Insane! You got to make a *mR. bERZERKELEY* out of that."

"You're right! But first, I gotta get my mother off my mind."

"What are you gonna do?"

"Where can I find some spray paint?"

"There's another one!" Josh says. "mR. bERZERKELEY spray paints the Federal Office Building in San Francisco. You've got a million of 'em if you just put your imagination to work."

"What about Roni? She's gone goofy."

"She's been naïve, a lesbian, and now a Goth who took a nasty drug and got sick. There's got to be several cartoons in there somewhere."

"You're right, Mr. Josh. But I have to get the evil bitch out of my mind first."

"I've got to go and take care of my girl's needs. She's a whole cartoon strip all by herself. You go do what you have to."

*　　　*　　　*

"No one treats me like this!" the vice-chancellor says behind a closed door in her office. "I own this place! No chancellor, no professor, and no little slut from nowhere are going to bring me down!"

Her intercom buzzes. "Vice-Chancellor?" her assistant says. "The file you wanted from human resources is here."

"Bring it in."

A tall, gorgeous African American female wearing a red power outfit and three-inch heels walks in and lays a folder on the vice-chancellor's desk. "I am giving you your notice," the vice-chancellor says to her assistant. "Don't let the door hit you in the ass on your way out."

The assistant turns and walks out, slamming the door behind her. "Bitch!" she says so the vice-chancellor can hear it through the door.

"I showed you, bitch! You want more?" the vice-chancellor yells at the closed door. She opens the folder. "Miss Asia, speaking of bitches, who are you?" She reads every word carefully. "You come from nowhere and have no last name. You went to a community college in Nevada and earned straight As. How many professors did you screw to get those grades?"

The vice-chancellor closes the folder. "I don't know anything more than I did before. There's got to be a way." She opens the folder again and looks through the papers. "There it is. You do have a driver's license, and a driver's license requires a birth certificate."

The vice-chancellor takes out her cell and punches in a number. "Special Agent Picard?" she asks. "Remember that favor I did for you when I got your daughter admitted to the university? I need a favor from you."

* * *

"Come on, boy," Michael says as he approaches the vice-chancellor's Victorian, crouching low to the ground. Trojan crouches with him. The dark night sky hides them in shadows. Michael takes out a black spray can and shakes it. With quick strokes he writes *bitch* on the side of the house, followed by *killer*. He finishes with the worst words he can think of—*child molester*—before sneaking back into the forest. Trojan watches, lifts his leg, and douses her favorite geraniums. Michael watches for a moment, and no lights come on. "Come on, boy. I've got it out of my system. Let's go make some cartoons."

* * *

Sarah, dressed in black, staggers into the kitchen from outside as the Campanile rings eight times. Her nose and mouth have been pierced, and silver rings adorn both.

"Well, what do we have here?" Bessie says, wiping the kitchen sink. "You're drunk and high and look like a jewelry store. What the fuck is going on?"

"My new friends and I have been in the park all day and night reading about the real Dracula. It's been so cool. Doom gave me a couple of little pills to make me relax and keep me going. I can hardly feel my feet touch the floor. I've never felt this good."

"Holy shit!" Bessie says. "We've got a druggie in the house. The mayor came home one time after sucking down some LSD. After I kicked his ass he didn't do that again. I don't know what to do with you."

"Can you make this our little secret? I don't want Mr. and Mrs. Churchill to know."

"You better get up to bed before they see you. Can I make you something to eat?"

"No. Doom gave me a pill that takes away my appetite. I want to be real thin like him—the scarier the better."

"There's Death and Doom. Who else is in your little group?"

"I can't remember all the names. It's so cool!"

"Get out of here!"

Sarah staggers upstairs as Asia walks in and sits at the block. "I suppose you heard?" she says.

"Yes! The chancellor got you off again, and you and Professor Spears started growing new cells."

"That's the good news. The bad news is the professor says it'll take a while to get the cells back to where the other ones were. We need you to stay healthy for a long time."

"Those super pills and the morphine they gave me at the hospital have kept me going all day. I feel almost as good as Sarah or Roni or Dream—whoever she is today—does after hitting on drugs in the park."

"Are you kidding me?"

"No. Her new friends have her higher than a kite, and she feels real good."

"I'll worry about her later. Right now you're the one we need to keep going."

"A couple more of those morphine bombs and I'm ready to see if needle dick has grown a new one."

"Time for you to get some rest. And nothing's changed. The professor is still the professor."

"I'll climb into the sack if you'll tell me all about it. I love fucking stories."

"Come on, Bessie. Time for bed."

* * *

"That was one of your best efforts," Jasmine says to Josh, lying in her bed. "I've inspired you."

"I can't help but think about Bessie and how she might die soon. I need to make the most of every minute."

"Speaking of minutes, I've made an appointment for you and me to visit a counselor tomorrow afternoon."

"For what?"

"To get you off this abortion kick you've been on. I talked to a few girls, and they say it is all part of the pregnancy thing. You've just got to get over it."

"You're taking me to a shrink?"

"I need you to stay with me through this pregnancy and beyond, my young, handsome, rich lover."

"You're really a sneaky snake, aren't you?" Josh says.

"Snake? That's your specialty, isn't it? I love it when you talk dirty. I told you, I am your inspiration. I think it's time again, don't you?"

"You DO inspire me."

"And, after we visit the shrink, we'll go home and see my parents."

"What? Drive to LA?"

"Don't worry. This snake will make the drive enjoyable."

"I have a big deadline to meet."

"Speaking of big ..."

Part Three
Road Warriors

Chapter Thirty-Eight
Stinking Shrink

"Is this the place?" Josh says, looking at a small house near the corner of McGee and Rose in the early morning, driving slowly in his old Honda. The cottage has a rickety white fence and is overgrown with vines and bushes and potted plants that haven't been tended to in decades. A tiny garden takes up one corner of a small swath of untamed devil grass. Silk curtains with a rainbow of colors frame the old windows.

"This is it," Jasmine says, her arm around Josh's shoulder as he pulls to the curb.

"I suppose tarot cards will be a part of the visit?" Josh says as he laughs slightly.

"Dr. Applegas has a PhD, an EdD, and an MBA. She's for real!"

"Applegas?" Josh says. "You have to be kidding."

"Come on, Daddy. Let's get this over with and be on our way to LA. The more time we spend in here, the less time we have to take care of my needs."

"Why go in?" Josh asks. "Let's take care of your needs right now and get on the road."

"I want you to get that abortion notion out of your head once and for all. I want this baby, and I want to be with you. Let's go!"

They walk up a cobblestone sidewalk onto a wooden porch. The front door opens, and a slightly stooped, diminutive, gray-haired female wearing a tie-dye top, a full skirt, and Birkenstocks greets them. "You must be Jasmine and Josh," she says. "I am Dr. Applegas. We've been expecting you."

"We?" Josh asks.

"Yes. The group Jasmine requested has gathered in the parlor. Shall we?"

"Group?" Josh whispers as they walk inside.

"Go with the flow," Jasmine says. "Think of my needs."

Josh and Jasmine walk through the house. The walls are covered with old, Victorian wallpaper. Incense wafts through the air, hiding the smell of high-grade pot. Three women and one man sit in a circle, leaving three chairs empty. "Have seats on either side of me," Applegas says, sitting down.

"I want you to meet the Anti-Abortion Support System, or ASS, as we call ourselves."

"Assholes, I call it," a balding, bearded man wearing loose walking shorts says as he shifts in his seat.

"That is Mr. Ruud," Applegas says. "And he is."

"Don't mind him, dear," a young African American female wearing a black turtleneck sweater and long skirt says. "His mind is always in the gutter."

"My mind?" Ruud interrupts. "No fucking, no abortions."

"Miss Parks, our resident unmarried mother of nine," Applegas says, "keeps us reminded about the consequences of not having an abortion."

"I'm the quiet one," an elderly female wearing a long wrap-around skirt and a wrinkled blue top says. "My parents tried to abort me sixty years ago and messed up. You want to see the scars on my pussy?"

"No, not now, Mathilda," Applegas says. "These young people are here to listen to the positive and negatives of having an abortion, not hear us beat each other up for the umpteenth time."

"I represent all the lesbians and gays in Berkeley," Mathilda says.

"She's so horny, she'll try to fuck both of you before you leave," Ruud says.

"I think you should have one or two abortions," a young, white woman wearing a low-cut top and tight, short skirt says. "Make sure it's right and then go all the way."

"She's Rhonda, our resident whore," Ruud says. "Never saw a dick she didn't like."

"Relax," Applegas says. "We all have our likes and dislikes."

"Are you sure you're pregnant and don't just have gas?" Mathilda asks.

"That's Applegas, you dumb shit!" Ruud says.

"Okay, okay," Applegas says. "Let's stay focused. Are you or aren't you?"

"I haven't had my period for almost two months and my breasts have swelled," Jasmine says. "I know I'm pregnant."

"What about one of those tests?" Miss Parks asks.

"No need," Jasmine says. "A woman knows these things."

"Knows?" Miss Parks laughs. "Hell. A couple of times I thought I was just putting on weight, and *bam!*, out comes another little black kid."

"Let's pretend, for the sake of our continuing discussion, you are pregnant," Applegas says. "Why do you, you handsome young man, want her to have an abortion? You want to be out playing around and not facing your responsibilities?"

"I want to hear more about her swelled breasts," Ruud says. "Have her take off her clothes so we can see."

"We all know what will swell," Rhonda says.

"I never asked her to have an abortion," Josh says. "I asked several times about abortions because I draw this comic strip and I used the conflict the discussion generates as part of humor."

"You draw cartoons?" Mathilda says. "Which one?"

"He draws two: *mR. bERZERKELEY* and *Veronica's Lives*," Jasmine answers. "And he makes a lot of money with his nudes, too."

"I've seen the one about our dumb-shit mayor," Ruud says. "He IS a cartoon."

"Thursday's *Veronica's Lives* is my favorite," Mathilda says. "I am that person sitting in my rocking chair thinking about old times."

"You don't want to her to have an abortion, young man?" Applegas asks. "You want to let nature take its course?"

"Yes, ma'am," Josh replies. "I really don't know why we're here."

"Neither do I," Ruud says. "I'd much rather be home tending my bees."

"Shit!" Miss Parks says. "Here we go with more of your honey talk again. Why don't you let a few of those bees fly up your ass and give us all a break?"

"I like his honey," Rhonda says. "It has a very distinct taste, especially when you put some on veggies."

"What about marriage?" Applegas says. "If you don't want to have an abortion, are you two gonna get married or live in sin and have a little bastard?"

"Hey, watch it!" Miss Parks says. "I got nine of those at home."

"That's what we're going to LA after this session for," Jasmine says. "We're gonna tell my mother and father and make arrangements."

"I've got a shotgun I can loan you," Ruud says.

"Why don't you pretend you're Hemingway," Miss Parks says. "That would be your gun's best use."

"Please," Applegas says. "I suggest, after hearing your story, you proceed to the altar posthaste and have a great life together."

"Will you sign the paper I gave you certifying that we had a counseling session?" Jasmine asks.

"Yes, dear," Applegas says. "Come back any time. My ASS takes Visa, Mastercard, and American Express."

Chapter Thirty-Nine
On the Road Again

"WHAT DO YOU THINK?" Mayor Sain asks Winnie as he stands in People's Park smoking a joint around a trash can fire with Jefferson and Sylvia.

"It's the middle of December, and everyone's attention has turned to the holidays, not the president's stimulus fund," Winnie says. "The pickets seem bored, and no one from the media has covered them for weeks. It's old news in Kansas. I don't think you're making any headway."

"Then we need to stir something up. Got any ideas? I can't let Berkeley go belly-up, and you can't let Bertha beat you in Kansas."

"I've still got a lot of time. You've got to take care of Berkeley."

"I don't know what else to do. I heard from the boys making the sizzle reel for the reality show. We could splash it all over the Internet, I suppose, but they say it needs a little more excitement. I need some of your political expertise."

"You are the best expertise I ever had," Sylvia slurs.

"Who you got supporting you?" Winnie asks. "Who are the big dogs on your side?"

"I got several big cities and a couple of governors."

"What about someone the president will listen to? Someone he counts on for support?"

"Such as?"

"How about Los Angeles? You get LA on board and things will happen."

"You're right. LA is key."

"I heard Josh say he is headed that way with his girl. You coulda hitched a ride if you woulda thought about all this earlier."

"And miss another evening in the park? No way. Cattle call, here I come!"

"I love cattle calls," Sylvia slurs.

*   *   *

Josh's old Honda pulls up the last hill on I-580 toward the I-5 on-ramp heading south to Los Angeles. Josh's silence and his focused stare give an indication that he is deep in thought. "You haven't said a word after we met with the support group," Jasmine says.

"I was reminiscing about my parents. I was remembering how they wanted to be around when I got married."

"That's right, you told me. They both died when you were a teenager."

"The part about getting married quickly so we don't have a bastard kinda got me, too," Josh says. "You and Applegas have a talk ahead of time?"

"We did have a consultation."

"I really don't want to go to LA. I left Michael to complete the cartoons for the end-of-the-year special. I have responsibilities. Going to LA right now isn't one of them."

"We have to arrange the wedding. My parents want to throw the biggest event of the holiday season. Married on Christmas! We won't forget our anniversary."

"I thought you were Jewish."

"We celebrate Christmas and Hanukkah. I love presents!"

"I know!"

"Come on now. Let's pull over at Harris Ranch," Jasmine says, rubbing Josh's chest.

"Me, married?"

* * *

Bertha paces back and forth in her office in front of four men in suits and Gerry Armstrong in casual clothes. "Things are not going well," Bertha says. "The polls have not moved in two weeks. We still lead Winston Churchill, narrowly, even with the pictures and his antics in Berkeley."

"You've been spending a lot of money, Bertha," one of the men says. "The central committee can only go so far. We need the money to take care of business here in Kansas, not in Berkeley."

"As hard as it is for me to say it, I think we need to steer away from good old mR. bERZERKELEY and try a new approach," Bertha says.

"What's next?" another man asks. "You going to call cousin Guido?"

The men chuckle as Bertha paces. "This is no laughing matter," she says. "Plan B is to have our friends in Washington cut whatever deal they need to cut with the president and have him take a fresh look at the stimulus funds and save Kansas from financial ruin."

"That'll make Winston look like a hero, won't it?" another man says.

"We'll make sure that Gerry gets all the credit," Bertha says. "So my old enemies in Berkeley win one. So what? We'll make Gerry the white knight and take all the credit before anyone else takes it. What do you say?"

"Bertha, you've done it again," a man says. "I'll get on our contacts immediately. We need to get pictures of Gerry with our Washington friends and the president. Can you handle that?"

"Gerry, what do you say?" Bertha asks. "You ready for a trip to DC?"

"I'm getting worried about Sarah in Berkeley, after seeing the pictures the pickets sent," Gerry says, holding several photographs. "She's dyed her hair black and wears black clothes. I think she's even pierced an ear."

"The pickets will be gone in the morning, and I'm sure your Sarah will be okay," Bertha says. "They may be weirdos, but Berkeley folks do take care of each other. She'll be fine. Go to DC and dazzle 'em. With our help you'll be a cinch in November, Governor."

* * *

At midnight, Josh's old Honda pulls up a winding, narrow road toward the top of Sherman Oaks. "I really don't like this road," Josh says. "There's hardly room for one car, let alone one coming the other way."

"You'll get used to it. I grew up here, and we never had a crash or even came close to one."

"No place to stop and get a little, that's for sure."

"You can wait a couple of minutes, can't you? And when have you ever gotten just a little?"

"Just a figure of speech, that's all."

"Sounds like another one of your cartoons."

"Not a bad idea. I'll have to remember that one."

"Park on the street. My parents are probably asleep by now. We can go in the side gate. My bedroom has an outside door."

"How does that not surprise me?"

Jasmine unlocks the door outside her bedroom and goes inside. Josh carries her luggage and a duffel bag.

"Jasmine, is that you?" A female voice asks on the other side of Jasmine's closed bedroom door.

"Mother? Yes. Josh and I just got here."

Jasmine opens the door to see her mother and father dressed in robes on the other side. Josh stands behind Jasmine. "Mother and Father—Marty and Carol—you remember Josh from last summer?"

"Ma'am, sir," Josh says, shaking their hands.

"We just got in, and we're tired. Can we talk over breakfast in a couple of hours?"

"Will you show Josh the guest room? You two aren't married yet, are you?" Jasmine's mother asks. "We have a big day tomorrow, selecting the dress I want you to wear, picking out invitations, and going to the announcement party. Get some sleep."

Jasmine's mother and father leave. Josh looks at Jasmine. "You've told them?"

"Not everything. I'll save the baby surprise for after our wedding."

"You've got a date?"

"I told you. Christmas is perfect. I can't wait."

"That's only three weeks away!"

"I know. Isn't it wonderful? We have a little time. What do you say?"

"Right now, I've got to get some sleep," Josh says.

"It's a long time until breakfast," Jasmine says, throwing her arms around Josh.

"Six hours?"

"You know my needs."

Jasmine's father reappears. "Josh," he says, "can I have a word with you?"

Josh follows Jasmine's father into a study and a well-stocked bar. "You want a drink, son?" Jasmine's father asks.

"Yes, sir. That sounds good!"

"Call me Marty. What'll it be?"

"You have any Jägermeister?"

"No. How about scotch or gin?"

"Whatever you're having will be fine with me."

Jasmine's father pours each of them a stiff gin with a splash of tonic and adds a lime. "This is how we do it here in Sherman Oaks," he says, handing a full glass to Josh.

"Thanks. It was a long drive."

"Jasmine tells me you are going to get married at Christmas," Marty says.

"Yeah, Christmas."

"Why don't you wait? Summer would be much better."

"You know your daughter. When she makes up her mind—look out!"

"Takes after her mother, that's for sure. Jasmine tells me you're quite an artist. Wasn't that what you were doing when you left LA last summer?"

"Yes. I gave up a career working for a major studio to chase her up north. Quite a daughter you have, but of course you know that."

"I do, and I want to make sure the one she marries takes care of her like I have for almost twenty years. You will do that, won't you?"

"Yes, sir."

"You are going to make sure she finishes Cal, aren't you? A college degree is like a life insurance policy in case of God knows what happens. What are you going to do to support her in the style she has been used to?"

"Continuing my cartoons and portraits is my plan."

"I read your *mR. bERZERKELEY* every day. They are a scream. Is that guy, the mayor, as kooky as he seems, or is that your imagination? No one could be that goofy. And your *Veronica's Lives*—is she a real person?"

"The mayor is who he is. There's no one like him. Most of what you see is for real with him. And the girl? That's where my imagination has gone wild."

"Jasmine says you're loaded and much different than the guy we all met last summer. To tell you the truth, we didn't give you much chance with her when you left. We thought you'd be long gone by now."

"Well," Josh starts, as Jasmine walks in, "things change."

Jasmine sits next to Josh. "Well, Father, how do you like Josh now?"

"We were just having some man talk," her father says. "He's assuring me he will take good care of you."

"He always does, Father. You have no idea."

*   *   *

Asia's cell rings as she lies in her bed, her eyes wide open. She looks at the clock. She picks up the cell and looks at the number. "A seven seven five number at 3:00 a.m.?" She puts the phone down and tries to close her eyes. The cell rings again. She picks it up. "Yes?"

"Lily Liu Lu, is this you?" a female voice says.

"Who is this?"

"Gretchen from the ranch."

"Lady Gretchen?" Asia says. "How did you find me?"

"I just had a visit with a Special Agent who spilled the beans while we were fucking. He was asking around Virginia City about someone named Asia a graduate student in Berkeley and had a picture of you. Some drunk at the Bucket of Blood sent him over here. He had your cell number, which I lifted from his wallet while he slept it off."

"I've been found out," Asia says. "How and why?"

"He said some bigwig at the university wanted the lowdown on you. Beyond that I have no idea. He was more interested in my thirty-eight double Ds than worrying about you. And you know those feds. They want all the freebies they can get."

"Shit! The vice-chancellor! Did he find out about Johnny Blood?"

"He didn't ask and I didn't tell. You in trouble over there?"

"No trouble, just one very angry enemy."

"Maybe you can take care of it like you did that bastard."

"You have no idea how tangled the web around Johnny Blood has become, Gretchen."

"Well, someone over there knows, Lily Liu Lu. What are you going to do? Hit the road again?"

"I can't. I have too much to do here."

"Then you'll get caught. It's only a matter of time. Maybe the road would be a good idea."

"I can't run away from the people I love anymore."

Chapter Forty
SoCal Stylin'

"Get up," Jasmine says, shaking Josh.

"Is it time again?" he says, still asleep.

"Forget my needs," Jasmine says. "Mother and Father are taking us to the club for breakfast. Then you and Mother and I are going to Rodeo Drive for wedding dress shopping. And there's the reception this evening, where we'll make our announcement."

"Club? Shopping? Reception? I was going to relax."

"No time for that. We've got to get ready for the wedding and get back to school so I can at least finish the semester before you know what happens."

"That's right. The baby."

"Shhh! Not so loud. Let's get going."

"There's no way I'm going to Rodeo Drive and shop. How did your father get out of it?"

"He's going to stay at the club and golf with his buddies. I told him you don't golf."

"Maybe I should learn."

"Come on, you spoilsport. Maybe there'll be a little time along the way to take care of my needs."

* * *

The taxi ride from LAX to downtown LA goes quickly in morning traffic. "Fucking palm trees," Mayor Sain says. "What are they good for, anyhow?"

"Whadda ya say?" the turban-wearing driver asks, turning down the chanting blasting from his radio.

"Nothing," Mayor Sain says. "Sure glad I live in Berkeley."

"Whadda ya say?"

"Nothing. Just babbling."

The taxi stops in front of Los Angeles City Hall, and Mayor Sain jumps out. "Keep the change," he says, throwing a hundred-dollar bill to the driver.

"Consider it a gift from the People's Republic of Berkeley." He looks at the tall structure. *Little bigger than Berkeley's.*

"I don't have an appointment," the mayor says to a well-dressed Hispanic female sitting behind the information window. "I am the mayor of Berkeley, and I need to see your mayor ASAP. I flew down here from Oakland this morning. It is very important."

"The mayor doesn't see anyone without an appointment, sir," the information officer says politely. "Is this an emergency?"

"Yes, I'd say it was. If we don't act quickly, LA will lose millions of dollars."

"Let me ring his assistant." The information officer works with a switchboard, talks, and listens. "His assistant is sending down one of the interns," she says.

"Thank you. That will be a start."

"You're from Berkeley?" the information officer says. "You ever see that crazy guy, mR. bERZERKELEY, walking around naked?"

"That's me," Mayor Sain says. "I am mR. bERZERKELEY."

"Oh my God!" the information officer says. "Wait until I tell the others. You will keep your clothes on, won't you?"

"I don't promise anything, especially being free in this beautiful Southern California weather."

"If I find a newspaper, will you autograph your cartoon for me?"

"Sure, why not?"

A Hispanic young man walks from an elevator. "Mayor Sain?" he asks. "Let's find an empty room."

Mayor Sain follows the young man to a conference room. "You wanted to see the mayor for some emergency or something?"

"Yes. I have been on a campaign to force the president to back off on the trouble his auditors are causing with the use of the stimulus funds. I met with a lot of the mayors a couple of weeks ago in Kansas, and most of them couldn't give the money back without causing financial ruin. In Berkeley's case, we would go bankrupt. I saw LA's numbers. There's no way you could survive. That's why I am here. I need your mayor to stand with me and fight the Feds."

"I guess you haven't heard," the intern says. "You were probably in the air when the news was sent."

"What's that?"

"The president has asked that his auditors reexamine the way the stimulus funds have been used and redo their reports. We got the message an hour ago."

"Any explanation?"

"We heard from one of our lobbyists that a bipartisan group from Congress approached him early this morning and cut some sort of deal."

"Well, I'll be damned!" Mayor Sain says. "That changes everything. I guess my little trip wasn't necessary after all."

"Stay in Los Angeles for a while and spend some of that Northern California green," the intern says. "I lost a bundle in Berkeley when I got in trouble at the USC game."

"You weren't …" Mayor Sain says taking a closer look at the young man. "Couldn't be."

"I ran on the field and was thrown in the jail with a bunch of naked people. I showed 'em."

"Are you kidding? I helped throw you back into the stands."

"It is a small world, isn't it? At least we won the game."

"Looks like we both won this game."

"Yes. Anything else I can do for you?"

"Got any free tickets to Disneyland?" Mayor Sain laughs.

"No. That's in a different city," the intern says.

There is a knock on the closed conference room door. The intern stands and pulls it open. Three women holding open newspapers stand outside giggling. "I told you it's him," the information officer says.

"I believe it's for you," the intern laughs. "That's right—you are mR. bERZERKELEY! Who needs to go to Disneyland when you are around? Will LA be in the next cartoon?"

"I'll make sure of it," Mayor Sain says, standing and walking to the giggling women.

"See you next year at the coliseum," the intern says as he walks out.

*   *   *

"What did you think about the quiche and slow gin fizz breakfast?" Jasmine's father asks Josh as they sit inside a restaurant at an exclusive country club. "We come at least twice a week."

"A style we have come to enjoy," Jasmine's mother says. "Nothing like it just before we head to Rodeo Drive and Marty enjoys a round of golf.

"We're ready, aren't we?" Jasmine says.

"That's why we brought both Beamers," Jasmine's father says. "Josh can be your escort while I break eighty and win the cost of breakfast back."

"What'll you shoot on the back nine?" Jasmine's mother laughs.

"Wiseass!" Jasmine's father says as he kisses Jasmine's mother on the cheek.

"Isn't being married going to be fun?" a bubbly Jasmine says, watching her parents tease each other.

"Yeah, fun," Josh says under his breath.

"What was that?" Jasmine says.

"Nothing. I was agreeing with you."

"Come on, you two," Jasmine's mother says. "Let's go shopping."

* * *

Winnie's cell rings as he sits at the block drinking coffee with Babe. "Pooh!" Mayor Sain says. "Did you hear?"

"I did. I got a call from Bertha this morning. The pickets are gone, and Gerry has saved the day with the stimulus fund."

"What? Gerry did what?"

"He's taking all the credit. Bertha has beaten me to the punch with the Kansas folks. It'll be all over the media by noon."

"All my worry, all the cartoons—all for nothing?"

"I'm sure it all added up and forced Bertha's hand. She's probably upset about letting you win one. But it'll give Gerry the upper hand in Kansas."

"At least Berkeley won't go bankrupt," Mayor Sain says. "Sorry about Kansas, old buddy."

"Don't be sorry for me. Maybe I'll just stay here a while longer and keep you out of trouble."

"Trouble? That's my middle name."

Black-haired Sarah, dressed Goth from head to toe, staggers down the stairs and out the kitchen door, passing Winnie without saying a word. "Sarah, Roni, Dream," Winnie says loudly.

"What's going on there?" Mayor Sain asks.

"Our Goth just left. Gerry may be winning Kansas, but his daughter is definitely on a losing streak here."

"How's Mom?"

"Asia came down and convinced her to get some rest. The whole thing with her liver and the vice-chancellor has us all in shock. When are you coming back?"

"I got a ticket for tonight."

"What are you going to do all day?"

"I don't know. A bunch of the girls from the mayor's office want me to go to lunch on Olvera Street with them."

"Isn't that where you and I got stinking drunk on margaritas and mooned USC cheerleaders after they kicked Cal's butt in the Coliseum?"

"One and the same. Say, I wonder what Josh is doing?"

*　　　*　　　*

A BMW makes its way through traffic to Beverly Hills and Rodeo Drive. Josh's cell rings as he drives. "What are you doing?" Mayor Sain asks. "I met with the mayor's office and I got a lot of time to kill before I head back to Berkeley. What can we do for fun?"

"I don't know, sir," Josh answers.

"Sir? You must have chicks in the car with you."

"I do. What's the problem?" Josh says, holding the cell phone tight to his ear so Jasmine and her mother can't hear.

Jasmine looks at Josh on the cell phone. "What are you doing? You can get a ticket for talking on your cell. Who in the hell is it?"

"It's Mayor Sain," Josh says. "It's very important."

"Go ahead and lie," Mayor Sain says. "Whatever you make up I'll back. Let's go get crazy!"

"You want me to represent you where?" Josh asks.

"I want you and me to find a couple of cuties and run naked on the beach."

"You want me to represent you with the studio about your reality show?"

"The only reality I want is a couple of big tits and several pitchers of margaritas."

"I interned there. I do have connections."

"Shake the broads and meet me at the Manhattan Beach pier in an hour."

"I don't know, sir. I have important business here. I am taking my girlfriend and her mother shopping on Rodeo Drive. We're looking at wedding dresses, tuxedos, the works."

"Marriage? No way. Get the fuck away from those women and meet me at the pier."

"Yes, sir, I know it's a once-in-a-lifetime chance, making a reality show."

"Does your girlfriend's mother have big tits? If so, excess the chick and bring her mother."

"Yes. It could be worth a lot of money."

"You're wasting time. Dump 'em, and let's go get naked!"

"You'll give me fifty percent for being your agent?"

"Fifty percent? You're a fucking crook! Let's go!"

"I'll talk it over with my girlfriend and her mother on the way to Rodeo Drive."

Josh folds his cell. "That sounds like a real opportunity," Jasmine's mother says.

"I guess if the mayor's reality show goes, we'll have to move to Los Angeles," Josh says.

"Now that sounds more like it," Jasmine says. "You better let us shop while you go and make a reality show. What will they call it?"

"*mR. bERZERKELEY*, after the cartoons, I'm guessing," Josh says with his tongue in his cheek. "That way I'll get creator money, too."

"I like the way this boy thinks," Jasmine's mother says. "I think the wedding dress is on him."

"I told you he was Mr. Moneybags," Jasmine says. "My kind of style!"

Chapter Forty-One
Flashing Before My Eyes

"I'm going to go on doing what I've been doing for fifty years. If I die doing it, then so what? I've lived a full life—or maybe it's just been full of it, with that naked commie bastard."

Bessie lies in her bed with a nervous Asia sitting on the edge. "Take it easy. Those pills they gave you will ease your pain. Something will come up to save the day."

"The only 'coming up' was flushed down the toilet a while ago. I feel like shit—though I look a whole lot better than you. What's the matter? Needle dick finally get to you?"

"My past might be catching up with me."

"All that fucking? You catch a disease or something? Maybe you need the drugs, not me."

"Nothing like that. Let's just say I did something premeditated before I left."

"You cut off someone's dick? I want to hear more."

"What I did needed to be done. Now, the vice-chancellor, in her devious way, has found out. It could be the end to my future and maybe go all the way to the chancellor."

"I totally agree with Michael. She is a real bitch and the most poisonous snake on the planet. I don't know how my son and she ever hooked up. Oops. Yes, I do. She's female. At least they produced one fine young man."

"Yes, they did. Did you see the cartoons in the paper? Those were his."

"I didn't have time. After Babe and Winnie got the word about Sarah's father taking credit, the pickets not showing up, Stephanie and Judy stomping off without eating the eggs and bacon I slaved over, and Trojan drinking the rest of my Jack, all I wanted to do was crawl back in bed. I'll read it later, if they aren't used to clean up Trojan's pee by the kitchen door."

"What are Stephanie and Judy so upset about?"

"All I heard was something about 'Asia promised' as they left arguing."

"Shit! How can I leave? I have so much to tie up here."

"Leave? You're not going to leave, are you?"

"It's tempting. When my past comes out the best thing for everyone is me disappearing."

"You said you'd find a way to help me stay alive, at least long enough to see my naked-ass commie son get his. You're my only hope."

"I am thinking about it. That's for sure."

"Well, if you have to, you have to. You've been a shining light for me these past few months. You've given me hope."

"I won't leave you, Bessie. You can count on it, no matter what. Right now, you've got to get some rest so you can carry on."

"It's almost lunch, and who knows who will be around? I think I'll start making dumplings for tonight. Might as well go out a winner."

Asia kisses Bessie on the forehead and tucks her in around the shoulders.

* * *

Sarah sits in the park next to the high school with several youths dressed in black. They pass clove cigarettes. "Dream! What did you see?" Death asks, petting her small, black cat. "When I took it, I saw my entire life flash before my eyes. I saw my horrible parents and my freaky sister and ugly brother yelling at me like they used to and calling me names. What did you see?"

"I saw the inside of a toilet," Sarah says. "I was so sick I thought I was going to die."

"That's what it's all about," a young man with three rings piercing his nose and two in his mouth says. "The closer you come to dying, the better it is."

"I don't like it," Sarah says. "I threw up all over myself, all over Mrs. Churchill and Josh. It was one of the worst experiences of my life."

"You'll get used to it," Death says.

"I don't know if I want to."

"Did you see last Friday's cartoon about you?" Death says. "The black crow with a piercing in its beak and beads leading to its tail, dropping black poop instead of white on the hat of an old man sitting below the wire?"

"That was Josh," Sarah says. "He's a jerk. I wish he would take some X and die!"

"Now we're talking," Death says. "You finally have become one of the group."

"You bring the Dracula book?" Death asks.

"I did," Sarah says. "I didn't have any time to read it. I did wipe off the puke, though."

* * *

The taxi leaves Josh in the Manhattan Beach pier parking lot. Mayor Sain is talking to three boys standing next to boogie boards. The mayor sees Josh. "Hey, Surfer Boy! What took you so long to get rid of the ball and chain? It's high noon and time to party!"

"Thanks for rescuing me. No way I'm gonna watch two women ogle wedding dresses on Rodeo Drive."

"You can't get married with all the chicks still left out there to make it with!"

"It ain't over yet," Josh says. "But it's getting close. How did you like the excuse I came up with?"

"You are the creative one. It's true, though. Those boys are cranking up the sizzle for the reality show. I don't know about the fifty percent."

"They bought it! What are we gonna do?"

"These boys, in addition to giving me some good skunk, have issued me a challenge. They say windsurfing out there is too dangerous. I say we prove them wrong."

"Windsurf near the pier?"

"I got a great idea! Let's see how long it takes to go from this pier to that one down there," Mayor Sain says, pointing south toward Hermosa Beach. "I say we do it naked. What do you say?"

"You want to windsurf naked from the Manhattan Pier to the Hermosa Pier?" Josh asks.

"Has it ever been done before?"

"Never," one of the surfers says. "This guy as crazy as he seems?"

"He's mR. bERZERKELEY," Josh laughs. "Crazy is his middle name."

"I got a couple of boards and sails at my house up the street we use at the lake," another of the surfers says. "I'll be right back."

"You guys want another hit while we wait?" a surfer asks. "This'll make all the news."

* * *

Willie's police car stops in front of Hamilton House. He hurries up the driveway and into the kitchen, almost stepping on Trojan making his move toward Mimi's house. "Bessie!" he yells as he enters the kitchen. "You gotta turn on the television."

"What the fuck is going on?" Bessie says, turning around at the stove. "We bomb somebody again?"

"No! It's your son."

Winnie walks from the stairs.

"Pooh!" Willie yells. "Turn on the TV. Jim is doing his thing again."

Winnie grabs the remote and turns on the flat screen.

"It's all over the news!" Willie says.

Winnie flips to a local station and brings up a live picture of the mayor and Josh windsurfing in the ocean, rocking up and down over large waves with sails stretched to the max. A helicopter shoots the picture from above, and a female voice narrates the scene. "Two men are windsurfing the ocean naked! The one wearing the backpack nearest the beach is said to be Jim Sain, the Mayor of Berkeley of *mR. bERZERKELEY* fame, according to a tweet we just received. We don't know who the other man is or where they are going. They seem to be headed toward the Hermosa Beach Pier. Crowds are gathering on that pier. This has never happened before! What a scene! Probably start a fad!"

"What a dumb shit!" Bessie says, wiping her hands with a towel as she watches the report. 'Shoulda had that abortion."

Babe comes walking down the stairs wearing a bathrobe. "What's the ruckus?"

"The mayor and it looks like Josh are windsurfing the LA beaches," Willie says. "Kinda looks like fun."

"The son-of-a-bitch has to keep it stirred up, doesn't he?" Bessie says.

The television picture switches to the Hermosa Pier and a male anchor. "They are almost here," he says as the camera focuses on the mayor and Josh racing toward them. "We don't know what they are going to do, but a large crowd of onlookers and two small Coast Guard chase boats are waiting. The Coast Guard wouldn't let us ride along, so we'll have to wait until the two men land somewhere along the beach to find out why they are trying this dangerous stunt—and naked to boot."

"He does know how to draw a crowd," Winnie says.

"I can't watch anymore," Bessie says. "I see my whole life and all my hard work trying to make something of the dumb shit going down the drain, along with my liver cells. I am going to finish up and go back to bed."

Bessie walks to the stove, leaving Winnie and Willie watching the television, Willie munching on a hot dumpling. An unmasked Michael moves quickly through the kitchen door to the television. "You guys already heard?" he asks. "The mayor and Josh are having fun in Los Angeles, aren't they?"

"Go ahead," Winnie says. "You can call him Dad or Father if you want.

"I'd call him dumb shit. Son or not!" Bessie yells from the stove. "He doesn't have two brain cells to rub together."

The television camera focuses on the mayor and Josh rounding the south side of the pier with the mayor waving to the large crowd that has gathered. "We'd provide closer pictures," the male news anchor says, "but we are not allowed to show certain body parts on television. Trust me. They are naked and heading for local police officers waiting on the beach."

"Shit!" Winnie says. "Who is gonna bail them out this time?"

Cameras follow the mayor and Josh toward the rolling surf. Their sails fall limp as they jump into the water. The mayor throws a bathing suit to Josh from the backpack he is wearing, and both dress before pushing their boards to shore. "How about that?" the male anchor says.

A camera on the beach focuses on the mayor and Josh walking from the surf and carrying their boards and sails. A gorgeous, blonde, female anchor talks. "And here he is—mR. bERZERKELEY, in person."

Three uniformed policemen walk up to them. "You two are under arrest," one of the officers says.

"What for?" Mayor Sain asks.

"For public nudity on the beach," a second officer answers.

"Do we look naked on the beach?" the mayor says. "I read the ordinances. We broke no law."

The officers look at each other. "I guess you are right," an officer says. "You are wearing suits now. We're going to have to get the board of supervisors to amend that law."

"Come to one of our city council meetings in Berkeley, the mayor says. "That amendment won't have a chance in our town. We believe in freedom for everything, including our privates."

The policemen look at each other and walk away. The female reporter walks up to the mayor. "So, mR. bERZERKELEY, what made you do such a stunt?"

The mayor looks at Josh and then back at the reporter. "It is all part of a reality show," he says. "The producers need to see me do something that has never been done before."

"We didn't see any cameras following you."

The mayor looks up at the news helicopter hovering overhead. "For a price, we'll get theirs."

"What reality show?" the anchor asks.

"*mR. bERZERKELEY*, what else?"

"When does it air?"

"It's still being developed," the mayor says. "All the networks will want it."

"What are you going to do next?" the anchor asks.

"I'm going to Disneyland!" the mayor answers with vigor.

"There you have it," the female anchor says. "Straight from the comic strip to your living room—mR. bERZERKELEY, in person."

The television resumes its regularly scheduled program.

"I'll give you fifty-to-one odds he asks her out," Willie says to Winnie with a mouth full of food.

"Don't bet!" Bessie yells. "You'll lose your ass on that one."

"What's fifty-to-one odds?" Michael asks.

"Maybe you should ask your father," Winnie says as he smiles.

* * *

Asia knocks on the front door of the chancellor's residence. Mrs. Lim, a pleasant Chinese woman in her sixties, answers. "I'm sorry to bother you, Mrs. Lim. Is the chancellor in?"

"You're the girl from Professor Spears' laboratory, aren't you?" she asks.

"Yes. We met at a reception."

"I remember. You caused quite a stir," she says as she smiles.

"I need to talk to the chancellor," Asia says. "It's important."

"I'll get him."

Mrs. Lim leaves and, after a moment, the chancellor greets Asia. "Miss Asia, is there a problem?"

"Is there somewhere we can talk privately?" Asia asks.

"I do have a small library. Follow me, please."

They walk into a small room lined from floor to ceiling with books. "Shall I shut the door?" the chancellor asks.

"Please."

"What is the problem?"

"It has come to my attention that the vice-chancellor has been snooping around Virginia City asking questions about me."

"Oh my God!" the Chancellor says, almost gasping and swallowing hard. "How do you know this fact?"

"A special agent visited the ranch and talked to at least one of my friends, Lady Gretchen. You remember—the tall, bosomy German woman. He found out who I really am and had my cell phone number in his pocket."

"She knows!"

"It's only a matter of time," Asia says. "If they dig deeper they can find logs and records and receipts and expose not only my past, but yours as well."

"I'm dead! If they find out I'll be ruined."

"So will I," Asia says.

"I told her if she didn't leave you alone I would fire her."

"That won't do any good now. You do that, and she'll run you out of town, along with me."

"What do we do?"

"I don't know if she'll go any further with her investigation, Chancellor. There's a good chance she has all she wants: me! I wanted to alert you that there may be a major crisis coming our way. It might just be me and not you. But the shit could hit the fan real soon."

"Is there any way you can keep me out of this? My career—the university—the scandal!"

"I don't know. Life has suddenly become more complicated. I can't hit the road because I have things I have to do. But if that's the only option, I will take the hit and keep her away from you."

"How can I ever repay you, Miss Asia—or should I say, Lily Liu Lu?"

"Let's leave that be for the moment. Let's see if we can both get out of this mess. We Chinese are born warriors! I don't know how, but there must be a way."

Chapter Forty-Two
Mickey Mouse

JOSH RETRIEVES HIS RINGING cell from his jeans. He looks at the number. "You'll never guess what just happened!"

"Happened? You windsurfing naked on television?" Jasmine screams. "I'll be the laughing stock of every Jew in LA when we get married. What are you thinking?"

"The mayor needed me to help him with part of the reality show shoot. That's all it was," Josh says, looking at the mayor, who has walked over to him holding a half-smoked joint. "They wanted an exciting scene so we gave them one."

"My father and mother are ready to disown you before we even get married. I was buying a wedding dress and the whole shop was watching you on television. My parents looked at me like I had the plague."

"We needed to do something to set up the reality show, the show that will bring in a whole lot of money—and you do want me to have a lot of money for you to spend, don't you?"

The mayor sticks a finger down his throat, dry heaving, mocking Josh's plea.

"Well, I guess so," Jasmine says. "When you coming back? My needs are way overdue."

"I have to check with the mayor and the reality show folks. What time is the reception?"

"It starts at six. You better be here soon so we can get ready. You want me to pick you up?"

"I'll take a cab after I talk to the mayor."

"I am so embarrassed," Jasmine says. "But money is money, and my friends understand that. You should see the dress I got!"

"I'm sure it is beautiful."

"Mother charged it and will have the bill for you. The reality show money will come in handy."

Josh folds his cell. "What's the little vixen up to now?" the mayor asks.

"Spending my money like water, as usual," Josh says, reaching for the mayor's joint.

"What say we grab a cab and hit Disneyland?" the mayor asks. "My flight isn't until seven."

"The only answer I can think of at the moment is fuck yeah!" Josh says, giving the mayor a high five.

*   *   *

"I'll bet they have some Jäger at the hotel bar," Mayor Sain says as he and Josh get on the monorail. "Did you see the hotties running the Pirates ride? I was ready to jump off and show them my sword."

"You already did that today once," Josh says.

"Thanks for coming along. That was the greatest. I thought shooting the water slide at the Splash Mountain standing up was awesome."

"The pictures of you mooning the camera came out good, too."

"I'm gonna have those sent to Mom. My butt mole stuck out like a sore thumb."

"What are you gonna do now that your little war with the president might be over?" Josh asks. "You want us to drop the *mR. bERZERKELEY*'s?"

"Nah. They are bringing me way too much publicity. It might come in handy in case the reality show really goes."

"You're serious, aren't you?" Josh says. "I thought the whole thing was just an excuse to get me away from Jasmine and shopping."

"I am serious. Those two guys I met on the way to Palo Alto—university boys—they seem to know what they are doing. After our little adventure, who knows?"

"My 50 percent still holds," Josh says.

"Fifty, sixty, who cares? All that really matters to me is Mom getting better and raising Michael."

"Your son has real talent," Josh says. "There's nothing Mickey Mouse about the way he cartoons."

"Life … it's a strange journey, isn't it?"

"Especially for mR. bERZERKELEY," Josh says.

"There's the hotel and several bars to hit. This place has really changed."

Josh and the mayor walk past the hotel to Main Street. "Look! Karaoke!" the mayor yells. "I'm right at home. They better have a lot of Jäger. I might even find a few juicy ones in the crowd."

The mayor and Josh are stopped by three large men with earpieces.

"You two," one of the men says. "You the guys who just mooned Splash Mountain?"

"My pants did fall off as we were coming down the water slide," the mayor says.

"You're that nut who windsurfed naked today, aren't you?" one of the men says. "mR. bERZERKELEY."

"That's me. You want my autograph?"

"No, but we are taking you to security to figure out how many laws you have broken while you've been in the park."

"What? I was just having a little fun."

Josh and Mayor Sain are led across a bridge to a door. They ride an elevator down inside Disneyland, under the park. "Where are you taking us?"

"This is Disneyland's underground city, where we have everything to keep the park going—including a jail for lawbreakers like you," one of the men says.

"What law did I break?" Mayor Sain says. "Walt Disney was for fun. We were just having fun!"

"There's fun and *fun*," one of the men says. "We're taking you to our supervisor."

The mayor and Josh follow the men down a long tunnel, passing a cafeteria, a dry cleaner, day care, gardens, and a uniform storage room. Men and women in costumes are everywhere. "Maybe I'll run into those hotties from the Pirates ride," Mayor Sain whispers to Josh. "I can still show them my sword."

They arrive at an office with *security* on the door. They walk inside and come face-to-face with a man who strongly resembles the vice-chancellor in a suit. Even his hair and facial expressions mirror hers exactly. "Shit!" the mayor says. "Am I seeing things, or am I seeing things?"

"I am Sergeant Wood of the Disneyland Special Security Force," the man says, sitting on one side of a wooden conference table with a small Mickey Mouse bobblehead in front of him. "Please sit down before we detain you."

"Detain us? You are going to throw us in jail?" Mayor Sain asks. "For mooning? In Berkeley, I walk naked down Shattuck."

"This is not Berkeley," Sergeant Wood says. "We have rules here, and rules are rules. You broke one on Splash Mountain and also when you urinated off the side of the boat during the Pirates of the Caribbean ride."

"All that water kinda got to me," Mayor Sain says.

"There were probably several other violations, like spitting at the hippopotamus on the safari and dumping your hot dog wrapper on the sidewalk in front of Space Mountain. But those we'll overlook and deal with the two major violations I cited."

"Do you know who I am?" Mayor Sain asks. "I am famous. I am mR. bERZERKELEY, the one and only."

"I know who you are, Mayor Sain. My cousin is the vice-chancellor of the university. She has told me all about you on more than one occasion."

"You and Vice-Chancellor Kris are cousins? I thought there was a family resemblance. Of course, the way you talk has confirmed that."

"Our mothers were twins," Sergeant Wood says.

"Same venom with a dick," Mayor Sain says.

"Are you going to get hostile with me?" Sergeant Wood asks. "That'll give you a few more days."

"Sir," Josh says, interrupting the feud that has suddenly erupted. "Can I explain?"

"Explain?" Sergeant Wood says. "What's there to explain?"

"This is all my fault," Josh says. "I decided to take the mayor on a road trip with me to help him get over the tragedies he is facing at home and have him relax a little."

"What tragedies?"

"His mother, Bessie, is dying and needs a new liver. Asia, one of the boarders, was growing a new one in the basement. She couldn't use the university laboratory because your cousin hates her."

"Whoa, whoa," Sergeant Wood says. "My cousin hates who?"

"Asia, one of Hamilton House boarders, where the mayor's mother is the cook."

"Why does she hate her?"

"Asia stripped in front of a biology class and was fired by your cousin but reinstated by the chancellor. Your cousin has had it in for her since then."

"Why couldn't I have a teacher like that?" Sergeant Wood says.

"So your cousin, who also is the mother of the mayor's son, Michael—a fact she refuses to admit—gets a search warrant, tears through Hamilton House, finds the liver cells, and flushes them down the drain, basically killing any chance the mayor's mother might survive."

"You and I are related?" Sergeant Wood asks.

"I suppose, in some manner of speaking," Mayor Sain says.

"She always had that mean streak," Sergeant Wood says. "But all of this doesn't resolve the problem we have with you and the violations you have committed in the park. Letting off steam isn't a reason to overlook the rules. You understand that, don't you?"

"I apologize for my actions," a humble Mayor Sain says. "Surfer Boy is right. I got a lot of shit going on back in Berkeley. Maybe this road trip wasn't such a good idea. I just keep causing more shit."

"Sir," Josh says. "I see that the wall clock says six o'clock. I am supposed to be at a reception in Sherman Oaks announcing my marriage to my college sweetheart. Can't we just go?"

"What is your connection here, anyhow?" Sergeant Wood asks. "Are you one of the boarders?"

"I am. I am also the cartoonist that draws *mR. bERZERKELEY* and *Veronica's Lives* for newspapers all over the world."

"You are? My wife and daughters especially like *Veronica's Lives*. I've got one that's five and another that's fifteen, just like your characters. That older one, the teen, is going through some pretty rough times right now."

"She sure is, sir," Josh says. "She's gone Goth."

"I saw that with the black crow. Pretty creative, the way you do it."

"Actually, your relative, Michael, the mayor and your cousin's son, drew that one. He's brilliant."

"Well, I'll be. And my cousin still doesn't admit he's hers?"

"The evil maiden is still all that," Mayor Sain says.

"Tell you what," Sergeant Wood says. "I learned a long time ago you never make an enemy of someone who buys ink by the barrel … or draws cartoons for several hundred newspapers. Uncle Walt would probably agree with what I am going to suggest. Just don't ever come back, you two. Escort them to their car or taxi or bus—however they got here—and get them on the road back to Berkeley or Sherman Oaks or wherever."

"Thank you, sir," Josh says.

"Cousin?" Mayor Sain says, extending his hand to shake with Sergeant Wood, who reaches out and grabs his hand.

"My sympathies, Mr. Mayor. For both your mother and dealing with my cousin."

"Can I?" Mayor Sain asks, looking at the Mickey Mouse bobblehead.

"Be my guest," Sergeant Wood says. "Maybe it'll appear in a future cartoon."

Chapter Forty-Three
Crash and Burn

LATE IN THE EVENING, a taxi drops Josh at Jasmine's house in Sherman Oaks. All the lights are on. The front door opens and Jasmine walks out with her arms crossed. "What the fuck have you been doing, as if I and the whole world didn't know?" she says, saliva spewing from her mouth in her rage.

"The mayor and I spent the day and half the night working with reality show folks," Josh says.

"You made me the laughing stock of Los Angeles!" Jasmine screams. "My mother and father are so mad they took off in our plane for Telluride without saying good-bye. My father was ready to get his rifle and blow holes in you!"

"Look. The mayor needed me. We're in this reality show business together."

"Surfing naked on national television! And Disneyland! I've never seen my father so mad."

"It's just business. That's all."

"We have a little business together, too," Jasmine says, patting her stomach. "Inside here we've got a living human being. Isn't our business important enough to show up for a reception in our honor? I had to make the announcement myself. Everyone there had seen you carousing naked on television and taking your clothes off at Disneyland."

"The reality show people took us to Club 33 to talk about the deal and the money they would offer. You do like money, don't you?"

"You could have called. I think this whole reality show gig is nothing but another figment of that fucked-up imagination of yours. Do you have anything to prove it is for real?"

"You know the Hollywood folks. They don't want anything on paper until the final deal."

"I knew it. Nothing but a sham. I am so embarrassed."

"It is for real. When we get back to Berkeley the producers will overnight a proposal. They promised."

"I don't know if I want to go back," Jasmine says. "I might stay here and make preparations."

"You have finals, don't you?"

"The only final I have is getting married on Christmas, and I don't know if that's such a good idea now. For all I know you will make up something else and disappear again."

"Come on," Josh says, putting his arms around Jasmine. "Let's go inside and discuss this further. How long has it been since your needs have been met?"

"You are way overdue. The house has been empty for at least an hour."

They hug tight. "What's that I feel?" Jasmine says. "You really missed me?"

Josh steps back and takes the Mickey Mouse bobblehead from the front pocket of his jeans and hands it to her. "This bulge is for you."

"It's so cute," Jasmine says holding it up.

"Come on inside and I'll show you 'cute,'" Josh says, hugging her tight again. "And that bulge is me."

* * *

Bertha sits behind her desk as Gerry walks in. "What is it this time?" Gerry asks. "It's midnight."

"I am filing a criminal complaint on your behalf against Winston in the morning," Bertha says.

"Why? You won! We've trumped Winnie. It's over."

"Over? It won't be over until he's been completely destroyed. I know him better than you. He can resurrect himself overnight. I've got to keep him down and out. He's crashed, but he's got to burn, too."

"What are the charges?"

"Child endangerment, underage drinking, and encouraging drug use," Bertha says, holding up a piece of paper.

"It's all about Sarah, isn't it?" Gerry says.

"You have seen the pictures," Bertha says. "He's killing her."

"I told you I should be there and bring her back home."

"I'll take care of her in the morning. We'll go for protective custody, too."

"She's eighteen!"

"It may not work, but it's at least worth a try. I need to keep the heat on Mr. Winston Churchill. He'll learn never to fuck with Bertha again."

"Did you see the mayor surfing naked in the Pacific?"

"What a joke! If I could wrap him up in this thing, I would, but the BAA is going to recall him for using city money for his little adventure in Los Angeles. They'll take care of him."

"You *are* going to make me governor, aren't you?"

"It's a sure thing, Gerry, and don't you forget who did it."

Chapter Forty-Four
Bucket List

Asia's scooter stops at the laboratory gate. She slides a card and enters. She walks inside and finds Professor Spears at a microscope. "Miss Asia? This is a surprise—a welcomed one at that."

"Professor. How are the cells coming?"

"I've been checking them every few minutes for any sign of splitting. None yet. I'm afraid they might not have responded to the boost I gave them. I'm sorry."

"Damn!" Asia says. "I was hoping they might take off. The mayor's mother is getting worse by the moment."

"Old Bessie is dying, isn't she? I remember her well. All woman."

"Yes, and her condition gets worse by the minute. I can't leave until she's better."

"Leave? You're not going to leave, are you?"

"The vice-chancellor has been at it again," Asia says. "She's determined to do me in, and she doesn't care who she takes with me."

"She doesn't know about us, does she?"

"No, and she never will."

"What can I do?"

"Nothing except keep trying to accelerate those cells. I can't leave without knowing there's hope for her. That tragedy would be worse than what I have been through."

"Speaking of keeping someone going ..."

"Sure, why not?" Asia says. "Let's make it quick. I've got quite a list of things I have to do before I hit the road."

"That's usually not a problem," the professor says.

*   *   *

Asia sits astride her scooter next to the Lawrence Hall of Science looking down at Berkeley, the Bay, San Francisco, and the Golden Gate with a full moon shining down. "Man, I don't want to leave," she says. "I can take care of Stephanie and Judy when Josh gets home and get the painting going. Sarah and I will have a little talk about drugs, Mr. and Mrs. Churchill can take care of themselves, and Michael seems to be doing okay. The mayor and I will have a little chat about the fact that we are stepbrother and step sister that will blow his mind. The fact that I killed our father Johnny Blood doesn't even have to come up. The key is making some progress on Bessie's liver."

She puts her helmet on and fires up her scooter. "One last tour, I guess."

Chapter Forty-Five
A True Warrior

Asia walks inside the kitchen. Stephanie, Judy, Michael, Winnie, and Babe sit at the block while Bessie heats up food on the stove. Sarah's head rests face down on the table. "What the?" Asia says. "It's after ten o'clock."

"Bessie wanted to make us all a snack," Babe says.

"Goddamn right," Bessie says. "I felt like shit all day and neglected my duties as chief cook and bottle washer. Sit your China ass down and have a little Jack. Who knows? This might be our last meal together."

"Come on, Bessie," Winnie says. The holidays are coming, and you don't want to miss those, do you?"

"Another feast?" Bessie says. "You're right. I guess I'll have to get a few more of those fucking pills and make it a while longer. I'll stay around as long as China Girl stays around."

"What?" Stephanie says. "You aren't leaving! You promised!"

"Don't worry," Asia says. "When Mr. Lover Boy gets back I'll do what I said I would do."

"We can't wait," an excited Judy says.

"What is this all about, if I might ask?" Babe says.

"Just a little deal we have made," Asia says.

"You can't leave us," Michael says. "You thought you might be able to help me with this." He touches the hole in the side of his head.

"Shit!" Asia says. "I didn't write that one down."

"You have a list? For what?" Babe asks.

"Things I have to finish before I—"

"Fucking leave," Bessie says. "I told you she's bailing out."

"Anything we can do?" Winnie asks. "Is it the vice-chancellor again?"

"She's a real bitch," Michael says. "I don't know what the mayor … my father ever saw in her."

"The same thing my naked-ass commie sees in every skirt: between her legs!" Bessie yells. "Wish they would have had some of those fucking pills fifty years ago."

"Pills?" Sarah says, her head suddenly rising. "Where?"

"Maybe you should take her up to bed," Babe says to Winnie.

"I want some more," Sarah says, beads dangling from piercings on the side of her face.

"I think you're right," Winnie says, standing up. "Come on, whoever you are today. I know where there are some pills upstairs."

Winnie helps Sarah up and supports her while she walks up the stairs.

"What's wrong with her?" Michael asks. "She used to be so nice and innocent and pretty."

"She's on my list, too," Asia says. "I've got a lot to take care of her before I leave."

"Why go?" Babe asks. "You've got a home here, a great job, and a PhD to finish."

"I can do that somewhere else. I'd rather not talk about why I should leave. It's a long story."

"More whoring?" Bessie says.

"What's a whoring story?" Michael asks.

"We'll let the mayor tell you about that," Babe says. "But Asia, whatever it is, you can't run away from it. Sometime, somewhere, it'll catch you."

"Just like the plague and my naked-ass commie son," Bessie says.

"Where else are you going to find the support system you have here?" Babe asks.

"You're going back to Kansas, aren't you?" Asia says.

"I don't know," Babe answers.

Trojan pops in through the doggy door, sees Asia, and goes for her leg.

"See! Even the mutt needs you!" Bessie says.

The mood grows serious as they wait for Asia to say something. "Well, I don't know," Asia says.

"Come on, China Girl," Bessie says. "You're a true warrior! Stay and fight!"

The door opens and a naked Mayor Sain walks in. "Hey, why so serious? Anybody miss me?"

Part Four
Peace Offerings

Chapter Forty-Six
Bite Me!

Winnie is at the stove cooking eggs and bacon. Asia peeks in Bessie's bedroom and sees her fast asleep and rocking the walls with loud snoring. "Thanks for letting me know about Bessie," Winnie says.

"When's the last time you cooked anything, Mr. Churchill?"

"I think it was on a campout with my son Billy when he was a cub scout a long time ago."

"Smells good! I haven't had anything to eat for a couple of days."

"Guess I've got to find a new avocation, since it looks like governor is out of the question."

"At least you have something to look forward to."

"You're really worried about something. Want to talk about it?"

"When the time is right."

Willie, in full uniform, walks into the kitchen holding a manila envelope. He sits down at the block next to Asia.

"Shit!" Willie says. "More burned bacon. I could smell it from the street."

"Asia says it smells pretty good. Bessie has spoiled you."

"You're right. How is she?"

"Sleeping like a baby," Winnie says.

"Sounds like she's snoring like a train," Willie says.

"What you got there?" a nervous Asia says. "You serving warrants?"

"Yes," Willie says. "It seems a certain vice-chancellor is still after Hamilton House."

"Is it for … me?" Asia asks with a quivering voice.

"No," Willie says. "Are you expecting one?"

"Whew!" Asia says as she exhales. "You had me there for a moment."

"It's for Pooh," Willie says, taking papers from the envelope. "It seems our darling vice-chancellor is serving you a claim for the dog biting her above the knee."

"A dog bite?" Winnie says. "I'll give it to my insurance company. I think we get one free bite, if I remember."

"She wants a grand for medical expenses and $50,000 for psychological trauma," Willie says. "She also demands the dog be put down."

"Kill Trojan?" Asia says. "Let's put *her* down!"

Trojan, on key, walks through the doggy door and over to Willie's leg. "Go ahead, little guy," Willie says. "It may be your last chance."

"There's no way," Winnie says. "He's a part of our Hamilton House family."

The kitchen door opens and the mayor walks in.

"Pooh cooking? Where's my camera? Where's Mom? I got some great news!"

"If you listen instead of blabber you'd hear her signature snoring in the other room," Willie says.

The mayor pauses and listens. "She okay?"

"I gave her a couple of pills to knock her out," Asia says.

"What are you doing here?" the mayor asks Willie. "Official business, or just looking for a handout?"

"The vice-chancellor is serving Pooh notice she wants money for the dog biting her above the knee the other day."

"Above the knee? I want to see that," Mayor Sain says.

"That's it," Winnie says. "That's my response to this ridiculous document, and you can so inform the vice-chancellor. I want to have a personal investigation of the crime committed by our house dog and copies of any and all professional examinations she has undergone with trained individuals."

"You are refusing to be served?" Willie says.

"Further, if she agrees to be examined, I am sending my assistant in this matter—the honorable mayor of Berkeley!"

"You want me to tell her that?" Willie asks.

"I second the motion!" Mayor Sain says. "I want to check her out. It's been a few years."

"You guys are full of shit!" Willie says. "I'll see you in court in a couple of hours."

"With the vice-chancellor?" Mayor Sain says.

"No. At my son's hearing. I think I'll pass on breakfast."

Willie walks out, leaving the mayor, Asia, and Winnie looking at each other. The smell of burning bacon fills the air. Bessie's door opens. "What the fuck is going on? I can't even die in peace without someone burning the bacon."

"Mom! I'm going to be famous."

"Shit," Bessie says. "What in the fuck did you do now?"

"I'm going to be a star! I got two calls this morning, one from New York and one from Los Angeles. They want to buy the reality show!"

"You *are* a fucking reality show," Bessie says as she groans. "At least I'll know you'll be able to survive after I'm gone."

"Come on, Mom. You're going to be okay. You're going to be a star in the show with me."

Bessie walks to the stove. "Give me that spatula, Pooh. A politician you might be. But a cook—there's no way. One bite of your shit will give them all the runs."

"Let me help," Mayor Sain says, moving toward the stove.

"The only help I want from you is to make peace with Michael's mother before I die," Bessie says.

"Wait a minute," the mayor says. "You want me to make peace with the iron maiden, the evil bitch from hell?"

"That will give me the peace I need, knowing that Michael has two parents who care for him and each other," Bessie says. "I've gone through the one-parent thing for fifty years and I know how painful it is. I don't want him to go through it."

"There are many things that are possible, and I've done most of them. But that? There's no way, even if I faked it, that she would come over to our side."

"It's me," Asia says. "If I were out of the way she would probably forgive everything else, eventually. But as long as I am around she'll keep being the bitch she is."

"There you have it, Mom," Mayor Sain says. "You want Asia to get you healthy, or the evil bitch to help you cook breakfast?"

"Both," Bessie says. "I want both before I die."

The mayor looks at Winnie, who shrugs his shoulders. "You are the star of newspapers and radio—and, I guess, now maybe television. If it can be done, you'll do it."

"Holy shit!" Mayor Sain says. "Turn me around three times and bite me on the ass. How in the world am I gonna pull this off?"

Chapter Forty-Seven
Chasing the Past

"Special Agent Picard is here to see you, Vice-Chancellor," the assistant's voice says over the intercom.

"Send him in," the vice-chancellor says tersely.

Special Agent Picard—middle-aged, cropped brown hair, stocky—walks into the office and shuts the door. "Well, give me what you got on Miss Asia. It better be good."

Picard sits down hard. "She's from Virginia City, Nevada, but you know that," he says. "Her real name is Lily Liu, the daughter of a prostitute at the ranch. What else do you need to know?"

"There's got to be more. Did you talk to the madam, any of the girls, any friends?"

"I did. They told me about how she was born early while her mother died as the result of a beating by a drunken customer. She was raised at the ranch and eventually became one of the whores. She was their most popular prostitute, using the name Lily Liu Lu. They said one day she ran away to go to college and made a new life for herself and hasn't been back since."

"I suppose you used all your investigative training to pry as much information from the girls as possible?"

"Of course. What I've told you is what they said. I appreciate what you did for my daughter in getting her accepted to the university. She is doing well, and her mother and I are very proud of her. I assume your favor has now been repaid?"

"There's more to this Lily Liu Lu than meets the eye, I know it. She and the chancellor have some secret she uses on him over and over to beat me up and almost get me fired. I need to know it all. There's something you didn't uncover."

"I'm telling you, that's all there is. Leave the young girl be. Just think what she has been through and how far she has come. Imagine, born to a dying whore and now earning a PhD at this prestigious university! Give her the peace she deserves."

"She'll get no peace from me. She's the bane of my existence. Trying to get me fired! After all I've done for this university! I won't rest until I run her out of Berkeley on a rail. You go back to Virginia City immediately and find out everything. There is something else, I know it!"

"I've been assigned to the Washington bureau. I can't go to Virginia City. I'll be the one getting fired."

"It's your choice, Special Agent Picard. Go back to Virginia City or buy your daughter a one-way ticket home."

"You wouldn't do that, would you?"

"Special Agent Picard," the vice-chancellor says, looking him straight in the eyes with an evil stare, "that's just for starters. You want to know what else I can do to your daughter?"

Chapter Forty-Eight
Protective Custody

"You again, counselor?" Judge Kelley says, sitting behind his bench in the Berkeley courtroom. "Any naked people, lesbian sex, or masked men this time?"

"No, sir," Winnie says, standing at a table next to Jamal. "Just this young man—the son of Berkeley Police Sergeant Willie Williams—who defended himself from being murdered by gang members on the Berkeley pier."

"The pier, the pier, why is it always the pier?" Judge Kelley says. Willie, in full uniform, sits behind a wooden barrier next to Babe, Mayor Sain, and a young African American male. "The document I am looking at says Jamal Williams is suspected of murdering a young man from San Francisco and then leaving the scene by jumping off the pier. Is that true?"

"Yes, your honor," Winnie says.

"How do you plead, young man?" the judge asks.

"Not guilty, your honor," Jamal says.

"He acted in self-defense, your honor," Winnie says. "We have a witness that will testify on his behalf, if you desire."

"Is that him sitting next to Mayor Sain?" Judge Kelley asks.

"Yes, your honor," Winnie says.

"I suppose he and Mr. Williams are buddies?" Judge Kelley asks.

"Yes, your honor," Winnie responds. "They have known each other since childhood."

"Is there anyone else?" Judge Kelley asks. "I can only assume that the young man, who is Mr. William's long-time buddy, will support his self-defense argument."

"There was another young man, your honor, but he was murdered by the young man my client stabbed," Winnie says.

"And killed," Judge Kelley says. "Whose knife was involved?"

"The evidence will show that the knife belonged to the young man who died at the hands of Jamal Williams. You can ask Sergeant Williams about the blood tests run on the knife. I believe you'll find a mixture of the blood of Jamal's deceased friend and the victim in question."

"Is this true, Sergeant Williams?" Judge Kelley asks.

Willie nods yes.

"Well, then, it does appear that self-defense may be involved," Judge Kelley says as he ponders. "But that will be up to the jury to decide when the case is heard."

"I would like to request that my client be released until the court date with no bail, your honor," Winnie says.

"It does seem appropriate in this case," Judge Kelley says. "I so order that Jamal Williams be released to his parents until the court can conduct a trial, with no bail set."

"No," Jamal says loudly.

"What?" Judge Kelley says. "Are you disagreeing with the court?"

"Is it possible that he can be released into my custody?" Winnie asks. "His parents are divorced, and, well, it would be in the best interest of the court to have him reside in Hamilton House."

"And not with his father, an officer of this city?" Judge Kelley asks.

"It's okay with me," Willie says standing up. "I am at Hamilton House from time to time, and I can make sure my son is a model citizen."

"I think I have given this case enough leeway already," Judge Kelley says. "But if that's the wish of your father, so be it. Let's keep peace in the family, at least until the trial."

Outside the courtroom, Willie stands with Winnie, Mayor Sain, Babe, Jamal, and the African American young man. "You will behave at Hamilton House, won't you?" Willie says with a finger in Jamal's face."

"Yes, sir," Jamal says. "Is it okay if I go to class now? School has already started, and we're late."

"You better be on your best behavior, or I will ask the judge to give you to me," Willie says. "Get out of my sight."

Jamal and his friend run off.

"Thanks for that," Winnie says. "We'll keep him on the up and up."

"Where's he going to sleep?" Babe says. "All our rooms are full."

"I've been thinking," Mayor Sain says. "I'll have Michael move in with me. That'll free up a room."

"Why not the basement?" Willie says. "Isn't that where Pooh slept through high school?"

"And let him sneak out through the windows and chase girls like he and I did?" Mayor Sain says.

"Wait a minute," Babe says. "More stories?"

"For another time," Winnie says. "I think it would be a good to have Michael move next door."

"I agree," an excited Mayor Sain says. "He and I can really be a family.

I gotta go and figure out what to do with the vice-chancellor, for Mom's sake."

"I want to go back to Hamilton House," Babe says. "I don't feel good."

"I gotta get back to arresting bad guys," Willie says. "By the way, the vice-chancellor has dropped her claim against you and the dog. She wants no part of the mayor examining her."

"Making peace with her *will* be impossible," Winnie says.

"I don't think that word is in her vocabulary," Babe says.

"Who's keeping peace at the store?" Winnie asks.

"Josh just arrived, and Michael is coming back after class," Babe says. "Let's go. I feel very sick all of a sudden."

"The morning kind?" Winnie asks.

Chapter Forty-Nine
The Anti-Bully

SARAH, DRESSED IN BLACK from head to toe with a string of beads attached to piercings in her nose and right ear, walks slowly by the art store, where Michael is busy working on cartoons. Unmasked Michael sees her and runs outside. "Hey!" he yells. "Can I walk to class with you?"

Sarah stops and turns around slowly, obviously in a stupor. "Yes? Oh, Michael, is that you?"

"It's me. Can I walk to class with you, if you can stand to be with someone that is deformed like me?"

"Sure, why not?" Sarah slurs. "Who cares what people think? I don't. You want something to pick you up?"

"What are you talking about?" Michael says, as they walk slowly toward campus.

"I've got a few extra pills, if you want any. I'm saving some for class. I need a boost. You need a boost?"

"I don't take pills," Michael says. "Is that part of being Goth?"

"No," Sarah slurs. "Some do and some don't. I prefer to be one that does. It makes life so interesting."

As they walk up Bancroft, they approach four young men, two white and two African American, talking. "Uh-oh," Michael says. "Those are the same guys that worked me over a couple of days ago. They go to high school and think they can push me around."

"Bullies?" Sarah says.

"I guess," Michael responds, trying to look down at the ground as they walk.

"Hey, Mr. Hole in the Head!" one of the boys yells. "How's your hearing?"

"You look like a fucking parking meter," another boy says.

"Who's the druggie with you?" another boy asks.

Sarah stops walking and approaches the boys. "You want to bully someone, bully me!" she yells. "You motherfuckers get out of here, or I'll go get my friends and show you what the word *bully* means."

"Okay, okay," one the boys says. "Let's go!"

The four boys walk down Bancroft toward Berkeley High School.

"That was really cool," Michael says. "I wish I could do that."

"I need to take a couple of pills," Sarah says. "That took it all out of me."

"Maybe we should skip class and go back to Hamilton House."

"We have finals next week," Sarah says. "I've missed a lot of class lately. I've got to get the prep sheets. Then I'll go back to the house."

"You are so brave," Michael says. "I want to be like you—a peacemaker."

"You ought to take pills," Sarah says. "You can change who you are immediately."

"Like you said, I really don't care if people don't like who I am. Do you?"

"No, I guess I really don't," Sarah says. "But pills sure make me feel different—like a warrior sometimes."

* * *

Josh arrives at Hamilton House and runs inside, passing Asia sitting at the block. Bessie's snoring can be heard in the background. "The traveler is back," Asia says. "How was Los Angeles?"

"You probably saw us on TV. That was a hoot."

"What's this about getting married?"

"That's her plan. I missed the reception where she made the announcement. My bad!"

"You and I have something to get done first, don't we?"

"The painting? Anytime! I'm more than ready."

"How about later tonight?" Asia says.

"I can't wait," Josh says. "Right now I've got to get to the store and catch up on the cartoons. Say, aren't you supposed to be at work?"

"It's a long story, but the professor gave me a couple of days off."

"How's Bessie's liver coming?"

"Bad. There's not much hope. She's on some pretty strong stuff to help ease the pain."

"What about Sarah? She's on some pretty bad stuff, I hear."

"I'm going to take care of that, too, before I pack up and leave."

"You can't leave. Not you. What's wrong?"

"That, too, is a long story that will probably come out sooner or later. It's all in the vice-chancellor's hands right now. It's probably best I leave to keep the peace."

"Don't let that bully take you out," Josh says. "Maybe we should blast her with a few cartoons."

"That won't stop her," Asia says. "Leaving is the best solution."

Josh's cell rings. "Yes, I will go with you to pick out baby clothes after I catch up on the cartoons," he says. "See you in a while, after you go to class."

"She pregnant?" Asia asks.

"You might as well know," Josh says. "She has missed a period and is sure she's got one in the oven. My life has disappeared."

"No wonder you kept asking about an abortion. You weren't kidding, were you?"

"My life is upside down. It doesn't feel right. But a life is a life."

"And a shotgun wedding?" Asia says.

"Yeah, and a shotgun wedding," Josh says. "Later tonight?"

"You got it, Surfer Boy," Asia says as she smiles. "I'll be ready for you."

Chapter Fifty
Fathers and Sons

MICHAEL WALKS INTO THE store where Josh is busy at his laptop. "I'm glad you're back. I was getting nervous about the phone calls from the Chronicle."

"What did Darby want? I gave him your cell number and told him we were partners."

"He really likes the new twists on *Veronica's Lives*."

"He liked the Goth bit? He must be on something," Josh says. "Speaking of our resident Goth, how's she doing?"

"I walked to class with her, and she took on some guys that were teasing me," Michael says. "Look!"

Josh looks at the cartoon of the high school age Roni, wearing a Supergirl suit, taking on boys wearing letterman's jackets. "You boys want to be bullies? Well, I'm the anti-bully. You're going to have to go through me first!"

"Now that is brilliant," Josh says. "You're the best. Darby will love this one, too. He was bullied unmercifully in school."

"He has an opening and wondered if you have any more ideas," Michael says.

"Another strip? I suppose, with you cranking them out like you are. The mayor wants to keep up the *mR. bERZERKELEY*'s until he knows what the Feds are gonna do."

"I've tried to think about another strip, but I don't know what to do," Michael says.

"I had one a long time ago that I thought was great, but no one else did."

"What was it?"

"I named it *Ham 'n' Eggs*, and it was about roommates, one cool and one as dumb as a stump. I've got it on my flash drive. Why don't you look at them when you get a chance? Right now, I've got to go shopping with my girl."

"*Ham 'n' Eggs*," Michael says to himself. "Sounds like a good idea to me."

*   *   *

Bessie stumbles from her room. Asia is still sitting at the block, writing on a legal pad. "You got it all figured out?" Bessie asks.

"I'm working on it. How do you feel?"

"Like taking a dump and going down the sewer with it," Bessie says as she makes her way to the stove. "You want some lunch or something?"

"No," Asia says. "I'm not hungry. I'm looking at all the options. I'll come up with something."

"Whatever happens, I am glad I met you. The world changes, people change, but you have always been just who you are, China Girl."

"Bessie the philosopher," Asia says as she smiles. "I am glad I met you, too."

"One thing positive has happened with my naked-ass commie son. He and his son are getting together, thanks to you."

"Glad to be a part of bringing families together," Asia says.

"If you're around, you can help with the cleaning," Bessie says.

"Whatever you need, Bessie. You can count on me."

"The cleaning's not for me, China Girl. Michael is moving next door. That pit hasn't been cleaned for years. There are probably several dead bodies inside and who knows what else. Willie the leech's son is moving to Michael's old room. Winnie's got him in protective custody. I'll have to double my food order. That boy can eat everything I make and still look for more."

"A chip off the old block, eh?"

"You got it, China Girl. Like father, like son. I wonder what it would have been like if my naked-ass commie's father was still around."

Asia's face turns gray, and she gulps hard, looking at Bessie bent over the stove.

*   *   *

"Michael," Mayor Sain says, walking into the art store. "Let's go to Hamilton House and move you over to my place. Isn't it exciting?"

"Me, move into your house?"

"Come on, father and son. Isn't it going to be great?"

"I've got a new cartoon strip to get out," Michael says. "Maybe later?"

"Ah, come on. I've got a council meeting tonight. After windsurfing you can keep at those cartoons."

"Me, windsurf? I can't swim."

"Swimming is highly overrated," Mayor Sain says. "That's what a lifejacket is for."

"I don't know," Michael says.

"Maybe it'll give you some more ideas for cartoons."

"You know, you're right, sir," Michael says.

"I'm not a sir. I'm your father."

"Yes, Father."

* * *

"Why are you picking out boy's clothes?" Josh asks Jasmine. "We might have a girl."

"It's a boy, that's for sure," Jasmine says, rubbing her stomach. "I've had indigestion for several weeks, just like my friend who had two boys."

"You had one friend who had boys, and you are basing buying boy's baby clothes on that?"

"You're not making fun of my friend or me, are you?" Jasmine asks.

"No, just making sure you know what you're doing."

"I'll keep the receipts just in case, funny boy," Jasmine says. "But I don't know if they have this store in Los Angeles. I never saw one on Rodeo Drive."

"I don't think there's a Ross there," Josh says as he laughs. "I'm sure we can find one in LA somewhere."

"I thought you'd like the fact that we're having a boy," Jasmine says. "You can have a father-and-son relationship and take him to tennis, gymnastics, swimming, golf, or a chess club."

"What about surfing and drawing cartoons?" Josh says.

"Silly boy! Our son is not going to be a beach bum like you were," Jasmine says. "We have a chance to really make him something special."

"You don't think I'm special?" Josh says.

"You are. Don't get me wrong," Jasmine says. "In the circles we will be in, you have to think about what other people would say. 'Where's your son? Tennis? Gymnastics? Golf?' Our crowd would think we're lesser if we would answer 'surfing.'"

"I'm doing okay," Josh says. "Sounds like you have our life and our son's life all planned out."

"Of course I do," Jasmine says. "You have a problem with that?"

* * *

Winnie parks the SUV in the driveway. Willie parks his police car at the curb. Winnie waits for Willie to walk up the driveway before entering the kitchen. Asia sits at the block, and Bessie struggles at the stove.

"China Girl," Bessie says. "Can you help me take this pot off? I got no energy."

"I'll help you," Willie says. "Smells like dumplings to me."

"Willie, the leech," Bessie says. "Might as well. You'll eat half of 'em later, and your son will eat the other half."

"The boy does have an appetite, that's for sure. Gets it from his mother."

"That's a crock and you know it," Bessie says. "If shit were edible you'd eat a whole sewer full."

"And you all said Bessie was dying," Willie says backing off. "Nothing has changed here!"

"I want to know if you and that handsome son of yours are gonna make up," Bessie says, turning around and holding her cleaver as she looks at Willie. "Before I go up or down I want peace around here."

Babe wanders from the stairway wearing her robe. "What's going on?"

"Willie and Bessie are having a discussion about a peace treaty between Willie and Jamal," Winnie says.

"That would be a good idea," Babe says. "We could all use a little peace around here. Now that Jamal is moving in, I suppose we'll be attracting the high school crowd."

"He better not bring any of his friends over here," Willie says. "There will be no peace in Hamilton House."

"I'm sure he'll do just fine," Winnie says.

"You bet he will," Bessie says, wielding her cleaver. "What do you say Willie the leech? You gonna be a good boy and leave your son be, or is Bessie gonna have to cut off some of that fat I put on your ugly body?"

"Peace, Bessie, peace. Guess I should get back to work and keep Berkeley safe. A little peace in this whole town would definitely be a change of pace."

"That would be wonderful," Asia says as she lets out a huge sigh.

Chapter Fifty-One
Strategy Shift

Winnie's cell rings as he sits in his bedroom relaxing, watching Babe take a rest. "Senator Churchill?" a female voice says. "This is the reporter who interviewed you before you left for Berkeley last August. Remember KNKC?"

"Oh, yes. How are you and Kansas doing?"

"We're fine. That's the question I want to ask you. You said I could check in with you from time to time."

"Everything in Berkeley is like it always is—active, energetic, crazy, and full of surprises."

"You mind elaborating live?"

"Why not? My life has always been an open book. You can check my record."

"Thanks. A press release from Gerry Armstrong's campaign says he took it upon himself to get the president to reexamine the stimulus funds Kansas was going to lose because you had been unable to make any progress using your Berkeley-style approach. Any comment?"

"I am pleased that the president has decided to take another look at how states and cities have used the funds that have been provided to simulate the economy and provide jobs. I hope the upcoming reviews by his staff will result in achieving the goals he set when the funds were approved."

"What about Gerry Armstrong's role in solving the problem?"

"Whether it was Gerry, the mayor of Berkeley, the cartoons that have been appearing nationwide, or the president himself wanting to keep the peace with the country during these horrible economic times, it doesn't matter to me. What matters is the fact it will be done. If it was Gerry, I will be the first to congratulate him on behalf of Kansas citizens and Americans everywhere."

"You sound gubernatorial, Mr. Churchill. Are you still planning on running next June?"

"It's December, and there's still time for me to decide. We still have a few things to get under control here in Berkeley, if that's possible."

"Like what?"

"Let's save that for the next interview. Right now, let's enjoy the fact that Kansas may be saved from returning millions of dollars and that the boost the dollars have already given to the economy may be maintained rather than eliminated."

"Thank you, Senator Churchill. This has been a live report from KNKC and the People's Republic of Berkeley."

"That was exciting," Babe says from under a large down comforter. "You did sound like a governor. Does that mean we're going home?"

"We still have a lot of issues to resolve here," Winnie says. "How are you feeling?"

"Like I've been kicked in the stomach by a mule," Babe says. "If I'm not pregnant I have a large mass of something—probably Bessie's dumplings—in my gut."

"We've got to get that checked," Winnie says. "You want me to rub it?"

"That's what got us into this mess in the first place."

* * *

Two large vans stop at the mayor's curb, and four men get out. Mayor Sain stands on the sidewalk. "Come on inside and bring all your cleaning equipment. My son is moving in, and two guys from a reality show are visiting in an hour. I want the pit I call my home cleaned from top to bottom."

"Maybe we should just burn it," one man says.

"Wiseass!" Mayor Sain says. "On second thought, that's not a bad idea."

The men follow Mayor Sain inside through the kitchen door. In a few moments, Mayor Sain reappears on the sidewalk as he sees Ken and Jed arrive on their bicycles. "Hey, guys!" Mayor Sain yells. "Welcome to my home. I've got news for you. I had two calls this morning from studios wanting to see the sizzle reel and make us a proposal for a reality show."

"All right!" Ken says. "That's great news."

"I'd invite you inside, but I have cleaners turning everything upside down. My son Michael is moving in."

"You have a son?" Jed asks.

"You bet. He's been living next door in Hamilton House since he got off on the rape charge. Now he's drawing cartoons."

"Sounds like more juicy stuff for the reality show," Ken says. "Maybe we should film inside Hamilton House for background. Isn't that where the people with you on the train live?"

"Most of them. My mother is the cook. Bad thing is she needs a new liver quick, or she won't be around to watch the reality show or anything else."

"My condolences," Jed says. "Can we go in anyhow?"

"Why not?"

Mayor Sain leads the two students, carrying a small camera and a boom mike, through the Hamilton House kitchen door, almost stepping on Trojan making a quick exit. "That's the house mutt, Trojan. He drinks booze like a fish. A dog that's a fish! That's good reality show stuff, isn't it?"

Ken, holding the camera, films Trojan as he scoots off.

"What the fuck are you doing?" Bessie says, holding her cleaver, as the mayor and the two students enter the kitchen. "You gonna make a movie of my last days on the planet?"

"Mom, these are the guys making the sizzle reel for the reality show I told you about."

"Better hurry up and get me on your film. I've been sizzling all morning with the new pills the fucking quacks gave me. It's coming out faster than I can guzzle water."

The mayor turns to Asia, sitting at the block with her notepad. "And this is Asia, PhD student and scientific genius. She also solved a rapist mystery with her DNA skills."

"Hello, fellows. The mayor is a reality show all by himself. You don't need me in it."

"You guys ought to see some of the tricks she has up her sweatshirt when she plays basketball. And that ain't all!"

"Thanks, but no thanks," Asia says. "You'll need me to sign a release or something. That won't happen."

"Leave her be, you naked-ass commie," Bessie says. "She's got a lot on her mind right now—especially a certain vice-chancellor."

"That's Michael's mother," Mayor Sain says.

"*The* vice-chancellor?" Ken asks.

"The one and only," Mayor Sain says. "You'll never get her to sign off either. Where's the rest of the brood?"

"The Lone Ranger and Josh are probably drawing cartoons at the store, our resident druggie is probably in the park with her ghoulish friends, and the lesbians are at work."

"What about Pooh and Babe?"

"Upstairs resting," Bessie says. "Why don't you take the film crew over to the dump you call your house and leave us alone?"

"I've got cleaners inside," Mayor Sain says. "I'm getting ready for my son, Michael, to move in. Hamilton House has this high school kid who murdered someone moving in after school gets out, and he needs a room. He's the son of a local police sergeant."

"Sounds like several reality shows to me," Jed says.

"The cleaners bring dump trucks?" Bessie asks. "You haven't cleaned it since I moved in here, and that was over twenty years ago."

"Gotta change once in a while, don't we?" Mayor Sain says.

"The only time you've ever been changed was when I could smell your diaper from a hundred yards."

"Bye, Mom and Asia," Mayor Sain says, leading Ken and Jed outside.

"Mr. Mayor," Ken asks. "Who keeps the peace in this place?"

"Why, I do, of course."

* * *

"Let's call Darby and tell him we'll do Ham 'n' Eggs," an excited Michael says, sitting at an artist's table near Josh in the store.

"With Darby, and probably most of the money people, you only get one chance. And Darby, he doesn't handle change well. You've got to make it a good one."

"Can I do it any way I want? I'll still help with *Veronica's Lives* and *mR. bERZERKELEY*."

"We're ten days ahead. I say do it!"

"This is better than I ever imagined. A few weeks ago, I was living in a basement wearing a mask. Now I am on top of the world."

"Yes, you are," Josh says. "And I've had papers drafted to form a partnership. That'll be icing on the cake."

"How can I ever thank you?"

"No thanks needed," Josh says. "Just keep doing the great things you are doing. It'll make us both rich. And the way I'm going, I'm going to need it. Putting our money together at least gives me some protection."

* * *

Sarah's backpack hits the floor next to the block as she slumps in a chair. Her black hair and the beads from her nose-to-ear piercing hit the table as she puts her head down. "What's the matter, Kansas?" Bessie asks from the stove. "Your uppers run out?"

"Yes," Sarah says. "I can't find my friends. They've disappeared."

"Probably watching some gory movie downtown."

"They get to have all the fun," Sarah says. "I think I'm going to drop out of school so I can have fun with them."

"What are you going to do with the rest of your life?" Bessie asks. "Hang around Berkeley with the homeless?"

"I think I'm going to be a witch like Death wants to be," Sarah says. "It sounds so neat."

"I'd give you some of my pain pills," Bessie says. "But it's all that's keeping me going, and I don't want to miss anything right up until the end."

"If I were a witch, I would whip up a potion to cure you. That's what I would do," Sarah says. "Witches can do anything they want—at least that's what Death says."

"I'll tell you what," Bessie says. "Why don't you have a couple of my dumplings and go take a nap? Then we'll talk about witches."

"I can't," Sarah says. "I'm going to go back to the university and drop out. Then I'm going to find my friends and tell them the good news."

"Kansas," Bessie starts, "take my advice for once. Eat and rest, and then talk. Bessie does know a few things about dropping out. Look at my naked-ass commie son. I kept him from dropping out of the reelection. Maybe you and I can find a reason for you to stay in school. Let's keep you on track and peace with Mr. and Mrs. Churchill and the state of Kansas."

"Maybe you're right. But I don't have any sleeping pills like I've been taking the past couple of days. They make me go to sleep instantly and have the craziest dreams."

"I'll give you one of those," Bessie says. "I've got enough for a couple of months, and I probably won't need all of them."

"Thanks, Bessie," Sarah says. "Want me to get it for you?"

"No!" Bessie yells. "I'll be right back."

* * *

Jamal slumps on the couch next to Asia, who is sitting and working feverishly on her laptop. "Whoa, girl," he says. "You're going to punch holes in that computer."

"I got a lot of loose strings to take care of, and they won't get done by themselves."

"How do you do that?"

"Take care of them?"

"No. Work like that on your laptop? I've never seen anyone work so fast, moving from one page to another. Where did you learn that?"

"I taught myself."

"I'd like to learn, too. It looks like a whole lot more fun than getting your head cracked open on the football field or running up and down a basketball court getting elbowed and shoved."

"I'll tell you what, Jamal. When I leave, you can have this laptop—as long as you promise not to play games all day and night."

"Leave? You're not leaving, are you?"

"It may be the only way to keep the peace around here."

* * *

"Miss Vice-Chancellor?" the assistant's voice says over the intercom. "There's a young woman here to see you without an appointment."

"I don't see anyone without an appointment. Tell her to come back next month or next year!"

"I think you'll want to see me, Vice-Chancellor Kris," Asia's voice says over the intercom.

"Oh, it's you. Please show Miss Asia inside."

Asia opens the vice-chancellor's door, closes it behind her, and settles into a wooden chair.

"You here to give me more grief? You almost got me fired. You know I'm not happy with you."

"I know I have been a problem, Vice-Chancellor. I am here to offer you an olive branch."

"Olive branch? What are you going to do? Stick it up my ass?"

"If I leave right now, pack up my stuff and disappear, will you leave everyone alone and get on with your life as if I never existed?"

"You've got to be kidding. There's no way after all the trouble you've caused me. And you wouldn't be here if there wasn't something you're afraid I might find if I dig a little deeper."

"I am making you an offer, Vice-Chancellor. I will leave immediately if you get off my case and go on about your business as second-in-command of the university."

"You are a smart girl—a very smart and tricky girl. The more you talk, the more I am convinced there is something else to find out. What have you done you don't want me to know? You are a prized whore from Virginia City—a prostitute selling yourself to men for sexual pleasure. That's legal in Nevada, so that's not what you're trying to hide. What is it? I will find out whether you leave or not."

"This is my final offer, Vice-Chancellor. I am offering you peace. I will leave, and you will never hear from me again. Isn't that enough?"

"And I am going to repeat myself. You stay, you leave—makes no difference to me. I am on to something, and you know it. It's only a matter of time until I find out what it is you're hiding. I know it has something to do with the chancellor. He reamed me, and no one does that and survives. I've run chancellors out before. Wu Lim will be next, once I find out what you and he have done that made him your protector."

"Vice-Chancellor Kris," Asia says, "you have refused my peace offering. You will ultimately be sorry for your decision. And when you fall, you will receive no sympathy from me."

"Are you through?" Vice-Chancellor Kris asks.

"You have made my decision for me," Asia says.

"What decision is that?"

"Whether to stay or leave."

Chapter Fifty-Two
We Want Babies!

WINNIE, BABE, ASIA, MICHAEL, Jamal, Stephanie, Judy, and Mayor Sain sit at the block, waiting for Bessie to finish cooking. Babe, in her robe, leans her head against Winnie's shoulder. "Hope you all like my special chicken fried steak," Bessie says. "Last time I cooked it was when my naked-ass commie son graduated from high school—or was it the university?"

"The university, mom," Mayor Sain says. "Where's the rest of them?"

"Josh left me at the store to finish the cartoons while he and his girlfriend went out to dinner to celebrate," Michael says.

"What?" Mayor Sain asks.

"I don't know, something about getting ready to get married."

"You got to him yet?" Stephanie whispers to Asia.

"Not yet," Asia says.

"Better hurry if he's getting married," Judy whispers.

"Trust me," Asia whispers. "It won't matter."

"Where's our Goth?" Mayor Sain asks.

"I talked her out of dropping out of school. She went to find out where her friends went."

"Dropping out of school?" Babe says sitting up. "That's all I need to send me back to bed. I haven't felt this lousy since I can't remember when."

"I can," Bessie says.

"Here we go with the fifty-years-ago routine," Mayor Sain chides.

"Reading my mind!" Bessie says. "Maybe it is time to go to bed permanently, especially with Asia leaving."

"I'm not leaving," Asia says. "I met with the vice-chancellor this afternoon, and leaving won't make any difference to her. She'll still wreak havoc."

"My mother!" Michael says. "What a joke!"

"The only joke bigger than her is sitting next to you," Bessie says. "Two peas in a pod."

"I will find a way to take care of you, Bessie," Asia says. "I don't know how, but there's got to be a way."

"That's why I am cooking my special steak. You never know when it will be my last meal."

"For God's sake, everyone," Mayor Sain says. "Let's break out the Jack and get drunk. Asia is staying and you will be saved from the grim reaper, Hamilton House has a new boarder, and my son and I will be living together for the first time ever. We should have a celebration!"

Trojan pops through the doggy door. "See? You mention booze, and the mutt shows up," Bessie says. "The little white puff next door plays second fiddle to my booze."

Bessie, with Michael's assistance, puts steaming trays of chicken fried steak on the table. Willie comes through the kitchen door just as the last tray is placed. "Ah, my favorite," he says as he takes a chair at the block.

"First the mutt and now the leech," Bessie says. "Glad I made twice as much as I should have. Between father and son, it'll all be gone, and you'll be looking for more."

"Which father and son are you talking about?" Mayor Sain asks.

"Wiseass!" Bessie yells.

* * *

Stephanie, Judy, and Asia sit in the living room off to one side. "You promised!" Stephanie says. "We want Josh to father our babies."

"I'll get plenty of sperm tonight, but I need the two of you to follow the instructions I worked on today to generate enough eggs for in vitro." Asia hands them a paper. "When your eggs are ready I will do the rest."

"You sure about this?" Judy asks.

"I had a little talk with Professor Spears, and he told me how to do it. Follow the instructions and it will be done."

"Thank you, Asia," Stephanie says. "What would we all do without you?"

As the girls leave, Asia is staring out the living room window into darkness. Michael sits next to her. "I am so glad you're not leaving," he says. "I have been thinking a lot about my condition and what I can do. There's got to be something that can be done—after taking care of Bessie, of course."

"There is," Asia says. "I did a lot of research on transplants this afternoon and was going to leave you some sources to investigate." She takes out a piece of paper and hands it to him. "All of these sources refer to various transplant techniques. I am going to leave it to you to dig deeper and see what you come up with."

"Is there information for Grandma, too?" Michael asks.

"I have liver transplants on another list," Asia says.

"Give me that one, too. I'll look up those first. My ear can wait."

"You are a really good young man," Asia says. "If I had a cousin I would want one just like you."

"Thanks, Miss Asia," Michael says as he takes the second piece of paper.

"By the way," Asia says, "that small suitcase I gave you for safe keeping—could you leave it on my bed? My door is unlocked."

"Sure. Then I'm going next door to my new room and stay up all night working on my laptop. I'm going to look at everything you've given me."

"Good night, Michael," Asia says and moves into the kitchen, where Jamal is helping Bessie with dishes while Willie finishes up the last steak.

"Leave the rest for Jamal and me," Asia says. "You are up way past your bedtime."

"And leave Willie the leech here to eat all the leftovers in the refrigerator?"

"I'm leaving," Willie says. "Just checking in, like the judge said."

"Your son will behave or feel my cleaver," Bessie says, reaching for her weapon.

"Trust me, son. She's a lot more dangerous than your mother."

"I can handle it, Dad," Jamal says. "Thanks for coming by."

"Good-bye," Willie says. "Get a good night's sleep."

"That's what I like to see. A little peace around here can go a long way. With that, I *will* leave you and Jamal alone to finish up," Bessie says to Asia, leaving the kitchen, returning to her room, and shutting the door to her room behind her.

"With you not leaving, that's a good thing," Jamal says.

"I'll get you your own laptop," Asia says. "I've got a few connections. But you've got to promise me—no games!"

"I do, I do," Jamal says.

"You get to bed, too," Asia says, pushing him lightly on the shoulder. "You got to get up early for school, don't you?"

"You got it," Jamal says. "And it has been a long day … but a day of peace."

Jamal leaves Asia alone rinsing dishes for the last dishwasher load. Sarah, black clothes scattered over her body and hair rustled, staggers in as the Campanile rings nine. "What in the hell?" Asia says.

"We were almost busted by the cops," Sarah says. "Death and I escaped by climbing through the bushes and running between buildings."

"What was the problem?"

"The cops wanted to arrest all of us for selling drugs," Sarah says. "Can you imagine? Me? Selling drugs? I don't want to sell them. I want to use them so I feel good—really good."

"You want some dinner?"

"No, I want drugs. I ran out, and the guy who had them was taken away. Death and I saw him being cuffed."

"Tell you what," Asia says. "How about a little Jack, two of Bessie's leftover dumplings, and some toast? Will that hold you over?"

"It might. But I need drugs like the one Bessie gave me to sleep this afternoon. Go and get me one of those, will you?"

"After you eat, I will," Asia says. "Do you remember what Bessie gave you?"

"I think she said it was vyke-something."

"Probably Vicodin," Asia says. "Let's hold back on the Jack. I'll see what I can do."

"Thanks, Asia," Sarah says. "I don't know what I would do without you."

* * *

"I don't care what the girls at the ranch say. Try again for the third time!" Vice-Chancellor Kris yells into her cell phone. "There's something going on. Maybe she had a baby, maybe she had sex with the chancellor … who knows? Stay there until you find out something, or your daughter will be expelled by noon tomorrow. Find something. They must keep records. You're supposed to be a special agent. Find me something special!"

* * *

The mayor sits in his basement playing his clarinet. Michael walks down the wooden stairs carrying the mayor's cell phone. "My music bothering you?" Mayor Sain asks. "I'll quit if you can't sleep."

"No, sir, it sounds great. I was working on my laptop in the kitchen when your phone rang."

The mayor looks at the clock on the wall. "Eleven thirty?"

He takes the cell. "Thanks, son," he says proudly. "I'm finished. Go to bed."

"Yes, sir."

"This is Mayor Sain. Who is this?"

"Mayor Sain?" a female voice says. "This is Gail Garcia from the White House."

"Which house? We have a lot of white ones here in Berkeley."

"*The* White House, Mr. Mayor. I am calling for the president."

"I just thought you said you are calling for the president from the real White House."

"That's correct, Mr. Mayor. I am calling for the president of the United States."

"Come on. Who's trying to pull mR. bERZERKELEY's leg? The joke is on me. You almost had me believing."

"Mr. Mayor. The president wants me to find out if you are going to stop those cartoons that have been putting him in an unfavorable light about the stimulus funds."

"You're not putting me on, are you? You are calling from DC?"

"Yes."

"It's after two thirty in the morning back there."

"Yes, it is. We never sleep."

"I suppose you could put the president on if I asked you too?"

"I could, if you want. But he's got to sleep for a few hours with his big day courting the prime minister of Ireland this morning. But if that's what you want, I'll wake him."

"No, no. What is it he wants?"

"The cartoons. Are you going to stop them?"

"We are letting them run out and waiting until we see what happens with his little team of auditors. I don't know when they are coming to review their findings. When that happens, depending on what they conclude, I will consider asking the artists to stop dinging him."

"That's all he asks, Mr. Mayor. With so much going on in the world and here at home, a little peace here and there is all we can hope for."

"Tell him good luck with the prime minister. And the next time he comes to Berkeley, we'll have a little game of one-on-one. And there's this female player I want him to take on. She has tricks he won't believe until he sees them."

"I will tell him, Mr. Mayor. Good night."

The mayor folds up his cell. "The president of the United States? Maybe I should go next door and see if Asia will pay off her promise to celebrate. No! I've got a son to look after. I guess I'll just have to have a juicy one before I hit the sack."

* * *

The clock reads midnight straight up when Asia's cell rings as she sits on the couch in the living room working on her laptop. "Lady Gretchen?" she says, looking at the seven seven five number. "What's up?"

"That special agent was here again looking for shit on you. He's on fire!"

"You didn't tell him anything, did you?"

"No, but he's becoming very insistent. He went from girl to girl and got nothing, at least no information. He musta spent a couple of thousand dollars."

"Where's my book?"

"We got it in the safe. He kept asking for a peek at your records, any records, but we didn't give in."

"The book has to be destroyed. Certain people's lives depend on it."

"The state will fine us big time. They use it to collect taxes, and we got to keep all our books."

"I don't care what it costs. I'll find the money. Burn it quick."

Josh walks in through the kitchen door. "I gotta go, Gretchen. Do it!"

"Hey, Asia," Josh says, sitting down hard next to her. "What are you doing up so late?"

"Waiting for you," Asia says, sexual tones dripping from her lips. "Waiting for the big, strong, handsome artist to get home."

"Uh-oh," Josh says. "Something tells me it's time to get out my charcoal and paint brushes."

"You are the smart one, aren't you? It is time. Why don't you go to your room, freshen up a little, and get ready for me?"

"I've been ready for you since the parade," Josh says. "See you soon?"

Josh follows Asia up the stairs and watches her disappear into her bedroom. Josh opens his room and quickly throws the clothes on the floor and his bed into a pile inside the closet. He goes into his bathroom and rustles through his hair with wet hands and looks at his unshaven face. He hears someone walk into his room and turns around. It is Asia, dressed in her red outfit with gold tassels. "Holy shit!" Josh says. "I am supposed to draw now?"

"How about you draw, and then we'll do whatever comes natural," Asia says, using her best sexual come-on.

"I don't know if I will be able to draw, if you know what I mean," Josh says.

"If you think you've got what you need memorized, I guess we don't have to wait, do we?"

"Memorized? I can think of nothing else," Josh says.

"Well, then, we can make good use of this, can't we?" Asia says holding a condom.

"You do have all the answers, don't you? I hope you have a couple more of those."

"I got a whole suitcase full, Josh. If you've got the gumption, I've got what you want."

*   *   *

Asia's scooter moves quickly up the winding road to the laboratory after midnight. She goes inside the tall wire fence, parks, and opens the door. She flips on a light switch and walks to the liquid nitrogen tank. She carefully takes out three condoms knotted at the top from a glass of ice and pours the semen into long tubes. "There's enough for several pregnancies," she says as she places the tubes in the unit.

"Doing a cryogenic experiment?" Professor Spears says, walking up behind her. Her hand jolts slightly in surprise.

"Professor? You almost scared me! What are you still doing here?"

"I never leave," he says. "I've been doing my best to grow those liver cells. They need 24-7 attention ... sort of like I do."

"Well, I'm here now. Let's take a look at those cells and then we'll take a look at you. What do you say about that?"

"Peace, that's all I ask for," Professor Spears says. "The vice-chancellor has left me alone for a whole day. It's been a good one, but it's now tomorrow."

"We'll start it off right, I promise."

*   *   *

Mayor Sain walks up the stairs from the basement. He hears scratching at his kitchen door. He walks over. "Trojan? What do you want? I don't have any Jack in here."

Trojan looks up at the mayor and then starts to run away. He stops and looks back at the mayor. He starts running again.

"You want me to follow you?"

Trojan barks softly.

"Okay, I guess," Mayor Sain says, following Trojan, who is running slowly toward Mrs. McPherson's house.

The mayor rounds the corner of Hamilton House and stops abruptly behind Trojan as they both confront five coyotes on the sidewalk. Trojan growls. "I get it," Mayor Sain says. "You want me to be the peacemaker. These guys been giving you trouble?"

Trojan barks.

"Shoo!" Mayor Sain says. "Get out of here!"

Mrs. McPherson's doggy door makes a noise, and Mimi sticks her head out. “Now I really get it,” Mayor Sain says. “You’re protecting the little beauty from next door. I’ll take care of these guys for you.”

Mayor Sain feigns moving toward the coyotes. All of them start to run away except one, who has his jowls raised and teeth showing. “Why is there always one who wants to fight?” Mayor Sain says. “Why don’t you just run away like the rest?”

Trojan walks up to the lone coyote, who towers over him and stops within three feet. Trojan raises his jowls, shows his teeth, and growls fiercely. The coyote looks at Trojan, then the mayor, and then Mimi, and then lifts his leg and pees on the sidewalk before turning and following the rest of the pack.

Trojan turns and looks at Mimi, his head held high. “Guess we showed them,” Mayor Sain says. “I think I’ll call the humane society in the morning. We need peace in the neighborhood.”

Part Five
Holidaze

Chapter Fifty-Three
Setting the Date

"It's so quiet with the pickets gone," Babe says, lying in bed next to Winnie.

"How do you feel? You've been a basket case since the Big Game."

"Just the mention of those words gives me the shakes. I will never attend another game."

"Come on, Babe. I think whatever is going on inside you is making you see only the negative in everything."

"There's something inside. That's for sure," Babe says. "And, when we're home for Christmas I'm going to have my doctor check it out."

"Aren't we staying here for Christmas and New Year's?"

"Christmas without seeing the grandchildren? You've got to be out of your mind. I've got all kinds of ideas what to buy them and want to see the looks on their faces when they open their presents in front of a great big tree in our beautiful home at the lake."

"We've got a few responsibilities here that need to be taken care of," Winnie says.

"You take care of them before we leave. It'll take every ounce of energy I have to pack."

Winnie's nose twitches. "Bessie's cooking breakfast. Guess it's time to see what all the boys and girls are doing."

"Bring me up a plate. I am going to lay here and keep dreaming about the lights around the frozen lake, the snow falling, and the hot toddies I am going to drink, no matter what the doctor finds inside of me."

Winnie walks to the block and sits. Sarah, Asia, Josh, Jamal, Stephanie, Judy, Mayor Sain, and Michael sit, waiting for Bessie to finish eggs and bacon. "Can I help?" Winnie asks.

"Might as well sit down," Mayor Sain says. "We've all offered, but she is determined to do her job."

"At least one of us is," Bessie growls. "If you had any sense in that fucking empty head, you'd go make peace with Michael's mother so I can at least smile once before I go knowing that the family is together."

"I promise I will try, Mom, just for you."

"She's a bitch, Grandma. I don't ever want to see her again."

"Knowing what she has gone through all these years because of your naked-ass commie father would turn anyone into a raving maniac."

"She's beyond that," Asia says. "I've known some bad ones in my short life. She tops the list."

"I thought the chancellor took care of her," Winnie says.

"She's on a roll. She's trying to find anything on me to get me out of here. If I leave or don't leave, it won't matter. So I decided to stay and see how it all plays out."

"That's great news," Mayor Sain says. "We'll have the best Christmas ever."

"Christmas?" Bessie says. "We better celebrate early. I got this feeling I won't be around much longer."

"Christmas?" Sarah says without her usual exuberance. "Does that mean we can have a tree and decorate it with black ornaments and voodoo dolls?"

"I say we celebrate Hanukkah instead," Bessie says. "That's a whole lot sooner this year."

"We always celebrate Kwanza," Jamal says. "It's our tradition."

"I've never celebrated Christmas," Asia says. "Whatever we do is all right with me."

"Michael," Mayor Sain asks, "what do you and your wicked mother celebrate?"

"She always went off on a short vacation and left me with enough food to survive while she was gone," Michael says.

"That's what we're going to do," Stephanie says.

"Yes! A weekend in Vichy Springs, hot tubs, mineral baths, massages," Judy says. "I can't wait."

"You might want to rethink that," Asia says as she winks at the both of them.

"Really?" Stephanie says. "Are you for sure?"

"I'm ready when you are," Asia says.

"I have no idea what the three of you are talking about," Mayor Sain says. "But I'm all in, too."

"What about you, Josh?" Winnie asks. "What are you going to do?"

"Get married, I suppose?" Josh says.

"You suppose?" Mayor Sain says. "Stay single, windsurf, draw those cartoons, smoke, and drink with me. Come on, buddy. No wedding."

"It's not as easy as all that," Josh says. "It seems I have no choice."

"It's okay with me," Sarah says. "You're not Goth, so you can go and do whatever you want."

"All right," Bessie says, walking to the block with a tray of food. "Enough of this. I say we do it the democratic way and vote. I propose we celebrate in a couple of days and give me enough time to prepare another feast. December 22 is the shortest day of the year. That's the day we celebrate, and we'll drink to everyone."

"That's the day I have to leave for LA," Josh says. "I'll miss it all."

"Anyone else have a conflict?" Bessie asks. After a pause, "Hearing no other objections, I say we have voted. December 22 it is! Bessie's rules one last time!"

"That was certainly democratic, Mom," Mayor Sain says.

"I got it from watching one of your fucking council meetings," Bessie says. "Now, eat breakfast, and then we'll plan the feast."

"Shall we invite the usual suspects?" Winnie says.

"Why not?" Bessie says. "I'd like to wish them all the best since it might be the last time I see them."

"Come on, Mom," Mayor Sain says. "Enough of the 'last time' shit. You're going to be around forever."

"Michael," Asia whispers, "did you have any luck with those lists I gave you?"

"I did," Michael says. "I got a few more to look through."

"Are you really sure?" Stephanie whispers to Asia.

"You two follow the instructions?" Asia whispers in return. "When you're ready, so am I."

"I have another idea," Bessie says, holding her cleaver. "Let's invite a certain vice-chancellor to use Josh's empty chair. A certain naked-ass commie is going to invite her, aren't you?"

"You've got to be kidding," Asia says. "I'll put arsenic in her Bloody Mary."

"There's no way I want to eat dinner with her," Michael says.

"You know she won't come," Mayor Sain says.

"Use the same lines on her you did a long time ago," Bessie says. "It worked once, didn't it? And it gave me a grandson."

"There's no way!" Mayor Sain says. "She'll give us all food poisoning just being in the same room."

"I'll cast a spell on her. That's what a real witch would do," Sarah says.

"She's the witch, not you," Bessie says.

"I got it!" Winnie says as he laughs. "We'll put her next to Jack R. Abbott and give him 'carve the turkey' as his dinner duty. If the smell doesn't get her the blood will."

"That's my Pooh," Mayor Sain says as he laughs. "That may be the answer."

Chapter Fifty-Four
Early Presents

WILLIE, IN FULL UNIFORM and carrying pieces of paper, walks into the kitchen as breakfast is being served. "Why don't you just take your old bed in the basement?" Bessie asks. "You're here more than at work."

"You checking on me again?" Jamal says.

"No," Willie says. "This is an official call. I have to serve another complaint." Willie hands the papers to Winnie.

"What's this?" Winnie says.

"Gerry Armstrong is filing a complaint against you for serving alcohol and drugs to an underage minor and exposing her to rape and possible molestation by a fraternity while under your supervision."

"What?" Winnie says. "Bertha is behind this one. I know it."

"My father is doing what?" Sarah says. "I'm going to put a hex on him he won't forget as soon as I get to the park."

"He got the booze right," Bessie says. "Anyone want some Jack to start the day?"

"Judge Kelley will set the date for a hearing," Willie says.

"Good ol' Judge Kelley," Mayor Sain says. "Maybe we should invite him to the feast, too."

"Speaking of feasts, that breakfast sure does look good," Willie says.

"I knew I should have ordered in a couple more dozen eggs and three packages of bacon," Bessie says. "Willie the leech and his bottomless pit!"

"I gotta go to school," Jamal says.

"You want to take my laptop?" Asia asks.

"Nah," Jamal says. "My boys aren't ready to see the studious me yet."

"There's a studious you?" Willie asks.

"You haven't seen anything, yet," Asia says.

* * *

A naked Mayor Sain walks up the steps into city hall, his backpack moving slightly on his broad shoulders and bare back. "Alice," he says to a female sitting behind a desk. "Happy almost holidays to you and that wonderful family."

"Same to you, Mr. Mayor," Alice says. "I saw you on television in Los Angeles. We taped it."

"That was a lot of fun," Mayor Sain says. "Got so much salt on my body I had to take three showers."

"We saw the picture of you at Disneyland on TV, too," Alice says. "We all want to try that one."

"A little tricky, but I still got the moves," Mayor Sain says. "Say hi to the family for me."

After the short elevator ride, Mayor Sain saunters to his office, where Queen stands, tapping her foot. "Well, Mr. World Traveler and celebrity. You finally decide to come back and do the people's business?"

"Queen. What would I ever do without you?"

"Like I said before, live on the streets with your homeless friends."

"You're probably right."

"Your other friends have an early Christmas present for you."

"My other friends?"

"Mr. Coolidge and the BAA. They left you a recall petition signed by over three thousand people. They say you have abandoned your position."

"Abandoned? I eat, sleep, and drink Berkeley."

"Don't forget 'smoke,'" Queen says sarcastically.

"Bastards. Is that all?"

"You got the agenda for the next council meeting with enough items to last for several days. Since you've been gone, they haven't been able to pass anything—all four-to-four votes."

"Nothing changes, does it?"

"Your other friends, the Feds, will be here in an hour to go over their revised report."

"Really? We'll see if the president came through."

"I wouldn't be so happy if I were you," Queen says. "I've been offered a job by the vice-chancellor at twice the meager wage you give me. She says she'll treat me real nice and wear clothes all the time."

"The iron maiden is really trying to mess with me, isn't she?"

"I guess she figures if I can put up with you for all these years, I can put up with anything."

"Come on, Queen. I'll double your coffee allowance."

"You know I don't drink coffee."

"I'll see what I can do. Don't be hasty. That evil female wants to destroy my life, and she'll take you down with her."

"That's not the way to talk about the woman who bore your son," Queen says.

"You know about Michael?"

"It's all over town," Queen says. "Maybe he'll be the next mayor."

"That he might," Mayor Sain says. "He is very talented."

"At least maybe he'd show up once in a while," Queen says, folding her arms.

"Okay, okay," Mayor Sain says. "You made your point. You're not really going to leave me, are you?"

"How could I?" Queen says. "I want to see how this whole thing works out. If they recall you, maybe I'll run for mayor."

* * *

"The stem cells don't seem to be growing very fast," Asia says, looking into a powerful microscope with Professor Spears behind her.

"I've done all I can, Miss Asia. They are growing, but I'm afraid there won't be enough to bolster Bessie's liver and keep her alive."

"I've got to find an answer, professor. They must grow and grow fast."

"The only thing that's growing fast is—" A buzzer breaks the professor's focus. "Who could that be?"

The professor opens the laboratory door and greets two deliverymen. "You Professor Spears?" one of the men asks. "This truckload is for you."

Professor Spears looks over the invoice. "My cloning equipment!" he yells. "I've got cloning equipment!"

Asia walks to him. "That's great, professor. Now you can live your dream."

"Yes, I can. You and I, we can reinvent the human race."

Professor Spears and Asia stand aside as the two men unload several boxes of equipment and place them in the middle of the laboratory.

"Just think!" an excited professor says as he shuts the door behind the men. "We can give birth to a superior race! We can create geniuses and super athletes. We can create animals that will sustain us forever. We can rule the world! This is an unbelievable present. This will be a great new year."

"If I'm here any longer," Asia says.

"You will be here. I will be here. We will be like we always are."

"You ready for the treat you were working on a little while ago?"

"After seeing all this equipment I don't think I'll be able, not for at least fifteen minutes."

* * *

"Can I look at it?" Michael says as Josh carries in a covered canvas.

"I don't know. It is a little racy."

"I can handle it," Michael says as he slowly pulls the cover up and over, unveiling Asia in her red outfit with gold tassels. "That's Asia?"

"That, Michael, is a real woman—a one-of-a-kind woman."

"That costume she has on—it's real ... sexy, isn't it?" Michael says slowly.

"It's more than that," Josh says. "No wonder the old man offered an additional half-million."

"Half a million ... dollars?"

"You are looking at a painting that is worth one and one-half million dollars, Michael," Josh says proudly. "I never thought I would do anything worth that much."

"When will you get the money?"

"Whenever he shows up," Josh says. "I think Babe knows how to get in touch with him. I've got to go take care of my girl at the sorority, if I have anything left after last night."

"What happened?"

"Nothing," Josh says. "Asia and I had a little ... chat after I dabbled with my charcoal."

"What do I do if the man shows up?"

"Take his money and put it in our business account. That way we both can get to it if we need it."

"I'll stay here until Babe shows up," Michael says. "One and a half million dollars! That a lot of money."

"That's a lot of woman!"

* * *

Sarah sits in the park across from Berkeley High School with several girls and guys dressed in various Goth ensembles. One of the boys hands her a pill container. "I don't know if I should?" Sarah says. "All I do is get sick."

"Come on, Dream. It'll help you become a witch, like you want," the boy says.

"I think I should be studying for finals or something. Maybe I'm not cut out to be a Goth."

"We all go through this phase," Death says, rubbing Voodoo's black head. "You don't have to do the drugs, you know. It's all about tragedy, not about drugs."

"Let me give you this as a present," the boy says, handing another pill container to Sarah. "When you get down, take one of the pink ones. When you are tired, take one of the blue ones. And if you really want to have some fun, take the green one."

"Or don't take any at all," Death says. "You can still be a Goth."

*　　　*　　　*

"You both said you were ready," Asia says, sitting on the bed in Stephanie and Judy's room.

"We are," Stephanie says. "Are you?"

"I've never done this before," Asia says. "I'm just doing what the professor told me to do. I've got the instrument loaded and ready. This might take a few tries, but the professor swears it will work."

"Go for it," Judy says. "Motherhood, here we come."

Asia inserts the instrument into Judy and releases sperm. "That was easy," Judy says. "Almost like sex."

"Don't get me started about sex," Asia says. "That's what's got me in trouble my whole life."

"What do you mean by that?" Stephanie says.

"Just feeling sorry for myself. I'll get over it."

"My turn," Stephanie says. "What Judy does, I do." Stephanie grabs Judy's hand.

Asia inserts the instrument and releases sperm inside Stephanie.

"You have enough for more tries if these don't work?" Judy asks.

"Josh gave me enough for a couple of months," Asia says. "That boy is a sperm machine!"

"How will we know if we are pregnant?"

"Wait a few days, buy a couple of tests, and hope for the best. If it doesn't take, we'll try again—if I'm still here."

"You aren't still talking about leaving, are you?" Stephanie asks.

"I may not have a choice," Asia says. "It's all out of my hands now."

"Don't we owe you something for doing this?" Judy asks.

"The best thing you can do is to be the best mothers you can be. That will be my present."

"What was your mother like?" Stephanie asks.

"That, my lesbian friends, is a whole other story."

*　　　*　　　*

Special Agent Picard walks into the Storey County Sheriff's Office in Virginia City. "So you're a special agent?" a uniformed sheriff asks.

"Yes," the agent says flashing a badge.

"Haven't seen one of those around here since one of the brothels fell behind paying their taxes."

"I'm investigating a young lady named Lily Liu Lu. I've been out at the ranch and they didn't give me much about her past."

"You know where she is?" the sheriff asks.

"Yes. That's why I've been asking around. She's causing trouble for someone in the Bay Area."

"We've been hoping someone would eventually lead us to her. We've got an old warrant for her arrest."

"For what?"

"For questioning in a murder a couple of years back."

"Lily Liu Lu murdered somebody?"

"Not just anybody. An old, belligerent drunk named Johnny Blood. Most everyone was glad he got his like he did—dick shot off!"

"And she did it?"

"That's what it looks like. We want to question her and get that case off our books. This whole thing doesn't sound worthy of a special agent."

"Let's just say I'm doing a favor for someone very important. Is there anything else you can tell me about Lily Liu Lu?"

"She sure was a popular one," the uniformed officer says. "She had visitors lined up waiting their turn, especially these rich guys from China."

"Who were they, these rich guys?"

"They all keep books for tax purposes. They got all the names."

"How do I get Lily Liu Lu's records? I was told they don't have any."

"If you break in and try to find it we'll have to throw you in the Storey County Jail. Otherwise, a court order is needed. And you need a good reason to get a court order. What crime has she committed that requires a review of her book?"

"None that I am aware of," Special Agent Picard says. "But you have given me information that is going to make a certain person very happy. Thank you, Sheriff."

Agent Picard stands outside the Storey County Jail holding his cell phone. He starts to dial and then stops. "I'm going to deliver this little present in person with a guarantee that she leaves my daughter alone. A little audio record might come in very handy."

Chapter Fifty-Five
Black Sox

"What is this?" Winnie says, walking down the stairs looking at the fireplace in the living room. "Black socks hanging on the fireplace?"

"The Kansas druggie hung one for everyone late last night," Bessie says, working over the stove. "She's been running around here like she has a red hot poker up her butt this morning. She's on something again."

Winnie walks to the block and sits down. Bessie grabs her chart. "You got 'take out the garbage' as your dinner duty," she says.

"At least it's not 'carve the turkey'," Mayor Sain says, walking through the kitchen door with Michael close behind. "And I was spared trash duty for once."

"Sit down, you naked-ass commie. You too, grandson."

"What is this all about?" Michael asks.

"A little game your grandmother plays when we have a holiday feast."

"Since this is probably my last one, pick something good," Bessie says.

Mayor Sain walks around the block twice and sits next to Winnie. Michael sits next to the mayor.

"Aha! You got 'wash the dishes' and your shadow has 'set the table,'" Bessie says reading her chart.

"At least it's not for several hours," the mayor says. "By then, after several joints and a bottle of Jäger, I won't care if my hands look like a washboard again."

"Should I set the table now?" Michael asks.

"Later, much later," Bessie says. "We got Bloody Marys, snacks, listening to shitty stories of past conquests from my naked-ass commie—your father, leftover dumplings, and who knows what else before we feast tonight."

"We've got special stockings to open, too," Sarah says, bouncing to the block holding small wrapped gifts. "Michael, can you help me?"

Michael pushes his chair back and goes to Sarah as Asia comes down the stairs. "What's all that?" she says, watching Michael follow Sarah to the fireplace and the black socks.

"The druggie is pretending it's a black Goth Christmas," Bessie says. "I don't think she even washed those socks she found."

"I do have to talk to that girl before things happen," Asia says, sitting down.

"I have automatically given you 'make Bloody Marys'," Bessie says. "I'll move a few things on the chart around."

"How about 'keep your promise,'" Mayor Sain says, smiling as Asia.

"How about 'I'm too tired,'" Asia says, smiling back. "You never give up, do you?"

"Not when you are on my mind," Mayor Sain says.

"And that's all the time," Bessie says.

Stephanie and Judy walk down the stairs, each carrying a travel bag. "You sure it's all right to go hot-tubbing?" Stephanie asks Asia.

"Shouldn't be a problem," Asia says. "You two have fun for me, too."

"What is that all about?" Mayor Sain asks. "You the lesbians' agent or something?"

"It's an inside joke. That's all," Asia says. "Where's the Bloody Mary fixin's? Time to get December 22 started right."

"Hey!" Sarah yells. "Don't leave without looking in your socks."

Stephanie and Judy walk to the fireplace and take down socks with their names pinned on. They each take out a small bottle of Fuzzy Navel with a red ribbon wrapped around the top.

"To remember me by," Sarah says, "when I was a lesbian before I was a Goth."

"Thanks," Stephanie says. "You'll always be our favorite lesbian friend."

Judy and Stephanie give Sarah a hug.

"Have fun for me, too," Sarah says as Stephanie and Judy leave.

Trojan pops in through the doggy door. He sniffs and walks to Sarah and Michael in the living room. "There you are," Sarah says. "This is for you." She reaches into a black sock and pulls out a small bone. Trojan sniffs the bone, clamps on it and runs out through the doggy door.

"Must be soaked in Jack or something," Bessie says. "It's too small to hump."

Josh walks down the stairs carrying a duffel bag. "Surfer Boy!" Bessie says. "You want some bacon and eggs before you hit the road to LA?"

"I promised my girl we'd stop for breakfast along the way," Josh says. "It's going to be a long trip, one I thought I'd never be taking."

"If she's the right one, it'll be worth it," Winnie says.

"The right one for what?" Babe says as she walks from the stairs and heads for the block. "Following you anywhere like a blind mutant?"

"Now, now," Bessie says. "Got you back here, didn't it?"

"That's what I am talking about," Babe says, sitting down. "Look where it got me!"

"You've got 'help Bessie with cooking' as your duty," Bessie says looking at her chart. "At least I got that one right. Thank God a certain naked-ass commie didn't sit there."

"This all sounds like fun, but I've got to run," Josh says. "Say, Michael, there's another one for our cartoons."

"Aren't you gonna look in your stocking?" Sarah says.

"Sure, why not?"

Josh drops his duffel bag and walks to the fireplace, taking down his black sock. He pulls out a rabbit's foot hanging on a small chain. "I thought you might need a little luck," Sarah says softly. "And it might remind you what we were like when we first met."

"Thanks," Josh says, looking at the good luck charm. "I'm going to need all the luck I can get."

Josh gives Sarah a light hug. "Happy holidays," he says. "I've got to go now."

Josh walks back to his duffel bag. "You all have a great time," he says. "I'll be thinking of you."

Josh leaves through the kitchen door. "Come on, everyone. I've got stocking stuffers for all of you!" Sarah yells.

"Me too?" Jamal says, walking down the stairs.

"A special one for you," Sarah says. "I'm going to make you a Goth like me."

Chapter Fifty-Six
Period

The morning is brisk and the wind slight as Josh's old Honda moves south quickly on I-5 past the Tracy turnoff. "Let's stop at Pea Soup Andersen's for breakfast," he says to Jasmine, whose head is resting on his shoulder.

"I have a better idea. Let's pull over at Pea Soup Andersen's to take care of my needs *and then* have breakfast."

"Sounds better," Josh says.

"This is what married life will be like for us, I know it," Jasmine says, snuggling around Josh's right shoulder. "You draw those funny little cartoons, and I'll keep it warm waiting for you."

"What about the baby?"

"I'm going to hire a live-in to do all that. My job is to keep you happy."

"I always thought parents were the ones who took care of their children."

"I've got a lot to teach you," Jasmine says. "You're flying high, and I'm going to be your pilot."

"Go on back to sleep. We'll be at Pea Soups in an hour."

Jasmine's cell rings. "Yes, Mother, we're on our way. We should be there in time to talk to the caterers and have a fitting. Josh needs to order his tuxedo, too. I'll talk to you when we get closer."

"Your mother is up early," Josh says. "She must be excited."

"Almost as much as I am. I'm having sweet dreams about our future. It's the best feeling I've ever had."

"I know what you mean," Josh says, thoughtfully looking down at the ignition and the rabbit's foot moving back and forth slightly.

*　　　*　　　*

A fully dressed Mayor Sain, holding two cups of Peet's coffee, stands nervously at the vice-chancellor's front door. The Campanile strikes eight times in the background. He rings the doorbell with his middle finger. "That's appropriate," he says to himself.

The vice-chancellor, dressed and ready to leave for her office, opens the door. "Shit!" she says. "What in the hell do you want?"

"Want a cup of coffee from an old friend?" Mayor Sain asks.

"You've got to be kidding," the vice-chancellor says. "You been smoking dope all night? You must be out of your fucking mind—again!"

"You haven't lost your venom, I see," Mayor Sain says. "I'm not here to make trouble for you, call you names, or bring you any stress."

"Then what do you want? I have a busy schedule of meetings and a chancellor who is all over my case for your shenanigans at the Big Game."

"We were wondering, with the upcoming holidays, what you are doing tonight for dinner. Bessie, my mother, asked me to invite you over to feast with us. Just a quiet gathering at Hamilton House."

"You *have* been up all night smoking dope!"

"Just trying to honor one of my mother's last wishes."

"From what I remember of your mother, Bessie she's doesn't want to see me anywhere near Hamilton House."

"She asked me to invite you."

"I suppose the usual cast of weirdos would be present to harass and humiliate me?"

"Most of the boarders would be there, that's true, including our son."

"I told you, I have no son."

"He's the real reason Bessie wants you to come over. No tricks, no harassment, no vitriolic carrying on. She wants our family together one time before she passes."

"Our family? You, me, and Michael? What a fucking joke! Now I've heard them all. I will never visit Hamilton House. Period!" The vice-chancellor slams the door in Mayor Sain's face. He looks at the two cups of coffee he is holding. He turns both of them upside down and empties them in flowerpots on both sides of the front door, unzips, and pisses on both.

"Jäger, a joint, and maybe a couple of coeds. That'll get me back on track. At least I tried."

* * *

"Where did everyone go?" Asia says, holding two Bloody Marys. "Guess I'll have to throw these out."

"Are you kidding, China Girl?" Bessie says, sitting at the block. "No sense wasting good booze."

"You shouldn't drink," Asia says.

"What is it going to do? Kill me? I'm already dead, if you listen to those quacks."

"I need time. We are trying to boost the stem cells and get enough to make a difference. You continuing to drink just makes it tougher, that's all."

"Who gives a shit?" Bessie says, grabbing a Bloody Mary from Asia. "Here's to life and living." Bessie lifts her glass to touch the one Asia holds.

"Bessie, you are one of a kind."

"China Girl, so are you." They drink.

"When is everyone coming over?"

"Later this evening," Bessie says. "I told them all I want to be in bed by ten, before my pills wear off."

"You better take a nap right now," Asia says. "You'll need all the energy you got to make it that late."

"Where's Sarah?" Asia asks.

"I sent her into my room to get my pills," Bessie says.

"You did what?" Asia asks.

"I was feeling woozy. She left them by the sink. Could you bring them to me?"

Asia brings a half-full pill bottle to Bessie. "These go great with booze," Bessie says, opening the container.

"Aren't you worried that Sarah might slip a few of these into her pocket?" Asia asks.

"Pills? What good are they?" Bessie groans, tossing two in her mouth and following up with a gulp of the Bloody Mary. "When you're over you're over."

Asia looks at the half-full pill bottle. "Shit!"

* * *

Sarah sits in the park with Jamal. "The Goths are usually here waiting for me."

"I see them every day from the high school. They are a bunch of freaks."

"They are not. They are my friends. They are sooo cool."

"What happened to you, girl? When I saw you the first time you were this bubbly, happy-go-lucky girl with long blonde hair. Where is that girl?"

"I was a lesbian then. But I saw the light when I met Death on the way to the Big Game. She and her friends have changed my life like I want to change yours."

"I like my life," Jamal says. "I keep screwing it up real good, but it's my life. I am in control."

Sarah takes out a pill bottle. "You haven't seen anything yet. These little pills can take you places you never thought you could go. You can get high, walk on water, float above the clouds, see people turn from black to white to green to red. They are amazing."

"You gotta get off that stuff," Jamal says, pushing the pills away. "Those things will destroy your life and maybe even kill you. They are nothing but evil."

"Evil? That's the name of one of the Goths. He's sooo cool."

"Look, girl," Jamal says, grabbing Sarah's arm. "Do not take those pills. I don't want to visit you in the morgue."

"The morgue? I heard one of the Goths talking about a field trip to look at dead people. That would be so neat!"

"Look," Jamal says, standing up. "I can't be here with you and those pills. If I get caught they'll throw me in juvie. Please don't take those pills. Go back to Hamilton House, get your blonde hair back, and take off those silly beads. Go back to being blondie the lesbian on the scooter."

A group of young men and women dressed in black walk toward Jamal and Sarah. "There are my friends!" Sarah yells. "I knew they would show up."

"Get back to being blondie, period!" Jamal says loudly.

"Good-bye, Jamal," Sarah says. "See you at the feast."

"If you're still with us," Jamal says as he walks off.

* * *

"What are we celebrating?" Winnie says, walking up to a naked Mayor Sain, Sylvia, and Jefferson standing in People's Park around a burning trash can.

"Two major developments," Mayor Sain says. "The Feds' review dinged me for $111.11 for the lunch I bought two visiting mayors. And the vice-chancellor turned down my invitation to join us at the holiday feast."

"Congratulations, I guess," Winnie says. "Berkeley has been saved, and we won't have indigestion after all. Great way to start the holidays."

"How's Babe?" the mayor asks. "She still sick?"

"Sick, depressed, who knows? She'll make a comeback."

"I can't wait for the feast," Sylvia slurs. "It'll be the best one I've ever had."

"Who else is coming over?" Jefferson asks.

"The four of us, Bessie, Babe, Sarah, Michael, Jamal, Jack R. Abbott, Doreen, and Asia."

"That makes twelve," Jefferson says. "What about Willie?"

"He'll clean up the leftovers," Winnie says. "He's on patrol."

"Good thing the evil maiden didn't accept my invitation," Mayor Sain says.

"She could have sat on your lap," Winnie says as he laughs.

"Yours is the best lap I ever had," Sylvia says.

"You want a hit?" Mayor Sain asks Winnie.

"Why not? Doesn't look like Kansas is in my future anymore."

"Your period of exile to the hinterlands is over?" Mayor Sain asks.

"Certainly seems that way, unless something highly unusual happens."

* * *

"Could you pull over?" Jasmine asks. "I've got a bad feeling in my stomach."

"Bad feeling?" Josh says.

"Pull over, goddamn it!" Jasmine yells.

Josh pulls off the road near a sign indicating they were ten miles to Buttonwillow.

"Maybe if I get out and go to the bathroom the pain will go away."

"That'll certainly give the truckers and others a sight to behold." Josh laughs.

"This is no fucking joke!" Jasmine yells. "I am in real pain. Open the fucking door!"

Josh waits until cars pass and moves around to the passenger's side.

Jasmine starts to slide from the front seat. "Blood!" she yells. "I'm sitting in a pool of blood. Get me to a hospital!"

Josh runs back to the driver's seat. "Let's hit Buttonwillow. There's got to be someone to help us."

The old Honda moves quickly back onto I-5 as Josh floors the accelerator. Jasmine cries loudly. "Hang on. We'll be there in a couple of minutes."

The old Honda takes an off-ramp and runs the stop sign, turning left and pulling into a gas station. Josh rolls down a window and yells at a man filling up his SUV. "Is there a hospital here?"

The man shrugs his shoulders and motions that he doesn't speak English. "Shit!" Josh says as he throws the car in park and runs inside to the counter. "Hospital? Doctor?" he yells.

The man behind the counter, speaking in broken English, points east. "Bakersfield!"

Josh jumps back in the old Honda. "We've got to get to Bakersfield. Hold on."

The Honda pulls onto SR-58 heading east at top speed as Jasmine screams, holding her crotch. "I'm dying!" she yells. "My baby is dying!"

After fifteen tense minutes, Josh sees a sign that reads "urgent care." He pulls into a small shopping mall and jams on his brakes. "Can you make it inside, or should I have them bring out a stretcher?"

"You bastard!" Jasmine yells. "Get me inside!"

Josh pulls her out. Blood covers her clothing and the car seat. He cradles her in his arms and moves toward the front door. Once inside, he carries her to the counter.

"Yes," a petite female dressed in a nurse's white uniform says in broken English. "What is the problem?"

"I am bleeding and losing my baby!" Jasmine yells. "Get me to the fucking doctor!"

"I'll need information first," the lady says. "Have you been here before?"

"Get me to a fucking doctor!" a crying Jasmine yells at the top of her lungs.

"You and I can take care of whatever we have to do," Josh says calmly. "Can we get her inside?"

"Follow me," the female says. "The doctor will be here shortly."

Josh takes Jasmine through double doors into a room with a hospital bed. He puts her down. "Get me something for the pain!" Jasmine yells.

"You'll have to wait for the doctor," the female says in broken English.

"I'm dying!" Jasmine yells. "I'm dying!"

"Let me have a look," the woman says. "Sir, you'll have to wait outside."

Josh leaves the room and takes a seat in a waiting area filled with Hispanic men, women, and children all looking at him. Josh smiles and takes out his smart phone. "Shit!" he says to himself. "So this is what marriage is going to be like?"

* * *

"Is this the painting?" Mr. Ying, an elderly Chinese gentleman, says to Michael as they stand in front of a covered canvas in the store. "Can I look at it?"

"Of course," Michael says, carefully pulling the cover up and off the painting.

"Beautiful! Unbelievable!" Mr. Ying says. "This is beyond my expectations. Where is the young man so I can personally congratulate him?"

"On his way to Los Angeles," Michael says. "He and I are partners."

"Then I should give you the money?" Mr. Ying asks.

"That's what he told me to do—take a check and deposit it immediately."

The elderly Chinese gentleman takes out a checkbook, uses a fountain pen, and hands a check to Michael. "That is the agreed upon amount, isn't it?" Mr. Ying asks.

"Yes sir. One million, five hundred thousand dollars," Michael says, his hands trembling. "That's a lot of money, period."

"Would you like me to go to the bank with you?" Mr. Ying asks.

"Would you mind?" Michael asks.

"Not at all. Let's make sure the store door is locked so no one can come in and take this most beautiful of all the world's portraits."

"Yes, sir."

* * *

Jasmine's screaming inside urgent care stops abruptly. In a few seconds, the female takes her seat behind the counter. "Sir," she says calmly in Josh's direction.

Josh walks to the counter. "She gave me her name and address. She said you would be responsible for payment. You are her husband or relative, aren't you?"

"Well, none of that yet," Josh says. "And I will pay whatever. What's wrong with her, anyway?"

"It seems your friend hasn't had a period for a couple of months. Whatever was inside all came out at once," the female says.

"The screaming and the pain?"

"The blood scared her, is my guess. She's okay now, resting and waiting for the doctor to determine what happened."

"Can I see her?"

"Go on back as long as you sign this paper making you the responsible party."

Josh sits on a chair beside Jasmine's bed. "You feeling better now?" Josh asks.

"Like a new person," Jasmine says. "I know it was a miscarriage. The doctor will tell us that. He'll also tell us how long we have to wait until we can get pregnant again."

"Pregnant again?" Josh says.

"After the wedding, we'll do it until we conceive again. It was the best feeling I've ever had."

A tall, handsome Hispanic man wearing a long, white coat walks into the room. "Miss Jasmine?" he asks with slightly broken English. "I am Doctor Silva. You have a problem?"

"That's my cue," Josh says standing up. "I'll wait outside."

Josh leaves the room and returns to the waiting area. He sits and looks at the sun setting through a window and then at the rabbit's foot dangling from the keys he is holding. "No fucking way!" he says out loud. He walks to the counter. "Do you have a piece of paper I can use to leave a note?"

*　　　*　　　*

"Special Agent Picard?" Vice-Chancellor Kris says into her cellphone. "Why haven't you called me?"

Picard sits with Lady Gretchen at the bar in the brothel. "I'm almost done with my investigation," he says, smiling.

"Get your ass back here and tell me what you found. It better be good."

"It's better than good," Picard says as Lady Gretchen rubs his arm. "You'll be back on top again."

"What are those sounds? Where are you?"

"I'm collecting the last bit of information now," Picard says. "There's a party going on, and the last person I'm interviewing will be free soon."

"Or very reasonable," Lady Gretchen mouths.

"I expect you in my office first thing tomorrow," Vice-Chancellor Kris says.

"I will be there, and I also want to talk about my daughter," Picard says. "You and I must reach an agreement before things get ugly."

"You want to see ugly? Don't show up, and I will show you ugly!"

"I am a special agent, Vice-Chancellor. I will take care of you if you take care of me."

"I will take care of you!" Lady Gretchen mouths.

"You bastard!" the vice-chancellor yells. "In the morning we will see who takes care of whom!"

*　　　*　　　*

Josh's old Honda speeds north on I-5, heading back to Berkeley. His cell rings. "You fucking bastard!" Jasmine yells. "What the fuck are you doing abandoning me in this shit hole?"

"You can get home with the credit card I left. There should be enough room on it that you haven't used already."

"I am going to sue you! My father is going to sue you! Your name will be mud, and you'll have nothing left when we get through."

"Better idea! Take the fucking credit card and stick it up your ass several times. You've been butt-fucking me for weeks with this pregnancy shit! It's over! Go marry yourself!"

"You bastard! You fucking asshole!"

Josh looks at the dangling rabbit's foot. "I belong elsewhere," he says. "Hope I'm back in time."

Chapter Fifty-Seven
The Last Hurrah

"All right, you bastards!" Bessie yells from the stove, holding her cleaver and waving it over her head. "This may be my last feast, so let's eat, drink, and be merry."

"But Mom, Jack R. Abbott got 'carve the turkey.' We're all going to get AIDS or herpes or something when he cuts off his finger."

"I've been practicing since last time," Jack says.

"That was twenty years ago," Bessie yells. "What the fuck have you been practicing on, one of your unfinished books?"

"Trust me," Doreen says. "You don't want to know."

"Jamal," Bessie yells. "You got 'prayer,' so get on with it."

"I don't know one," Jamal says.

"Shit!" Bessie yells. "God bless this fucking food! Let's eat. I have to do everything around here!"

"Amen," Mayor Sain says.

"I'm not very hungry," Babe says to Winnie. "I'm going back upstairs and lie down. Can you take 'pass out dessert' for me?"

"Sure. Maybe we should go to the doctor and see what's wrong."

"When we get to Kansas," Babe says.

"I thought we were going to stay here for the holidays," Winnie says.

"I am going home tomorrow whether you're on the plane with me or not," Babe says.

"I guess I'd better make reservations," Winnie says.

"I already got mine," Babe says. "If you're going, you'd better make 'em pretty fast."

Jack R. Abbott slices white meat off the turkey while everyone watches in anticipation. "Two joints says he cuts his pinky again," Jefferson says to Mayor Sain. "Three joints he cuts his middle finger."

"Can I get in on this?" Asia says. "I say he doesn't cut anything but the turkey."

"No way!" Mayor Sain says. "How about a side bet? And you have to pay off this time. No excuses."

"You never give up, do you?"

"Not when it comes to sex and Jack R. Abbott."

"Anyone want more Jack?" Doreen says. "That's what I drew."

"Jack for Jack?" Mayor Sain says.

Jack R. Abbott looks up and slices his pinky at the same time. Blood starts dripping on the white meat. "You distracted me!" Jack yells.

"Quick," Bessie yells. "Take the piece he bloodied off the plate. The rest will be good. No sense wasting a whole fucking turkey this time."

"I brought a couple of Band-Aids just in case," Doreen says, reaching into her pocket.

"That's two joints, Mr. Mayor," Jefferson says.

"And that's you and me later," Mayor Sain says to Asia.

"In your dreams," Asia says.

Babe pushes back, stands, and heads for the stairs. "What's the matter, Babe?" Bessie yells. "Can't stand the sight of blood?"

"She's feeling a little sick," Winnie says.

"I'd be sick, too, if I hadn't seen the dumb shit cut his hand before a couple of times," Bessie says. "Doreen, can you finish what your boyfriend started?"

"Michael," Mayor Sain says. "You and Sarah or Roni—"

"Dream," Sarah interrupts.

"—Dream," Mayor Sain continues, "have been real quiet. Everything okay?"

"Everything is great, sir," Michael says.

"He's your fucking father!" Bessie yells. "Call him Father or Dad, because he ain't no sir."

"I had a surprise for Josh, but he isn't here," Michael says. "I'll save it until I see him again."

"He's off getting married," Sarah says. "I hope he wrecks his car and drives off a cliff or something."

The kitchen door opens and Josh walks in. All eyes turn his way. "Any food left?" Josh says.

"Josh? What?" Sarah says.

"Come on, Surfer Boy," Bessie says. "Sit your ass down in Babe's chair and eat some of my finest. Stay away from the white meat, though. Jack R. Abbott drew 'carve the turkey,' and he did the usual."

"You were off to get married," Sarah says. "What happened?"

"I think I got a little lucky," Josh says. "Something about a rabbit's foot." He holds the key chain up.

"You got lucky at the store, too," Michael says. "The guy took the painting and gave us the money."

"You got $1,500,000 in cash around here?" Bessie says.

"It's already in the bank," Michael says.

"That means I am rich, too," Asia says.

"All right, everyone," Bessie says, holding up her water glass half-full of Jack. "Here's to all of us. We are all rich, because we have each other and we're together for the holidays."

"Here's to many, many more," Mayor Sain adds.

"I can only hope," Bessie says.

Chapter Fifty-Eight
Getting Out

"There's an airport shuttle outside," Bessie says as Winnie carries two suitcases down the stairs. "You and Babe gonna be gone when I die?"

"You seem okay to me. That was a great feast last night," Winnie says.

"I am about out of those fucking pills. When they're gone so am I."

"I told Asia to make sure you get more pills," Winnie says. "Just keep taking them like you're supposed to and cut back on the Jack, and you'll be here when we get back."

"When *he* gets back," Babe says, walking behind Winnie. "I don't know if I'm coming back or not."

"Well, then, give old Bessie a hug. It's been nice knowing you."

"Come on, Bessie," Winnie says. "If you think your time is up it will be. Think positive."

"How am I supposed to think positive with what's his name next door bugging me all the time?"

"Bessie, you're one of a kind," Babe says, hugging her tight.

"Go on, get out of here," Bessie says, with a slight quiver in her voice. "That fucking shuttle won't wait forever."

Mayor Sain walks into the kitchen. "See what I told you?" Bessie says. "Just can't leave me alone."

"You guys aren't really leaving, are you?" Mayor Sain says. "I got a recall getting underway, you got a criminal complaint, Jamal goes to trial pretty soon, and Mom's health is worrying us all."

"I'm only a couple of hours away," Winnie says. "If you need me during the holidays I can be here."

"What about you, Babe?" Mayor Sain asks. "The house will fall apart without you here."

"This may be good-bye," Babe says. "I don't know what's wrong with me, but I need to go home—and I mean to Lake Quivira."

"I hope it's nothing I have done," Mayor Sain says.

"Of course it is, you dumb shit," Bessie says. "Leave them be. They gotta go."

Babe gives Mayor Sain a big hug. "It's not you, Jim. It's me. I'll be back."

*　　　*　　　*

"Has a Mr. Picard called?" Vice-Chancellor Kris yells into her intercom.

"No, ma'am," her female assistant answers.

"When he does, show him in immediately."

"Yes, Vice-Chancellor."

The vice-chancellor's cell rings. "Special Agent Picard? It's Monday morning, and you are not here. We had an arrangement."

"I'm still in Virginia City. I am meeting with two more girls who said they had details about Lily Liu Lu. I should be back in a couple of days."

"Our deal was for you to return and give me the information I want. Otherwise, your daughter's days at the university are done."

"You can't do that! Finals are over, and she's on break."

"I can and I will. We are sending out failure notices as we speak."

"Do that and you will get nothing from me," Special Agent Picard says.

"Don't mess with me, Special Agent. Those that do always lose."

*　　　*　　　*

"Michael," Asia says, sitting at the block eating breakfast. "Any luck with your research?"

"Actually, I did find one guy who might be able to help, but I have to look into his work further."

"Great," Asia says. "I have a feeling we're gonna need to do something pretty quick."

"You two talking about me again?" Bessie yells with her back to the block. "Do it while you can. I ain't gonna be around too much longer."

"Don't talk like that, Grandma. We will find an answer."

"You don't know how long I have waited for someone to call me that," Bessie says. "Here, in my final hours, it finally happens."

Josh walks from the stairs. "Michael, Asia, Bessie," he says with a happy voice. "I'm sure glad to be back. What are you two doing?"

"Planning my funeral," Bessie yells. "Might as well join in the fun. It'll give you a whole bunch of new cartoons."

"That's right," Michael says. "I forgot to tell you. Your editor called and wants to drop *Veronica's Lives* and focus on *Ham 'n' Eggs*."

"Drop *Veronica*? Never," Josh says. "I'll talk to that son of a bitch. Where is she, by the way?"

"She left early to meet her friends," Bessie says. "They are going to the morgue. I told her to sign me up for a slab."

"Got to get her off those drugs," Asia says. "That's my job."

"Let me help," Josh says. "I want the naïve Sarah to come back."

"So do I," Michael says. "She's the nicest, sweetest, most beautiful girl I've ever known."

"Sounds like we've got a little competition in the air," Bessie says. "I'd like to stay around a little longer to see who wins."

*   *   *

Josh and Asia are alone in the living room. Josh touches her on the shoulder. "That was some sex a couple of nights ago. The best I ever had."

"That was just to get you into the mood to paint," Asia says.

"You mean … no repeats?" Josh asks.

"Right now I have too much on my mind," Asia says. "Maybe in the future, if I am still here."

"You can't leave," Josh says. "One of the reasons I came back was you."

"Sex! All men can think about is sex, sex, sex."

"There's sex and *sex*," Josh says. "And you are definitely *sex*."

"That's been the story of my life," Asia says. "Why did you *really* come back?"

"I now know what I want," Josh says. "I am going to stay around a little longer and see if I can get her to come back to me."

"You mean Sarah, of course," Asia says. "You've made a good choice, whenever she finally settles down."

"In the meantime," Josh says, "is there anything I can do for you, since we're financial partners of a sort?"

"Just hang onto that money. We may need it to take care of a few problems we have."

"Anything else?" Josh asks.

*   *   *

Sam, Winnie's driver, waits at baggage at Kansas City International Airport. Snow covers the ground outside and a chill fills the air. "Senator! Mrs. Churchill. Welcome home and merry Christmas."

"Merry Christmas," Babe says. "I feel better already. It's been only a month since we were here last. Seems like a year."

"How's mR. bERZERKELEY doing?" Sam asks.

"Nothing's changed with him, Sam," Winnie answers.

"Still walking around naked?"

"Every chance he gets."

The long, black limousine pulls into the Churchill's plowed driveway. Their estate glistens in the early evening snow.

"There's my home. There's where I live," Babe says. "Look! There's a Christmas tree all lit up!"

"Your daughter wanted to surprise you," Sam says. "They're waiting inside. They've been up all night."

Babe moves quickly from the limousine to the front door and inside. "Allison, Jennifer, Katrina. I missed you all so much."

Inside the limousine Winnie sits in the backseat. "She really wants out of Berkeley, doesn't she?" Sam says.

"I've never seen her so negative, Sam. She hasn't been herself for quite a while. I'm a little worried."

"The doctor's appointment you asked me to arrange is in the morning," Sam says. "I hope she's all right."

"We could be in for quite a surprise, Sam. It could change everything."

Part Six
Life Goes On

Chapter Fifty-Nine
Dreams

"That's beautiful!" Michael says, watching Josh at a canvas, painting the sun setting through the Golden Gate with dark clouds forming on the horizon and the ocean rolling.

"It's what I see when the mayor and I windsurf in the late afternoon. The wind is blowing, and the air is cool and the water cold on our naked bodies. It's hard to turn and go back to shore. There's times when I want to just keep going to see what's out there, what's behind those dark clouds, what distant shores the water touches."

"You don't need to be looking at what you are painting?" Michael says.

"It's all in my mind—a vision that doesn't fade away. I have used my memory to help a lot of people and make a lot of money."

"I just want to help Grandma," Michael says. "I want her to be around to see me paint like you, have children, and grow old."

"That's what life is all about, Michael. The past is the past. This painting is a snapshot of a time passed. You can't change what has gone before. You can cry over it, mourn a lot, blame, and point fingers, but what has gone before is a memory. The sun will rise every day and disappear in the evening. The water will rise with the incoming tide and fall and rise again. Those little cars will drive into the city in the morning and back at night and get ready to do it all over again tomorrow."

"There will never be another Grandmother," Michael says. "We must save her. And Sarah, Miss Asia, and my father—we must help them, too."

"We are doing our part, and we'll do more," Josh says, concentrating on the colors in the fading sun and the glistening sea. "We've got the money and the will and the dreams. Life will go on, and so will Hamilton House."

Chapter Sixty
Tears for Years

Asia's scooter stops at the top of the driveway after a quick trip to the laboratory to check on the liver cells. She takes off her helmet and walks inside the kitchen. Bessie sits at the block, sobbing. "Bessie!" Asia says, sitting down next to her and putting one arm around her shoulders.

"You better organize a farewell party soon," Bessie sobs. "I keep shitting my drawers and I can't stop. I'm wearing a fucking diaper! I'm sure it's time."

"Probably something you ate. That juice Stephanie and Judy brought back from Vichy Springs—what was it? Some concoction of herbs and veggies and fat-eating bacteria?"

"I tell you, I'm almost over. I can feel it in my gut. I swell up like a balloon, and then *swoosh*, the dam breaks and I pee like a racehorse. I know I'm through. And where is everyone who cares about me? Gone."

"Michael and Josh are drawing cartoons, Stephanie and Judy are at work, Sarah is probably over in the park with her Goth friends, Jamal is practicing basketball, and the mayor had an emergency meeting at city hall."

"Winnie and Babe abandoned me, too."

"They are back in Kansas, but you know they're coming back. No one is abandoning you."

Trojan pops in through the doggie door.

"Look, there's Trojan. He hasn't abandoned you, either."

"He would, if the little white puff next door was available. After years of taking care of everybody, who is here to take care of me? And who will take care of Hamilton House in a few days when I'm gone, China Girl?"

"I'm here, at least for now," Asia says. "I will never leave you, unless I have no other choice."

"Why would that happen? No one will take you away from me."

"I say live for the moment," Bessie. "You never know what might happen the next minute, the next hour, the next day. Might as well live every second to the max."

"Is there something you're not telling me?"

*   *   *

"Thank you for coming over, Miss Asia," Chancellor Lim says, sitting behind his desk in his office.

"I came as soon as you called, Chancellor. What's the problem?"

His voice starts to tremble and he holds back tears as he speaks. "What have you heard?"

"The vice-chancellor has sent someone to Virginia City again to try and dig up information on both of us. No problem. No one will be able to find anything on you. She is determined. We did keep records of our clients for tax purposes. I made sure that my book was destroyed. There should be no record."

"Should be?"

"She'd never get it. My friends will protect your honor."

"I can't sleep or eat. All I think about is the years I have put in to raise the money needed to make this university the best. If the word about some of my fund-raising activities gets out, I'll be a laughing stock and lose the best job anyone could have. I'll be destroyed. What can I do?"

"She hasn't come up with anything yet, Chancellor. Maybe a little Chinese luck can take care of both of us."

*   *   *

"What did the doctor say?" Winnie asks Babe, waiting in a doctor's outer office. "Why are you crying?"

"Wait until we get home," a sobbing Babe says.

They ride back to Lake Quivira in the limousine in silence. Babe works hard to keep from sobbing, wiping her eyes every few minutes. "Thanks, Sam," Winnie says as he closes the car door and waves. "I'll give you a call if we need a ride."

Babe walks inside and breaks out bawling as she throws her purse on a chair and walks to the kitchen. "Okay, what's wrong?" Winnie says. "Why all the tears?"

"You bastard," Babe says. "Look what you've done to me!'

"What are you talking about?"

"You knocked me up! I'm fifty years old, and you got me pregnant."

"That's wonderful," Winnie says, walking toward her.

"Stay away," Babe says, crying.

"Why? You're going to have a child, our child. Why cry? That's great news—a little surprising at our age, but great!"

"Not a baby, you bastard. Babies!"

"What? Twins?"

"Yes! Twins!" Babe cries as she walks to Winnie and throws her arms around him. "You're better than ever. Twins, you Berkeley bastard!"

Chapter Sixty-One
Try and Try Again

Asia's scooter speeds around curves on the winding road above the university and stops at the laboratory gate. Asia swipes a card and moves inside. She parks and walks to the door. Once inside, she sees the professor bending over a microscope. "How are they doing?" she says, out of breath.

"Just like this morning, these stem cells seem to be moving in the right direction, Miss Asia. But I'm afraid there won't be enough of them anytime soon to make any difference in a dying liver."

"There must be something you can do to boost their activity. You're the world's foremost scientist. Bessie has to live."

"I am the world's most foremost scientist. But I am not God."

"What am I supposed to do? She can't die."

"There is someone who might be able to help," Professor Spears says. "He used to work in the laboratory a long time ago. I heard he has done some pretty incredible things with stem cells."

"Who is he?"

"A former student, Ainsley Bassette. I've lost touch with him. I have no idea where you might find him."

"If he's that talented, he must be at some laboratory, some university."

"He's been terminated from every place he's worked. He has a horrible habit that he can't kick."

"What habit?"

"I'd rather not say. Find him and he might be able to help. Habit or no habit, he may be your only choice other than getting Bessie a new liver from a donor."

"The hospital administrator said flat-out no."

"Maybe you should keep trying," the professor says. "He's only a man, and you have a way with men."

"You're right," Asia says. "I will go to the hospital right now and ask him one more time."

"After you and I, you know?"

"It'll have to wait," Asia says. "I gotta help Bessie."

"A rain check?"

"You got it, professor. At least two."

*   *   *

Josh nudges Sarah, who is sitting at the block eating a sandwich. "You are pretty good with peanut butter and jelly," he says.

Sarah pushes the string of beads from the side of her face and tosses her black hair to the side so she can eat.

"You trying to hit on me?"

"Just trying to be friends again."

"You want to be friends?" Sarah says. "Get rid of that horrible cartoon about me, become a Goth, and get me some of those little pills. Other than that, you can keep being the asshole you have been forever."

"Come on," Josh says, nudging Sarah playfully again. "This whole Goth thing doesn't fit you. That bubbly, excited, beautiful young girl that loved life is still in there. She'll come out again."

"Not hardly! I hate life. The dead are beautiful. There's no excitement anymore. The only real fun is getting stoned and flying above ground."

"Can I paint you again?"

"Like you did Asia and your girlfriend? What a joke!"

"Just like you are," Josh says. "In your Gothness."

"I don't do naked anymore, and I don't do you."

"I'll give you time to come around. You do make a mean PB&J."

*   *   *

"Dr. Forman, please," Asia says, standing in front of a receptionist inside the hospital administrator's office.

"Do you have an appointment?"

"No. It's real important that he see me. It's life or death."

A middle-aged man of slight build and wearing a blue suit and black, horned-rimmed glasses walks from the office behind the receptionist's desk. "Sir," Asia asks, "Are you Dr. Forman?"

"Last time I checked," the man answers.

"I must see you. Someone important to many of us is about to die unless you give her priority for a liver transplant. Please see me."

"Come in, Miss …?"

"Asia."

"Please come in, Miss Asia."

The hospital administrator sits behind his desk. "Who? What?" he asks.

"Bessie Sain, the mayor's mother, is dying and needs a new liver. She has been admitted several times lately if you need to check records."

Dr. Forman uses his computer keyboard and searches the hospital database. "Ah, yes, Bessie Sain," he says sitting back. "She has been treated for cirrhosis recently. The outlook is not good."

"You've got to put her at the top of the list, Dr. Forman. She can't die."

"I see here there have been other requests of a similar nature on her behalf. They were all denied because of her age. We do not perform liver transplants on those seventy or older. It's against hospital policy."

"What if I bought one and made it available? Would you do it then?"

"That, too, is against hospital policy. Our insurance company would not allow it, and there's no surgeon that would risk a career to transplant a liver that has not been properly processed."

"Look," Asia says, loosening the buttons on her blouse so her large breasts hang out as she leans over and presses them on top of the administrator's desk. "I can take you places you have never been. I can do things men only dream of. I would be yours forever, anytime, anywhere."

"Well, Miss Asia," Dr. Forman says, trying to look away. "What you say would be very exciting and adventurous if I had an urge toward women. But, since I am an openly gay man, it doesn't do anything for me. I suggest you leave."

"Bessie will not die, sir!" Asia says with a firm voice. "I won't let her. Someway, somehow, there will be a transplant, even if I have to turn out the entire Berkeley community and run you out of town."

"Be my guest," the administrator says. "That has been tried before and failed. But it's Berkeley. Go for it."

"I just might," Asia says.

*   *   *

Michael works on his laptop at the store. Josh works on cartoons at his table. "What was that name Asia gave us?" Michael asks.

"Ainsley Bassette," Josh says.

"Bassette," Michael says. "I remember it was a dog of some kind."

"You tried to talk any sense into Sarah?" Josh asks.

"Nah," Michael says as he focuses on his laptop screen. "She's really way out there lately. I've got this hole in my head, and I'm normal compared to her."

"I figure it's just another one of her adventures," Josh says. "We've got to get her off this one. She could really hurt herself."

"Maybe we should turn our *Veronica's* into Goth tragedies or something dark to get her attention."

"Darby would freak out again," Josh says. "Things are pretty touchy in the cartoon business."

"The name Ainsley Bassette doesn't come up," Michael says. "Maybe I'm spelling it wrong."

"Try everything," Josh says. "'Dr. Ainsley Bassette,' 'Dr. A. Bassette,' 'I. M. A. Bassette'—anything you can think of."

"'I. M. A. Bassette'—that's a good one," Michael says as he works on the keyboard. "Look! An article on organ transplants comes up!"

"Where is he located?" Josh asks.

"He is listed as chief surgeon in Lafayette, Louisiana. But the article was written six years ago."

"Keep trying," Josh says. "A transplant is what we're after. We've got to find him!"

* * *

Asia sits at the block with Mayor Sain, Michael, Josh, Stephanie, Judy, Jamal, and Sarah. Trojan is busy humping Michael's leg. "Thanks, everyone, for meeting tonight after Bessie has gone to bed. She won't hear us because the pills have knocked her out. Bessie is dying and needs a new liver immediately. I can't grow stem cells fast enough, and the hospital administrator refuses to put her at the top of the transplant list. He won't even let me buy one and bring it in."

"What?" Mayor Sain says. "Wait till I get ahold of Dr. Forman. I'll ring his little neck until he gives in."

"He's pretty set in his ways," Asia says. "I threatened the biggest protest Berkeley has ever held, and he just shrugged his shoulders."

"Protest? I'll burn down the fucking place," Mayor Sain says. "I'll run his ass out of town on a rail. I'll get the naked people to chase all his patients away. I'll—"

"There is a real chance none of that will work," Asia says. "Bessie is in deep trouble. Michael, any luck finding the guy I told you about?"

"I'm still looking," Michael says. "He's dropped out of sight."

"Don't give up," Asia says. "That's one thing Bessie has taught us all."

"Worked for us during my reelection," Mayor Sain says.

"We'll ask around our community and see if anyone can help," Stephanie says.

"I'll pass the word at the high school," Jamal says.

"We'll work it into our cartoons," Josh says.

"We'll find one and someone who *will* put it in," Mayor Sain says. "Mom can't die on us."

"She did make a request," Asia says. "She wants a rocking party—or, as she calls it, her last New Year's party."

"I've got the song," Mayor Sain says. "I'll need all of you to practice with me."

"Why not?" Josh says. "If she wants a party, let's give her a party."

"Jäger and joints in my basement in ten," Mayor Sain says. "Let's do her proud!"

* * *

"What do you have for me?" Vice-Chancellor Kris says to Special Agent Picard, who is standing at the front door of her Victorian as the Campanile rings nine times in the cool night air. "It took you long enough."

"I had to spend a few extra days to make sure my information was correct."

"In a whorehouse?" she says, ushering him inside in front of her blazing fireplace.

"The scene of the crime," Picard says.

"What crime?" the vice-chancellor says, moving to the edge of a chair.

"First, before I give you the information on Miss Asia—or Lily Liu Lu, as she was called—I want to make sure you and I come to an understanding. You were the one that called me about my daughter's entrance status in the beginning. You said you were admitting her because you might need a favor from me one day. Isn't that correct?"

"Yes. Why are you bringing that up?"

"I want to make sure you don't threaten to expel her again if what I give you doesn't meet your need to terminate Miss Asia."

"I never make promises before I get what I am looking for," the vice-chancellor says, sitting back.

"You've done this before?" Special Agent Picard asks.

"I always get what I want," the vice-chancellor says. "I do what is necessary."

"So you have?" Picard asks.

"That's immaterial. What do you have for me on Miss Asia? If it's what I need to get even with her for all the trouble she has caused me and helps me get the goods on the chancellor, I might leave your daughter alone."

"This is blackmail, Vice-Chancellor Kris."

"Call it what you want. What do you have?"

Special Agent takes two pieces of paper from his inside coat pocket. "It seems your Miss Asia left Virginia City overnight after allegedly killing one of her customers. According to this newspaper account, she took out a pistol and shot the old man's genitals 'clean off,' neutering him on the spot before putting a bullet between his eyes." He hands a reproduction of the newspaper article to the vice-chancellor.

"Ouch! Anything else? Anything on the chancellor? Was he one of her customers?"

"A lot of folks remember several wealthy Chinese gentlemen visiting the ranch to have sex with Lily Liu Lu on several occasions. None of the names you gave me were familiar."

"They must have records."

"They do, but they wouldn't give them up. You'd have to get them some other way. I tried my best."

"I'll bet you did," the vice-chancellor says with a smirk. "That little devil! I'd bet this house on the fact that she and the chancellor had met before she came into his office a few months back."

"Is that enough for you to keep my daughter in the university?" Special Agent Picard asks.

"For now," Vice-Chancellor Kris says. "You gave me the goods on Miss Asia, but I'm after a bigger fish. No one talks to me like the chancellor did. He'll regret the day he threatened to fire me."

Special Agent Picard walks from the vice-chancellor's house, stops, and turns off the hidden tape recorder in his coat pocket. He smiles and walks off.

The vice-chancellor dials the phone. "Information? Virginia City? The sheriff's office, please."

* * *

"That call was from Asia," Winnie says to Babe upstairs in their Lake Quivira estate master suite. "She says Bessie is dying and there's no cure in sight. They are going to throw a huge last New Year's party in The Hole for her and say good-bye."

"I suppose you'll want to pack me up and head back there. Is that it, Governor?"

"At least I want to try," Winnie says, sitting on the bed. "She's been like a mother to me, and I know you think a lot of her."

"I do, poor woman. But I have a couple of little ones I'm thinking about now. Flying on airplanes isn't exactly what the doctor wants me to do."

"I've got to go back and see if there's any way I can help. I owe her that."

"You do what you have to. I'll be all right here. Katrina and the girls are moving in to help me."

"They are? What about her husband?"

"Nelson? He's off chasing an exotic pole dancer around Kansas. He hasn't been home for days."

"Nothing changes, does it?" Winston says.

"I knew you'd be off doing something—running for governor or God knows what. So I asked them to stay awhile."

"I hate to leave you like this. Pregnant. I can hardly believe it. I thought you had your tubes tied. Anything else you have been keeping from me?"

"Remember how sex-crazed I was when I was pregnant with Billy and Katrina?"

"How could I forget?" Winnie says.

"Well, with twins it's twice as bad. Are you sure you want to leave?"

* * *

Trojan walks around the corner of Hamilton House, headed for McPherson's. As he nears, he hears the doggie door open and Mimi's tiny bell ring as it touches heavy plastic. *Finally? Try and try again is my motto, especially when it comes to a moment's pleasure.*

He rounds a bush and comes face-to-face with several coyotes, fangs bared. *What the? I'm dust!*

The lights from Josh's old Honda shine directly in the coyotes' eyes as he approaches. Josh honks his horn and the coyotes scatter. *Saved by the horn! Love that Surfer Boy.*

Josh stops his car and Michael, sitting in the passenger seat, opens the door. "Get in, boy. You got to stay away from those coyotes."

Love Michael, too! Trojan hops into Michael's lap. *There's always another day. Those coyotes got off lucky again!*

* * *

"What do you mean Storey County won't issue a warrant for her arrest?" Vice-Chancellor Kris yells into the phone. "She shot off some old guy's dick and killed him, and you are going to let her walk?"

"Nothing was ever proved at the scene that it was her," an aging Sheriff Viscovich says. "The other girls said the guy she shot was beating up whores and knocking down doors. He was shot in self-defense by one of the girls."

"That's not what the newspaper article says. It cites one of the girls laying it all on Lily Liu Lu, who is now Miss Asia, an employee here at the university. Aren't you gonna at least investigate?"

"We got enough trouble up here, ma'am," Sheriff Viscovich says. "We got bikers taking off their clothes and parading through Virginia City, a bunch of religious zealots trying to close down the bordellos, and a group of computer freaks hacking into our slots. We don't have the time to look into the killing of some old crackpot who probably deserved to have his pecker shot off."

"You are a disgrace to law and order!" the vice-chancellor yells before she slams the phone down. She taps her long fingernails, thinking. She picks up the phone again and dials. "Bertha Potts? This is Vice-Chancellor Kris. You have any good legal contacts near Virginia City, Nevada? I think I might have something that will help you bring down Winston Churchill and his old buddy Mayor Sain. Can you help?"

*   *   *

Michael is sitting on his bed, busy at his laptop. Josh taps on his door. "You have any luck?"

"No," Michael says looking up. "This guy Ainsley Bassette has basically disappeared after publishing that article. I can't find him anywhere. What can we do?"

"I've been thinking," Josh says, leaning against the door jam. "You and I have the power to reach millions of people all over the planet. Maybe we should follow Bessie's advice and use what comes naturally, like I did when I started *mR. bERZERKELEY*."

"You mean start a new cartoon?"

"No. I mean, let's work the search for Ainsley Bassette into our cartoons starting immediately—like the naked mayor looking under a bush with the caption 'Where is Ainsley Bassette?'"

"Or searching a trash can or the sewer with the same question," Michael says, perking up.

"And the old lady in the rocking chair on Thursday, pregnant as hell, with the same question: 'Where is Ainsley Bassette?'" Josh says excitedly.

"And my Ham 'n' Eggs digging through a mountain of garbage with the same question: 'Where is Ainsley Bassette?'" Michael says.

"Let's get on it!" Josh says. "I'll do *bERZERKELEY* and you do *Veronica* and *Eggs*. I'll call Darby and tell him to hold for our stuff and put it in the papers starting tomorrow."

Chapter Sixty-Two
The Last New Year's Party

A SQUAD CAR ARRIVES in front of Hamilton House, windshield wipers moving slowly to clear the mist that fell as night arrived. "Come on, Mom," Mayor Sain says, walking into the kitchen, where Bessie sits at the block. "Our chariot has arrived."

"Chariot?" Bessie says. "That's what your fucking father said when we climbed into the backseat at the drive-in."

"The rest are already at the Hole. This is going to be one great party."

"The last New Year's party, you naked-ass commie."

"Winnie called and said he was arriving at eight tonight. The whole gang will be there."

"I didn't think Babe would show," Bessie says. "She's got more sense than to fly back just to party."

"Winnie said she would have, but there's been a complication with her health. He said he would tell us all about it."

"I still say she has more brains than all the rest."

Willie opens the kitchen door. "You need help, Mr. Mayor?"

"I don't need any help from you two," Bessie growls. "Just a long sleep, and that's coming pretty soon."

The squad car stops in front of the Hole. Mayor Sain helps Bessie from the backseat. "That's what I should have done fifty years ago," Bessie says. "Beat the shit out of your son-of-a-bitch father and be hauled off to jail in the backseat of a cop car."

"I'm glad you didn't, Mom. We couldn't have grown up like we did without you being the rock in all our lives."

"You're not going to get sentimental now, are you? We might as well get in the car and go back to Hamilton House."

"It's going to be the best party you ever had," Mayor Sain says.

"And the last," Bessie says. "Let's get it over with."

Mayor Sain helps her down the steps into The Hole, where Josh, Sarah, Michael, Stephanie, Judy, Jamal, Jefferson, Sylvia, Jack R. Abbott, and Doreen stand waiting. When the mayor opens the glass door, the cheering and clapping begins. "Yay for Bessie! Happy last New Year!"

"Take it easy!" Bessie yells. "I ain't dead yet."

Bessie walks to the head of a long table that has been set up in front of the pizza counter. Blue and gold crepe paper streamers hang from the ceiling. Willie grabs the mayor's arm and holds him back. "Did you see the cartoons today?" he asks.

"No. I didn't have time, making all the arrangements and finishing a special surprise for Mom."

"'Where's Ainsley Bassette?' was in all three."

"Ainsley Bassette? I haven't heard that name in years … decades. What are the boys doing?"

The mayor and Willie walk to Josh and Michael, who are standing off to one side waiting for Bessie to sit down. "Guys," Mayor Sain says. "What's with the cartoons and Ainsley Bassette?"

Asia is standing near and overhears the question. "He may be the only one who can save Bessie's life," Asia says. "We need to find him."

"You have to be kidding," Mayor Sain says. "Do you have any idea who and what Ainsley Bassette is?"

"No," Asia says. "What I do know is he has a radical way of treating a dying liver, and we need him here ASAP."

"He has one very bad habit," Mayor Sain says. "He's a habitual masturbator—and I do mean habitual."

"Remember that time in our chemistry class when Jessica wore that perfume and sent him into the chemicals locker and he got caught by Miss Davidson?" Willie says.

"Or the time he saw the big Swede's panties when she got up from her seat in history and he got caught beating his meat in the coat room by Principal Anderson," Mayor Sain says with a chuckle. "He lived in Hamilton House for a while until he got kicked out of the university for peeping in the girl's locker room while he did his deed. He did it so often we made him live in the basement so the rest of the boarders could sleep."

"I don't care what he has done," Asia says. "He may be our only hope."

"Does Bessie know?" Mayor Sain asks. "She made him wash his hands ten times a day. I don't think she'll want him working on her."

"Do you want us to stop the cartoons?" Josh says. "It's only been two days."

"We're getting a lot of hits on our Twitter account," Michael says. "No Ainsley Bassette, but lots of admirers."

"We might have to check out those tweets," Asia says. "One of them might actually know where he is."

"Ainsley Bassette, a life saver? Who would have believed? But he's not here, and we have a party to throw for Mom. What say we do it up right? Jäger and joints all around!" Mayor Sain yells.

The sound of the Campanile ringing eight times can barely be heard in the background as Winnie walks in. "I'll take one of each," he says, walking up to Mayor Sain. "I hear there's a party going on."

"Pooh, old buddy!" Mayor Sain yells giving Winnie a bear hug. "You made it!"

"I did. What's this about our old classmate Ainsely?" Winnie says, pulling a folded piece of paper from his pocket."

"It's a long story," Mayor Sain says. "Let's save it for at least two Jägers and joints."

"Made me look for a bar of soap and a wash basin," Winnie laughs. "The human testosterone machine!"

"Come on, old buddy. Sit next to me and Mom. This is gonna be fun. Hey, what's this I hear about Babe? She okay?"

"That'll be after three Jägers and joints—and Ainsley Bassette," Winnie says, sitting down.

"Okay, guys and girls!" Mayor Sain yells. "We got several different kinds of pizza, salad, and pasta. To get us going, I dug out an old home movie. Jefferson …"

Jefferson turns on an old projector and a sound Super 8 begins to flicker on a white wall. Winnie, Willie, and the mayor are having a water fight with hoses on the Hamilton House front lawn. "That looks like me," Jamal says.

"Why do you think I want you to make it?" Willie says to Jamal, who is sitting next to him. "We are like twins, and I don't want to see you go down the tubes like I did."

"That's the best mayor I ever had," a stoned Sylvia says, looking at Mayor Sain flex while being pummeled with water by Winnie.

The film turns to a young, curvy Bessie wearing a white dress with red flowers being soaked by Winnie, Willie, and Mayor Sain. Her nipples can be seen poking through the white fabric. She begins to strip as if she were listening to music. "That's my mom!" Mayor Sain yells.

"You were a real looker," Asia says. "No wonder the men chased you."

"I did most of the chasing, as I recall," Bessie says. "When the men would take one look at the bastard I gave birth to, they all took off."

"Bessie! You're hot!" Stephanie says.

"Maybe I *should* have gone lesbian!" Bessie says.

"Who's taking the pictures?" Josh asks. "If you are all in it, who is making this movie?"

"The whacker," Bessie says. "Got him out of the closet long enough to point the camera. After he saw me undressed he went back upstairs into a room."

"Ainsley Bassette?" Asia asks. "Got any pictures of him?"

"Never could get him to stand still long enough without thinking he's gonna use you like a *Playboy* centerfold."

The Super 8 pans the old Berkeley High School, downtown Shattuck Avenue, and the university stadium. Willie, in his football uniform, flexes his muscles. "I remember that shot," Willie says to Winnie. "That was just before my last game, the one where I busted my knee for good."

"We had a great party in the hospital, didn't we?" Mayor Sain says. "I snuck in joints and a couple of beers."

"I married your mother on crutches three days later," Willie says to Jamal. "I coulda been a pro if I hadn't busted myself up so bad and gave it all up for Esmeralda."

The film ends with Bessie sitting on the lawn and Mayor Sain playing his guitar and singing "Auld Lang Syne." "You had a great voice then too," Michael says.

"Thanks, son."

"You got any pictures of my mother?" Michael asks.

"She came later, much later," Mayor Sain answers. "I think they were still shots I used for target practice."

"What does Ainsley Bassette look like?" Asia asks Bessie.

"He's as tall as a tree, bent over slightly, weighs just enough to keep from blowing in the wind, and his hands are big and his fingers longer than knives," she says. "Of course, that's when he's not doing his thing behind closed doors somewhere. He makes our mutt seem like a saint!"

"He's really Bessie's only hope?" Winnie asks Mayor Sain.

"That's what our Chinese beauty thinks," Mayor Sain answers. "Can you imagine what he's gonna do when he first lays eyes on her?"

"What else you got to embarrass me with, you naked-ass commie?" Bessie says. "That was like watching my whole life fall apart in front of me."

"I've got another surprise." Jefferson turns on a video. "It's the sizzle reel the university guys made in hopes of landing a reality show."

Jefferson turns on the television and a recorder.

"You're gonna contaminate the airwaves with your shit!" Bessie says. "I can't wait until I get out of this life!"

The sizzle reel starts with naked Mayor Sain walking on Berkeley streets toward city hall past men, women, and children, who pay him no attention with the caption 'mR. bERZERKELEY on his way to do the people's business.' The opening follows with scenes of pickets protesting loss of the president's stimulus fund, the mayor feeding the homeless on Martin Luther King Jr. Way, the group singing "Axe, Axe, Axie" on the train to Palo Alto, the naked skydiver at the game and the mayor mooning the Stanford crowd, the celebration after the Big Game, and the members of Hamilton House sitting at the block with Trojan humping his leg.

"This is too painful to watch," Bessie says. "It's like having to eat secondhand garbage."

The sizzle reel closes with naked Mayor Sain and Josh windsurfing on the open sea from Manhattan Beach to Hermosa Beach and the answer to the question "What are you going to do now?": "Go to Disneyland, of course."

The final shot, with credits, shows pictures of the mayor as a baby, as a high school athlete, hanging from the Campanile, and mooning Splash Mountain. "This piece of shit will never make the big screen," Bessie says. "Thank God for little favors!"

"I thought it was the best movie I ever saw," a stoned Sylvia says.

"I got ideas for several books," Jack R. Abbott says.

"What did you think?" Josh asks Sarah, whose head is face down on the table.

"I think she's asleep," Asia says. "Been hitting those pills pretty hard."

"I am not either," Sarah says, sitting up quickly. "I can hear every word you've said. I'm just tired."

Winnie stands. "Here's a toast," he says. "To our infamous friend, neighbor, and now Hollywood star, Mayor Jim Sain—and the wonderful mother who brought him into this world."

"Hear, hear" is the response in unison before drinks are downed.

"This is supposed to be my party," Bessie says. "He's trying to take all the credit, just like always."

"Mom, we have a surprise for you."

"What now? A retroactive abortion?"

"We've been practicing a song, just for you. Okay, gang, let's arrange ourselves." Mayor Sain stands along with everyone except Winnie and Bessie. Signaling Jefferson, a soundtrack starts. Everyone is behind the mayor, forming a chorus.

"Every night in our dreams,
"We see you; we feel you.
"That is how we know you go on.
"Far across the distance
"and spaces between us,
"You have come to show you go on.

"Near, far,
"wherever you are,
"We believe that the heart does go on."

Customers sitting in booths away from the long table sing along as the music continues. Bessie, her face red, wipes small tears from her face.

"Josh, did you bring it?" Mayor Sain says at the song's conclusion.

Josh walks behind the counter and brings out an oil painting of Bessie. "That's beautiful," Asia says. "That's your best yet!"

"You should have seen the one I painted of you," Josh says to Asia.

"Maybe I shoulda worn her whoring outfit, too," Bessie says.

"Come on, Mom. Isn't it the best painting you've ever seen?"

"You can throw darts at it in a few days after I'm gone."

"No way," Mayor Sain says. "This will stay in my house with Michael and me."

"Time for the scrapbooks?" Jefferson asks.

"Sure," Mayor Sain says. "The party is just starting."

"Maybe for you," Bessie says. "I'm so tired I might just go to the morgue right now. But I have a few words to say myself."

Asia helps Bessie stand. "Okay, group. This is Bessie's last stand. First, I'll start with the lesbians, Stephanie and Judy. Yes, I know your names. I want to apologize for calling you 'the lesbians,' something I probably shoulda been myself. I wish you two the very best forever. Second, Josh, the great cartoonist and the sneakiest person ever to live at Hamilton House—if my naked-ass commie son had a room, you'd be number two—let your talents take you to wherever you want to go, and I don't mean to bed with every two-legged pussy you meet, like someone who will go unmentioned. Sarah—will someone wake up Sarah, our house druggie?"

"I am awake," Sarah says with her head on the table. "And my name is Dream, not Sarah—ugh!"

"Our little, formerly innocent Kansas beauty, who copies everything and everyone she sees, someday, you are gonna have to be yourself, a one-of-a-kind that copies no one and determines what she is, not what someone else wants her to be."

"I love you, Bessie," Sarah says, her head still on the table.

"Jamal," Bessie says, "my advice to you is to also be yourself. Don't get sucked into anything like a certain leech that has been hanging around Hamilton House since he was in high school. Start using that brain of yours instead of other body parts, like a certain other bastard that will go unnamed."

"Yes, ma'am." Jamal says. "I love you, too."

"Asia, China Girl," Bessie says, "you have been my inspiration and the only thing that's kept me going these past few months. You gave me a grandson, hope, and a friendship I will carry with me the few remaining hours of my life. My only advice is to stay away from the naked-ass commie who lives next door. Who knows where that pecker has been?"

"Bessie, you are the best!" Asia says.

"Willie the leech," Bessie says. "Forget all the bad things I've said about you these past forty years. Of course, there might not be anything left to think about. You've been the biggest appetite Hamilton House has ever seen. And you have the biggest heart sitting here at the table. Use that forgiveness that has always been inside you to take care of your prized possession. Jamal can be anything he wants if you stand at his side and help him. Got it?"

"Yes, ma'am. I love you, too," Willie says, wiping a small tear from his eye.

"Jack R. Abbott and Doreen, the odd couple," Bessie says. "You two have been my naked-ass commie son's friends for decades. Although I can't compliment you on your choice of friends, I can thank you for standing beside him and at least trying to keep him out of trouble. Jack, keep writing, and put the ashes of your first book in my urn. Doreen, stick a plug up the bulldog's ass for all of us, will you? I can smell him from across town."

"We love you, too," Doreen says.

"I will write the best book ever," Jack R. Abbott says. "I've got several choices to finish."

"Jefferson and Sylvia, more of my naked-ass commie's friends from way back. If things were different, I'd be calling Sylvia my son's wife. But you got smart and chose LSD instead. Probably would have turned out the same anyhow. And Jefferson, someday organize a protest that runs the bastard that calls himself my son out of town, will you please?"

"We love you, too," Jefferson says.

"You're the best mother-in-law I almost ever had," Sylvia slurs.

"Winnie the Pooh," Bessie says. "As your second mother, I must say I used all my good luck on you—a successful lawyer, politician, senator and maybe a governor. I followed your career from afar and wished my naked-ass commie would have done just a little of what you have done. You have made me proud. I only wish Babe were here so I could thank her for keeping you on the straight and narrow. She coulda given me a lot of tips over the years about what's-his-name."

"We love you, too," Winnie says. "Babe couldn't make it because she has a little problem—actually, two little problems. It seems I got a little excited returning to my birthplace."

"Are you telling us she's pregnant?" Mayor Sain says. "With twins?"

"That's what the doctor said a couple days ago. Guess it must be in the Berkeley water or something."

"Twin Poohs!" an excited Mayor Sain says. "That calls for another round of Jäger and joints."

"Judy and I have an announcement," Stephanie says. "We think we're pregnant, too."

"Pregnant lesbians! Twin Poohs! Life *will* march on without me!" Bessie says. "Give me one of those joints. It won't hurt what's left of my liver. Maybe give me something else, though."

"Didn't you forget a couple of people?" Asia asks.

"I can't," Bessie says. "I don't want to shed tears talking about Michael. And my naked-ass commie son—I've said enough about him already."

"That's okay, Mom," Mayor Sain says. "We know you love us, and we love you, too. You've been the best mom anyone could want."

"Grandma, too," Michael says. "I love you the most."

"Come on, Asia," Bessie says. "Call me a taxi and get me out of here before I have to take a shit and my diaper runs over."

"Yes, Bessie."

"Good night, everyone," Bessie says. "May the party continue forever."

Chapter Sixty-Three
Who Shot Johnny Blood?

EVERYONE STANDS AND CLAPS for Bessie as she hobbles out feebly, supported by Asia. They stop at a large scrapbook sitting on the counter. Bessie opens the book, and they stare at the picture of Johnny Blood on the first page. "There is the no-good prick that started this whole thing," Bessie says. "Let's get out of here before I do shit my drawers."

"He was a looker," Asia says. "No wonder you gave in."

"He was hung like a horse, but he was a horse's ass, if you know what I mean. No-good Johnny Blood. Johnny Blood—I hate that name. I'd like to thank whoever did him in. Saved me and the whole world from his sorry butt."

"Sounds like the son-of-a-bitch got what he deserved," Asia says, shaking slightly. "Come on, Bessie. Let's get you to bed."

Bessie can't see the look on Asia's face or the tiny beads of sweat forming on her forehead. The arm around Bessie's middle shakes slightly.

"What's the matter, China Girl? Old Bessie getting too heavy for you?"

"Just want to make sure you get home all right," Asia says. "You are very special, and I want to make sure you're comfortable."

"I'll be comfortable when I'm in that urn," Bessie says. "I only hope that fucking Johnny Blood's dick is still being barbequed in hell."

"You don't have to worry about that, Bessie. That's not where you're going."

"China Girl, you are the only one I can really trust."

Beads of sweat continue to form on Asia's forehead.

"You're from Virginia City, aren't you? My naked-ass commie son's fucked-up father was there. Did you ever hear of him?"

"His name does sound familiar."

"Johnny Blood. You'd never forget him if you ever met him. What a bastard!"

"Sounds like it, Bessie. Let's get you home to bed."

*　　　*　　　*

Sitting in his plush Reno office, lawyer Peter Smith talks into a speaker on his polished desk. "Vice-Chancellor Kris? This is Peter Smith. Bertha Potts said you had something I can help you with."

"Are you the lawyer Bertha Potts referred me to?" Vice-Chancellor Kris says.

"Yes."

"I am having a problem dealing with the Storey County sheriff, and I was hoping you could help me."

"You have a speeding ticket or get caught in one of the bordellos?"

"Hardly. I've never been to Virginia City. A university employee has not been forthcoming about her past. She grew up in Virginia City and was a prostitute. I have it on good authority she shot and killed a customer and disappeared, ending up here as a student and now an employee. I have been in contact with the sheriff, and he refuses to investigate. I find that appalling. Don't you?"

"The sheriff has that authority," Smith says. "He can do pretty much whatever he wants. If he doesn't want to go any further, he can do that."

"Isn't there something you can do to make him reopen the case? I mean, isn't murder the same in Virginia City as it is in the rest of the world?"

"What case are you referring to?"

"Look up 'who shot Johnny Blood' on your search engine, and the article will come up."

"Just a second, Vice-Chancellor."

Smith pauses. Someone is trying to cut through on the vice-chancellor's cell. She looks at the number and lets it go to voice mail.

"I remember that case," Smith says. "I read the article and am grabbing myself just thinking about getting my privates shot off."

"What can you do to get them to reopen the case and go after my employee?"

"Why does it matter? Apparently the sheriff had good reason not to pursue any leads. Your employee is safe. Why reopen the case?"

"It goes deeper than that," the vice-chancellor says. "I have every indication our employee, when she was a prostitute, was servicing several international clients, including, possibly, the university chancellor. As the university watchdog, I need to make sure nothing like that happened or could ever happen. Can you think of the harm it would do the university if such a scandal got out?"

"I see your point, Vice-Chancellor. Since the sheriff is an elected position and Virginia City is highly political, perhaps an inquiry from me about the possibility of the case receiving national exposure from a cold case script being developed for a television series would stir him to action. It really does sound like a good tale to me, no pun intended."

"Bertha was right. You are the one to make this happen."

"Bertha does have a way with words, doesn't she?"

Chapter Sixty-Four
Leper's Leap

On a small Bahamian island covered with scrub trees and bushes, bare-chested, full-bearded Ainsely Bassette stretches his six-foot-eight frame in a grass shack overlooking blue water. A warm morning breeze rustles his jet-black hair and the smell of wood burning in open fires causes his nose to twitch. "Doctor, Doctor," a half-naked young boy with black lesions on his face says, running toward him.

"What is it, Frog?" Bassette says as he yawns.

"It's Lizard. She's having fits again."

Ainsley grabs a black leather duffel bag and follows the young boy. They cross a hill and enter a wooden building. Several young children with black lesions on their half-naked bodies watch as Ainsley Bassette bends over a naked young woman covered from head to toe with black lesions, moving from side to side. He touches her forehead and takes out a syringe and a small vile. He withdraws a small amount of liquid and injects it into her leg. The young woman moves for a few moments and then relaxes. "She'll sleep and then be okay," Bassette says.

"Thank you, Doctor," Frog says, wrapping his arms around Ainsley's leg. "You have saved her."

Ainsely looks at the curvaceous, large-breasted, beautiful, black-haired, naked young lady covered with black lesions lying on the straw bed. "In the old days, that's not all I'd be doing."

Ainsley walks back to his hut. An older man with black lesions on his face carrying a stack of newspapers and a mailbag waits for him. "It's this week's mail and papers from Nassau, Doctor Lazurus."

"Thanks, Lion," Ainsley says. "They send any Jagermeister with the mail?"

"A case waits at the dock for you, Doctor, along with a crate of medical supplies."

"Great! I'd better go and bring them up here before all the animals decide to explore."

Ainsley walks to the dock and brings the case of Jäger to his shack. He opens the cardboard box and loads his almost empty floor freezer with the booze. He takes out a half-full bottle and downs a swig and then another. "Thank you, mR. bERZERKELEY, for bringing Jäger into my life."

"Oh," he says to himself, "almost forgot the medical supplies."

After stashing the supplies in a stand-up refrigerator, Ainsley sits down on a chair in front of the shack and opens a newspaper. "Let's see what good ol' Jim is up to today." He goes through the paper and comes to the cartoon section. He sees the naked mayor digging through a trash bin at People's Park and the caption "Where is Ainsley Bassette?" "My God! I don't believe it!" He looks at *Veronica's Lives* and sees the five-year-old girl peddling through a junkyard with the same caption. He looks at *Ham 'n' Eggs* and sees Eggbert walking into the humane society saying, "I wonder if Ainsley Bassette is in here?" "What is going on? I better see what mR. bERZERKELEY wants, but not before I finish my Jäger."

* * *

Josh sits at the block. Jamal is at the stove cooking eggs and bacon. "These smell real good," Josh says. "You've got all kinds of talent."

"I had plenty of practice at my mother's house. She stayed pretty busy at night, if you know what I mean. It was either learn how to cook or starve."

Mayor Sain and Michael walk into the kitchen from next door and sit at the block. "Guess we found Bessie's replacement already," Mayor Sain says.

"She's still sleeping off last night," Jamal says. "Asia asked if I would cook until she gets back from the laboratory."

"Smells really good, Jamal," Mayor Sain says.

"Have you looked at all the tweets?" Josh asks Michael.

"I did. What a bunch of wackos! There were several who said they were his wives."

"Who are we talking about?" Mayor Sain asks.

"Ainsley Bassette," Josh says. "We've already counted at least twenty children, and how many wives, Michael?"

"Six so far."

"I guess our Ainsley finally found out what it was used for," the mayor says.

"I heard Winnie say this Ainsley used to go to high school with you guys and even lived here for a while," Michael says.

"We also heard he had this problem," Jamal says.

"His father was a sheepherder, so he had plenty of females to keep him going all hours of the day and night. A gypsy woman happened by one day, and the world greeted Ainsley Bassette nine months later."

"Bassette?" Jamal asks.

"The gypsy's favorite dog with a French twist. His mother eventually made her way to Berkeley and took up tarot cards near the campus."

"Shit!" Josh says. "Sounds like a new cartoon strip to me."

"We have enough Ainsley stories to last several hours," Mayor Sain says. "And we will tell them all to you later, because I have to go to city hall. I've got a council meeting tonight, and the sheep are restless again. Gotta go!"

Mayor Sain leaves after grabbing two strips of bacon. "Ready for a big day at the drawing boards, Michael?" Josh asks.

"I'm ready. I also want to keep looking at the transplant doctors. Believe it or not, I found one that does ears."

"You don't want to get one, do you?" Josh asks.

"Michael," Jamal says, walking from the stove. "That wouldn't be you."

"I would like to look normal, like you and Josh," Michael says. "Two ears would be a start and cover up this hole in my head."

"We dig you just like you are," Jamal says. "No need to be different on my account."

"Thanks, guys. I don't want to do it for you. I want it for me. Maybe if I'm normal someone will look at me."

"You mean Sarah?" Josh says as he laughs. "All she's looking for is some more of those little pills and beads to string around her pale face."

"She will get away from all that stuff, won't she?" Michael asks.

Jamal and Josh look at each other. "We can only hope," Josh says.

* * *

A dressed Mayor Sain walks into his office. "Dressed? What's the occasion?" Queen asks. "You sick?"

"We've got a council meeting today, don't we?" Mayor Sain says. "I got to get my game face on. Might as well start with clothes."

"The BAA are demanding to meet with you before tonight."

"Is this about the upcoming bond election? We need to build an overpass so the handicapped can cross the freeway and enjoy the pier, the marina and the restaurants like everyone else."

"Also, there's some crazy kook that keeps calling for you saying you've been looking for him."

"Did he give you a name?"

"He refuses. He thinks the phones are tapped. He's the strangest one we've had in a long time."

"Got to be him," Mayor Sain says to himself. "Did he leave a number?"

"No. He'll probably call and bug me again, soon."

The phone rings. Queen picks it up and listens. "It's him. Want me to put him through or call the police?"

Mayor Sain goes inside his office and sits at his desk. He picks up the phone. "Ainsley, it that you? *Arf, arf!*"

"I haven't been barked at in years," Ainsley says, sitting in a chair in front of his shack. "I read you're looking for me, mR. bERZERKELEY."

"You still doing your thing, you old dog, you?"

"Finally found a place where I don't get the urge, at least not more than once a day," Ainsley says.

"Pooh and I were talking about the one time in chemistry," Mayor Sain says as he laughs.

"You guys start telling those kind of stories … I've got a bunch, too, like the time you climbed up the drainpipe to look into the girl's locker room and it broke. What do you want? Your phone isn't bugged, is it?"

"We are in desperate need of your talents," Mayor Sain says.

"Which talent?"

"You wrote an article a few years back about a new way to treat a dying liver."

"Oh, I thought …"

"Not that talent. We searched everywhere and couldn't find any trace of you. You just disappeared."

"My lifelong battle with my urge has caused me to move quickly. I have several wives and at least fifteen children I know about ready to string me up for back alimony, child support, you name it."

"Many of them responded to twitter. A whole lot of people want to find you."

"I am on an isolated island living with a leper colony. I keep them alive, and they keep me from wanting to, you know, do my thing 24-7. Those little black lesions on their bodies do something to my psyche, and I reach for my medical kit instead of my pecker. Works great most of the time."

"How do you survive?"

"I get all the food and drink I want and free housing—if you call a hut housing. And I get a lot of royalties from my books."

"What books?"

"Erotica, what else? I use several pen names. What's going on with you? Why the rush?"

"Bessie—Mom—needs your help, Ainsley," Mayor Sain says. "Without a new liver or some miracle she's going to leave us. Soon."

"Those dumplings were the best things I've ever tasted. They turned me on and almost made me want to—"

"She needs your help. Is there anything you can do?"

"I haven't dabbled with my theories in years. Over here there's been no need yet. And leaving would be impossible."

"Why impossible?"

"If I got caught they'd throw away the key. And I'd have to get there somehow. Can you imagine me on an airplane? Perfume? Beautiful—or even ugly—stewardesses? Even a large dog with a cute butt … I'd be on a no-fly list immediately."

"You've got to find a way, Ainsley. Mom will be dead if you don't."

"It will cost a lot of money, too. I need a team to work with me. You think the hospital will let us use their equipment?"

"You get here and we will take care of the rest."

"Thank you for turning me on to Jägermeister, mR. bERZERKELEY."

"Get out here and I will buy you a lifetime supply."

"Maybe a little gull dung for the nostrils, black tape over my sunglasses, and ear plugs? It might work."

* * *

"How are you feeling?" Winnie asks Babe.

"Other than the fact that you are in Berkeley and I'm lying naked in our soft, comfortable, plush bed overlooking a frozen lake, I'm fine," Babe says romantically.

"I'd be there in a moment and you'd have a couple more babies inside talking like that," Winnie says. "But I've still got a few things to wrap up here."

"How's Bessie?"

"She thinks she's a going to breathe her last at any moment," Winnie says as he sighs. "Asia gives her some time, but not much. I got to stay around a little longer to make sure everything is stabilized before I come back. Once Bessie gets into the hospital and we find a cook, then I can come back for a little while."

"Bertha is cranking up again," Babe says. "The paper ran an article about your criminal complaint and Gerry's daughter and Jim's recall caused by trying to help you."

"Leave it to her," Winnie says. "Nothing changes."

"I'm going to lie in bed all day. Katrina and the girls will move in tomorrow, and I'm worn out just thinking about what's next."

"I love you," Winnie says. "I'll call if anything exciting happens here."

"Are you kidding?" Babe says. "Everything is exciting there. That's why I'm here."

Chapter Sixty-Five
The Last Rodeo

THE JANUARY MORNING IS crisp and cold, and a layer of fog covers Berkeley, waiting for the sun to warm the air. Winnie, Mayor Sain, Josh, and Michael sit at the block waiting for Jamal to finish cooking eggs and bacon. "Where's Asia?" Mayor Sain asks. "Taking care of Mom?"

"In the bedroom with her," Winnie says. "Bessie was groaning all night. I could hear her through the vents."

"What about Sarah and the others?" Mayor Sain asks.

"The Goth never came home last night," Jamal says. "Or if she did, she snuck by my door like a ghost. I couldn't sleep either with the groaning going on. The lesbians? They left for some baby training class."

"He's already talking like Bessie," Mayor Sain says as he laughs. "Must have rubbed off on the stove or something."

"When you guys going to find another cook? I've got to start school in a couple of days, and I gotta get going. Finals are coming, and I'm student now."

"We are interviewing three possible cooks today," Winnie says.

"You talk to Alice Waters about using one of her subs?" Mayor Sain asks.

"I did, and she is the first one in about an hour," Winnie answers. "You gonna like gourmet breakfasts and healthy lunches and dinners?"

"I like Alice Waters," Mayor Sain says. "Anything she and Chez Panisse do is okay with me. I'll show her what I use to peel an artichoke."

"Speaking of the ridiculous," Winnie says, "have any of you heard from Ainsley Bassette?"

"The tweets are going wild," Michael says. "There's been at least seven different women who say if we heard from him they want to know so they can call the cops and have him arrested. We even heard from at least twenty others who say they are his children."

"Our editor has been calling about the use of the caption," Josh says. "He thinks we are going to get sued or something. The paper is being bombarded by the same ones who are tweeting us."

"I was going to save this for a surprise," Mayor Sain says. "And it is probably better that you don't know anything so you don't have to lie when asked. But the aforementioned Mr. Bassette did call me yesterday at city hall."

"I thought you were closed for the holidays."

"We had a special meeting of the council about the sheep's concerns over the bond for the handicapped overpass."

"I missed that one," Winnie says. "Babe and I must have talked for two hours on the phone. All I did was listen."

"Just like the council meeting. We listened and listened and listened."

"What did you do?" Winnie asks.

"Probably the same thing you did," Mayor Sain says. "Agreed to check on everything they mentioned and get back to them."

"Is he coming to save Bessie?" Michael asks.

"He's going to try. He's living on some island treating lepers. He's afraid if he leaves he might resort to his old ways and never make it here."

"He's taking a big risk coming," Josh says. "If anything gets out, he's history, reading the tweets."

"He'd come for Bessie," Winnie says. "She was both our mothers when we lost ours. I'm here, too."

Jamal walks from the stove carrying a steaming plate of eggs and bacon. "That's why I want to stay here, Mr. Churchill," he says. "You guys all care for each other. At my house it's nothing but arguing and fighting. When the court thing is all over, can I stay here?"

"You can stay here as long as you are allowed," Winnie says. "And that brings up another subject. I am going back to Kansas to take care of my better half. I need someone to take over and be house manager. I'll be back and forth, but someone needs to keep the lid on here, assuming this is Bessie's last rodeo."

"I don't want to even think about that," Mayor Sain says. "She'll recover. Something will happen. Bessie can't die."

"She can't," Michael says. "I just found my grandmother, and I don't want to lose her."

"I'll do it," Josh says. "Michael and I can keep the cartooning up either here or at the store. I'll watch both places for you."

"That'll be great, Josh," Winnie says. "And I have faith in your ability to keep an eye on Sarah, too."

"Now that is a whole other ballgame," Josh says.

"I'll keep my eyes on her," Michael says.

Asia comes running from the bedroom. "Can you guys call an ambulance? Bessie's ready."

"Is she ... dead?" Mayor Sain asks.

“No,” Asia says. “She’s resting, but it’s time to get her where they have the equipment and drugs and know how to take care of her.”

“How long?” Mayor Sain asks.

“I’m no expert,” Asia says. “They may be able to keep her alive for a few weeks longer. Any luck finding the guy?”

“He may be headed our way,” Mayor Sain says. “May or may not.”

“He is our only hope,” Asia says.

Chapter Sixty-Six
Grand Arrivals

"WHAT ARE YOU SNIVELING bastards doing hanging out here?" Bessie says, lying in a hospital bed and hooked up to machines and intravenous drip systems. "You come to watch an old lady kick the bucket?"

Mayor Sain, Winnie, and Asia sit in chairs in the private room. "We are going to be with you around the clock, Mom, just like we have the past week," Mayor Sain says. "We want to spend every minute with you."

"Can't you leave me alone for a little privacy?" Bessie says. "How am I supposed to take a pee? I gotta get used to being alone, anyhow. Why don't you perverts go out and do something positive, like feed the homeless or clean up the mutt's shit around Hamilton House?"

Michael, Stephanie, and Judy stand in the doorway.

"Shift change!" Bessie yells. "Get out of here so my grandson and the lesbians can have a seat. And when you come back bring me some Jack and cheese."

Mayor Sain, Winnie, Asia, and Michael stand at the door while Stephanie and Judy take seats. "Any news?" Mayor Sain asks.

"I keep searching everything," Michael says. "The tweets keep pouring in."

"More of Ainsley's wives and children?"

"Yes, sir. He has a lot of them."

"He *did* find out what it was used for," Winnie says.

"Where's Josh?" Mayor Sain asks.

"Our editor is supposed to call in a few minutes," Michael says. "He says it's urgent."

As a cold wind blows paper across Oxford, Josh sits in the store working on his laptop. His cell rings. "Yes, Darby? What do you want this time?"

"You guys have stirred up a national phenomenon with this Ainsley Bassette business. The media that carry your cartoons have been besieged with calls, e-mails, tweets about the guy—I assume Ainsley Bassette is a guy. The networks have been calling, too. They are in a bidding war to find out more and do specials. Who is this guy, anyway?"

"A figment of our imagination," Josh says, tongue in cheek. "What's it to you, anyhow? It's making you lots of money, isn't it?"

"Ainsley Bassette better be real!" Darby yells. "This is a money-making opportunity I don't want to pass up, and neither do my bosses."

"You are truly a cocksucker, Darby. Did you make friends with me in college just so you might use me to make money? Can't you lighten up and enjoy a little spoof? Go bug someone else. We can always take our cartoons elsewhere. mR. bERZERKELEY can buy another paper if he wants."

"Don't threaten me! Try any funny business—you and that hole-in-the-head kid—and you'll be blacklisted worldwide."

"Fuck you, Darby, and the horse you rode to work on!"

"There better be an Ainsley Bassette, that's all I have to say. Your career and my job depend on it."

"Fucking bastard!" Josh slams his cell shut.

Outside the store, Ainsley Bassette, looking like a full-bearded homeless man in a dirty, tattered, long black overcoat sits with a scrub cap turned up, waiting for a few coins. A large red bandana covers his nose and mouth. Large, blackened sunglasses cover his eyes. Earplugs dangle around his neck. Josh slams the store door shut, stops, drops a dollar bill in Ainsley's cap, and continues on to his old Honda parked a few steps away. "Fucking Darby," he says as he gets into the car. He speeds off toward Durant and heads to Hamilton House. Ainsley's eyes follow the car.

Winnie pulls the SUV into the driveway. Mayor Sain and Asia step out and inside Hamilton House, where Josh sits at the block drinking a beer, still fuming about Darby. "Got any more of those?" Mayor Sain asks. "I think I'm going to have a few beers, down a bottle of Jäger, and smoke several joints before I go back to the hospital. I love Mom, but she's becoming a real pain in the ass!"

"Sounds like turnabout is fair play," Winnie says.

"What are you so pissed about?" Asia asks Josh, sitting down beside him. "Your girlfriend call you or something?"

"I don't have one of those anymore," Josh says. "One of her sorority sisters said she ran off with the doctor that treated her and is enrolling at Cal State Bakersfield. It was our editor, my dear old friend. He's all over my case about Ainsley Bassette. He tried to get me to give him up and I wouldn't. His bosses and the networks want to do a big splash about finding him. It's all about money—like everything else."

"We don't want to do that," Winnie says. "That would scare him off for sure. You did the right thing."

"Knowing Darby, he won't give up, especially if it means a whole lot of money," Josh says after taking a gulp of beer.

Ainsley has followed the old Honda and stands at the kitchen door. Trojan walks up the steps, sniffs his tattered pants, and keeps on going through the doggy door. The noise causes the group to look at the door. The sight of Ainsley filling the doorway with his six-foot-eight frame sets them back. "What the?" Mayor Sain says.

"Want me to call Willie?" Asia asks.

"That's the homeless guy that was sitting in front of the store," Josh says. "Maybe he's hungry."

"I'll see what he wants," Mayor Sain says. "One of you grab Bessie's cleaver to back me up?"

Mayor Sain opens the door. "Can we help you?"

"Only if you got a fresh bottle of Jäger," Ainsley says. "What the fuck are you doing publishing my name all over the world?"

"Ainsley!" Mayor Sain yells. "It's you!"

Mayor Sain goes to shake his hand, thinks better of it, and gives him a slight bear hug. "It's all right, Jim. I washed my hands an hour ago. Wouldn't have been all right before that after I saw two naked lesbians getting it on in People's Park."

"Ainsley!" Winnie says, walking to the door. "Get your sorry ass in here. You look like shit!"

"It's good to see you, too, Pooh," Ainsley says, shaking Winnie's hand. His eyes turn to Asia. "Holy shit!" he says. "The basement still available?"

"Come over to my house," Mayor Sain says. "I got a change of clothes, a shower, plenty of Jäger and joints, and several rooms where you can take care of your frustrations after seeing China Girl."

"We have a lot of work to do," Asia says. "You won't be long, will you?"

"Shit!" Mayor Sain says. "You keep talking and he'll be holed up all day and night."

Mayor Sain pulls Ainsley toward his house across the driveway, forcing him to take his eyes off Asia.

"My God!" Josh says. "There *is* an Ainsley Bassette, and he looks like a comic strip all by himself!"

Trojan watches the mayor drag Ainsley across the driveway, looks at Josh and Asia's legs, and then decides to jump up on the couch and rest.

"The competition has arrived, eh, Trojan?" Josh says, patting the mutt on the head.

* * *

Sarah, dirt and grass covering her black clothes and pale face, walks in stoned and slams down hard in a seat at the block. "Is it morning or evening? I don't know."

"Shit! The druggie has arrived," Asia says.

"I tried out some little pink ones and blue ones and an oxi. I can't feel my feet. It was so neat." Sarah puts her head on the block and passes out.

Asia feels Sarah's pulse and listens carefully to her breathing. "I'd say she's asleep. An oxi? That's bad news."

"What can we do?" Josh asks.

"Maybe we should get her to the hospital," Winnie says.

"I'll put her in bed while we wait for Ainsley to come back over and talk about Bessie. You guys chill."

"Chill?" Winnie says. "That reminds me. I've got to call Babe and see how she's doing with the grandkids."

Asia lies in her bed looking up at the dark ceiling. She doesn't need her red outfit to bring a vision of holding a revolver and killing Johnny Blood, who fathered both she and the mayor. What will Bessie do when she finds out? What will Michael do when he finds out Johnny Blood was his grandfather and she is his aunt? What a tangled web she has spun! As she stares upward, she hears the sound of Sarah barfing. "That's good," she says to herself. "Get those drugs out of your system quick."

Asia opens Sarah's door and sees her in the bathroom on her knees, her face buried in the toilet while she barfs. She walks up to her and pats her on the back. "Get it all out, sweetie, every last bit."

"I feel so terrible!" Sarah cries before she vomits. "Am I going to die?"

"Isn't that what Goths think about? Death, dying, torture, and vampires? You want to be Goth, you gotta get with the program."

"I don't want to be like this!" Sarah cries just before she vomits again. "I *am* going to die."

Asia pulls her face out of the toilet bowl and looks at her eyes. "What else did you take?"

"They gave me this other pill in case I got sick!" Sarah cries. "I can't feel my body."

"Shit!"

Asia grabs Sarah's vomit-covered cell phone from the floor. "911? We need paramedics over here immediately. We got an overdose on our hands."

Sirens approach and stop in front of Hamilton House. Winnie runs down the stairs and sees Asia looking out the living room window. "What is going on?" Winnie asks.

Asia stands at the open front door and yells, "Send them in here!"

She turns to Winnie. "Our little Goth has OD'ed and needs to get to the hospital ASAP."

Two male paramedics rush up the stairs and into Sarah's room. "She's taken several pills and I'm guessing another dose of X," Asia says. "She needs it all pumped out immediately."

"You the girl's parent?" one attendant yells at Winnie.

"No, but I'll take responsibility for her. Get Sarah to the hospital! Now!"

*   *   *

Ainsley, Mayor Sain, Winnie, Michael, and Josh sit at the block. Asia, wearing black spots that look like lesions on her face and chest, sits across from Ainsley. "Thanks for wearing those, Miss Asia," Ainsley says. "Asia—what a pretty name!"

"Shit!" Mayor Sain says. "Even your name. We'll never get anything done!"

"It's okay," Ainsley says. "I just have to concentrate, and it will be hard—shit! I did it again."

"Come on," Asia says. "We got to talk about Bessie."

"You sure it's okay for Jamal to sit with her all night?" Mayor Sain asks.

"Willie is with him," Winnie says. "Stephanie and Judy are sitting with Sarah."

"Shit!" Mayor Sain says. "We got the whole hospital full."

"Look!" Asia says with authority. "Bessie needs a new liver, and we don't have much time."

"Or a liver to give her," Mayor Sain interjects.

"You are our only hope," Asia says, looking at Ainsley, who tries not to look into her eyes. "I read the paper you published a long time ago. You can help her. You're the only one."

"We need someone else with the same blood type and a lot of common DNA markers to give up enough liver stem cells to fire up Bessie's liver," Ainsley says. "I did it with pigs, and I know it will work with humans."

"I've been growing stem cells in Professor Spears's laboratory," Asia says. "He doesn't think there are enough of them."

"The professor?" Ainsley says. "I'll bet you make him wiggle and shake, too."

"Enough of the sex talk," Asia says. "This is serious business."

"I've got to see it," Ainsley says. "The cells, I mean. When can we go up there?"

"You could take him on the back of your scooter, but you'd never make it. You'd end up rolling around in the botanical gardens or some ditch," Mayor Sain says.

"We'll take the SUV," Winnie says.

"Is that it?" Asia says. "All we need are stem cells, same blood type, common DNA markers?"

"There is the little matter of finding a place to do the operation and a trained surgeon to do the work," Ainsley says.

"The work?" Asia asks.

"I do the talking; someone else who knows how to cut and slice does the work," Ainsley says.

"I doubt we'll have any volunteers around here," Winnie says. "The hospital is pretty tight, and when they hear about what they are going to do and who they are going to listen to—forget it."

"There is a surgeon who owes me big time," Ainsley says. "We could get him, but it will cost a lot of money."

Asia looks at Josh, who looks back. "We've got money. How much?"

"Probably a half mill," Ainsley says.

"That's a lot for a surgeon," Mayor Sain says.

"That's two hundred for him and three for me," Ainsley says. "I got wives and kids all over the globe to support. I give them a few bucks when one of my books hits big. This'll make them all happy … for a little while."

"Who is this guy?" Asia asks. "Michael'll look him up."

"Dr. Vernon Muler," Ainsley says. "He's chief surgeon over in San Francisco."

"Will he do it?"

"He'd better. He had a problem with one of his wives and mistresses at the same time. I promised them all sex therapy, and they dropped him like the plague, except for the one he really wanted to be with. A real who's who of San Francisco society."

"Sex therapy?" Winnies asks.

"Yes. I gave them sex 24-7-365. Knocked up two of them and turned the third lesbian. He owes me big time. Shit! We got a little time?"

* * *

Vice-Chancellor Kris, dressed in a red power suit with three-inch heels, walks into the chancellor's residence and is greeted by a doorman dressed in a black tuxedo. "The guests are waiting in the wine cellar, Vice-Chancellor," the doorman says, bowing slightly.

As she walks down the stairs into the cellar, all eyes are on her. Four

Chinese men stand talking to the chancellor while their wives talk to each other. The vice-chancellor walks up to the group of men. "Greetings from the academic side," she says. "I hope your visit has been pleasant."

"Vice-Chancellor Kris," the chancellor says. "These are my friends from China. You met them a few months ago."

"Yes, I did. Mr. Ling, Mr. Yen, Mr. Chee, Mr. Wong. I did get all your names right, didn't I?"

"You have a very good memory, Vice-Chancellor," Mr. Ling says, bowing slightly.

"Yes, I do. And when I want to find out something, I know how to find it out."

"Very noble and helpful to the chancellor," Mr. Yen says with a slight bow.

"What major projects are you doing, Vice-Chancellor?" Mr. Chee says with a slight bow.

"I am studying Nevada. Have any of you heard of Virginia City?"

"Isn't that where silver was discovered in the west?" Mr. Wong says, also bowing slightly.

"Yes. It is a very unique city, and I am going to find out all about it—its past and present, where visitors come from and why, and what contributions it has made to the history of America and its institutions such as this university."

"As I said, Vice-Chancellor, a very noble undertaking," Mr. Ling says.

"Have you ever been to Virginia City, Chancellor?"

"I have, Vice-Chancellor. Have you?"

"No, but I'm going there soon."

An African American man in a tuxedo rings a chime. "Dinner is served."

"It seems we are being called to dinner, my friends," the chancellor says. "Vice-Chancellor, can you join us?"

"I can only stay for a moment," the vice-chancellor says. "I am meeting with some investigators on a very important matter in a few minutes. You all enjoy your meal. The chancellor only gives his guests the finest experiences, as you all know."

"Thank you, Vice-Chancellor," the chancellor says.

"Oh, would you mind?" the vice-chancellor says, taking out her cell phone. "This is one picture I will hang on my wall." She snaps a photo. "Thanks, gentlemen."

The vice-chancellor leaves the five men, who watch her as she saunters up the wine cellar stairs.

"What are we going to do?" Mr. Ling says in Mandarin.

"We are all in big trouble," Mr. Yen says, also in Mandarin.

"She knows!" Mr. Chee says.

"Everything!" Mr. Wong says.

"I will call Miss Asia after dinner," the chancellor responds. "I will find out the truth."

*　　　*　　　*

"I knew there's no way I could fly with my, shall we say, unique situation. So I hopped on a freighter and got off in Mexico. Then I rode a bus to the border and snuck across with some illegals. I rode with the men all night to Stockton and hitchhiked with two truckers to Oakland. I walked from the wharf."

"You didn't have any problems?" Winnie says, steering his SUV around curves on the road to the laboratory with Ainsley sitting next to him.

"None, except for this beautiful Spanish dancer that was sneaking over. Do we have time to stop before we hit the professor's laboratory?"

"We don't have time!" Asia yells from the backseat, picking at the black lesions pasted on her face.

"Just once?" Mayor Sain says from the backseat. "That's a record for you."

"Well, there was another time in the back of the van on the way to Stockton."

"Think about Bessie," Asia says. "You've got to think about Bessie."

"I used to when she was younger. She had a hell of a shape. Sure you can't make one short stop?"

"Here's the laboratory gate," Winnie says pulling in and stopping. "Asia, can you get us in?"

Asia uses her card and the gate opens. "I'll bet the professor will be surprised to see me," Ainsley says.

Asia punches in a code and opens the door. The professor walks to them as they all enter. "What a surprise!" Professor Spears says, reaching to shake Ainsley's hand but thinking better. "To what do I owe this pleasure? The whole group!"

"Mr. Bassette wants to look at the liver stem cells you and I have been growing," Asia says.

"Miss Asia. What are you afflicted with?"

"Nothing, Professor Spears. Mr. Bassette insisted I wear them to keep him from getting excited looking at me."

"Just her name—Asia—turns me on," Ainsley says. "Can I use the bathroom for a moment?"

"I see nothing's changed," Professor Spears says.

"We have to look at the cells, professor," Mayor Sain says. "Ainsley needs to know if there are enough to save Mom's life."

"Follow me."

Ainsley looks in the microscope for several minutes. He pokes a metal rod into the mass. "I hate to say it, folks. Those are the finest liver stem cells I have ever seen, but there are hardly enough of them to make a difference. I haven't seen Bessie's liver, but I'm guessing there's only a little left that can function. These would give her a slight boost, but not enough to keep her alive for long."

"You mean Mom's going to die?"

"Not unless you can find me a cell mass that's a whole lot bigger, with the same blood type and a lot of common DNA markers, like I said before."

Asia looks at the flash drive on her key chain. She walks to a computer and puts it in. She stares at the data. "I'd say we have at least one possibility," she says, walking back to the group.

"What?" Mayor Sain asks.

"You."

"Me?"

"You have the same blood type, and you are her son, giving you a lot of the same DNA markers."

"She's right," Ainsley says. "But if we have to take too much of your liver to meld into hers, you might die. It's very risky for both of you. I'd say, knowing how much you have abused your liver, it's probably out of the question."

"Maybe not," Asia says, looking at data again. "There another possibility."

"No," Mayor Sain says. "You are talking about Michael, aren't you?"

"He's young and hasn't been abusing his liver," Asia says. "I'll bet there's enough stem cells between the two of you to restart Bessie's liver and give her a new life."

"Maybe," Ainsley says. "But the risk is the same. I have to remove most of Bessie's liver, a lot of the mayor's, and enough of Michael's, meld them all together, and hope the mass regenerates to save Bessie life—and that the remaining cells in both the mayor and Michael regenerate and keep them alive. A grand challenge and enough to turn me on just thinking about it."

"How do you meld them together?" Professor Spears asks.

"I think you're looking at it," Ainsley says, staring at the liver stem cells through the microscope again. "These are so hot! They'll be like superglue!"

"I don't want Michael touched," Mayor Sain says. "If there's a chance he might die I don't want to take it. He deserves to live a long and glorious life whether Bessie or I are here with him or not. I just can't do it."

"mR. bERZERKELEY would rather die than take a chance?" Ainsley says. "Come on. Trust old Ainsley. I haven't let you down before, have I?"

"Oh, please," Mayor Sain says. "Do we have time to tell all the stories?"

"I say we ask Michael and let him make the decision," Asia says. "I'd say we have a plan."

"Now that we have a plan," Ainsley says, "can I use the bathroom?"

*   *   *

"I walked right up to them and did everything but tell them I know about their little game with Miss Lily Liu Lu," the vice-chancellor says into her cell phone, sitting in front of her fireplace and holding a glass of red wine. "I'll bet their little peckers twitched and turned and shriveled listening to my every word. And the chancellor—I'll bet he shit his drawers!"

"I got the picture you sent," Peter Smith says. "I'll have one of my investigators nose around Virginia City and see if any of them are recognized."

"I'd appreciate it if you did it yourself," Vice-Chancellor Kris says. "I don't want anyone else to know what is going on. I want this to be a big surprise—the biggest—the grandest! I'll show the chancellor he can't treat me like a second-class citizen."

"Is that what this is all about?" Smith says. "Revenge?"

"That's right," the vice-chancellor says. "No one takes me down."

Chapter Sixty-Seven
The Type

WINNIE, MAYOR SAIN, AND Michael sit at the block waiting for breakfast. "Are you sure you don't want me to cook?" Jamal says, walking from the stairs.

"No," Winnie answers. "We want you to get to school early, go into the library, and study for finals. That's the most important thing right now. The temporary cook we hired will show, I hope."

"I'll get off early and head to the hospital to sit with Bessie," Jamal says.

"No!" Winnie says emphatically. "Josh, Asia, Stephanie, and Judy are there with Bessie and Sarah. You've got a big job to do: study."

"Yes, sir."

"Your trial is coming up, and we need to prove you are now giving it your all. Study!"

"Yes, Mr. Churchill."

Jamal leaves through the kitchen door, almost stepping on Trojan coming in. Trojan looks at the set of legs at the block and heads toward Michael. The door is shut and, almost as quickly, reopened by Ainsley. Trojan sees him walk in, stops heading for Michael's leg, and goes to the couch to lie down and watch.

"Where's the food? I'm starved," Ainsley says. "I had quite a night!"

"We heard," Mayor Sain says. "I almost barked like the old days. *Arf, arf!*"

"Have you talked to Michael yet?" Ainsley asks.

"About what?" Michael says.

"About saving Bessie's life."

"I was about to," Mayor Sain says. "I was hoping we would have something to eat first."

"Michael," Winnie says, "we have a very important question to ask you."

"No," Mayor Sain says. "It's out of the question."

"What do you want, Mr. Churchill?"

"It seems there is a possibility that Bessie can be saved by Ainsley here if he can take enough liver cells from someone else and put them in Bessie's liver. It seems both you and your father have the right type of blood and enough DNA markers to do the job."

"It's out of the question, Winnie," Mayor Sain says. "I will never consent."

"Your father is going to give all the cells he can to Bessie. It might not be enough, and it also might injure your father's liver to the point it won't be enough to keep him alive."

"So you need some from me?" Michael says. "You don't even have to ask. Of course you can use whatever you need."

"It could be very dangerous for both of you," Ainsley says. "It's highly experimental, and if I take too much, you will never recover."

"I will never consent," Mayor Sain says. "Let's not talk about it anymore."

"I am eighteen, and I don't need your consent," Michael says. "Without question, I want to save Bessie's life."

There is a knock at the front door, interrupting the serious discussion. Winnie stands and heads to answer. "Yes?" he says, looking at a balding, six-foot, four-hundred-pound individual with rolls of fat hanging in front, dressed in white chef's clothing.

"Hello. Is this Hamilton House? I was sent by the agency to cook for you."

"This is Hamilton House, and we need a cook. Come on in."

"Thanks. My name is Jessica. It used to be Jesse, but when the 151 I was using on the Bananas Foster burned the wrong banana, I had it lopped off and became a woman—a bald-headed woman, can you imagine? I hope that doesn't scare you off."

"Jessica, around here, you have no idea how normal what you just told me sounds," Winnie says. "Can you cook?"

"Oh, yes. You want to see my credentials?" Jessica starts to dig under a roll of fat.

"No. We have hungry men to feed and a trip to the hospital to make. I'll show you to the kitchen."

Winnie leads a hobbling Jessica to the kitchen. "You all right?" Winnie says.

"They left me my right nut to have fun once in a while, and it rubs me a little when I walk. No problem."

"Jessica," Winnie says. "This is Mayor Sain, his son Michael, and our house guest, Mr.?"

"Lazurus," Ainsley interrupts. "Mr. Lazurus."

"And over on the couch is our house dog Trojan."

Trojan looks at Jessica, starts to get off the couch to sniff her legs, looks at her again, and lies back down.

"Mayor Sain?" Jessica says. "I've always wanted to meet you. I love your naked people and those great cartoons. Can I get you to write 'mR. bERZERKELEY' on my uniform just above the crotch?"

"Sure, why not?"

"The refrigerator is stocked, and we're very hungry," Winnie says. "They'll be others over later after they get back from the hospital."

"Do you have a bathroom I could use? The walk from BART almost killed me, and I don't want to poop all over the potatoes, as they say."

"That's Bessie's room," Winnie says. "There's a bathroom inside."

"Thank you. A tinkle in time save's nine!"

Jessica walks into Bessie's room. "Want to mount that one?" Mayor Sain asks Ainsley.

"She just set me back at least an hour."

"She used to be Jesse until her dick burned off," Winnie says. "And when they gave her a sex change they left one testicle dangling."

"Shit! Sounds like several more cartoons for Josh and Michael," Mayor Sain says.

"Josh and I were talking, and we're going to end the 'where is Ainsley Bassete' idea now that you've shown up," Michael says.

"No, no, don't do that," Ainsley says. "If they stop, the vultures will know I *did* show and come looking. Keep 'em going as long as you have ideas."

"Around here, the ideas never stop," Winnie says.

"Where did you get her or him or whatever?" Mayor Sain asks.

"Alice didn't have anyone available, and the other two cooks never showed up," Winnie says. "I used the local temp agency."

Jessica reappears. "Well, that was a pleasant experience. Took ten pounds off. I feel like a new person. What'll you all have for breakfast?"

"I think I'll eat at the hospital," Winnie says.

"Me too," Michael says.

"Not me," Mayor Sain says. "Give me your best stuff, whatever it is. I am starved and so is Mr. Lazurus."

"I make an unbelievable eggs Benedict and links. You boys ready for the best and most luscious sausage you ever tasted?"

"Shit!" Ainsley says. "You mind if I use Bessie's bathroom?"

* * *

"How is she doing?" Asia asks a male doctor walking away from a sleeping Sarah in the intensive care unit.

"She coming out of it," the doctor says. "She took enough drugs to kill an elephant. With the black clothes, white makeup, and jet-black hair, she looks the type."

"She's blonde, beautiful, full of life, and fresh out of immaturity and innocence," Asia says. "Damn drugs. I've seen it all."

"Those piercings new?"

"Piercings, beads, hair dye—all new. A few weeks ago she was a lesbian, and now she's a Goth. She went to the Big Game and wanted to play a tuba. I have no idea what's next."

"She'll be released soon, once the drugs are clear. You think she'll go back to them?"

"Can you do us a big favor, Doctor? Can you keep her a little longer, maybe have her room with someone that might get her out of the Goth stage?"

"We'll have to clear it with her insurance, but yes, we can do that."

"She's quite a girl, and we need to keep her around. I know two boys that want to make sure she recovers."

* * *

Josh, Winnie, Michael, and Asia sit in Bessie's room, trying to keep from laughing as Bessie's loud snoring shakes the curtains. She wakes suddenly. "What the fuck? You still here? What are those little black things on your face?" she says to Asia.

"It's a long story, but it's the only thing that keeps Ainsley from doing his thing," Asia says.

"He's here?" Bessie asks. "Has he washed his hands?"

"He came a long way to save you," Winnie says.

"He comes all the time," Bessie says.

"We want to talk to you about something," Winnie says. "He might have a way to save your life."

"You find a transplant?" Bessie asks. "Probably one of my naked-ass commie son's homeless winos. What good would it do trading one dead liver for another?"

"We have been to the laboratory and looked at the liver cells Professor Spears has been growing," Asia says. "Ainsley says they are the best he's ever seen, but there are not enough of them to make a difference. He needs a whole lot more."

"I don't want that boy touching me," Bessie says. "I'd probably get pregnant."

"We have found enough cells to make a difference," Asia says. "Both your son and Michael together can possibly bring your liver back to life."

"Take from my son? If I did, I'd go around all day scratching my crotch and checking out every skirt in town. And Michael—what would it do to him? I don't want to do anything to hurt my only grandson."

"It is the only way to give you a possibility of surviving, Bessie," Asia says. "You do want to live, don't you?"

"I'll have to think about it," Bessie says. "I don't want the whacker to touch me or have any part of my naked-ass commie son inside of me. And I don't want to take a chance at hurting Michael. You've given me a lot to think about."

"You mind if Michael and I go and see Sarah?" Josh asks.

"I heard the nurses talking about the druggie that came in," Bessie says. "Is that Sarah?"

"Yes," Winnie says. "She's in pretty bad shape."

"Probably better than me if I give in to Ainsley's plan."

* * *

"Where's Sarah?" Michael and Josh ask a female nurse as they look at the empty bed she occupied.

"She's been moved to room 1111," the nurse answers. "We're keeping her here under observation until she's completely recovered."

"Can we see her?" Michael asks.

"Of course."

Michael and Josh walk down a long hallway to room 1111. Sarah is sleeping. Across from her is another patient with a marine's uniform folded across a chair. "She your friend?" the female marine asks.

"Yes," Josh says. "We're all from Hamilton House."

"I expected some folks in black and beads and voodoo dolls," the marine says. "My name is Captain Axelrod, or Lady X as the troops call me behind my back."

"That's what got her in trouble," Josh says. "X."

"Bad stuff," the captain says. "Drugs can take it all out of you. Is that what happened to her?"

"Pretty much," Josh says. "I hope it's all over when she wakes up."

"We want the old Sarah back, or Roni, or whatever she wants to call herself," Michael says.

“Are you guys talking about me?” Sarah says opening her eyes. “My name is Dream.”

“Sarah,” Josh says. “I am so glad you’re okay.”

“Okay? I’m in prison here. They won’t let me out to see my friends.”

“We’ll take care of you,” Michael says.

“You guys don’t understand. The Goths—they love me. They will be my friends forever.”

“Hon,” Captain Axelrod says. “There haven’t been any of your Goth friends coming to visit you the past two days. Just these guys and a few others from that place you live.”

“Who are you?” Sarah says. “Have I been in the same room with you for a while?”

“I am Captain Axelrod. I am a marine.”

“What’s wrong with you?”

“I had a hysterectomy. Seems crawling around in Afghanistan did things that weren’t supposed to happen. Might as well get rid of it anyhow. I never want children.”

“Maybe we should leave the two of you alone to have girl talk,” Josh says. “We’ve got to save Bessie.”

“You can leave her in my hands, boys,” Axelrod says. “Lady X will protect her.”

*   *   *

Ainsley sits alone at the block. Jessica works at the stove. “How many more are there?” Jessica asks.

“Make enough for ten. You never know how many will show up. You do know how to make dumplings, don’t you?”

“I heard about Bessie’s specialty. I don’t think I want to compete. I make a mean shepherd’s pie.”

“Shit! My father was a shepherd. Screwed himself to death.”

“Fucking?”

“No, he was doing the ram’s favorite, and out of nowhere, he was knocked on his ass and run over by the herd.”

“Sounds like my type of man,” Jessica says. “I make excellent pigs in a blanket, too.”

“That reminds me too much of this chick I knew in Guatemala,” Ainsley says. “Wrapped her snatch in a tortilla and served it for breakfast. You do anything like that?”

“You ever do a one-balled transsexual that hasn’t had any for months?”

"No. But there's always the first time."

*　　　　*　　　　*

"Miss Asia?" the chancellor says on his cell phone, sitting in his wine cellar with four Chinese gentlemen. "We need to talk to you immediately."

Asia, sitting on her bed, talks slowly. "Yes, Chancellor. What's the matter? Need more help raising funds?"

"The vice-chancellor knows," the chancellor says. "She came to a party we were having last night and basically told us she knows about our trips to see you in Virginia City and raising money. She knows."

"Vice-Chancellor," Asia says, "she knows nothing. She's the type that wants to let you think she knows. There is no way she can prove you or any of your friends visited me."

"She took our picture. I'd bet she has someone talking to everyone in town trying to identify us."

"Chancellor, you and your guys came into the ranch in a limousine and left in a limousine. No one saw you except the girls at the ranch, and they are all sworn to secrecy for a lot of reasons. You are safe."

"You don't know the vice-chancellor. She will stop at nothing to get the goods on you and me. You must guarantee that no matter what she does, you will not give us up."

"Chancellor, that will never happen. You are safe. But you know our Chinese custom. Someday I will call on you and collect."

"Yes, Miss Asia. We are aware you have us over a barrel, so to speak. But we are willing to make that deal to save our lives, our families, and the university."

"Chancellor, tell your friends Asia will never let you or them down. The vice-chancellor may be a snake in the grass, but I'm not that type. I never go back on my word."

Chapter Sixty-Eight
Promises, Promises

"What happened to Jessica the cook?" Winnie asks Ainsley, who is frying burgers and pouring Jägermeister on top of them as he, Mayor Sain, Michael, and Josh walk into the kitchen.

"I saw her or him or whatever hobbling down Durant toward Oxford, holding his ball and screaming."

"What did you do?" Winnie says.

"I was demonstrating my donut-hole-making technique on the soufflé."

"Shit!" Mayor Sain says. "You did that once to Bessie, and she threw the cleaver at you."

"There's no time to call the agency," Winnie says.

"I'm making my special burgers and onion rings," Ainsley says. "I was going to show Jessica how I peeled the onions with no hands, but that's when she or he took off."

Winnie looks at the deep fryer and the onion rings dancing in the boiling oil. "I think I might go over to Chez Panisse and talk to Alice about a sub," he says.

"Me too," Josh says, watching Ainsley scratch his butt with a free hand. "You need some help convincing her, don't you? And we need to talk about this house manager idea."

"You guys go ahead," Mayor Sain says. "Michael and I are going to have the feast of a lifetime. Imagine. Jäger burgers and deep-fried onion rings. What a treat. Maybe Ainsley should take over the cooking duties."

Winnie and Josh look at each other. "You're the house manager now," Winnie says to Josh with a smile.

"Let's go see Alice Waters," Josh says.

"When you come back, we need to talk about the operation," Mayor Sain says to Winnie. "If it's as dangerous as Ainsley says, I need to make sure Berkeley is going to stay Berkeley if I don't make it. I need a few promises from everyone!"

"When we get back, it's a deal," Winnie says. "Anything but taking over the naked people."

"Chicken!" Mayor Sain yells as they leave. "Come on, Ainsley. Michael and I are starved."

"How does he make donuts, anyhow?" Michael asks.

* * *

Asia, Jamal, and Willie sit with Bessie in her hospital room as she eats food from a tray. "Goddamn hospital food!" she yells. "I need my spices, a little grease, and a jug of Jack to make it even close to edible."

"You have to do what the doctors and nurses want," Asia says. "You have to hang on a little longer while they get ready to do the operation."

"I don't know if I really want to go through with it. I don't mind my naked-ass commie son possibly giving up his life for me; he got me into this mess. But Michael? I don't want to hurt his chances of a long and happy life."

"He'll be okay," Asia says. "I promise."

"You need to promise me that you'll stay around and keep the house from falling apart while I recover, won't you? And if I don't make it, you'll make sure Hamilton House goes on forever, won't you?"

"I will, Bessie. I will," Asia says. "Winnie has asked Josh to be house manager while he's away. Josh and I will take care of everything."

"I will too," Jamal says. "I already feel like part of the family."

"I will always look out for Hamilton House," Willie says. "We will keep all the memories going forever."

"And you will keep your fucking hands off Jamal here, won't you?" Bessie says to Willie.

"Yes, ma'am, I promise," Willie says. "He's been a changed person since he moved in. He'll have no problem with me. I can't promise the same for his mother. But for me, I'm going to be a doting father."

"Now I just need promises from Kansas," Bessie says. "Which room is she in?"

"Stephanie and Judy are with her," Asia says. "I'll get her on the phone."

Asia dials room 1111. She waits a moment. "Stephanie? Is Sarah awake? Bessie wants to talk to her."

"She's moving around in her bed, but she's still out of it," Stephanie says.

"Please tell her to call Bessie when she wakes. Room 222."

Asia hangs up the phone. "She will call, Bessie. Stephanie will make sure."

"Those lesbians turned out to be pretty good girls, didn't they?" Bessie says. "And they are both pregnant? What happened? The immaculate conception twice?"

"I had a little hand in it," Asia says.

"I thought it was a different part of the body," Bessie says. "Shit! I did it the hard way—and I do mean hard—with good old Johnny Blood."

"The conversation is getting kinda rough," Willie says. "Come on, Jamal. Let's grab a burger at Oscar's. I hear Ainsley is cooking, and I know what that means."

"Ainsley Bassette is using my stove? Shit! When he was younger it got all stuck up and burned. He had better wash his hands this time."

*　　　*　　　*

"Chez Panisse is closed already," Winnie says. "I didn't realize it was that late."

"I know a place around the corner on Walnut," Josh says. "Jasmine and I used to stop by before and after, if you know what I mean."

"I was young once," Winnie says.

They walk up Shattuck, turn east on Vine, walk to Walnut, and turn south. "Chester's? Looks like my kind of place," Winnie says.

They walk inside. The bartender sees them. "Josh—mR. bERZERKELEY—haven't seen you in a while. Where's the hottie?"

"Hugh," Josh says, reaching out to shake. "I dumped her in Bakersfield. I'm a free man again. This is Mr. Churchill—Winnie."

"I remember you from the cartoons," Hugh says as he sticks out his hand to shake. "You're mR. bERZERKELEY's best friend."

"We go way back," Winnie says. "Way back."

"What do you guys want to eat or drink? It's on the house."

"I promised Josh a great meal to celebrate him being in charge of Hamilton House while I'm back in Kansas."

"We have a really good menu and the best cook in town," Hugh says. "Have a seat. I'll get the menu."

"The best cook in town?" Josh says. "Maybe I should take a look."

Josh follows Hugh toward the rear of Chester's and looks into the kitchen, where a gaunt African American female of average height with black hair in cornrows wrapped around her head stands in front of a stove. Josh walks back to the bar, where Winnie sits drinking a cold beer. "Well?" Winnie asks as Josh sits down in front of his beer.

"Cute, wiry, and muscular-looking," Josh says.

"Maybe we should see if she can cook," Winnie says. "Let's order a bunch of different items and check her out. You don't think she'd let the mayor and Ainsley get to her, do you?"

"If she's half as tough as she looks, there's no way."

*　　　*　　　*

"What does she want, anyway?" Sarah says, sitting up in her hospital bed.

"She wants to talk to you," Judy says. "Maybe she wants to say goodbye."

"That's so sad," Sarah says. "How can I do that?"

"Hey," Captain Axelrod says from the next bed. "You got to be tough if you want to be a marine. Do what you have to do and suck it up and then cry later."

"You want to be a marine?" Stephanie says. "That's so cool. I wish I would have thought of that."

"There's no way I'm going to let you leave me alone," Judy says, putting an arm around her shoulder. "Besides, we've got other responsibilities on the way."

"That's right!" Sarah says. "It wasn't my imagination. You're both pregnant. You've got to promise me I can help pick out names."

"You two are pregnant?" the captain says. "I thought ..."

"We are lesbians," Stephanie says.

"And proud of it," Judy adds.

"Lesbian mothers," the captain says. "Now that's a real responsibility."

"Can I get pregnant and still be a marine?" Sarah asks.

"Having a baby might get in the way," the captain says. "But anything is possible when you serve your country."

"How neat!" Sarah says.

"You gonna call Bessie?" Stephanie asks.

"I am! I am going to be a marine, and I promise to be rough and tough like Captain Axelrod and defend my country's honor against all sorts of bad people. Give me the phone!"

*　　　*　　　*

Ainsley sits in the kitchen at the block eating a burger and drinking Jägermeister when Winnie and Josh walk in. Trojan lies on the couch, watching. The mutt thinks about getting up and humping an incoming leg but doesn't budge, wanting to see what will happen next. "Where's the group?" Winnie asks, pulling up a chair.

"Jim went next door to grab a couple of juicy ones, and the rest aren't back from the hospital. I've got their food warming."

Mayor Sain walks into the kitchen. "Hey, guys. You made it back. How was sweet Alice?"

"Her place was closed, so we went around the corner," Winnie says. "We think we found a cook."

"You are replacing me?" Ainsley says. "I was going to prepare a special soufflé in the morning covered with roasted huckleberries dipped in chocolate without using my hands."

"We don't have to ask what body parts you are going to use, do we?" Winnie asks.

"You guys take away all the fun," Ainsley says.

"You've got to get ready for the operation of a lifetime—my lifetime, Bessie's, and Michael's," Mayor Sain says. "What say we hop in the SUV, go down to the pier like the old days, and smoke these juicy ones out at the end?"

"I'm game," Ainsley says. "Last time I was out there, I thought I saw a mermaid, and well, you know what happened next."

"I think I will pass," Josh says. "I've got several cartoons to catch up on. The operation still on for tomorrow night?"

"Yes, it is," Ainsley says. "And don't forget to keep up the 'where's Ainsley Bassette' scam."

"I promise."

*　　　*　　　*

Willie and Jamal sit in a squad car eating thick, juicy hamburgers. "You really are turning over a new leaf?" Willie says to Jamal. "You're not just jivin' the folks like you have been doing your whole life?"

"I promise. I am a new person. Those people—Mr. and Mrs. Churchill, Bessie, the mayor, Josh, Michael, the lovers—they are all free and smart and using everything they got to do good things. Sarah or Roni or Dream? She'll straighten out. I know it. And Miss Asia? She is not only smart; she's wise. I want to be like her."

"What about Ainsley Bassette?"

"Well, I guess there's got to be one," Jamal says as he laughs.

"You are right about that," Willie says as he laughs. "He's been freaky since high school. Never saw, smelled, or heard anything or anyone that he didn't want to do his thing thinking about."

"I am going to straighten out my grades, get back into shape, and see what happens," Jamal says. "I am going to make you proud again."

"Promise?" Willie asks.
"Promise."

*   *   *

Ainsley, Winnie and Mayor Sain stand at the end of the Berkeley pier, smoking joints and taking hits from the mayor's bottle of Jägermeister. San Francisco's lights dance in the cool night to the enjoyment of twinkling stars and a full moon overhead. "Here we are, thirty years later," Mayor Sain says. "Who would want to be anywhere else? A beautiful night, the ocean under our feet, great joints, Jägermeister, and best friends."

"I agree," Winnie says. "But I've got a pregnant wife lying in bed naked at our estate on a lake in Kansas."

"You gotta stop talking like that," Ainsley says. "The bathroom is at the other end of the pier."

"Sorry, I forgot," Winnie says.

"When you gonna get ED or something to turn a page on that habit of yours?" Mayor Sain asks.

"Don't mention those initials in my presence," Ainsley says. "My dick has a mind of its own and may turn on me."

"Your brain and your dick are the same thing," Mayor Sain says.

"I was born with it," Ainsley says. "I hear I got hard when I hit the air and saw a female nurse attending my mother."

"You've got to promise me you'll at least come back and visit Mom if I don't make it," Mayor Sain says.

"I can't make that promise," Ainsley says taking a hit. "If I get caught, they'll throw me in the slammer forever. What I can promise is I will do my very best to pull off this operation tomorrow."

"And you, Pooh—you got to promise that you will become the next mayor of Berkeley if I don't make it. A new mR. bERZERKELEY!"

"That will be difficult with a certain person demanding to have our babies in Kansas. But for you, I will make that promise. What about the others?"

"I got Mom to promise she will swear at a picture of me every day of her life if she makes it and I don't. Michael promises to smoke a joint, drink Jägermeister, run my beer and pizza place, and join the Black Hole if he makes it and I don't. Jefferson promises to take care of Sylvia forever. Jack R. Abbott promises to finish a book and dedicate it to me. And Doreen promises to make one of her special casseroles and put a portion inside my urn. Stephanie and Judy promised to consider *Jim* if one of their babies is a boy, and Miss Kansas is so out of it I didn't even try."

"What about Asia?" Winnie asks.

"She promises to go through with the deal we made before the Big Game if I make it."

"What deal was that?" Ainsley asks.

"I probably shouldn't tell you," Mayor Sain says. "You'll be running toward the bathroom holding your dick. I don't want to fire up your imagination any further."

"It's okay," Ainsley says. "It's already been a good day."

Chapter Sixty-Nine
Operation Liver or Let Live

WINNIE LIES IN BED talking on his cell. "I couldn't sleep all night. How about you?"

"Like a baby," Babe says. "The wind off the lake was whistling through the windows all night, and the morning sun was bright and beautiful off the ice."

"I am more than ready to get back to Kansas," Winnie says. "Today is going to be either the best day ever or a complete disaster. At breakfast, Ainsley is going over his plan—which he calls 'Operation Liver or Let Live,' believe it or not."

"Someday I would like to meet that one," Babe says.

"No, I don't think you would," Winnie says as a buzzer rings.

"Was that what I think it was?" Babe says. "It's only 6:30 out there, isn't it?"

"Yes, it is, and yes, that was the doorbell. I have to get downstairs. I'll call you later and give you an update. I love you."

"I love you too. Good luck today."

Winnie throws on a robe and hustles down the stairs. "Got to get that elevator," he says as he jumps the last two steps and heads for the front door.

The wiry, muscular African American female cook he and Josh saw last night is standing on the porch carrying one small male baby. Another little boy is wrapping his arms around one of her legs.

"Good morning," Winnie says.

"Good morning, Mr. Churchill," she says. "I'm Jazzleen, and these are my two baby boys, Rhashan and Devontae. I hope you don't mind. I can't afford a babysitter, and my grandmother is very ill."

"Come on in. Jazzleen, is it? Let me show you the kitchen."

Winnie holds the door while the young woman walks inside. The young boy holding on to his mother's leg lets loose and runs inside toward Trojan, who is napping on the couch. "Doggy, doggy!" the young boy yells, grabbing Trojan's ears.

"Devontae!" Jazzleen yells. "Get away from that mutt. He may bite your little black ass, and I won't be able to take care of you while I cook."

Stephanie and Judy, ready for work, are walking down the stairs. "Look!" Stephanie says. "Babies!"

"Could you girls take care of them for a few minutes while our new cook gets us some breakfast?"

"We would love to," Judy says. "A little advance practice couldn't hurt."

"I got a bottle for Rhashan in my backpack on the porch," Jazzleen says. "He'll drink it cold."

"Got it," Stephanie says. "What a treat!"

"Excuse me while I go back upstairs and get dressed," Winnie says. "The kitchen is fully stocked."

"You care what I make?" Jazzleen asks.

"Surprise us," Stephanie says.

*   *   *

Mayor Sain, Michael, and Ainsley sit at the table in the mayor's kitchen. "You have to fast all day," Ainsley says. "Both of you. Your lives depends on it."

"No food, no drink, no joints?" Mayor Sain whines. "What'll we do?"

"Do what I do when I need to take my mind off my stomach," Ainsley says.

"All day?" Mayor Sain whines again as his cell rings. "Yes?" He hands the cell to Ainsley after answering. "It's for you."

"I gave your number to Vernon. I hope you don't mind."

"I am starved and thirsty," Mayor Sain says as Ainsley takes the cell.

"I'm going to draw cartoons all day," Michael says. "Maybe you can help me."

"Shit!" Mayor Sain says. "I guess I can go to the basement and play my instrument."

"I told you that's what I do to take my mind off my stomach," Ainsley says.

"Shit!" Mayor Sain says as he slides back from the table.

"Vernon, listen to me," Ainsley says with a stern tone. "You get over to the hospital by ten o'clock sharp. I don't care what or who you're supposed to be doing tonight. Everything is set up, the room has been booked in your name, and an assistant and nurses have been hired. You have to show up. You hear me? Show up or else."

"The doctor who is going to do the operation on us?" Michael asks as he watches Ainsley slam the cell shut.

"Prima donnas—all prima donnas," Ainsley says angrily and then changes his tone. "Donna, I remember her. Michael, can you excuse me for a moment?"

*　　　*　　　*

Winnie walks down the stairs and over to the block where Stephanie and Judy are feeding Jazzleen's babies. Josh is helping Jazzleen with breakfast. Jamal follows Winnie to the block.

"What do we have for breakfast?" Winnie asks, sniffing at smells that have never existed before in Bessie's kitchen.

"Fried hush puppies, garlic mashed potatoes, and liver and onions," Jazzleen says as she turns around. "Just stuff I found in the refrigerator. I'm still looking for some meat."

"Jazzleen?" Jamal says. "What are you doing here?"

"Jamal! You live here, too?"

"You two know each other?" Winnie asks.

"She was in my classes at Berkeley High as a freshman," Jamal says. "It looks like I know why she dropped out."

"Sit down and enjoy a little soul food breakfast," Jazzleen says. "You and I can catch up later."

"I've never eaten breakfast like this," Winnie says.

"I know," Jazzleen answers. "For some of my folks, this is the only meal they get all day, so they get it while they can."

"I thought of the liver," Josh says. "It's appropriate, don't you think?"

The kitchen door opens and Ainsley walks in. "Well, what do we have here? Day care?"

"This is Jazzleen, our temporary cook," Winnie says.

"Holy shit! I'll be right back," Ainsley says, walking out of the kitchen.

*　　　*　　　*

The rest of the day is a mixture of soul-searching, contemplation, and anticipation mixed with the constant bitching of a starved Mayor Sain. Finally the time has come and darkness has fallen over Berkeley and the Bay as the Campanile rings eight times. Winnie, Mayor Sain, Michael, and Ainsley sit at the block. "Pooh, we'll drive to the hospital and drop off Jim and Michael and then go to Ashby BART to pick up Vernon Muler. Josh and Asia are already at the hospital making sure all arrangements have been made and paid for, and Bessie is ready."

"You sure about all this?" Mayor Sain asks.

"Don't chicken out on me now," Ainsley says. "Operation Liver or Let Live is in full swing." Ainsley burps.

"That smelled like onions to me," a starving Mayor Sain says.

"The best soul food I've ever gotten indigestion from," Ainsley says.

"You are a cock, Ainsley Bassette," Mayor Sain says. "A real big one!"

"Keep talking like that and you'll put the plan off schedule," Ainsley replies.

"Shit!" Mayor Sain says.

"Let's go!" Ainsley yells, heading for the door.

The SUV stops at the hospital. Mayor Sain and Michael greet Asia and Josh. "How did it go inside?" Ainsley asks from the passenger side.

"Everything is set," Asia says. "We had a lot of trouble with the CEO, but apparently your friend Dr. Muler had called him."

"The money up front also helped a lot," Josh says.

"Great," Ainsley says. "Get them inside, prepped, and ready."

"How's Mom?" Mayor Sain asks.

"She has been spewing more one liners than you can believe. I got enough good stuff for a whole year's worth of mR. bERZERKELEYs."

"Let's go," Ainsley says. "BART from the city should be arriving."

The SUV waits at the curb on Adeline. A tall, tanned, muscular man in a long black overcoat carrying a doctor's small satchel walks up the steps from BART. "There!" Ainsley says pointing at the man. "That's Vernon Muler."

Winnie pulls the SUV up to the man. "Get in the fucking car," Ainsley says through an open window.

"Good to see you again, too," Muler says to Ainsley as he climbs into the backseat.

"This is my old high school friend, Winston Churchill," Ainsley says. "You ready to travel where no man has gone before?"

"When this is over, you and I have settled all scores," an angry Vernon Muler says.

"Agreed, you cheating bastard," Ainsley says. "Teach you to keep your stethoscope around your neck and not in some chick's pussy."

"Hearing you talk like that and not grab for your dick is encouraging," Muler says.

"I am focused," Ainsely says. "Besides, there'll be a lot of time later after this is over."

"You want me to do what at the hospital?" Muler says.

"It's simple," Ainsely says as the SUV moves up Ashby toward Telegraph. "With me guiding you, remove some of the dying liver from the mayor's mother. Remove some of the mayor's liver and some of his son's and attach them like superglue to what's left of the mayor's mother's liver using some of the finest liver stem cells I have ever seen."

"Oh, is that all?" Vernon Muler says as he laughs. "Has this ever been done before?"

"I did it several times years back on pigs," Ainsley says.

"On pigs? Shit! Did they live?"

"All but one, but it was the best bacon I ever tasted," Ainsley says.

"Shit! Why don't you do it yourself?" Muler asks.

"I am not licensed anymore in California, and the hospital would shut the doors on me fast. That's why I need you."

"My friend the hospital administrator isn't very happy about all this, as you know. I had to assume all liability in writing."

"Piece of cake," Ainsley says as they pull into the hospital parking garage. "Go to the top and park next to the edge closest to the hospital."

"Why?" Muler asks.

"You are going to wear this," Ainsley says, handing a small device to Muler. "It's a video camera and picks up sound. Wear it around your head so I can see and hear. I will talk to you through this earpiece." Ainsely hands Muler a wireless earpiece.

"You are not going to be next to me in surgery?"

"No. Just in case of any trouble, I will be sitting right here. Got it?"

"You are crazy," Muler says.

"Just think," Ainsley says. "No more blackmail from me. Isn't that a wonderful thought?"

"Shit!" Muler says as he gets out of the SUV.

"You sure about all this?" Winnie says.

"Trust me," Ainsley says. "Go inside and keep everything running smoothly like you always try to do."

"Okay," Winnie says, reaching for the door. "I'll see you when this is over, and we'll talk about old times."

"If I'm still here," Ainsley says. "If not, think about me the next time you smoke a juicy one and have a glass of Jäger."

Ainsley puts out a hand to shake. Winnie starts to shake and pulls back. "It's okay, Pooh. I washed my hands before we left Hamilton House out of pure habit."

"You get the traveler's checks from Asia?" Winnie asks.

"In my pocket," Ainsley says. "Signed and ready to go."

"Travel safe, old friend," Winnie says, shaking his hand. "I hope our paths cross again."

"Maybe when you become governor of Kansas."

"Shit!" Winnie says as he leaves the car.

Chapter Seventy
Where's Ainsley Bassette?

The Campanile rings eleven times as twelve weapon-carrying men with "FBI" on the back of their windbreakers jump from two vans and encircle Hamilton House under dark skies. Trojan, on coyote watch next door, dives under a bush as the men hurry across the lawn. One of the men uses hand signals to send several agents around the back. Four men approach the front door and wait. With a steel ram, they force the door open and storm inside. The men in back charge in through the kitchen door. They quickly move from room to room. Finding no one on the first floor or in the basement, they move up the stairs. Once upstairs, they move from room to room. They arrive at Stephanie and Judy's room. They listen. The use the ram and smash open the door. Stephanie and Judy are naked, making love.

"What?" Stephanie screams.

"Where is Ainsley Bassette?" one of the FBI agents asks.

"Get the fuck out of our room!" Judy yells.

"Where is he?" the agent says.

"They are all at the hospital!" Stephanie yells. "Get out of here!"

"Where's the owner?"

"At the hospital, you dumb shit," Judy yells. "Get the fuck out of our bedroom!"

The agents leave the room, the door splintered in several pieces. After searching the rest of the rooms and the owner's suite on the third floor, they run from Hamilton House and climb into their vans. They speed off toward the hospital.

Winnie's cell rings as he watches the operation from an observation room above. "Mr. Churchill!" Stephanie screams. "The FBI just raided Hamilton House, destroyed our room, and are coming to the hospital looking for you and that tall, weird guy!"

"Shit!"

"What's wrong?" Asia says, sitting next to Winnie.

"The FBI is on its way, looking for Ainsley. They just raided Hamilton House."

"Shit is right," Asia says. "It looks like the operation is about half done.

They got the two liver pieces in Bessie using the professor's stem cells. They got to use what's left to take care of the mayor and Michael."

"I'll go tell Ainsley," Winnie says.

"Wait for the FBI and lead them off. That may give the surgeon enough time to finish."

As the FBI vans screech to a halt in front of the emergency room, Winnie starts running toward the garage. The agents jump from their vans and give chase. Winnie runs up several flights of stairs to the top and over to his car. The agents surround him. Winnie has his hands raised. "On the ground!" one of the agents yells. Winnie lies on the pavement. The agents open all the SUV's door at once, but there's no sign of Ainsley Bassette.

"What's this all about?" Winnie says from the pavement.

"You were running away from us," an agent says. "Who are you?"

"Can I at least sit up?" Winnie says.

"Stand up and give us your identification," an agent says.

Winnie stands and takes out his wallet and his driver's license. "You are the owner of Hamilton House?" an agent asks, reading his name.

"Yes. What's the problem?"

"We're looking for a fugitive wanted in several states and territories," an agent says. "We found his DNA all over a transsexual who was being treated in a San Francisco hospital."

"Treated for what?"

"Sexual molestation and battery," the agent says. "The nurses needed a straightjacket to keep the victim from committing suicide."

"We did have one of our former friends and boarders, Mr. Ainsley Bassette, stop by and visit."

"Where is he?"

"I have no idea," Winnie says. "He came and left. He could be anywhere by now."

"When's the last time you saw him?"

"Earlier today. Frankly, I've been so concerned about the mayor, his mother, and his son and their operation I haven't been thinking about Ainsley."

"mR. bERZERKELEY?" the agent in charge says. "What's wrong with him?"

"An experimental liver transplant," Winnie says. "He and his son are giving pieces of their livers to save the mayor's mother."

"I suppose that will be in one of his cartoons?" the agent in charge says. "What were you running to your car for?"

"I left my checkbook," Winnie says. "You know how these hospitals are. They won't let them out before we pay."

"Sorry to bother you, Mr. Churchill. You will contact us if Mr. Bassette shows up again, won't you?"

"Yes, sir. You have my word."

"Let's go check the hospital," the agent in charge says.

The agents move quickly from the top of the parking garage. From above, Winnie can see several agents enter the hospital while others move around the outside of the building, looking in bushes.

Winnie watches and then walks toward the stairs. As he starts to leave the parking garage, he hears a voice from inside a large trash bin. "They all gone?" Ainsley asks.

Winnie walks over to the bin and leans against it, looking straight ahead, pretending to catch his breath. "What did you do to that one-balled cook, anyhow?"

Chapter Seventy-One
Visitation Rights.

Gerry Armstrong walks into Bertha's office and slumps into a chair. "Bertha," he says, obviously exhausted, "we have to talk. I have to go to Berkeley immediately."

"Be patient, Gerry. The criminal complaint has been filed and the recall started. The polls have you ahead by sixty points."

"We received a letter from the vice-chancellor saying that Sarah is one step from being kicked out of the university. We also got a call from our insurance company wanting us to approve her stay in the hospital in the detox unit. I have to go and see what I can do. No matter what, I am her father."

"If it weren't for me talking to the vice-chancellor, your daughter would have been kicked out of the university. She didn't take most of her finals. I took care of you like I always do." Bertha thumbs through pictures. "She does look pretty good in black," she says, handing the picture to Gerry. "Daddy's little Goth!"

"I've got to go take care of my daughter."

"Take it easy, Gerry. She's going to be more ammunition for media events, YouTube, you name it, all blaming Winston for everything we find highlighted in the polls. By the time we're through, he won't be able to run for dogcatcher."

"Say what you want, Bertha. But I'm on the next plane to Berkeley, and I won't be back until Sarah's with me."

* * *

The vice-chancellor, dressed for work, walks into the hospital early in the morning. "Michael Kris?" she asks the volunteer behind the information counter.

"ICU, third floor."

"Intensive Care?"

"Yes, ma'am, and he has a 'no visitors except family' sign. Are you one of his family members?"

"I used to be his mother."

The vice-chancellor takes the elevator to the third floor and walks through doors marked ICU to a nurses' station. "Michael Kris, please."

"And you are?"

"I was his mother once."

"Just a moment," the nurse says, reaching for a phone. "Room 333."

The vice-chancellor walks a few steps and greets Asia, who is stepping from room 333 and closing the door behind her. "You! What are you doing here?"

"Screening who goes into this room," Asia says. "I am helping the hospital keep unwanted visitors out."

"Unwanted? I get a call this morning saying my son—or at least someone who used to be my son—is breaking my health insurance plan. Whatever they did here last night has a ten-thousand-dollar deductible."

"I have already paid the deductible, Vice-Chancellor. I'll tell them in accounting. You won't be bothered anymore."

"What exactly happened here last night?"

"Michael helped save Bessie's life—the life you put in danger when you flushed those stem cells down the drain. If he hadn't given some of his liver to Bessie, she would have died for sure. Now all we can do is wait and see if both of them and the mayor recover. They may all die, but at least they tried to help, which is more than I can say for you."

"The mayor gave up part of his liver, too? I'm surprised that bastard had any to give."

"They both have gone the extra mile to save someone they love. You ought to try it sometime."

"You are real poison, aren't you, Miss Lily Liu Lu? Yes, I know all about you and the murder you committed on some poor john. I know about your friends at the ranch, your history, and your lies. But in the spirit of helping you, I am willing to forget what I have found out if you'll do one thing for me. I want you to give up the chancellor and his wealthy Chinese friends. Give me what you know about them, and all will be forgotten."

"I have no idea what you are talking about, Vice-Chancellor. Lily Liu Lu is gone. I am Asia, a PhD student at the university and a boarder at Hamilton house with some really nice and honorable people. I grew up a whore, and I can't undo that. Anything else you're talking about is beyond me."

"Then I will get what I need to bring the chancellor down without you, and you will spend the rest of your sorry life behind bars for murder. I'll make sure of that."

"I wouldn't expect anything less from you, Vice-Chancellor. Do what you have to do."

"Count on it, bitch." The vice-chancellor starts to walk away.

"You want to see Michael?" Asia asks.

"I don't have a son named Michael," she says, walking away.

Asia watches Vice-Chancellor Kris leave, her heels making noise on the polished floor. She goes inside the room, where Bessie, Mayor Sain, and Michael lie in hospital beds connected to several machines. "Who was that?" Michael asks.

"No one. A real nobody," Asia answers.

* * *

"It was a long night—a really long night," Winnie says into his cell, lying in bed at Hamilton House. "The operation took four hours and, according to the surgeon, went as well as expected. Thanks for waiting up."

"I guess this Ainsley Bassette knows his stuff?"

"He didn't do the actual operation. He was directing it from a trash bin out in the parking garage."

"You've got to be kidding."

"He left before the FBI could catch him. I suppose he's on his way back to wherever he came from."

"The FBI? What in the hell?"

"He's wanted worldwide."

"What for?"

"I didn't take time to ask the agents when they had me on the ground with weapons pointed at me."

"Get out of there! Come home to Kansas. I can't believe what I am hearing."

"I've got to visit them in the hospital and make sure they're going to be all right before I hit the airplane."

"What about me? I have visitation rights too."

"I'll be home as soon as I can. I've got to make sure our temporary cook is going to last."

"Temporary cook?"

"We went through one two days ago, and we're trying out a young girl again this morning for whoever is still here."

"What?"

"Stephanie and Judy checked into the Golden Bear on San Pablo, and Bessie, Jim, Michael, and Sarah are in the hospital. That leaves just Josh, Jamal, and I here to enjoy real soul food."

"Don't tell me any more. I am glad I'm here in good old Lake Quivira babysitting while Katrina drives around Kansas looking for Nelson."

"Don't tell me any more either. Sounds like we've got our hands full in both places."

"The newspaper has a story in it accusing you of turning Sarah into a druggie and buying her black clothes and having her nose and ears pierced. It has a picture that isn't exactly how I remember her."

"Bertha will never stop, will she?"

* * *

Asia's cell rings. She looks at the number and steps from room 333. "Lady Gretchen, what's up?"

"The Storey County sheriff is on his way to arrest you," Lady Gretchen says. "I heard there's some high-powered attorney from Reno making big trouble about them not going after you. The sheriff is worried about his reelection. You are going to get a visit this afternoon, probably."

"Great! Did you take care of my book like I asked?"

"Long gone in the fireplace. You don't have to worry. We're covering that pretty little ass of yours."

"My ass is in a sling," Asia says. "Looks like I'll be seeing you sooner than I thought."

"We'll all come and visit you. You're gonna bring us a whole lot of new customers when the headlines get out."

"At least Lily Liu Lu will be good for something!"

* * *

Josh and Jamal sit at the block waiting for Jazzleen to finish cooking grits and collard greens. Josh is giving a bottle to Rhashan, and Jamal is feeding Devontae, who is sitting in a high chair. "I gotta go to the store and finish up several cartoons," Josh says.

"Go ahead," Jazzleen says. "I am almost done, and he can play on the floor for a few minutes. You want me to wrap some food for you?"

"I am very late already. My editor is going to crucify me. Keep some in the refrigerator for me, will you? Smells great."

"Yes, sir. I will."

Josh places the baby on the floor and walks quickly out the kitchen door. "So do you mind if I ask who the lucky man or men are?"

"You remember Antonio?"

"The stud? The pro football player?"

"That's him. He said he was going to show me his trophies. Instead I became one—twice."

"Where is he now? I haven't heard his name on television for a while."

"He got drunk in a bar, waived a gun around, shot some dude in the leg, and is in prison for a few years."

"That's no good. When will he get out?"

"He just got five more years added to his sentence for fighting. He'll never get out."

"You get divorced?"

"Divorced? Got to get married first. All we got is no money and visitation rights."

"Maybe you should come back to school and finish up. You've still got a lot of friends."

"Friends? I need money, honey. I got two mouths other than my own to feed, rent to pay, clothes to buy. I gotta survive. That's why I got my first fight next month. Five hundred dollars for two rounds. I don't make that in a month around here."

"Fight? You?"

"MMA. Gotta kick some ass and make some dough."

"You gonna let us know when and where?"

"If I'm still cooking here when the mayor's mother gets better."

"That could be a long time or never," Jamal says.

"I met her once at Longfellow when the mayor sang her a song. From what I saw, she's so tough she'll be back in a couple of days."

"I don't know. For what it's worth, I hope you stay around a lot longer."

*　　　*　　　*

Trojan is frustrated. He doesn't dig the soul food being prepared for meals, Bessie isn't around to put Jack in his dish, and most of the legs he uses to keep his tool fresh and ready are gone. The only good thing is that madman Ainsley Bassette, who gives humping a bad name, has disappeared. *Maybe Mimi will come out and thank me for keeping those coyotes at bay. Maybe Mrs. McPherson will invite me inside. Maybe she will give me the visitation rights I deserve for being the great protector. Then again … maybe not. Oh, well, might as well try. There's nothing else to do.*

Chapter Seventy-Two Gotcha!

GERRY ARMSTRONG WALKS INTO the hospital in the late afternoon. "Sarah Armstrong's room, please?"

The candy striper behind the information desk looks in her computer. "There's no one named Sarah Armstrong here."

"I was informed she was in a detox unit. At least that's what my insurance company said."

"We have a Roni Armstrong."

"That's probably her. I understand she has changed her name at least once since she got to this wacko place."

"Room 1111."

Gerry enters Sarah's room and does a double take. He looks at the two women, and neither one is the Sarah he raised. "Daddy!" Sarah says, seeing him in the doorway. "What are you doing here?"

"I didn't recognize you," Gerry says. "Jet black hair, beads hanging from your nose to your ear—what is going on?"

"I am a Goth," Sarah says, "and my name is Dream. At least it was when I got here. Of course, I don't remember that. I was stoned and almost dead."

"I've got to get you out of this place and back to Kansas. You'll kill yourself. You need to come back where sane, normal people live."

"I'm not a Goth anymore, Daddy. When they let me out I'm going to be a marine."

"What?"

"Yes. That's Lady X sleeping over there. She's had a hysterectomy, and they have her in here because there are no other beds. She's a marine. I'm going to enlist. Isn't that cool?"

"Let me get this straight. You're going to be a marine? Did I hear you right?"

"I am, and I'm going to change my name back to Sarah. You'd like that, wouldn't you?"

"Yes, well, the name yes. But a marine? Are you going to leave school and go to basic and learn how to shoot guns and kill people?"

"They let me stay in school until I graduate and pay me. When I get out I serve as long as I was in school. Isn't that neat?" Asia walks into the room. "Asia, this is my father."

Asia looks at Gerry Armstrong, then at Sarah, and then back at Gerry with a strange, piercing stare. Gerry does likewise.

"So *you* are Sarah's father?" Asia says as she extends a hand to shake.

"I am. I am Gerry Armstrong. Nice to meet you."

"I am one of Hamilton House's boarders. We were all concerned about Sarah's well-being and have asked that she be kept here until all those nasty things she was taking are out of her system and she doesn't want to take them anymore."

"I don't. I am going to be a marine, get very healthy, and bulk up so I can be strong—very strong."

Winnie walks into the room. "Gerry," he says, extending both hands to shake one of his now trembling hands. "What are you shaking for? Doesn't Sarah look great? She's getting out tonight, and we're going to have a get-Sarah-blonde-and-beadless party at Hamilton House. Now that you're here, you'll have to stay with us."

"I don't know. I was thinking the worst when I got a letter from the university and the insurance company called me for authorization. It seems she is on the road to rapid recovery. I don't know about the marine thing, though."

"Come on, look at all the votes you'll get back in Kansas from veterans and rednecks. Your daughter, in the US Marines! Bertha will be ecstatic. Come on, let's go get a drink, and you can tell me how your election is coming."

"You go bring the car around. I want to say good-bye to Sarah," Gerry says, looking at Asia as Winnie leaves.

"Daddy," Sarah says, "thank you so much for coming to visit me. Tell Mother I love her, and I love you."

Asia and Gerry walk out and stop in the middle of the hall, away from Sarah's room. "Gerry Armstrong? Sarah's father?" Asia says. "You're Phil from Iowa, the wealthy banker who came to visit me every six months with his gang of buddies."

"Shit!" Gerry says. "I hoped I would never see you again."

"Well, Lily Liu Lu is here, and so are you. Wait until all those voters back in Kansas hear about your little escapades in Virginia City and 'round the world and the extra five hundred you would give me to play with these." Asia pulls up her loose sweatshirt to show her braless breasts. "Remember?"

"How could I forget?"

"And I suppose those buddies of yours—who were they? Chet, Tim, and Bruce? I'll bet they are Kansas political bigwigs, too. Wait until the press gets hold of this!"

"You can't do that. It'll ruin everything. You've got to be reasonable and realize how many lives you will destroy."

"You are going to start sending Sarah money to attend the university. You are going to stop harassing Mr. Churchill and Mayor Sain and drop all charges, suits, or whatever Bertha has conjured up. You are going to halt all legal maneuvers against me. And you are going to drop out of the race for governor. If you don't do these things, I will make life miserable for you and your friends. Got it?"

"You won't go public if I do those things, will you? I can't undo what Bertha has already done for the vice-chancellor. Those two women are two of a kind."

"Take care of Sarah, stop harassing Mr. Churchill and the mayor, and drop out of the race immediately. I'll wait awhile to see what happens to me before I promise to keep your transgressions a secret."

"Please, have mercy."

Chapter Seventy-Three
Potty Time!

WINNIE, SARAH, JOSH, ASIA, Willie, Jamal, Jack R. Abbot, Doreen, Sylvia, and Jefferson crowd into the hospital room occupied by Mayor Sain, Bessie, and Michael. Constant low-frequency noises and occasional beeps come from the monitoring machines.

"What the fuck is this?" Bessie says, groaning. "A gang wake?"

"Sarah has been released, so we thought we'd have a party," Winnie says. "Stephanie and Judy would have come, but they are having stomach trouble."

"Better wake up mR. bERZERKELEY and Michael over there," Bessie says with much effort. "They wouldn't want to miss anything. I don't think they're dead. Or maybe they are."

"You talking about me again?" Mayor Sain says, opening his eyes and looking around the room. "Where's Ainsley?"

"You and the FBI," Winnie says. "He's long gone to where I have no idea—at least that's what I told the law."

"Shit!" Mayor Sain says. "I owe him a big one, a great big one."

"You want a juicy one?" Jefferson says, leaning against his bed. "I harvested a bumper crop, and I got plenty left over since you been in here."

"I want to keep a clear head," Mayor Sain says softly. "The nurse has got a real cute ass."

"Shit!" Bessie says. "He's not dead. He's still got his brains in his dick."

"You've got the clearest head I ever had," Sylvia says.

Josh and Sarah lean against Michael's bed. "Hey, boy wonder," Josh says. "How are you doing?"

"I am very tired," Michael says, waking up. "How about you guys?"

"I got a couple of weeks ahead on the cartoons," Josh says.

"How did you handle Ainsley Bassette?"

"I introduced a Basset hound in all three of them with the caption "There you are, Ainsley! I've been looking for you."

"That's great, Josh. You are very smart."

"He may be smart, but I'm going to be a marine," Sarah says.

"A marine?" Josh asks. "A real marine?"

"You bet," Sarah says, saluting. "A real fighting machine."

"Better get your licks in now, Michael," Josh says. "She's going to bulk up and lift weights."

"Wow!" Michael says.

Willie and Jamal stand in the middle of the room. "See what happens when you have friends?" Willie says to Jamal. "They all stick together."

"I know. Hamilton House is the best place I've ever been."

"I hear you're making eyes at the new cook," Willie says. "You falling into the same trap I did?"

"Jazzleen and her babies are great," Jamal says. "But I've got my eye on the prize, and she won't get in the way."

"Better watch out! Women have a way."

"I thought of a new mystery last night," Jack R. Abbott says to Mayor Sain. "It's called *Murder by Masturbation* and stars Ainsley Bassette. What do you think?"

"Sounds like a best seller to me. You gonna finish it?" Mayor Sain asks.

"As soon as you get out and help me with the details," Jack R. Abbott says.

"I can't wait. Mom's snoring is about to drive me into another room."

"My snoring? You've been letting out enough gas to blow us all up. You've already knocked a couple of water cups off the table."

"What is going on in here?" a middle-aged female nurse says, walking in. "You've all got to get out of here. This is the ICU, and these people are in very serious condition. It's time for their enemas."

"They are our friends," Mayor Sain says. "This is Hamilton House—well … except for our little mutt."

"I don't care who or what they are. They've got to get out of here, now! It's potty time!"

"I'm gone," Josh says. "See you in the funny papers."

"Me, too," Sarah says. "I want out of this hospital to spend my first night as a marine!"

"Come on, Jamal," Willie says. "I hear there's some soul food left over at Hamilton House."

"Doreen and I are leaving," Jack R. Abbott says. "We have a date at the kennel. I've got new inspiration to write a mystery novel."

"Shit!" Doreen says. "His little dance has already started."

"Sylvia and I will be back," Jefferson says. "I'll smoke one for you."

"You're the best mayor I ever had," Sylvia says.

"Well, old friends," Winnie says to Mayor Sain on one side of him and Bessie on the other, "I'll be hitting the airport tonight on my way back to Kansas. A pregnant woman needs a little attention."

"That's what got her pregnant in the first place," Bessie says, scoffing.

"You are coming back, aren't you?" Mayor Sain asks.

"I will always be just a few hours away," Winnie says.

"How do you know we're gonna make it?" Mayor Sain says. "What if something happens?"

"Asia will be here, won't you?" Winnie says to Asia, who is standing behind him. "Nothing will happen to anybody with her around. I've gotta go or I will miss my flight."

Winnie waves good-bye to all three as he leaves the room. Asia walks over to Michael's bed. "What can I do for you?"

"I was thinking," Michael says. "If we make it out of here—if I make it out of here—do you think I might be able to find someone to give me an ear transplant?"

"All things are possible. Just get better."

Asia joins Winnie in the hallway, where he is talking to a doctor. "How are they doing?" Winnie asks.

"This is a first for me," the doctor says. "We are monitoring them closely. As far as we can tell, none of the stem cells in the older woman have started to bring her new liver together. And the other two—they are hanging on by a thread. They barely have enough of a liver left to keep them alive for long. It'll be a few days."

"That's not encouraging," Winnie says. "Maybe I should stay awhile."

"Go ahead and go," Asia says. "There's nothing you can do. I'll keep you informed, unless I have to suddenly depart myself."

"You leave? Why you?"

"I have a feeling," Asia says. "I won't leave you or Hamilton House in the lurch, though. The group will take care of business. Bessie, Mayor Sain, and Michael will all get better."

"Do you have medical training?" the doctor asks. "This operation has never been done before. We are on pins and needles around here."

"Doctor, I know more about the human body than anyone in Berkeley—especially the male body. And Bessie? She's too tough to die!"

"Then I'm leaving," Winnie says. "What you've said has always been true. Don't disappear, you hear?"

"Not if I can help it, Mr. Churchill. Fly safe."

Chapter Seventy-Four
The Reality of Life

ASIA'S SCOOTER ROUNDS THE corner and heads up Durant to Hamilton House. As she approaches, she sees a Storey County Sheriff Department vehicle parked at the curb. She slows and keeps going toward Telegraph. Inside, two uniformed sheriffs sit at the block talking to Sarah, Josh, Stephanie, Judy, and Jamal. "If you see Lily Liu Lu, tell her to surrender peacefully and go back to Virginia City with us," one the men says. "She has an appointment with Judge Slaby about the murder of Johnny Blood."

"Who is Lily Liu Lu?" Sarah asks.

"They described Asia," Josh says. "Are you arresting her?"

"We are extraditing her voluntarily to answer a few questions, that's all. We can do it the formal way, if she resists."

"I'm sure there's some misunderstanding," Stephanie says. "Asia will clear it all up when she gets back from the hospital."

"Is there any place we can get a nice, thick steak and a baked potato in this town?" one of the officers asks.

"You might try one of the places at the marina," Josh says. "Berkeley is more into healthy foods."

"What could be healthier than a big, juicy steak?" one of the men asks.

"We got a little soul food left," Jamal says.

"Come on, let's go spend our per diem," one of the men says to the other. "Who knows when we'll get to come to the big city again? Tell Miss Lily Liu Lu we will be back in a couple of hours."

The men push back and leave. Asia, parked out of sight, watches the sheriffs' car leave. She pulls up the driveway and walks into the kitchen, where the stunned group sits.

"Those men are here to arrest you," Sarah says. "Who is Lily Liu Lu?"

"Bessie leave any Jack?" Asia says. "I don't drink, at least not much, but now's the time. Any takers?"

"We're pregnant, and Jamal is in training," Stephanie says.

"Sarah," Josh says, "does the marine want to drink with me and Asia?"

Asia sits down at the table.

"Maybe I shouldn't, either. I don't want to go back to that horrible hospital."

"It's just you and me, Asia, or Lily Liu Lu—whoever you are," Josh says.

"You all know or think you know about my past. I was born to a whore and became a whore named Lily Liu Lu before I left to become Asia, a student at the university. The reason I left is hanging in Bessie's room. Let me go get it."

Asia leaves and returns with the picture of Johnny Blood Bessie keeps in her bathroom. She sets it on the table. "This is Johnny Blood. He killed my mother for getting pregnant by him. He beat her to death, forcing me to be born early. Years later, when he got out of prison, he came for me. When he walked into my room naked, I shot his dick off and then gave him one between the eyes."

"You killed him dead?" Sarah says.

"Deader than a doornail. I watched him twitch and die before I climbed out a window and left forever."

"Shit!" Jamal says.

"Why is his picture hanging in Bessie's room?" Judy asks.

"Johnny Blood is the mayor's father and Michael's grandfather."

"Wait a minute!" Josh says. "If he is the mayor's father and Michael's grandfather and your father—holy shit!"

"Yes, I am the mayor's half-sister."

"This is fucking cool," Jamal says.

"You are related to Mayor Sain and Michael?" Sarah says.

"You killed the mayor's father?" Stephanie says.

"Blood spurted all over the room," Asia says. "Got a little on my red outfit."

"Too bad the reality show guys aren't around," Josh says. "This is unbelievable! Have you told the mayor, Bessie, and Michael yet?"

"No, but I am off to the hospital to do just that before the sheriffs come back."

"How I would like to be a little mouse in the corner," Josh says.

* * *

Asia puts on a helmet and fires up her scooter. "Time to face reality," she says. The scooter moves down the driveway, and she slams on the brakes. "What the?"

Two humane society trucks are parked in the middle of Durant, blocking traffic. Four men with nets are chasing several coyotes. Asia gets off her scooter and walks toward Mrs. McPherson's house. "Kill them all!" Mrs. McPherson yells, standing on her lawn and holding her little white poodle. "They are after my Mimi."

Asia walks over to the screaming woman. "What happened?"

"I heard this racket. When I came outside, the horny mutt from next door was holding off a pack of fucking coyotes from attacking my little darling. I called 911."

"What? Where is he?"

One of the men steps back, and Trojan lies on his side in the middle of the street. Mimi struggles with Mrs. McPherson and jumps from her arms, running quickly to the fallen Trojan. Asia runs close behind. "Trojan, my little man!" Asia cries, stroking his head.

Mimi goes to him and licks his mouth. His eyes open.

"I'm afraid he's a goner," one of the humane society men says. "He took quite a mauling from those coyotes. We got 'em all but one."

"No!" Asia yells. "He can't die. I won't let him."

"I'm afraid there's not much you can do," the man says. "He's is still breathing, but I don't give him much of a chance. Those bastards go right for the kill. They don't mess around."

"My poor baby!" Asia cries. "My poor little man."

Mimi licks Trojan several more times on the face. Mrs. McPherson walks over and grabs her little poodle. "Your dog is quite a hero, miss. I hope he makes it."

"He will, if it's the last thing I do," Asia says, reaching for her cell as Mrs. McPherson walks away, Mimi looking over her shoulder at Trojan. "Professor Spears? How do you clone a dog?"

END